IT IS FAR, FAR INTO THE FUTURE—THE EVE OF THE WORLD'S EXISTENCE. AND PEOPLE ARE EVACUATING THE GALAXY BY AIRCRAFT, SPACESHIP, OR ANY MEANS TO AVOID BEING SWALLOWED BY THE EARTH.

HUMANITY'S FUTURE IS BEYOND PRAYER—AND PERHAPS EVEN BEYOND SCIENCE. OUR ONLY HOPE IS THE INGENUITY OF ONE HUMAN BEING ... ONE SINGLE SURVIVOR ...

THE LAST MAN ON EARTH.

THE LAST MAN ON EARTH

**Isaac Asimov,
Martin Harry Greenberg and
Charles G. Waugh**

Fawcett Crest • New York

A Fawcett Crest Book
Published by Ballantine Books
Copyright © 1982 by Isaac Asimov, Martin H. Greenberg and
Charles G. Waugh

ISBN 0-449-24531-4

Printed in Canada

First Ballantine Books Edition: August 1982

CONTENTS

The editors and publisher are grateful for permission to reprint the following:

"The Underdweller" by William F. Nolan Copyright © 1957 by King-Size Publications. Reprinted by permission of the author.

"Flight to Forever" by Poul Anderson Copyright © 1950 by Fictioneers, Inc.; copyright renewed. Reprinted by permission of the author and the author's agents, Scott Meredith Literary Agency, Inc., 845 Third Avenue, New York, N.Y. 10022

"Trouble with Ants" by Clifford Simak Copyright © 1951 by Ziff-Davis Publishing Company. Reprinted by permission of the author and his agents, Kirby McCauley Ltd.

"The Coming of the Ice" by G. Peyton Wertenbaker Copyright © 1926 by E.P. Inc.; by arrangement with Forrest J Ackerman, 2495 Glendower Ave., Hollywood, California 90027

"The Most Sentimental Man" by Evelyn E. Smith Copyright © by King-Size Publications. Reprinted by permission of the author and her agents, Henry Morrison Inc.

"Eddie for Short" by Wallace West Copyright © 1953 by Ziff-Davis Publications. Reprinted by permission of Mrs. Wallace West.

"Knock" by Frederic Brown Copyright © 1948 by Standard Magazines. Reprinted by permission of International Creative Management, Inc.

"Original Sin" by S. Fowler Wright Copyright © 1949 by S. Fowler Wright; by arrangement with Forrest J Ackerman, 2495 Glendower Ave., Hollywood, California 90027

"A Man Spekith" by Richard Wilson Copyright © 1969 by Galaxy Publishing Corporation. Reprinted by permission of the author.

"In the World's Dusk" by Edmund Hamilton Copyright© 1936 by Popular Fiction Company; copyright renewed. Reprinted by the agents for the author's estate, Scott Meredith Literary Agency, Inc., 845 Third Avenue, New York, N.Y. 10022

"Kindness" by Lester del Rey Copyright © 1944 by Street and Smith Publications; copyright renewed. Reprinted by permission of

THE LAST MAN ON EARTH

INTRODUCTION

By Isaac Asimov

WHAT IS THE OLDEST SURVIVING last-man-on-Earth story?

Well, it's almost as old as history. History begins with writing, for it is only through writing that we can get a connected story of events. We can deduce things from various nonwritten artifacts—pottery, paintings, jewelry, tools—but that's not the same thing. What we deduce from such items is "prehistory."

History, then, begins about 3100 B.C. in the land that is now called Iraq. Along the lower course of the Tigris and Euphrates rivers, there lived a people we call Sumerians, who were the first to invent writing and various other things. (They were very clever people, obviously.)

As is monotonously true of all peoples, the Sumerians had to deal with natural disasters, and about 2800 B.C. they had a really bad one. The rivers, which were their source of life, thanks to irrigation and agriculture, overflowed. They did this periodically, as rivers will, but this time they *really* overflowed.

Why the incident was so unusually disastrous—whether because of particularly heavy rains, particularly high tides, a tsunami, a meteor splashing into the Persian Gulf—we don't know. In any case, much of the valley seems to have been flooded, and there must have been great loss of life.

Eventually, the flood receded, and there was a recovery, but forever after, the Sumerians dated everything as having happened "before the flood" or "after the flood." Naturally, since they didn't know what caused the flood any more than we do, they blamed the gods. (That's the advantage of religion. You're never without an explanation for anything.)

People being what they are, there was a science fiction writer in Sumeria who got the brilliant idea of telling the story of the flood, but of improving a bit on it and wringing a little more drama out of it than had actually existed. Why just drown thousands? Drown everybody!—Well, except for one family, so that they could account for the fact that there were still human beings on Earth.

The story grew (I daresay other writers added their own bits), and eventually there came into existence the Epic of Gilgamesh, king of Uruk. As part of the tale, the writer described how and why the gods decreed a flood that would (and did) drown *the whole Earth*. (In the first place, most of the Sumerians probably thought Sumeria and the immediately surrounding nations *were* the whole Earth, and in the second, did you ever know a writer who could resist embroidering the facts?—except me, of course.)

He then described how *one* man—just *one*—managed to escape by the kindness and guidance of one of the gods. The man was Ut-Napishtim, and he was the first person we know of, by name, who was "the last man on Earth" in a science fiction story.

The tale of Gilgamesh was extraordinarily popular, and it was still to be found in the library of Ashurbanipal, the last great king of Assyria, over two thousand years after it was written. (We found it in the ruins of that library over two thousand years after it was destroyed.) It undoubtedly spread through the entire ancient world and helped inspire other "strong men" stories—Hercules among the Greeks, Samson among the Israelites, Rustem among the Persians, and so on.

What's more, the story of the flood was seized upon. In the first place, it was very dramatic; in the second place, it was considered actual history; and in the third place, most cultivated people lived along rivers or coasts and were familiar with floods.

The result was that the Greeks had their story of Deucalian and the Israelites their story of Noah. The Israelites picked up much of the material in the first eleven chapters of Genesis during the period of the Babylonian captivity in the seventh century B.C., and that included the story of the flood. Except for getting rid of the polytheistic bits, they stayed pretty close to the details as given in Gilgamesh. (In our cynical modern world, we would call it plagiarism.)

There are two things I want to note about this first last-man story. In the first place, Noah wasn't really the last man; he had three sons with him. In the second place, there were also four women present—his wife and the wives of his three sons. The women weren't important, though; the Bible doesn't even bother to give their names. (In the Greek tale, Deucalian has a wife, too, and although the Greeks weren't great shakes at women's rights—quite the reverse—they at least gave her a name. It was Pyrrha, if you're curious.)

The second thing I want to note is that the biblical version of the tale of Gilgamesh was accepted as sober history for thousands of years. It wasn't until about 1800 that geologists began to realize that there had never been a worldwide flood on Earth.

And even *today* there are many who are certain there was indeed a worldwide flood "because the Bible says so." This includes the "creationists," who are very anxious to teach their version of Babylonian mythology in the schools as "science," by George—so don't tell *me* that science fiction writers don't have influence.

There is such a thing as progress, however. We have come a long way since we have had to drag in some god throwing a tantrum to account for humanity's being reduced to a last fragment.

It was only a few years ago that scientists described a natural disaster that may really have happened and may very nearly have sterilized Earth—the impact of a sizable asteroid. It did (many say) succeed in wiping out the dinosaurs, and such a thing may have happened half a dozen times before in Earth's history.

There are also vast pandemics, such as the Black Death, which is supposed to have wiped out a third of the human species in a third of a century. There are imaginative exercises of more modern science fictional views than were available to the Sumerians—time travel to the far future, invasions of conquering extraterrestrial hordes, and so on. Most of all, there are the prospects of a deadly nuclear war, which seems the most likely of all paths to last-mandom, if paths there must be.

So here in this book we ring seventeen changes on the theme —seventeen successors, in a manner of speaking, to Ut-Napish-tim. Just for fun, see if you can think up an eighteenth.

William F. Nolan

Best-known in the science fiction world for his novel *Logan's Run* (1967), William F. Nolan has been a very active and very good free-lance writer since 1956. He is also a fine screenwriter, with such films as *Burnt Offerings* (1976) and television plays like *Melvin Purvis, G-Man* to his credit. And as if this were not enough, he also is a first-rate anthologist, both within science fiction—*Man Against Tomorrow* (1965) and *Science Fiction Origins* (1980) among others—and in the small field of automobile lore, where his collaborations with the late Charles Beaumont, *Omnibus of Speed* (1958) and *When Engines Roar* (1964), are considered classics.

"The Underdweller" also rates as at least a minor classic about the struggle to survive in sewers of Los Angeles.

THE UNDERDWELLER

By William F. Nolan

IN THE WAITING, WINDLESS DARK, Lewis Stillman
pressed into the building-front shadows along Wilshire Boulevard. Breathing softly, the automatic poised and ready in
his hand, he advanced with animal stealth toward Western
Avenue, gliding over the night-cool concrete past ravaged
clothing shops, drug and ten-cent stores, their windows shattered, their doors ajar and swinging. The city of Los Angeles,
painted in cold moonlight, was an immense graveyard; the
tall, white tombstone buildings thrust up from the silent
pavement, shadow-carved and lonely. Overturned metal
corpses of trucks, buses, and automobiles littered the streets.

He paused under the wide marquee of the Fox Wiltern.
Above his head, rows of splintered display bulbs gaped—sharp
glass teeth in wooden jaws. Lewis Stillman felt as though
they might drop at any moment to pierce his body.

Four more blocks to cover. His destination: a small corner
delicatessen four blocks south of Wilshire, on Western. Tonight
he intended bypassing the larger stores like Safeway and
Thriftimart, with their available supplies of exotic foods; a
smaller grocery was far more likely to have what he needed.
He was finding it more and more difficult to locate basic
foodstuffs. In the big supermarkets, only the more exotic and
highly spiced canned and bottled goods remained—and he
was sick of caviar and oysters!

Crossing Western, as he almost reached the far curb, he
saw some of *them*. He dropped immediately to his knees
behind the rusting bulk of an Oldsmobile. The rear door on
his side was open, and he cautiously eased himself into the
back seat of the deserted car. Releasing the safety catch on

the automatic, he peered through the cracked window at six or seven of them, as they moved toward him along the street. God! Had he been seen? He couldn't be sure. Perhaps they were aware of his position! He should have remained on the open street, where he'd have a running chance. Perhaps, if his aim were true, he could kill most of them; but, even with its silencer, the gun might be heard and more of them would come. He dared not fire until he was certain they had discovered him.

They came closer, their small dark bodies crowding the walk, six of them, chattering, leaping, cruel mouths open, eyes glittering under the moon. Closer. Their shrill pipings increased, rose in volume. Closer. Now he could make out their sharp teeth and matted hair. Only a few feet from the car . . . His hand was moist on the handle of the automatic; his heart thundered against his chest. Seconds away . . .

Now!

Lewis Stillman fell heavily back against the dusty seat cushion, the gun loose in his trembling hand. They had passed by; they had missed him. Their thin pipings diminished, grew faint with distance.

The tomb silence of late night settled around him.

The delicatessen proved a real windfall. The shelves were relatively untouched and he had a wide choice of tinned goods. He found an empty cardboard box and hastily began to transfer the cans from the shelf nearest him.

A noise from behind—a padding, scraping sound.

Lewis Stillman whirled about, the automatic ready.

A huge mongrel dog faced him, growling deep in its throat, four legs braced for assault. The blunt ears were laid flat along the short-haired skull and a thin trickle of saliva seeped from the killing jaws. The beast's powerful chest muscles were bunched for the spring when Stillman acted.

His gun, he knew, was useless; the shots might be heard. Therefore, with the full strength of his left arm, he hurled a heavy can at the dog's head. The stunned animal staggered under the blow, legs buckling. Hurriedly, Stillman gathered his supplies and made his way back to the street.

How much longer can my luck hold? Lewis Stillman wondered, as he bolted the door. He placed the box of tinned goods on a wooden table and lit the tall lamp nearby. Its flickering orange glow illumined the narrow, low-ceilinged room.

Twice tonight, his mind told him, twice you've escaped them—and they could have seen you easily on both occasions if they had been watching for you. They don't know you're alive. But when they find out . . .

He forced his thoughts away from the scene in his mind, away from the horror; quickly he began to unload the box, placing the cans on a long shelf along the far side of the room.

He began to think of women, of a girl named Joan, and of how much he had loved her . . .

The world of Lewis Stillman was damp and lightless; it was narrow and its cold stone walls pressed in upon him as he moved. He had been walking for several hours; sometimes he would run, because he knew his leg muscles must be kept strong, but he was walking now, following the thin yellow beam of his hooded lantern. He was searching.

Tonight, he thought, I might find another like myself. Surely, *someone* is down here; I'll find someone if I keep searching. I *must* find someone!

But he knew he would not. He knew he would find only chill emptiness ahead of him in the long tunnels.

For three years, he had been searching for another man or woman down here in this world under the city. For three years, he had prowled the seven hundred miles of storm drains which threaded their way under the skin of Los Angeles like the veins in a giant's body—and he had found nothing. *Nothing.*

Even now, after all the days and nights of search, he could not really accept the fact that he was alone, that he was the last man alive in a city of seven million . . .

The beautiful woman stood silently above him. Her eyes burned softly in the darkness; her fine red lips were smiling. The foam-white gown she wore continually swirled and billowed around her motionless figure.

"Who are you?" he asked, his voice far off, unreal.

"Does it matter, Lewis?"

Her words, like four dropped stones in a quiet pool, stirred him, rippled down the length of his body.

"No," he said, "Nothing matters, now, except that we've found each other. God, after all these lonely months and years of waiting! I thought I was the last, that I'd never live to see—"

"Hush, my darling." She leaned to kiss him. Her lips were moist and yielding. "I'm here now."

He reached up to touch her cheek, but already she was fading, blending into darkness. Crying out, he clawed desperately for her extended hand. But she was gone, and his fingers rested on a rough wall of damp concrete.

A swirl of milk-fog drifted away in slow rollings down the tunnel.

Rain. Days of rain. The drains had been designed to handle floods, so Lewis Stillman was not particularly worried. He had built high, a good three feet above the tunnel floor, and the water had never yet risen to this level. But he didn't like the sound of the rain down here: an orchestrated thunder through the tunnels, a trap-drumming amplified and continuous. Since he had been unable to make his daily runs, he had been reading more than usual. Short stories by Welty, Gordimer, Aiken, Irwin Shaw, Hemingway; poems by Frost, Lorca, Sandburg, Millay, Dylan Thomas. Strange, how unreal this present day world seemed when he read their words. Unreality, however, was fleeting, and the moment he closed a book the loneliness and the fears pressed back. He hoped the rain would stop soon.

Dampness. Surrounding him, the cold walls and the chill and the dampness. The unending gurgle and drip of water, the hollow, tapping splash of the falling drops. Even in his cot, wrapped in thick blankets, the dampness seemed to permeate his body. Sounds . . . Thin screams, pipings, chatterings, reedy whisperings above his head. They were dragging something along the street, something they'd killed, no doubt: an animal—a cat or a dog, perhaps . . . Lewis Stillman shifted, pulling the blankets closer about his body. He kept his eyes tightly shut, listening to the sharp, scuffling sounds on the pavement, and swore bitterly.

"Damn you," he said. "Damn all of you!"

Lewis Stillman was running, running down the long tunnels. Behind him, a tide of midget shadows washed from wall to wall; high, keening cries, doubled and tripled by echoes, rang in his ears. Claws reached for him; he felt panting breath, like hot smoke, on the back of his neck. His lungs were bursting, his entire body aflame.

He looked down at his fast-pumping legs, doing their job with pistoned precision. He listened to the sharp slap of his heels against the floor of the tunnel, and he thought: I might die at any moment, but my *legs* will escape! They will run on, down the endless drains, and never be caught. They move so fast, while my heavy, awkward upper body rocks and sways above them, slowing them down, tiring them—making them angry. How my legs must hate me! I must be clever and humor them, beg them to take me along to safety. How well they run, how sleek and fine!

Then he felt himself coming apart. His legs were detaching themselves from his upper body. He cried out in horror, flailing the air, beseeching them not to leave him behind. But the legs cruelly continued to unfasten themselves. In a cold surge of terror, Lewis Stillman felt himself tipping, falling toward the damp floor—while his legs raced on with a wild animal life of their own. He opened his mouth, high above those insane legs, and screamed, ending the nightmare.

He sat up stiffly in his cot, gasping, drenched in sweat. He drew in a long, shuddering breath and reached for a cigarette, lighting it with a trembling hand.

The nightmares were getting worse. He realized that his mind was rebelling as he slept, spilling forth the bottled-up fears of the day during the night hours.

He thought once more about the beginning, six years ago—about why he was still alive. The alien ships had struck Earth suddenly, without warning. Their attack had been thorough and deadly. In a matter of hours, the aliens had accomplished their clever mission—and the men and women of Earth were destroyed. A few survived, he was certain. He had never seen any of them, but he was convinced they existed. Los Angeles was not the world, after all, and since he had escaped, so must have others around the globe. He'd been working alone in the drains when the aliens struck, finishing a special job for the construction company on B tunnel. He could still hear the weird sound of the mammoth ships and feel the intense heat of their passage.

Hunger had forced him out, and overnight he had become a curiosity. The last man alive. For three years, he was not harmed. He worked with them, taught them many things, and tried to win their confidence. But, eventually, certain ones came to hate him, to be jealous of his relationship with the others. Luckily, he had been able to escape to the drains. That was three years ago, and now they had forgotten him.

His subsequent excursions to the upper level of the city had been made under cover of darkness—and he never ventured out unless his food supply dwindled. He had built his one-room structure directly to the side of an overhead grating—not close enough to risk their seeing it, but close enough for light to seep in during the sunlight hours. He missed the warm feel of open sun on his body almost as much as he missed human companionship, but he dared not risk himself above the drains by day.

When the rain ceased, he crouched beneath the street gratings to absorb as much as possible of the filtered sunlight. But the rays were weak, and their small warmth only served to heighten his desire to feel direct sunlight upon his naked shoulders.

The dreams . . . always the dreams.

"Are you cold, Lewis?"

"Yes. Yes, cold."

"Then go out, dearest. Into the sun."

"I can't. Can't go out."

"But Los Angeles is your world, Lewis! You are the last man in it. The last man in the world."

"Yes, but they own it all. Every street belongs to them, every building. They wouldn't let me come out. I'd die. They'd kill me."

"Go out, Lewis." The liquid dream-voice faded, faded. "Out into the sun, my darling. Don't be afraid."

That night, he watched the moon through the street gratings for almost an hour. It was round and full, like a huge yellow floodlamp in the dark sky, and he thought, for the first time in years, of night baseball at Blues Stadium in Kansas City. He used to love watching the games with his father under the mammoth stadium lights when the field was like a pond, frosted with white illumination, and the players dream-spawned and unreal. Night baseball was always a magic game to him when he was a boy.

Sometimes he got insane thoughts. Sometimes, on a night like this, when the loneliness closed in like a crushing fist and he could no longer stand it, he would think of bringing one of them down with him, into the drains. One at a time,

they might be handled. Then he'd remember their sharp,
savage eyes, their animal ferocity, and he would realize that
the idea was impossible. If one of their kind disappeared,
suddenly and without trace, others would certainly become
suspicious, begin to search for him—and it would be all over.

Lewis Stillman settled back into his pillow; he closed his
eyes and tried not to listen to the distant screams, pipings,
and reedy cries filtering down from the street above his head.

Finally he slept.

He spent the afternoon with paper women. He lingered
over the pages of some yellowed fashion magazines, looking
at all the beautifully photographed models in their fine
clothes. Slim and enchanting, these page-women, with their
cool enticing eyes and perfect smiles, all grace and softness
and glitter and swirled cloth. He touched their images with
gentle fingers, stroking the tawny paper hair, as though, by
some magic formula, he might imbue them with life. Yet, it
was easy to imagine that these women had never *really* lived
at all—that they were simply painted, in microscopic detail,
by sly artists to give the illusion of photos.

He didn't like to think about these women and how they
died.

"A toast to courage," smiled Lewis Stillman, raising his
wine glass high. It sparkled deep crimson in the lamplit
room. "To courage and to the man who truly possesses it!" He
drained the glass and hastily refilled it from a tall bottle on
the table beside his cot.

Aren't you going to join me, Mr. H.?" he asked the seated
figure slouched over the table, head on folded arms. "Or must
I drink alone?"

The figure did not reply.

"Well, then—" He emptied the glass, set it down. "Oh, I
know all about what one man is supposed to be able to do.
Win out alone. Whip the damn world single-handed. If a fish
as big as a mountain and as mean as all sin is out there, then
this one man is supposed to go get him, isn't that it? Well,
Papa H., what if the world is *full* of big fish? Can he win over
them all? One man, alone? Of course he can't. Nosir. Damn
well right he can't!"

Stillman moved unsteadily to a shelf in one corner of the
small wooden room and took down a slim book.

"Here she is, Mr. H. Your greatest. The one you wrote cleanest and best—*The Old Man and the Sea*. You showed how one man could fight the whole damn ocean." He paused, voice strained and rising. "Well, by God, show me, *now,* how to fight this ocean! My ocean is full of killer fish, and I'm the one man and I'm alone in it. I'm ready to listen."

The seated figure remained silent.

"Got you now, haven't I, Papa? No answer to this one, eh? Courage isn't enough. Man was not meant to live alone or fight alone—or drink alone. Even with courage, he can only do so much alone and then it's useless. Well, I say it's useless. I say the hell with your book, and the hell with *you!*"

Lewis Stillman flung the book straight at the head of the motionless figure. The victim spilled back in the chair; his arms slipped off the table, hung swinging. They were lumpy and handless.

More and more, Lewis Stillman found his thoughts turning to the memory of his father and of long hikes through the moonlit Missouri countryside, of hunting trips and warm campfires, of the deep woods, rich and green in summer. He thought of his father's hopes for his future, and the words of that tall, gray-haired figure often came back to him.

"You'll be a fine doctor, Lewis. Study and work hard, and you'll succeed. I know you will."

He remembered the long winter evenings of study at his father's great mahogany desk, poring over medical books and journals, taking notes, sifting and resifting facts. He remembered one set of books in particular—Erickson's monumental three-volume text on surgery, richly bound and stamped in gold. He had always loved those books, above all others.

What had gone wrong along the way? Somehow, the dream had faded; the bright goal vanished and was lost. After a year of pre-med at the University of California, he had given up medicine; he had become discouraged and quit college to take a laborer's job with a construction company. How ironic that this move should have saved his life! He'd wanted to work with his hands, to sweat and labor with the muscles of his body. He'd wanted to earn enough to marry Joan and then, later perhaps, he would have returned to finish his courses. It all seemed so far away now, his reason for quitting, for letting his father down.

Now, at this moment, an overwhelming desire gripped

him, a desire to pore over Erickson's pages once again, to recreate, even for a brief moment, the comfort and happiness of his childhood.

He'd once seen a duplicate set on the second floor of Pickwick's bookstore in Hollywood, in their used book department, and now he knew he must go after it, bring the books back with him to the drains. It was a dangerous and foolish desire, but he knew he would obey it. Despite the risk of death, he would go after the books tonight. *Tonight.*

One corner of Lewis Stillman's room was reserved for weapons. His prize, a Thompson submachine gun, had been procured from the Los Angeles police arsenal. Supplementing the Thompson were two automatic rifles, a Luger, a Colt .45, and a .22 caliber Hornet pistol equipped with a silencer. He always kept the smallest gun in a spring-clip holster beneath his armpit, but it was not his habit to carry any of the larger weapons with him into the city. On this night, however, things were different.

The drains ended two miles short of Hollywood—which meant he would be forced to cover a long and particularly hazardous stretch of ground in order to reach the bookstore. He therefore decided to take along the .30 caliber Savage rifle in addition to the small hand weapon.

You're a fool, Lewis, he told himself as he slid the oiled Savage from its leather case, risking your life for a set of books. Are they *that* important? Yes, a part of him replied, they are that important. You want these books, then go *after* what you want. If fear keeps you from seeking that which you truly want, if fear holds you like a rat in the dark, then you are worse than a coward. You are a traitor, betraying yourself and the civilization you represent. If a man wants a thing and the thing is good, he must go after it, no matter what the cost, or relinquish the right to be called a man. It is better to die with courage than to live with cowardice.

Ah, Papa Hemingway, breathed Stillman, smiling at his own thoughts. I see that you are back with me. I see that your words have rubbed off after all. Well, then, all right—let us go after our fish, let us seek him out. Perhaps the ocean will be calm . . .

Slinging the heavy rifle over one shoulder, Lewis Stillman set off down the tunnels.

*   *   *

Running in the chill night wind. Grass, now pavement, now grass beneath his feet. Ducking into shadows, moving steathily past shops and theaters, rushing under the cold, high moon. Santa Monica Boulevard, then Highland, then Hollywood Boulevard, and finally—after an eternity of heartbeats—Pickwick's.

Lewis Stillman, his rifle over one shoulder, the small automatic gleaming in his hand, edged silently into the store.

A paper battleground met his eyes.

In the filtered moonlight, a white blanket of broken-backed volumes spilled across the entire lower floor. Stillman shuddered; he could envision them, shrieking, scrabbling at the shelves, throwing books wildly across the room at one another. Screaming, ripping, destroying.

What of the other floors? *What of the medical section?*

He crossed to the stairs, spilled pages crackling like a fall of dry autumn leaves under his step, and sprinted up the first short flight to the mezzanine. Similar chaos!

He hurried up to the second floor, stumbling, terribly afraid of what he might find. Reaching the top, heart thudding, he squinted into the dimness.

The books were undisturbed. Apparently they had tired of their game before reaching these.

He slipped the rifle from his shoulder and placed it near the stairs. Dust lay thick all around him, powdering up and swirling as he moved down the narrow aisles; a damp, leathery mustiness lived in the air, an odor of mold and neglect.

Lewis Stillman paused before a dim, hand-lettered sign: MEDICAL SECTION. It was just as he remembered it. Holstering the small automatic, he struck a match, shading the flame with a cupped hand as he moved it along the rows of faded titles. Carter . . . Davidson . . . Enright . . . *Erickson*. He drew in his breath sharply. All three volumes, their gold stamping dust-dulled but legible, stood in tall and perfect order on the shelf.

In the darkness, Lewis Stillman carefully removed each volume, blowing it free of dust. At last, all three books were clean and solid in his hands.

Well, you've done it. You've reached the books and now they belong to you.

He smiled, thinking of the moment when he would be able to sit down at the table with his treasure and linger again over the wondrous pages.

He found an empty carton at the rear of the store and placed the books inside. Returning to the stairs, he shouldered the rifle and began his descent to the lower floor.

So far, he told himself, my luck is still holding.

But as Lewis Stillman's foot touched the final stair, his luck ran out.

The entire lower floor was alive with them!

Rustling like a mass of great insects, gliding toward him, eyes gleaming in the half-light, they converged upon the stairs. They'd been waiting for him.

Now, suddenly, the books no longer mattered. Now only his life mattered and nothing else. He moved back against the hard wood of the stair rail, the carton of books sliding from his hands. They had stopped at the foot of the stairs; they were silent, looking up at him with hate in their eyes.

If you can reach the street, Stillman told himself, then you've still got half a chance. That means you've got to get through them to the door. All right then, *move*.

Lewis Stillman squeezed the trigger of the automatic. Two of them fell as Stillman rushed into their midst.

He felt sharp nails claw at his shirt, heard the cloth ripping away in their grasp. He kept firing the small automatic into them, and three more dropped under his bullets, shrieking in pain and surprise. The others spilled back, screaming, from the door.

The pistol was empty. He tossed it away, swinging the heavy Savage free from his shoulder as he reached the street. The night air, crisp and cool in his lungs, gave him instant hope.

I can still make it, thought Stillman, as he leaped the curb and plunged across the pavement. If those shots weren't heard, then I've still got the edge. My legs are strong; I can outdistance them.

Luck, however, had failed him completely on this night. Near the intersection of Hollywood Boulevard and Highland, a fresh pack of them swarmed toward him.

He dropped to one knee and fired into their ranks, the Savage jerking in his hands. They scattered to either side.

He began to run steadily down the middle of Hollywood Boulevard, using the butt of the heavy rifle like a battering ram as they came at him. As he neared Highland, three of them darted directly into his path. Stillman fired. One doubled over, lurching crazily into a jagged plate glass store front. Another clawed at him as he swept around the corner to Highland, but he managed to shake free.

The street ahead of him was clear. Now his superior leg power would count heavily in his favor. Two miles. Could he make it before others cut him off?

Running, reloading, firing. Sweat soaking his shirt, rivering down his face, stinging his eyes. A mile covered. Halfway to the drains. They had fallen back behind his swift stride.

But more of them were coming, drawn by the rifle shots, pouring in from side streets, from stores and houses.

His heart jarred in his body, his breath was ragged. How many of them around him? A hundred? Two hundred? More coming. God!

He bit down on his lower lip until the salt taste of blood was on his tongue. You can't make it, a voice inside him shouted. They'll have you in another block and you know it!

He fitted the rifle to his shoulder, adjusted his aim, and fired. The long rolling crack of the big weapon filled the night. Again and again he fired, the butt jerking into the flesh of his shoulder, the bitter smell of burnt powder in his nostrils.

It was no use. Too many of them. He could not clear a path.

Lewis Stillman knew that he was going to die.

The rifle was empty at last; the final bullet had been fired. He had no place to run because they were all around him, in a slowly closing circle.

He looked at the ring of small cruel faces and thought, The aliens did their job perfectly; they stopped Earth before she could reach the age of the rocket, before she could threaten planets beyond her own moon. What an immensely clever plan it had been! To destroy every human being on Earth above the age of six—and then to leave as quickly as they had come, allowing our civilization to continue on a primitive level, knowing that Earth's back had been broken, that her survivors would revert to savagery as they grew into adulthood.

Lewis Stillman dropped the empty rifle at his feet and threw out his hands. "Listen," he pleaded, "I'm really one of you. You'll *all* be like me soon. Please, *listen* to me."

But the circle tightened relentlessly around Lewis Stillman. He was screaming when the children closed in.

Poul Anderson

The illustrious Poul Anderson is the recipient of no less than six Hugo Awards and two Nebulas, as well as the Tolkien Memorial Award. This last award recognizes his substantial contributions to the field of fantasy, since Anderson is one of the few writers currently working who is capable of producing high-quality "hard" science fiction and outstanding fantasy, frequently in the same year. A full-time writer for more than thirty years, he served as President of the Science Fiction Writers of America in 1971–1972. He has contributed more than seventy novels and story collections to the science fiction/fantasy field, and is still going strong, as in this fine tale of a man who went too far into the future.

FLIGHT TO FOREVER

by Poul Anderson

THAT MORNING IT RAINED, a fine, summery mist blowing over the hills and hiding the gleam of the river and the village beyond. Martin Saunders stood in the doorway letting the cool, wet air blow in his face and wondered what the weather would be like a hundred years from now.

Eve Lang came up behind him and laid a hand on his arm. He smiled down at her, thinking how lovely she was with the raindrops caught in her dark hair like small pearls. She didn't say anything; there was no need for it, and he felt grateful for silence.

He was the first to speak. "Not long now, Eve." And then, realizing the banality of it, he smiled. "Only why do we have this airport feeling? It's not as if I'll be gone long."

"A hundred years," she said.

"Take it easy, darling. The theory is foolproof. I've been on time jaunts before, remember? Twenty years ahead and twenty back. The projector works, it's been proven in practice. This is just a little longer trip, that's all."

"But the automatic machines, that went a hundred years ahead, never came back—"

"Exactly. Some damn fool thing or other went wrong with them. Tubes blew their silly heads off, or some such thing. That's why Sam and I have to go, to see what went wrong. We can repair our machine. We can compensate for the well-known perversity of vacuum tubes."

"But why the two of you? One would be enough. Sam—"

"Sam is no physicist. He might not be able to find the trouble. On the other hand, as a skilled mechanic he can do

31

things I never could. We supplement each other." Saunders took a deep breath. "Look, darling—"

Sam Hull's bass shout rang out to them. "All set, folks! Any time you want to go, we can ride!"

"Coming." Saunders took his time, bidding Eve a proper farewell, a little in advance. She followed him into the house and down to the capacious underground workshop.

The projector stood in a clutter of apparatus under the white radiance of fluoro-tubes. It was unimpressive from the outside, a metal cylinder some ten feet high and thirty feet long with the unfinished look of all experimental setups. The outer shell was simply protection for the battery banks and the massive dimensional projector within. A tiny space in the forward end was left for the two men.

Sam Hull gave them a gay wave. His massive form almost blotted out the gray-smocked little body of MacPherson. "All set for a hundred years ahead," he exclaimed. "Two thousand seventy-three, here we come!"

MacPherson blinked owlishly at them from behind thick lenses. "It all tests out," he said. "Or so Sam here tells me. Personally, I wouldn't know an oscillograph from a klystron. You have an ample supply of spare parts and tools. There should be no difficulty."

"I'm not looking for any, Doc," said Saunders. "Eve here won't believe we aren't going to be eaten by monsters with stalked eyes and long fangs. I keep telling her all we're going to do is check your automatic machines, if we can find them, and make a few astronomical observations, and come back."

"There'll be people in the future," said Eve.

"Oh, well, if they invite us in for a drink we won't say no," shrugged Hull. "Which reminds me—" He fished a pint out of his capacious coverall pocket. "We ought to drink a toast or something, huh?"

Saunders frowned a little. He didn't want to add to Eve's impression of a voyage into darkness. She was worried enough, poor kid, poor, lovely kid. "Hell," he said, "we've been back to nineteen fifty-three and seen the house standing. We've been ahead to nineteen ninety-three and seen the house standing. Nobody home at either time. These jaunts are too dull to rate a toast."

"Nothing," said Hull, "is too dull to rate a drink." He poured and they touched glasses, a strange little ceremony in the utterly prosaic laboratory. "Bon voyage!"

"Bon voyage." Eve tried to smile, but the hand that lifted the glass to her lips trembled a little.

"Come on," said Hull. "Let's go, Mart. Sooner we set out, the sooner we can get back."

"Sure." With a gesture of decision, Saunders put down his glass and swung toward the machine. "Good-by, Eve, I'll see you in a couple of hours—after a hundred years or so."

"So long—Martin." She made the name a caress.

MacPherson beamed with avuncular approval.

Saunders squeezed himself into the forward compartment with Hull. He was a big man, long-limbed and wide-shouldered, with blunt, homely features under a shock of brown hair and wide-set gray eyes lined with crow's feet from much squinting into the sun. He wore only the plain blouse and slacks of his work, stained here and there with grease or acid.

The compartment was barely large enough for the two of them, and crowded with instruments—as well as the rifle and pistol they had along entirely to quiet Eve's fears. Saunders swore as the guns got in his way, and closed the door. The clang had in it an odd note of finality.

"Here goes," said Hull unnecessarily.

Saunders nodded and started the projector warming up. Its powerful thrum filled the cabin and vibrated in his bones. Needles flickered across gauge faces, approaching stable values.

Through the single porthole he saw Eve waving. He waved back and then, with an angry motion, flung down the main switch.

The machine shimmered, blurred, and was gone. Eve drew a shuddering breath and turned back to MacPherson.

Grayness swirled briefly before them, and the drone of the projectors filled the machine with an enormous song. Saunders watched the gauges, and inched back the switch which controlled their rate of time advancement. A hundred years ahead—less the number of days since they'd sent the first automatic, just so that no dunderhead in the future would find it and walk off with it. . . .

He slapped down the switch and the noise and vibration came to a ringing halt.

Sunlight streamed in through the porthole. "No house?" asked Hull.

"A century is a long time," said Saunders. "Come on, let's go out and have a look."

They crawled through the door and stood erect. The machine lay in the bottom of a half-filled pit above which grasses waved. A few broken shards of stone projected from the earth. There was a bright blue sky overhead, with fluffy white clouds blowing across it.

"No automatics," said Hull, looking around.

"That's odd. But maybe the ground-level adjustments—let's go topside." Saunders scrambled up the sloping walls of the pit.

It was obviously the half-filled basement of the old house, which must somehow have been destroyed in the eighty years since his last visit. The ground-level machine in the projector automatically materialized it on the exact surface whenever it emerged. There would be no sudden falls or sudden burials under risen earth. Nor would there be disastrous materializations inside something solid; mass-sensitive circuits prevented the machine from halting whenever solid matter occupied its own space. Liquid or gas molecules could get out of the way fast enough.

Saunders stood in tall, wind-rippled grass and looked over the serene landscape of upper New York State. Nothing had changed, the river and the forested hills beyond it were the same, the sun was bright and clouds shone in the heavens.

No—no, before God! Where was the village?

House gone, town gone—what had happened? Had people simply moved away, or . . .

He looked back down to the basement. Only a few minutes ago—a hundred years in the past—he had stood there in a tangle of battered apparatus, and Doc and Eve—and now it was a pit with wild grass covering the raw earth. An odd desolation tugged at him.

Was *he* still alive today? Was—Eve? The gerontology of 1973 made it entirely possible, but one never knew. And he didn't want to find out.

"Musta give the country back to the Indians," grunted Sam Hull.

The prosaic wisecrack restored a sense of balance. After all, any sensible man knew that things changed with time. There would be good and evil in the future as there had been in the past. "—And they lived happily ever after" was pure myth. The important thing was change, an unending flux out of which all could come. And right now there was a job to do.

They scouted around in the grass, but there was no trace of

the small automatic projectors. Hull scowled thoughtfully. "You know," he said, "I think they started back and blew out on the way."

"You must be right," nodded Saunders. "We can't have arrived more than a few minutes after their return-point." He started back toward the big machine. "Let's take our observation and get out."

They set up their astronomical equipment and took readings on the declining sun. Waiting for night, they cooked a meal on a camp stove and sat while a cricket-chirring dusk deepened around them.

"I like this future," said Hull. "It's peaceful. Think I'll retire here—or now—in my old age."

The thought of transtemporal resorts made Saunders grin. But—who knew? Maybe!

The stars wheeled grandly overhead. Saunders jotted down figures on right ascension, declination and passage times. From that, they could calculate later, almost to the minute, how far the machine had taken them. They had not moved in space at all, of course, relative to the surface of the earth. "Absolute space" was an obsolete fiction, and as far as the projector was concerned Earth was the immobile center of the universe.

They waded through dew-wet grass back down to the machine. "We'll try ten-year stops, looking for the automatics," said Saunders. "If we don't find 'em that way, to hell with them. I'm hungry."

2063—it was raining into the pit.

2053—sunlight and emptiness.

2043—the pit was fresher now, and a few rotting timbers lay half buried in the ground.

Saunders scowled at the meters. "She's drawing more power than she should," he said.

2023—the house had obviously burned, charred stumps of wood were in sight. And the projector had roared with a skull-cracking insanity of power; energy drained from the batteries like water from a squeezed sponge; a resistor was beginning to glow.

They checked the circuits, inch by inch, wire by wire. Nothing was out of order.

"Let's go." Hull's face was white.

It was a battle to leap the next ten years; it took half an hour of bawling, thundering, tortured labor for the projector to fight backward. Radiated energy made the cabin unendurably hot.

2013—the fire-blackened basement still stood. On its floor lay two small cylinders, tarnished with some years of weathering.

"The automatics got a little farther back," said Hull. "Then they quit, and just lay here."

Saunders examined them. When he looked up from his instruments, his face was grim with the choking fear that was rising within him. "Drained," he said. "Batteries completely dead. They used up all their energy reserves."

"What in the devil is this?" It was almost a snarl from Hull.

"I—don't—know. There seems to be some kind of resistance which increases the further back we try to go—"

"Come on!"

"But—"

"Come on, God damn it!"

Saunders shrugged hopelessly.

It took two hours to fight back five years. Then Saunders stopped the projector. His voice shook.

"No go, Sam. We've used up three quarters of our stored energy—and the farther back we go, the more we use per year. It seems to be some sort of high-order exponential function."

"So—"

"So we'd never make it. At this rate, our batteries will be dead before we get back another ten years." Saunders looked ill. "It's some effect the theory didn't allow for, some accelerating increase in power requirements the farther back into the past we go. For twenty-year hops or less, the energy increases roughly as the square of the number of years traversed. But it must actually be something like an exponential curve, which starts building up fast and furious beyond a certain point. We haven't enough power left in the batteries!"

"If we could recharge them—"

"We don't have such equipment with us. But maybe—"

They climbed out of the ruined basement and looked eagerly towards the river. There was no sign of the village. It must have been torn down or otherwise destroyed still further back in the past at a point they'd been through.

"No help there," said Saunders.

"We can look for a place. There must be people somewhere!"

"No doubt." Saunders fought for calm. "But we could spend a long time looking for them, you know. And—" his voice wavered. "Sam, I'm not sure even recharging at intervals would help. It looks very much to me as if the curve of energy consumption is approaching a vertical asymptote."

"Talk English, will you?" Hull's grin was forced.

"I mean that beyond a certain number of years an infinite amount of energy may be required. Like the Einsteinian concept of light as the limiting velocity. As you approach the speed of light, the energy needed to accelerate increases ever more rapidly. You'd need infinite energy to get beyond the speed of light—which is just a fancy way of saying you can't do it. The same thing may apply to time as well as space."

"You mean—we can't ever get back?"

"I don't know." Saunders looked desolately around at the smiling landscape. "I could be wrong. But I'm horribly afraid I'm right."

Hull swore. "What're we going to do about it?"

"We've got two choices," Saunders said. "One, we can hunt for people, recharge our batteries, and keep trying. Two, we can go into the future."

"The future!"

"Uh-huh. Sometime in the future, they ought to know more about such things than we do. They may know a way to get around this effect. Certainly they could give us a powerful enough engine so that, if energy is all that's needed, we can get back. A small atomic generator, for instance."

Hull stood with bent head, turning the thought over in his mind. There was a meadowlark singing somewhere, maddeningly sweet.

Saunders forced a harsh laugh. "But the very first thing on the agenda," he said, "is breakfast!"

The food was tasteless. They ate in a heavy silence, choking the stuff down. But in the end they looked at each other with a common resolution.

Hull grinned and stuck out a hairy paw. "It's a hell of a roundabout way to get home," he said, "but I'm for it."

Saunders clasped hands with him, wordlessly. They went back to the machine.

"And now where?" asked the mechanic.

"It's two thousand eight," said Saunders. "How about—well—two thousand five hundred A.D.?"

"Okay. It's a nice round number. Anchors aweigh!"

The machine thrummed and shook. Saunders was gratified to notice the small power consumption as the years and decades fled by. At that rate, they had energy enough to travel to the end of the world.

Eve, Eve, I'll come back. I'll come back if I have to go ahead to Judgment Day....

2500 A.D. The machine blinked into materialization on top of a low hill—the pit had filled in during the intervening centuries. Pale, hurried sunlight flashed through wind-driven rain clouds into the hot interior.

"Come," said Hull. "We haven't got all day."

He picked up the automatic rifle. "What's the idea?" exclaimed Saunders.

"Eve was right the first time," said Hull grimly. "Buckle on that pistol, Mart."

Saunders strapped the heavy weapon to his thigh. The metal was cold under his fingers.

They stepped out and swept the horizon. Hull's voice rose in a shout of glee. "People!"

There was a small town beyond the river, near the site of old Hudson. Beyond it lay fields of ripening grain and clumps of trees. There was no sign of a highway. Maybe surface transportation was obsolete now.

The town looked—odd. It must have been there a long time; the houses were weathered. They were tall peak-roofed buildings, crowding narrow streets. A flashing metal tower reared some five hundred feet into the lowering sky, near the center of town.

Somehow, it didn't look the way Saunders had visualized communities of the future. It had an oddly stunted appearance, despite the high buildings and—sinister? He couldn't say. Maybe it was only his depression.

Something rose from the center of the town, a black ovoid that whipped into the sky and lined out across the river. *Reception committee,* thought Saunders. His hand fell on his pistol butt.

It was an airjet, he saw as it neared, an egg-shaped machine with stubby wings and a flaring tail. It was flying slowly now, gliding groundward toward them.

"Hallo, there!" bawled Hull. He stood erect with the savage wind tossing his flame-red hair, waving. "Hallo, people!"

The machine dove at them. Something stabbed from its nose, a line of smoke—tracers!

Conditioned reflex flung Saunders to the ground. The bullets whined over his head, exploding with a vicious crash behind him. He saw Hull blown apart.

The jet rushed overhead and banked for another assault. Saunders got up and ran, crouching low, weaving back and forth. The line of bullets spanged past him again, throwing up gouts of dirt where they hit. He threw himself down again.

Another try.... Saunders was knocked off his feet by the bursting of a shell. He rolled over and hugged the ground, hoping the grass would hide him. Dimly, he thought that the jet was too fast for strafing a single man; it overshot its mark.

He heard it whine overhead, without daring to look up. It circled vulture-like, seeking him. He had time for a rising tide of bitter hate.

Sam—they'd killed him, shot him without provocation— Sam, red-haired Sam with his laughter and his comradeship, Sam was dead and they had killed him.

He risked turning over. The jet was settling to earth; they'd hunt him from the ground. He got up and ran again.

A shot wailed past his ear. He spun around, the pistol in his hand, and snapped a return shot. There were men in black uniforms coming out of the jet. It was long range, but his gun was a heavy war model; it carried. He fired again and felt a savage joy at seeing one of the black-clad figures spin on its heels and lurch to the ground.

The time machine lay before him. No time for heroics; he had to get away—fast! Bullets were singing around him.

He burst through the door and slammed it shut. A slug whanged through the metal wall. Thank God the tubes were still warm!

He threw the main switch. As vision wavered, he saw the pursuers almost on him. One of them was aiming something like a bazooka.

They faded into grayness. He lay back, shuddering. Slowly, he grew aware that his clothes were torn and that a metal fragment had scratched his hand.

And Sam was dead. Sam was dead.

He watched the dial creep upward. Let it be 3000 A.D. Five hundred years was not too much to put between himself and the men in black.

He chose nighttime. A cautious look outside revealed that he was among tall buildings with little if any light. Good!

He spent a few moments bandaging his injury and changing into the extra clothes Eve had insisted on providing—a heavy wool shirt and breeches, boots, and a raincoat that should help make him relatively inconspicuous. The holstered pistol went along, of course, with plenty of extra cartridges. He'd have to leave the machine while he reconnoitered and chance its discovery. At least he could lock the door.

Outside, he found himself standing in a small cobbled courtyard between high houses with shuttered and darkened windows. Overhead was utter night, the stars must be clouded, but he saw a vague red glow to the north, pulsing and flickering. After a moment, he squared his shoulders and started down an alley that was like a cavern of blackness.

Briefly, the incredible situation rose in his mind. In less than an hour he had leaped a thousand years past his own age, had seen his friend murdered and now stood in an alien city more alone than man had ever been. *And Eve, will I see you again?*

A noiseless shadow, blacker than the night, slipped past him. The dim light shone greenly from its eyes—an alley cat! At least man still had pets. But he could have wished for a more reassuring one.

Noise came from ahead, a bobbing light flashing around at the doors of houses. He dropped a hand through the slit in his coat to grasp the pistol butt.

Black against the narrowed skyline four men came abreast, filling the street. The rhythm of their footfalls was military. A guard of some kind. He looked around for shelter; he didn't want to be taken prisoner by unknowns.

No alleys to the side—he sidled backward. The flashlight beam darted ahead, crossed his body, and came back. A voice shouted something, harsh and peremptory.

Saunders turned and ran. The voice cried again behind him. He heard the slam of boots after him. Someone blew a horn, raising echoes that hooted between the high dark walls.

A black form grew out of the night. Fingers like steel wires closed on his arm, yanking him to one side. He opened his mouth, and a hand slipped across it. Before he could recover balance, he was pulled down a flight of stairs in the street.

"In heah." The hissing whisper was taut in his ear. "Quickly."

A door slid open just a crack. They burst through, and the other man closed it behind them. An automatic lock clicked shut.

"Ih don' tink dey vised use," said the man grimly. "Dey better not ha'!"

Saunders stared at him. The other man was of medium height, with a lithe, slender build shown by the skin-tight gray clothes under his black cape. There was a gun at one hip, a pouch at the other. His face was sallow, with a yellowish tinge, and the hair was shaven. It was a lean, strong face, with high cheekbones and narrow jaw, straight nose with flaring nostrils, dark, slant eyes under Mephisto-phelean brows. The mouth, wide and self-indulgent, was drawn into a reckless grin that showed sharp white teeth. Some sort of white-Mongoloid half-breed, Saunders guessed.

"Who are *you?*" he asked roughly.

The stranger surveyed him shrewdly. "Belgotai of Syrtis," he said at last. "But yuh don't belong heah."

"I'll say I don't." Wry humor rose in Saunders. "Why did you snatch me that way?"

"Yuh didn' wanna fall into de Watch's hands, did yuh?" asked Belgotai. "Don't ask mih why Ih ressued a stranger. Ih happened to come out, see yuh running, figgered anybody running fro de Watch desuhved help, an' pulled yuh back in." He shrugged. "Of course, if yuh don' wanna be helped, go back upstaiahs."

"I'll stay here, of course," he said. "And—thanks for rescuing me."

"*De nada,*" said Belgotai. "Come, le's ha' a drink."

It was a smoky, low-ceilinged room, with a few scarred wooden tables crowded about a small charcoal fire and big barrels in the rear—a tavern of some sort, an underworld hangout. Saunders reflected that he might have done worse. Crooks wouldn't be as finicky about his antecedents as officialdom might be. He could ask his way around, learn.

"I'm afraid I haven't any money," he said. "Unless—" He pulled a handful of coins from his pocket.

Belgotai looked sharply at them and drew a whistling breath between his teeth. Then his face smoothed into blankness. "Ih'll buy," he said genially. "Come Hennaly, gi' us whissey."

Belgotai drew Saunders into a dark corner seat, away from the others in the room. The landlord brought tumblers of rotgut remotely akin to whiskey, and Saunders gulped his with a feeling of need.

"Wha' name do yuh go by?" asked Belgotai.

"Saunders. Martin Saunders."

"Glad to see yuh. Now—" Belgotai leaned closer, and his voice dropped to a whisper—"Now, Saunders, *when*'re yuh from?"

Saunders started. Belgotai smiled thinly. "Be frank," he said. "Dese're mih frien's heah. Dey'd think nawting of slitting yuh troat and dumping yuh in de alley. But Ih mean well."

With sudden great weariness, Saunders relaxed. What the hell, it had to come out sometime. "Nineteen hundred seventy-three," he said.

"Eh? De future?"

"No—the past."

"Oh. Diff'ent chronning, den. How far back?"

"One thousand and twenty-seven years."

Belgotai whistled. "Long ways! But Ih were sure yuh mus' be from de past. Nobody eve' came fro' de future."

Sickly: "You mean—it's impossible?"

"Ih do' know." Belgotai's grin was wolfish. "Who'd you visit dis era fro' de future, if dey could? But wha's yuh story?"

Saunders bristled. The whiskey was coursing hot in his veins now. "I'll trade information," he said coldly. "I won't give it."

"Faiah enawff. Blast away, Mahtin Saundahs."

Saunders told his story in a few words. At the end, Belgotai nodded gravely. "Yuh ran into de Fanatics, five hundred yeahs ago," he said. "Dey was deat' on time travelers. Or on most people, for dat matter."

"But what's happened? What sort of world is this, anyway?"

Belgotai's slurring accents were getting easier to follow. Pronunciation had changed a little, vowels sounded different, the "r" had shifted to something like that in twentieth-century French or Danish, other consonants were modified. Foreign words, especially Spanish, had crept in. But it was still intelligible. Saunders listened. Belgotai was not too well versed in his history, but his shrewd brain had a grasp of more important facts.

The time of troubles had begun in the twenty-third century with the revolt of the Martian colonists against the increasingly corrupt and tyrannical Terrestrial Directorate. A century later the folk of Earth were on the move, driven by famine, pestilence and civil war, a chaos out of which rose the religious enthusiasm of the Armageddonists—the Fanatics, as they were called later. Fifty years after the massacres on Luna, Huntry was the military dictator of Earth, and the rule of the Armageddonists endured for nearly three hundred years. It was a nominal sort of rule, vast territories were always in revolt and the planetary colonists were building up a power which kept the Fanatics out of space, but wherever they did have control they ruled with utter ruthlessness.

Among other things they forbade was time travel. But it had never been popular with anyone since the Time War, when a defeated Directorate army had leaped from the twenty-third to the twenty-fourth century and wrought havoc before their attempt at conquest was smashed. Time travelers were few anyway, the future was too precarious—they were apt to be killed or enslaved in one of the more turbulent periods.

In the late twenty-seventh century, the Planetary League and the African Dissenters had finally ended Fanatic rule. Out of the postwar confusion rose the Pax Africana, and for two hundred years man had enjoyed an era of comparative peace and progress which was wistfully looked back on as a golden age; indeed, modern chronology dated from the ascension of John Mteza I. Breakdown came through internal decay and the onslaughts of barbarians from the outer planets, the Solar System split into a multitude of small states and even independent cities. It was a hard, brawling period, not without a brilliance of its own, but it was drawing to a close now.

"Dis is one of de city-states," said Belgotai. "Liung-Wei, it's named—founded by Sinese invaders about tree centuries ago. It's under de dictatorship of Krausmann now, a stubborn old buzzard who'll no surrender dough de armies of de Atlantic Master're at ouah very gates now. Yuh see de red glow? Dat's deir projectors working on our energy screen. When dey break it down, dey'll take de city and punish it for holding out so long. Nobody looks happily to dat day."

He added a few remarks about himself. Belgotai was of a dying age, the past era of small states who employed mercenaries to fight their battles. Born on Mars, Belgotai had hired out over the whole Solar System. But the little mercenary companies were helpless before the organized levies of the rising nations, and after the annihilation of his

band Belgotai had fled to Earth, where he dragged out a
weary existence as thief and assassin. He had little to look
forward to.

"Nobody wants a free comrade now," he said ruefully. "If de
Watch don't catch me first, Ih'll hang when de Atlantic take
de city."

Saunders nodded with a certain sympathy.

Belgotai leaned close with a gleam in his slant eyes. "But
yuh can help me, Mahtin Saundahs," he hissed. "And help
yuhself too."

"Eh?" Saunders blinked wearily at him.

"Sure, sure. Take me wid yuh, out of dis damned time. Dey
can't help yuh here, dey know no more about time travel dan
yuh do—most likely dey'll throw yuh in de calabozo and
smash yuh machine. Yuh have to go on. Take me!"

Saunders hesitated, warily. What did he really know? How
much truth was in Belgotai's story? How far could he trust—

"Set me off in some time when a free comrade can fight
again. Meanwhile Ih'll help. Ih'm a good man wid gun or
vibrodagger. Yuh can't go batting alone into de future."

Saunders wondered. But what the hell—it was plain enough
that this period was of no use to him. And Belgotai had saved
him, even if the Watch wasn't as bad as he claimed. And—
well—he needed someone to talk to, if nothing else. Someone
to help him forget Sam Hull and the gulf of centuries separating him from Eve.

Decision came. "Okay."

"Wonnaful! Yuh'll no be sorry, Mahtin." Belgotai stood up.
"Come, le's be blasting off."

"Now?"

"De sooner de better. Someone may find yuh machine. Den
it's too late."

But—you'll want to make ready—say good-by—"

Belgotai slapped his pouch. "All Ih own is heah." Bitterness underlay his reckless laugh. "Ih've none to say good-by
to, except mih creditors. Come!"

Half dazed, Saunders followed him out of the tavern. This
time-hopping was going too fast for him, he didn't have a
chance to adjust.

For instance, if he ever got back to his own time he'd have
descendants in this age. At the rate at which lines of descent
spread, there would be men in each army who had his own
and Eve's blood, warring on each other without thought of

the tenderness which had wrought their very beings. But then, he remembered wearily, he had never considered the common ancestors he must have with men he'd shot out of the sky in the war he once had fought.

Men lived in their own times, a brief flash of light ringed with an enormous dark, and it was not in their nature to think beyond that little span of years. He began to realize why time travel had never been common.

"Hist!" Belgotai drew him into the tunnel of an alley. They crouched there while four black-caped men of the Watch strode past. In the wan red light, Saunders had a glimpse of high cheekbones, half-Oriental features, the metallic gleam of guns slung over their shoulders.

They made their way to the machine where it lay between lowering houses crouched in a night of fear and waiting. Belgotai laughed again, a soft, joyous ring in the dark. "Freedom!" he whispered.

They crawled into it and Saunders set the controls for a hundred years ahead. Belgotai scowled. "Most like de world'll be very tame and quiet den," he said.

"If I get a way to return," said Saunders, "I'll carry you on whenever you want to go."

"Or yuh could carry me back a hundred years from now," said the warrior. "Blast away, den!"

3100 A.D. A waste of blackened, fused rock. Saunders switched on the Geiger counter and it clattered crazily. Radioactive! Some hellish atomic bomb had wiped Liung-Wei from existence. He leaped another century, shaking.

3200 A.D. The radioactivity was gone, but the desolation remained, a vast vitrified crater under a hot, still sky, dead and lifeless. There was little prospect of walking across it in search of man, nor did Saunders want to get far from the machine. If he should be cut off from it . . .

By 3500, soil had drifted back over the ruined land and a forest was growing. They stood in a drizzling rain and looked around them.

"Big trees," said Saunders. "This forest has stood for a long time without human interference."

"Maybe man went back to de caves?" suggested Belgotai.

"I doubt it. Civilization was just too widespread for a lapse into total savagery. But it may be a long ways to a settlement."

"Le's go ahead, den!" Belgotai's eyes gleamed with interest. The forest still stood for centuries thereafter. Saunders scowled in worry. He didn't like this business of going farther and farther from his time; he was already too far ahead ever to get back without help. Surely, in all ages of human history—

4100 A.D. They flashed into materialization on a broad grassy sward where low, rounded buildings of something that looked like tinted plastic stood between fountains, statues, and bowers. A small aircraft whispered noiselessly overhead, no sign of motive power on its exterior.

There were humans around, young men and women who wore long colorful capes over light tunics. They crowded forward with a shout. Saunders and Belgotai stepped out, raising hands in a gesture of friendship. But the warrior kept his hands close to his gun.

The language was a flowing, musical tongue with only a baffling hint of familiarity. Had times changed that much?

They were taken to one of the buildings. Within its cool, spacious interior, a grave, bearded man in ornate red robes stood up to greet them. Someone else brought in a small machine reminiscent of an oscilloscope with microphone attachments. The man set it on the table and adjusted its dials.

He spoke again, his own unknown language rippling from his lips. But words came out of the machine—English!

"Welcome, travelers, to this branch of the American College. Please be seated."

Saunders and Belgotai gaped. The man smiled. "I see the psychophone is new to you. It is a receiver of encephalic emissions from the speech centers. When one speaks, the corresponding thoughts are taken by the machine, greatly amplified, and beamed to the brain of the listener, who interprets them in terms of his own language.

"Permit me to introduce myself. I am Hamalon Avard; dean of this branch of the College." He raised bushy gray eyebrows in polite inquiry.

They gave their names and Avard bowed ceremoniously. A slim girl, whose scanty dress caused Belgotai's eyes to widen, brought a tray of sandwiches and a beverage not unlike tea. Saunders suddenly realized how hungry and tired he was. He collapsed into a seat that molded itself to his contours and looked dully at Avard.

Their story came out, and the dean nodded. "I thought you were time travelers," he said. "But this is a matter of great interest. The archeology departments will want to speak to you, if you will be so kind—"

"Can you help us?" asked Saunders bluntly. "Can you fix our machine so it will reverse?"

"Alas, no. I am afraid our physics holds no hope for you. I can consult the experts, but I am sure there has been no change in spatiotemporal theory since Priogan s reformulation. According to it, the energy needed to travel into the past increases tremendously with the period covered. The deformation of world lines, you see. Beyond a period of about seventy years, infinite energy is required."

Saunders nodded dully. "I thought so. Then there's no hope?"

"Not in this time, I am afraid. But science is advancing rapidly. Contact with alien culture in the Galaxy has proved an immense stimulant—"

"Yuh have interstellar travel?" exploded Belgotai. "Yuh can travel to de stars?"

"Yes, of course. The faster-than-light drive was worked out over five hundred years ago on the basis of Priogan's modified relativity theory. It involves warping through higher dimensions— But you have more urgent problems than scientific theories."

"Not Ih!" said Belgotai fiercely. "If Ih can get put among de stars—dere must be wars dere—"

"Alas, yes, the rapid expansion of the frontier has thrown the Galaxy into chaos. But I do not think you could get passage on a spaceship. In fact, the Council will probably order your temporal deportation as unintegrated individuals. The sanity of Sol will be in danger otherwise."

"Why, yuh—" Belgotai snarled and reached for his gun. Saunders clapped a hand on the warrior's arm.

"Take it easy, you bloody fool," he said furiously. "We can't fight a whole planet. Why should we? There'll be other ages."

Belgotai relaxed, but his eyes were still angry.

They stayed at the College for two days. Avard and his colleagues were courteous, hospitable, eager to hear what the travelers had to tell of their periods. They provided food and living quarters and much-needed rest. They even pleaded Belgotai's case to the Solar Council, via telescreen. But the answer was inexorable: the Galaxy already had too many barbarians. The travelers would have to go.

Their batteries were taken out of the machine for them and

a small atomic engine with nearly limitless energy reserves installed in its place. Avard gave them a psychophone for communication with whoever they met in the future. Everyone was very nice and considerate. But Saunders found himself reluctantly agreeing with Belgotai. He didn't care much for these over-civilized gentlefolk. He didn't belong in this age.

Avard bade them grave good-by. "It is strange to see you go," he said. "It is a strange thought that you will still be traveling long after my cremation, that you will see things that I cannot dream of." Briefly, something stirred in his face. "In a way I envy you." He turned away quickly, as if afraid of the thought. "Good-by and good fortune."

4300 A.D. The campus buildings were gone, but small, elaborate summerhouses had replaced them. Youths and girls in scanty rainbowhued dress crowded around the machine.

"You are time travelers?" asked one of the young men, wide-eyed.

Saunders nodded, feeling too tired for speech.

"Time travelers!" A girl squealed in delight.

"I don't suppose you have any means of traveling into the past these days?" asked Saunders hopelessly.

"Not that I know of. But please come, stay for a while, tell us about your journeys. This is the biggest lark we've had since the ship came from Sirius."

There was no denying the eager insistence. The women, in particular, crowded around, circling them in a ring of soft arms, laughing and shouting and pulling them away from the machine. Belgotai grinned. "Le's stay de night," he suggested.

Saunders didn't feel like arguing the point. There was time enough, he thought bitterly. All the time in the world.

It was a night of revelry. Saunders managed to get a few facts. Sol was a Galactic backwater these days, stuffed with mercantile wealth and guarded by nonhuman mercenaries against the interstellar raiders and conquerors. This region was one of many playgrounds for the children of the great merchant families, living for generations off inherited riches. They were amiable kids, but there was a mental and physical softness about them, and a deep inward weariness from a meaningless round of increasingly stale pleasure. Decadence.

Saunders finally sat alone under a moon that glittered with the diamond-points of domed cities, beside a softly lapping artifical lake, and watched the constellations wheel overhead—the far suns that man had conquered without mastering himself. He thought of Eve and wanted to cry, but the hollowness in his breast was dry and cold.

Belgotai had a thumping hangover in the morning which a drink offered by one of the women removed. He argued for a while about staying in this age. Nobody would deny him passage this time; they were eager for fighting men out in the Galaxy. But the fact that Sol was rarely visited now, that he might have to wait years, finally decided him on continuing.

"Dis won' go on much longer," he said. "Sol is too tempting a prize, an' mercenaries aren' allays loyal. Sooner or later, dere'll be war on Eart' again."

Saunders nodded dispiritedly. He hated to think of the blasting energies that would devour a peaceful and harmless folk, the looting and murdering and enslaving, but history was that way. It was littered with the graves of pacifists.

The bright scene swirled into grayness. They drove ahead.

4400 A.D. A villa was burning, smoke and flame reaching up into the clouded sky. Behind it stood the looming bulk of a ray-scarred spaceship, and around it boiled a vortex of men, huge bearded men in helmets and cuirasses, laughing as they bore out golden loot and struggling captives. The barbarians had come!

The two travelers leaped back into the machine. Those weapons could fuse it to a glowing mass. Saunders swung the main-drive switch far over.

"We'd better make a longer jump," Saunders said, as the needle crept past the century mark. "Can't look for much scientific progress in a dark age. I'll try for five thousand A.D."

His mind carried the thought on: *Will there ever be progress of the sort we must have? Eve, will I ever see you again?* As if his yearning could carry over the abyss of millennia: *Don't mourn me too long, my dearest. In all the bloody ages of human history, your happiness is all that ultimately matters.*

As the needle approached six centuries, Saunders tried to ease down the switch. Tried!

"What's the matter?" Belgotai leaned over his shoulder.

With a sudden cold sweat along his ribs, Saunders tugged harder. The switch was immobile—the projector wouldn't stop.

"Out of order?" asked Belgotai anxiously.

"No—it's the automatic mass-detector. We'd be annihilated if we emerged in the same space with solid matter. The detector prevents the projector from stopping if it senses such a structure." Saunders grinned savagely. "Some damned idiot must have built a house right where we are!"

The needle passed its limit, and still they droned on through a featureless grayness. Saunders reset the dial and noted the first half millennium. It was nice, though not necessary, to know what year it was when they emerged.

He wasn't worried at first. Man's works were so horribly impermanent; he thought with a sadness of the cities and civilizations he had seen rise and spend their little hour and sink back into the night and chaos of time. But after a thousand years. . .

Two thousand . . .

Three thousand . . .

Belgotai's face was white and tense in the dull glow of the instrument panel. "How long to go?" he whispered.

"I—don't—know."

Within the machine, the long minutes passed while the projector hummed its song of power and two men stared with hypnotized fascination at the creeping record of centuries.

For twenty thousand years that incredible thing stood. In the year 25,296 A.D., the switch suddenly went down under Saunder's steady tug. The machine flashed into reality, tilted, and slid down a few feet before coming to rest. Wildly, they opened the door.

The projector lay on a stone block big as a small house, whose ultimate slipping from its place had freed them. It was halfway up a pyramid.

A monument of gray stone, a tetrahedron a mile to a side and a half a mile high. The outer casing had worn away, or been removed, so that the tremendous blocks stood naked to the weather. Soil had drifted up onto it, grass and trees grew on its titanic slopes. Their roots, and wind and rain and frost, were slowly crumbling the artificial hill to earth again, but still it dominated the landscape.

A defaced carving leered out from a tangle of brush. Saunders looked at it and looked away, shuddering. No human being had ever craved that thing.

The countryside around was altered; he couldn't see the old river and there was a lake glimmering in the distance which had not been there before. The hills seemed lower, and forest covered them. It was a wild, primeval scene, but there was a spaceship standing near the base, a monster machine with its nose rearing skyward and a sunburst blazon on its hull. And there were men working nearby.

Saunders' shout rang in the still air. He and Belgotai scrambled down the steep slopes of earth, clawing past trees and vines. Men!

No—not all men. A dozen great shining engines were toiling without supervision at the foot of the pyramid—robots. And of the group which turned to stare at the travelers, two were squat, blue-furred, with snouted faces and six-fingered hands.

Saunders realized with an unexpectedly eerie shock that he was seeing extraterrestial intelligence. But it was to the men that he faced.

They were all tall, with aristocratically refined features and a calm that seemed inbred. Their clothing was impossible to describe; it was like a rainbow shimmer around them, never the same in its play of color and shape. So, thought Saunders, so must the old gods have looked on high Olympus, beings greater and more beautiful than man.

But it was a human voice that called to them, a deep, well-modulated tone in a totally foreign language. Saunders remembered exasperately that he had forgotten the psychophone. But one of the blue-furred aliens were already fetching a round, knob-studded globe out of which the familiar translating voice seemed to come: ". . . time travelers."

"From the very remote past, obviously," said another man. Damn him, damn them all, they weren't any more excited than at a bird which rose, startled, from the long grass. You'd think time travelers would at least be worth shaking by the hand.

"Listen," snapped Saunders, realizing in the back of his mind that his annoyance was a reaction against the awesomeness of the company, "we're in trouble. Our machine won't carry us back, and we have to find a period of time which knows how to reverse the effect. Can you do it?"

One of the aliens shook his animal head. "No," he said. "There is no way known to physics of getting farther back than about seventy years. Beyond that, the required energy approaches infinity and—"

Saunders groaned. "We know it," said Belgotai harshly.

"At least you must rest," said one of the men in a more kindly tone. "It will be interesting to hear your story."

"I've told it to too many people in the last few millennia," rasped Saunders. "Let's hear yours for a change."

Two of the strangers exchanged low-voiced words. Saunders could almost translate them himself: *"Barbarians—childish emotional pattern—well, humor them for a while."*

"This is an archeological expedition, excavating the pyramid," said one of the men patiently. "We are from the Galactic Institute, Sarlan-sector branch. I am Lord Arsfel of Astracyr, and these are my subordinates. The nonhumans, as you may wish to know, are from the planet Quulhan, whose sun is not visible from Terra."

Despite himself, Saunders' awed gaze turned to the stupendous mass looming over them. "Who built it?" he breathed.

"The Ixchulhi made such structures on planets they conquered, no one knows why. But then, no one knows what they were, or where they came from, or where they ultimately went. It is hoped that some of the answers may be found in their pyramids."

The atmosphere grew more relaxed. Deftly, the men of the expedition got Saunders' and Belgotai's stories and what information about their almost prehistoric periods they cared for. In exchange, something of history was offered them.

After the Ixchulhi's ruinous wars the Galaxy had made a surprisingly rapid comeback. New techniques of mathematical psychology made it possible to unite the peoples of a billion worlds and rule them effectively. The Galactic Empire was egalitarian—it had to be, for one of its mainstays was the fantastically old and evolved race of the planet called Vro-Hi by men.

It was peaceful, prosperous, colorful with diversity of races and cultures, expanding in science and the arts. It had already endured for ten thousand years, and there seemed no doubt in Arfel's calm mind that it could endure forever. The barbarians along the Galactic periphery and out in the Magellanic Clouds? Nonsense! The Empire would get around to civilizing them in due course; meanwhile they were only a nuisance.

But Sol could almost be called one of the barbarian suns, though it lay within the Imperial boundaries. Civilization was concentrated near the center of the Galaxy, and Sol lay in what was actually a remote and thinly starred region of space. A few primitive landsmen still lived on its planets and had infrequent intercourse with the nearer stars, but they hardly counted. The human race had almost forgotten its ancient home.

Somehow the picture was saddening to the American. He thought of old Earth spinning on her lonely way through the emptiness of space, he thought of the great arrogant Empire and of all the mighty dominions which had fallen to dust through the millennia. But when he ventured to suggest that this civilization, too, was not immortal, he was immediately snowed under with figures, facts, logic, the curious para-mathematical symbolism of modern mass psychology. It could be shown rigorously that the present setup was inherently stable—and already ten thousand years of history had given no evidence to upset that science. . . .

"I give up," said Saunders. "I can't argue with you."

They were shown through the spaceship's immense interior, the luxurious apartments of the expedition, the looming intricate machinery which did its own thinking. Arsfel tried to show them his art, his recorded music, his psychobooks, but it was no use; they didn't have the understanding.

Savages! Could an Australian aborigine have appreciated Rembrandt, Beethoven, Kant, or Einstein? Could he have lived happily in sophisticated New York society?

"We'd best go," muttered Belgotai. "We don't belong heah."

Saunders nodded. Civilization had gone too far for them; they could never be more than frightened pensioners in its hugeness. Best to get on their way again.

"I would advise you to leap ahead for long intervals," said Arsfel. "Galactic civilization won't have spread out this far for many thousands of years and certainly whatever native culture Sol develops won't be able to help you." He smiled. "It doesn't matter if you overshoot the time when the process you need is invented. The records won't be lost, I assure you. From here on, you are certain of encountering only peace and enlightenment . . . unless, of course, the barbarians of Terra get hostile, but then you can always leave them behind. Sooner or later, there will be true civilization here to help you."

"Tell me honestly," said Saunders. "Do you think the negative time machine will ever be invented?"

One of the beings from Quulhan shook his strange head. "I

doubt it," he said gravely. "We would have had visitors from
the future."

"They might not have cared to see your time," argued
Saunders desperately. "They'd have complete records of it. So
they'd go back to investigate more primitive ages, where
their appearance might easily pass unnoticed."

"You may be right," said Arsfel. His tone was disconcert-
ingly like that with which an adult comforts a child by a
white lie.

"Le's go!" snarled Belgotai.

In 26,000 the forests still stood and the pyramid had
become a high hill where trees nodded and rustled in the
wind.

In 27,000 a small village of wood and stone houses stood
among smiling grain fields.

In 28,000 men were tearing down the pyramid, quarrying
it for stone. But its huge bulk was not gone before 30,000 A.D.,
and a small city had been built from it.

Minutes ago, thought Saunders grayly, they had been
talking to Lord Arsfel of Astracyr, and now he was five
thousand years in his grave.

In 31,000, they materialized on one of the broad lawns that
reached between the towers of a high and proud city. Aircraft
swarmed overhead and a spaceship, small beside Arsfel's but
nonetheless impressive, was standing nearby.

"Looks like de Empire's got heah," said Belgotai.

"I don't know," said Saunders. "But it looks peaceful,
anyway. Let's go out and talk to people."

They were received by tall, stately women in white robes of
classic lines. It seemed that the Matriarchy now ruled Sol,
and would they please conduct themselves as befitted the
inferior sex? No, the Empire hadn't ever gotten out here; Sol
paid tribute, and there was an Imperial legate at Sirius, but
the actual boundaries of Galactic culture hadn't changed for
the past three millennia. Solar civilization was strictly home-
grown and obviously superior to the alien influence of the
Vro-Hi.

No, nothing was known about time theory. Their visit had
been welcome and all that, but now would they please go on?
They didn't fit in with the neatly regulated culture of Terra.

"I don't like it," said Saunders as they walked back toward
the machine. "Arsfel swore the Imperium would keep expand-

ing its actual as well as its nominal sphere of influence. But it's gone static now. Why?"

"Ih tink," said Belgotai, "dat spite of all his fancy mathematics, yuh were right. Nawthing lasts forever."

"But—my God!"

34,000 A.D. The Matriarchy was gone. The city was a tumbled heap of fire-blackened rocks. Skeletons lay in the ruins.

"The barbarians are moving again," said Saunders bleakly. "They weren't here so very long ago; these bones are still fresh, and they've got a long ways to go to dead center. An empire like this one will be many thousands of years in dying. But it's doomed already."

"What'll we do?" asked Belgotai.

"Go on," said Saunders tonelessly. "What else can we do?"

35,000 A.D. A peasant hut stood under huge old trees. Here and there a broken column stuck out of the earth, remnant of the city. A bearded man in coarsely woven garments fled wildly with his woman and brood of children as the machine appeared.

36,000 A.D. There was a village again, with a battered old spaceship standing hard by. There were half a dozen different races, including man, moving about, working on the construction of some enigmatic machine. They were dressed in plain, shabby clothes, with guns at their sides and the hard look of warriors in their eyes. But they didn't treat the new arrivals too badly.

Their chief was a young man in the cape and helmet of an officer of the Empire. But his outfit was at least a century old, and he was simply head of a small troop which had been hired from among the barbarian hordes to protect this part of Terra. Oddly, he insisted he was a loyal vassal of the Emperor.

The Empire! It was still a remote glory, out there among the stars. Slowly it waned, slowly the barbarians encroached while corruption and civil war tore it apart from the inside, but it was still the pathetic, futile hope of intelligent beings throughout the Galaxy. Some day it would be restored. Some day civilization would return to the darkness of the outer worlds, greater and more splendid than ever. Men dared not believe otherwise.

"But we've got a job right here," shrugged the chief. "Tautho

of Sirius will be on Sol's necks soon. I doubt if we can stand
him off for long."

"And what'll yuh do den?" challenged Belgotai.

The young-old face twisted in a bitter smile. "Die, of
course. What else is there to do—these days?"

They stayed overnight with the troopers. Belgotai had fun
swapping lies about warlike exploits, but in the morning he
decided to go on with Saunders. The age was violent enough,
but its hopelessness daunted even his tough soul.

Saunders looked haggardly at the control panel. "We've got
to go a long ways ahead," he said. "A hell of a long ways."

50,000 A.D. They flashed out of the time drive and opened
the door. A raw wind caught at them, driving thin sheets of
snow before it. The sky hung low and gray over a landscape of
high rocky hills where pine trees stood gloomily between
naked crags. There was ice on the river that murmured
darkly out of the woods.

Geology didn't work that fast; even fourteen thousand
years wasn't a very long time to the slowly changing planets.
It must have been the work of intelligent beings, ravaging
and scoring the world with senseless wars of unbelievable
forces.

A gray stone mass dominated the landscape. It stood enormous a few miles off, its black walls sprawling over incredible acres, its massive crenellated towers reaching gauntly
into the sky. And it lay half in ruin, torn and tumbled stone
distorted by energies that once made rock run molten, blurred
by uncounted millennia of weather—old.

"Dead," Saunders' voice was thin under the hooting wind.
"All dead."

"No!" Belgotai's slant eyes squinted against the flying
snow. "No, Mahtin, Ih tink Ih see a banner flying."

The wind blew bitterly around them, searing them with its
chill. "Shall we go on?" asked Saunders dully.

"Best we go find out wha's happened," said Belgotai. "Dey
can do no worse dan kill us, and Ih begin to tink dat's not so
bad."

Saunders put on all the clothes he could find and took the
psychophone in one chilled hand. Belgotai wrapped his cloak
tightly about him. They started toward the gray edifice.

The wind blew and blew. Snow hissed around them, covering the tough gray-green vegetation that hugged the stony
ground. Summer on Earth, 50,000 A.D.

As they neared the structure, its monster size grew on them. Some of the towers which still stood must be almost half a mile high, thought Saunders dizzily. But it had a grim, barbaric look; no civilized race had ever built such a fortress.

Two small, swift shapes darted into the air from that clifflike wall. "Aircraft," said Belgotai laconically. The wind ripped the word from his mouth.

They were ovoidal, without external controls or windows, apparently running on the gravitic forces which had long ago been tamed. One of them hovered overhead, covering the travelers, while the other dropped to the ground. As it landed, Saunders saw that it was old and worn and scarred. But there was a faded sunburst on its side. Some memory of the Empire must still be alive.

Two came out of the little vessel and approached the travelers with guns in their hands. One was human, a tall well-built young man with shoulder-length black hair blowing under a tarnished helmet, a patched purple coat streaming from his cuirassed shoulders, a faded leather kit and buskins. The other. . .

He was a little shorter than the man, but immensely broad of chest and limb. Four muscled arms grew from the massive shoulders, and a tufted tail lashed against his clawed feet. His head was big, broad-skulled, with a round half-animal face and cat-like whiskers about the fanged mouth and the split-pupiled yellow eyes. He wore no clothes except a leather harness, but soft blue-gray fur covered the whole great body.

The psychophone clattered out the man's hail: "Who comes?"

"Friends," said Saunders. "We wish only shelter and a little information."

"Where are you from?" There was a harsh, peremptory note in the man's voice. His face—straight, thin-boned, the countenance of a highly bred aristocrat—was gaunt with strain. "What do you want? What sort of spaceship is that you've got down there?"

"Easy, Vargor," rumbled the alien's bass. "That's no spaceship, you can see that."

"No," said Saunders. "It's a time projector."

"Time travelers!" Vargor's intense blue eyes widened. "I heard of such things once, but—time travelers!" Suddenly: "When are you from? Can you help us?"

"We're from very long ago," said Saunders pityingly. "And I'm afraid we're alone and helpless."

Vargor's erect carriage sagged a little. He looked away. But the other being stepped forward with an eagerness in him. "How far back?" he asked. "Where are you going?"

"We're going to hell, most likely. But can you get us inside? We're freezing."

"Of course. Come with us. You'll not take it amiss if I send a squad to inspect your machine? We have to be careful, you know."

The four squeezed into the aircraft and it lifted with a groan of ancient engines. Vargor gestured at the fortress ahead and his tone was a little wild. "Welcome to the hold of Brontothor! Welcome to the Galactic Empire!"

"The Empire?"

"Aye, this is the Empire, or what's left of it. A haunted fortress on a frozen ghost world, last fragment of the old Imperium and still trying to pretend that the Galaxy is not dying—that it didn't die millennia ago, that there is something left besides wild beasts howling among the ruins." Vargor's throat caught in a dry sob. "Welcome!"

The alien laid a huge hand on the man's shoulder. "Don't get hysterical, Vargor," he reproved gently. "As long as brave beings hope, the Empire is still alive—whatever they say."

He looked over his shoulder at the others. "You really are welcome," he said. "It's a hard and dreary life we lead here. Taury and the Dreamer will both welcome you gladly." He paused. Then, unsurely, "But best you don't say too much about the ancient time, if you've really seen it. We can't bear too sharp a reminder, you know."

The machine slipped down beyond the wall, over a gigantic flagged courtyard to the monster bulk of the—the donjon, Saunders supposed one could call it. It rose up in several tiers, with pathetic little gardens on the terraces, toward a dome of clear plastic.

The walls, he saw, were immensely thick, with weapons mounted on them which he could see clearly through the drifting snow. Behind the donjon stood several long, barracks-like buildings, and a couple of spaceships which must have been held together by pure faith rested near what looked like an arsenal. There were guards on duty, helmeted men with energy rifles, their cloaks wrapped tightly against the wind, and other folk scurried around under the monstrous walls, men and women and children.

"There's Taury," said the alien, pointing to a small group

clustered on one of the terraces. "We may as well land right there." His wide mouth opened in an alarming smile. "And forgive me for not introducing myself before. I'm Hunda of Haamigur, general of the Imperial armies, and this is Vargor Alfri, prince of the Empire."

"Yuh crazy?" blurted Belgotai. "What Empire?"

Hunda shrugged. "It's a harmless game, isn't it? At that, you know, we are the Empire—legally. Taury is a direct descendant of Maurco the Doomer, last Emperor to be anointed according to the proper forms. Of course, that was five thousand years ago, and Maurco had only three systems left then, but the law is clear. These hundred or more barbarian pretenders, human and otherwise, haven't the shadow of a real claim to the title."

The vessel grounded and they stepped out. The others waited for them to come up. There were half a dozen old men, their long beards blowing wildly in the gale, there was a being with the face of a long-beaked bird and one that had the shape of a centauroid.

"The court of the Empress Taury," said Hunda.

"Welcome." The answer was low and gracious.

Saunders and Belgotai stared dumbly at her. She was tall, tall as a man, but under her tunic of silver links and her furred cloak she was such a woman as they had dreamed of without ever knowing in life. Her proudly lifted head had something of Vargor's looks, the same clean-lined, high-cheeked face, but it was the countenance of a woman, from the broad clear brow to the wide, wondrously chiseled mouth and the strong chin. The cold had flushed the lovely pale planes of her cheeks. Her heavy bronze-red hair was braided about her helmet, with one rebellious lock tumbling softly toward the level, dark brows. Her eyes, huge and oblique and gray as northern seas, were serene on them.

Saunders found tongue. "Thank you, your majesty," he said in a firm voice.

"If it please you, I am Martin Saunders of America, some forty-eight thousand years in the past, and my companion is Belgotai, free companion from Syrtis about a thousand years later. We are at your service for what little we may be able to do."

She inclined her stately head, and her sudden smile was warm and human. "It is a rare pleasure," she said. "Come

inside, please. And forget the formality. Tonight let us simply be alive."

They sat in what had been a small council chamber. The
great hall was too huge and empty, a cavern of darkness and
rustling relics of greatness, hollow with too many memories.
But the lesser room had been made livable, hung with
tapestries and carpeted with skins. Fluorotubes cast a white
light over it, and a fire crackled cheerfully in the hearth. Had
it not been for the wind against the windows, they might
have forgotten where they were.

"—and you can never go back?" Taury's voice was sober.
"You can never get home again?"

"I don't think so," said Saunders. "From our story, it
doesn't look that way, does it?"

"No," said Hunda. "You'd better settle down in some time
and make the best of matters."

"Why not with us?" asked Vargor eagerly.

"We'd welcome you with all our hearts," said Taury, "but I
cannot honestly advise you to stay. These are evil times."

It was a harsh language they spoke, a ringing metallic
tongue brought in by the barbarians. But from her throat,
Saunders thought, it was utter music.

"We'll at least stay a few days," he said impulsively. "It's
barely possible we can do something."

"I doubt that," said Hunda practically. "We've retrogressed,
yes. For instance, the principle of the time projector was lost
long ago. But still, there's a lot of technology left which was
far beyond your own times."

"I know," said Saunders defensively. "But—well, frankly—
we haven't fitted in any other time as well."

"Will there ever be a decent age again?" asked one of the
old courtiers bitterly.

The avian from Klakkahar turned his eyes on Saunders.
"It wouldn't be cowardice for you to leave a lost cause which
you couldn't possibly aid," he said in his thin, accented
tones. "When the Anvardi come, I think we will all die."

"What is de tale of de Dreamer?" asked Belgotai. "You've
mentioned some such."

It was like a sudden darkness in the room. There was
silence, under the whistling wind, and men sat wrapped in
their own cheerless thoughts. Finally Taury spoke.

"He is the last of the Vro-Hi, counselors of the Empire.
That one still lives—the Dreamer. But there can never really

be another Empire, at least not on the pattern of the old one. No other race is intelligent enough to coordinate it."

Hunda shook his big head, puzzled. "The Dreamer once told me that might be for the best," he said. "But he wouldn't explain."

"How did you happen to come here—to Earth, of all planets?" Saunders asked.

Taury smiled with a certain grim humor. "The last few generations have been one of the Imperium's less fortunate periods," she said. "In short, the most the Emperor ever commanded was a small fleet. My father had even that shot away from him. He fled with three ships, out toward the Periphery. It occurred to him that Sol was worth trying as a refuge."

The Solar System had been cruelly scarred in the dark ages. The great engineering works which had made the other planets habitable were ruined, and Earth herself had been laid waste. There had been a weapon used which consumed atmospheric carbon dioxide. Saunders, remembering the explanation for the Ice Ages offered by geologists of his own time, nodded in dark understanding. Only a few starveling savages lived on the planet now, and indeed the whole Sirius Sector was so desolated that no conqueror thought it worth bothering with.

It had pleased the Emperor to make his race's ancient home the capital of the Galaxy. He had moved into the ruined fortress of Brontothor, built some seven thousand years ago by the nonhuman Grimmani and blasted out of action a millennium later. Renovation of parts of it, installation of weapons and defensive works, institution of agriculture . . . "Why, he had suddenly acquired a whole planetary system!" said Taury with a half-sad little smile.

She took them down into the underground levels the next day to see the Dreamer. Vargor went along too, walking close beside her, but Hunda stayed topside; he was busy supervising the construction of additional energy screen generators.

They went through immense vaulted caverns hewed out of the rock, dank tunnels of silence where their footfalls echoed weirdly and shadows flitted beyond the dull glow of fluorospheres. Now and then they passed a looming monstrous bulk, the corroded hulk of some old machine. The night and loneliness weighed heavily on them, they huddled together and did not speak for fear of rousing the jeering echoes.

"There were slideways here once," remarked Taury as they started, "but we haven't gotten around to installing new ones. There's too much else to do."

Too much else—a civilization to rebuild, with these few broken remnants. How can they dare even to keep trying in the face of the angry gods? What sort of courage is it they have?

Taury walked ahead with the long, swinging stride of a warrior, a red lioness of a woman in the wavering shadows. Her gray eyes caught the light with a supernatural brilliance. Vargor kept pace, but he lacked her steadiness, his gaze shifted nervously from side to side as they moved down the haunted, booming length of the tunnels. Belgotai went cat-footed; his own restless eyes had merely the habitual wariness of his hard and desperate lifetime. Again Saunders thought what a strange company they were, four humans from the dawn and the dusk of human civilization, thrown together at the world's end and walking to greet the last of the gods. His past life, Eve, MacPherson, the world of his time, were dimming in his mind, they were too remote from his present reality. It seemed as if he had never been anything but a follower of the Galactic Empress.

They came at last to a door. Taury knocked softly and swung it open—yes, they were even back to manual doors now.

Saunders had been prepared for almost anything, but nonetheless the appearance of the Dreamer was a shock. He had imagined a grave white-bearded man, or a huge-skulled spider-thing, or a naked brain pulsing in a machine-tended case. But the last of the Vro-Hi was—a monster.

No—not exactly. Not when you discarded human standards; then he even had a weird beauty of his own. The gross bulk of him sheened with iridescence, and his many seven-fingered hands were supple and graceful, and the eyes—the eyes were huge pools of molten gold, lambent and wise, a stare too brilliant to meet directly.

He stood up on his stumpy legs as they entered, barely four feet high though the head-body unit was broad and massive. His hooked beak did not open, and the psychophone remained silent, but as the long delicate feelers pointed toward him Saunders thought he heard words, a deep organ voice rolling soundless through the still air: "Greeting, your majesty. Greeting, your highness. Greeting, men out of time, and welcome!"

Telepathy—direct telepathy—so that was how it felt!

"Thank you ... sir." Somehow, the thing rated the title, rated an awed respect to match his own grave formality. "But I thought you were in a trance of concentration till now. How did you know—" Saunders' voice trailed off and he flushed with sudden distaste.

"No, traveler, I did not read your mind as you think. The Vro-Hi always respected privacy and did not read any thoughts save those contained in speech addressed solely to them. But my induction was obvious."

"What were you thinking about in the last trance?" asked Vargor. His voice was sharp with strain. "Did you reach any plan?"

"No, your highness," vibrated the Dreamer. "As long as the factors involved remain constant, we cannot logically do otherwise than we are doing. When new data appear, I will reconsider immediate necessities. No, I was working further on the philosophical basis which the Second Empire must have."

"What Second Empire?" sneered Vorgar bitterly.

"The one which will come—some day," answered Taury quietly.

The Dreamer's wise eyes rested on Saunders and Belgotai. "With your permission," he thought, "I would like to scan your complete memory patterns, conscious, subconscious, and cellular. We know so little of your age." As they hesitated: "I assure you, sirs, that a nonhuman being half a million years old can keep secrets, and certainly does not pass moral judgments. And the scanning will be necessary anyway if I am to teach you the present language."

Saunders braced himself. "Go ahead," he said distastefully.

For a moment he felt dizzy, a haze passed over his eyes and there was an eerie thrill along every nerve of him. Taury laid an arm about his waist, bracing him.

It passed. Saunders shook his head, puzzled. "Is that *all?*"

"Aye, sir. A Vro-Hi brain can scan an indefinite number of units simultaneously." With a faint hint of a chuckle: "But did you notice what tongue you just spoke in?"

"I—eh—huh?" Saunders looked wildly at Taury's smiling face. The hard, open-voweled syllables barked from his mouth: "I—by the gods—I can speak Stellarian now!"

"Aye," thought the Dreamer. "The language centers are peculiarly receptive; it is easy to impress a pattern on them. The method of instruction will not work so well for information involving other faculties, but you must admit it is a convenient and efficient way to learn speech."

"Blast off wit me, den," said Belgotai cheerfully. "Ih allays was a dumkoff at languages."

When the Dreamer was through, he thought: "You will not take it amiss if I tell all that what I saw in both your minds was good—brave and honest, under the little neuroses which all beings at your level of evolution cannot help accumulating. I will be pleased to remove those for you, if you wish."

"No, thanks," said Belgotai. "I like my little neuroses."

"I see that you are debating staying here," went on the Dreamer. "You will be valuable, but you should be fully warned of the desperate position we actually are in. This is not a pleasant age in which to live."

"From what I've seen," answered Saunders slowly, "golden ages are only superficially better. They may be easier on the surface but there's death in them. To travel hopefully, believe me, is better than to arrive."

"That has been true in all past ages, aye. It was the great mistake of the Vro-Hi. We should have known better, with ten million years of civilization behind us." There was a deep and tragic note in the rolling thought-pulse. "But we thought that since we had achieved a static physical state in which the new frontiers and challenges lay within our own minds, all beings at all levels of evolution could and should have developed in them the same idea.

"With our help, and with the use of scientific psychodynamics, and the great cybernetic engines, the coordination of a billion planets became possible. It was perfection, in a way—but perfection is death to imperfect beings, and even the Vro-Hi had many shortcomings. I cannot explain all the philosophy to you; it involves concepts you could not fully grasp, but you have seen the workings of the great laws in the rise and fall of cultures. I have proved rigorously that permanence is a self-contradictory concept. There can be no goal to reach, not ever."

"Then the Second Empire will have no better hope than decay and chaos again?" Saunders grinned humorlessly. "Why the devil do you want one?"

Vargor's harsh laugh shattered the brooding silence. "What indeed does it matter?" he cried. "What use to plan the future of the universe, when we are outlaws on a forgotten planet? The Anvardi are coming!" He sobered, and there was a set to his jaw which Saunders liked. "They're coming, and there's little we can do to stop it," said Vargor. "But we'll give them a fight. We'll give them such a fight as the poor old Galaxy never saw before!"

"Oh, no—oh no—oh no—"

The murmur came unnoticed from Vargor's lips, a broken cry of pain as he stared at the image which flickered and wavered on the great interstellar communiscreen. And there was horror in the eyes of Taury, grimness to the set of Hunda's mighty jaws, a sadness of many hopeless centuries in the golden gaze of the Dreamer.

After weeks of preparation and waiting, Saunders realized matters were at last coming to a head.

"Aye, your majesty," said the man in the screen. He was haggard, exhausted, worn out by strain and struggle and defeat. "Aye, fifty-four shiploads of us, and the Anvardian fleet in pursuit."

"How far behind?" rapped Hunda.

"About half a light-year, sir, and coming up slowly. We'll be close to Sol before they can overhaul us."

"Can you fight them?" rapped Hunda.

"No, sir," said the man. "We're loaded with refugees, women and children and unarmed peasants, hardly a gun on a ship— Can't you help us?" It was a cry, torn by the ripping static that filled the intersteller void. "Can't you help us, your majesty? They'll sell us for slaves!"

"How did it happen?" asked Taury wearily.

"I don't know, your majesty. We heard you were at Sol through your agents, and secretly gathered ships. We don't want to be under the Anvardi, Empress; they tax the life from us and conscript our men and take our women and children. . . . We only communicated by ultrawave; it can't be traced, and we only used the code your agents gave us. But as we passed Canopus, they called on us to surrender in the name of their king—and they have a whole war fleet after us!"

"How long before they get here?" asked Hunda.

"At this rate, sir, perhaps a week," answered the captain of the ship. Static snarled through his words.

"Well, keep on coming this way," said Taury wearily. "We'll send ships against them. You may get away during the battle. Don't go to Sol, of course; we'll have to evacuate that. Our men will try to contact you later."

"We aren't worth it, your majesty. Save all your ships."

"We're coming," said Taury flatly, and broke the circuit.

She turned to the others, and her red head was still lifted. "Most of our people can get away," she said. "They can flee into the Arlath cluster; the enemy won't be able to find them in that wilderness." She smiled, a tired little smile that tugged at one corner of her mouth. "We all know what to do, we've planned against this day. Munidor, Falz, Mico, start readying for evacuation. Hunda, you and I will have to plan our assault. We'll want to make it as effective as possible, but use a minimum of ships."

"Why sacrifice fighting strength uselessly?" asked Belgotai.

"It won't be useless. We'll delay the Anvardi, and give those refugees a chance to escape."

"If we had weapons," rumbled Hunda. His huge fists clenched. "By the gods, if we had decent weapons!"

The Dreamer stiffened. And before he could vibrate it, the same thought had leaped into Saunders' brain, and they stared at each other, man and Vro-Hian, with a sudden wild hope. . . .

Space glittered and flared with a million stars, thronging against the tremendous dark, the Milky Way foamed around the sky in a rush of cold silver, and it was shattering to a human in its utter immensity. Saunders felt the loneliness of it as he had never felt it on the trip to Venus—for Sol was dwindling behind them, they were rushing out into the void between the stars.

There had only been time to install the new weapon on the dreadnought; time and facilities were so cruelly short, there had been no chance even to test it in maneuvers. They might, perhaps, have leaped back in time again and again, gaining weeks, but the shops of Terra could only turn out so much material in the one week they did have.

So it was necessary to risk the whole fleet and the entire fighting strength of Sol on this one desperate gamble. If the old *Vengeance* could do her part, the outnumbered Imperials would have their chance. But if they failed . . .

Saunders stood on the bridge, looking out at the stellar host, trying to discern the Anvardian fleet. The detectors were far over scale, the enemy was close, but you couldn't visually detect something that outran its own image.

Hunda was at the control central, bent over the cracked old dials and spinning the corroded signal wheels, trying to coax another centimeter per second from a ship more ancient than the Pyramids had been in Saunders' day. The Dreamer stood quietly in a corner, staring raptly out at the Galaxy. The others at the court were each in charge of a squadron, Saunders had talked to them over the inter-ship visiscreen—Vargor white-lipped and tense, Belgotai blasphemously cheerful, the rest showing only cool reserve.

"In a few minutes," said Taury quietly. "In just a few minutes, Martin."

She paced back from the viewport, lithe and restless as a tigress. The cold white starlight glittered in her eyes. A red cloak swirled about the strong, deep curves of her body, a Sunburst helmet sat proudly on her bronze-bright hair. Saunders thought how beautiful she was—by all the gods, how beautiful!

She smiled at him. "It is your doing, Martin," she said. "You came from the past just to bring us hope. It's enough to make one believe in destiny." She took his hand. "But of course it's not the hope you wanted. This won't get you back home."

"It doesn't matter," he said.

"It does, Martin. But—may I say it? I'm still glad of it. Not only for the sake of the Empire, but—"

A voice rattled over the bridge communicator: "Ultrawave to bridge. The enemy is sending us a message, your majesty. Shall I send it up to you?"

"Of course." Taury switched on the bridge screen.

A face leaped into it, strong and proud and ruthless, the Sunburst shining in the green hair. "Greeting, Taury of Sol," said the Anvardian. "I am Ruulthan, Emperor of the Galaxy."

"I know who you are," said Taury thinly, "but I don't recognize your assumed title."

"Our detectors report your approach with a fleet approximately one-tenth the size of ours. You have one Supernova ship, of course, but so do we. Unless you wish to come to terms, it will mean annihilation."

"What are your terms?"

"Surrender, execution of the criminals who led the attacks

on Anvardian planets, and your own pledge of allegiance to me as Galactic Emperor." The voice was clipped, steel-hard.

Taury turned away in disgust. Saunders told Ruulthan in explicit language what to do with his terms, and then cut off the screen.

Taury gestured to the newly installed time-drive controls. "Take them, Martin," she said. "They're yours, really." She put her hands in his and looked at him with serious gray eyes. "And if we should fail in this—good-by, Martin."

"Good-by," he said thickly.

He wrenched himself over the panel and sat down before its few dials. *Here goes nothing!*

He waved one hand, and Hunda cut off the hyperdrive. At low intrinsic velocity, the *Vengeance* hung in space while the invisible ships of her fleet flushed past toward the oncoming Anvardi.

Slowly then, Saunders brought down the time-drive switch. And the ship roared with power, atomic energy flowed into the mighty circuits which they had built to carry her huge mass through time—the lights dimmed, the giant machine throbbed and pulsed, and a featureless grayness swirled beyond the ports.

He took her back three days. They lay in empty space; the Anvardi were still fantastic distances away. His eyes strayed to the brilliant yellow spark of Sol. Right there, this minute, he was sweating his heart out installing the time projector which had just carried him back. . . .

But no, that was meaningless, simultaneity was arbitrary. And there was a job to do right now.

The chief astrogator's voice came with a torrent of figures. They had to find the exact position in which the Anvardian flagship would be in precisely seventy-two hours. Hunda rang the signals to the robots in the engine room, and slowly, ponderously, the *Vengeance* slid across five million miles of space.

"All set," said Hunda. "Let's go!"

Saunders smiled, a mirthless skinning of teeth, and threw his main switch in reverse. Three days forward in time. . . .

To lie alongside the Anvardian dreadnought!

Frantically Hunda threw the hyperdrive back in, matching translight velocities. They could see the ship now, it loomed like a metal mountain against the stars. And every gun in the *Vengeance* cut loose!

Vortex cannon—blasters—atomic shells and torpedoes—gravity snatchers—all the hell which had ever been brewed in the tortured centuries of history vomited against the screens of the Avardian flagship.

Under that monstrous barrage, filling space with raving energy till it seemed its very structure must boil, the screens went down, a flare of light searing like another nova. And through the solid matter of her hull those weapons bored, cutting, blasting, disintegrating. Steel boiled into vapor, into atoms, into pure devouring energy that turned on the remaining solid material. Through and through the hull that fury raged, a waste of flame that left not even ash in its track.

And now the rest of the Imperial fleet drove against the Anvardi. Assaulted from outside, with a devouring monster in its very midst, the Anvardian fleet lost the offensive, recoiled and broke up into desperately fighting units. War snarled between the silent white stars.

Still the Anvardi fought, hurling themselves against the ranks of the Imperials, wrecking ships and slaughtering men even as they went down. They still had the numbers, if not the organization, and they had the same weapons and the same bitter courage as their foes.

The bridge of the *Vengeance* shook and roared with the shock of battle. The lights darkened, flickered back, dimmed again. The riven air was sharp with ozone, and the intolerable energies loosed made her interior a furnace. Reports clattered over the communicator: "—Number Three screen down—Compartment Number Five doesn't answer—Vortex turret Five Hundred Thirty-seven out of action—"

Still she fought, still she fought, hurling metal and energy in an unending storm, raging and rampaging among the ships of the Anvardi. Saunders found himself manning a gun, shooting out at vessels he couldn't see, getting his aim by sweat-blinded glances at the instruments—and the hours dragged away in flame and smoke and racking thunder. . . ."

"They're fleeing!"

The exuberant shout rang through every remaining compartment of the huge old ship. *Victory, victory, victory*—She had not heard such cheering for five thousand weary years.

Saunders staggered drunkenly back onto the bridge. He could see the scattered units of the Anvardi now that he was behind them, exploding out into the Galaxy in wild search of refuge, hounded and harried by the vengeful Imperial fleet.

And now the Dreamer stood up, and suddenly he was not a stump-legged little monster but a living god whose awful thought leaped across space, faster than light, to bound and roar through the skulls of the barbarians. Saunders fell to the floor under the impact of that mighty shout, he lay numbly staring at the impassive stars while the great command rang in his shuddering brain:

"Soldiers of the Anvardi, your false emperor is dead and Taury the Red, Empress of the Galaxy, has the victory. You have seen her power. Do not resist it longer, for it is unstoppable.

"Lay down your arms. Surrender to the mercy of the Imperium. We pledge you amnesty and safe-conduct. And bear this word back to your planets:

"Taury the Red calls on all the chiefs of the Anvardian Confederacy to pledge fealty to her and aid her in restoring the Galactic Empire!"

They stood on a balcony of Brontothor and looked again at old Earth for the first time in almost a year and the last time, perhaps, in their lives.

It was strange to Saunders, this standing again on the planet which had borne him after those months in the many and alien world of a Galaxy huger than he could really imagine. There was an odd little tug at his heart, for all the bright hope of the future. He was saying goodby to Eve's world.

But Eve was gone, she was part of a past forty-eight thousand years dead, and he had *seen* those years rise and die, his one year of personal time was filled and stretched by the vision of history until Eve was a remote, lovely dream. God keep her, wherever her soul had wandered in these millennia—God grant she had had a happy life—but as for him, he had his own life to live, and a mightier task at hand than he had ever conceived.

The last months rose in his mind, a bewilderment of memory. After the surrender of the Anvardian fleet, the Imperials had gone under their escort directly to Canopus and thence through the Anvardian empire. And chief after chief, now that Ruulthan was dead and Taury had shown she could win a greater mystery than his, pledged allegiance to her.

Hunda was still out there with Belgotai, fighting a stubborn Anvardian earl. The Dreamer was in the great Polarian

System, toiling at readjustment. It would be necessary, of course, for the Imperial capital to move from isolated Sol to central Polaris, and Taury did not think she would ever have time or opportunity to visit Earth again.

And so she had crossed a thousand starry light-years to the little lonely sun which had been her home. She brought ships, machines, troops. Sol would have a military base sufficient to protect it. Climate engineers would drive the glacial winter of Earth back to its poles and begin the resettlement of the other planets. There would be schools, factories, civilization; Sol would have cause to remember its Empress.

Saunders came along because he couldn't quite endure the thought of leaving Earth altogether without farewell. Vargor, grown ever more silent and moody, joined them, but otherwise the old comradeship of Brontothor was dissolving in the sudden fury of work and war and complexity which claimed them.

And so they stood again in the old ruined castle, Saunders and Taury, looking out at the night of Earth.

It was late, all others seemed to be asleep. Below the balcony, the black walls dropped dizzily to the gulf of night that was the main courtyard. Beyond it, a broken section of outer wall showed snow lying white and mystic under the moon. The stars were huge and frosty, flashing and glittering with cold crystal light above the looming pines, grandeur and arrogance and remoteness wheeling enormously across the silent sky. The moon rode high, its scarred old face the only familiarity from Saunders' age, its argent radiance flooding down on the snow to shatter in a million splinters.

It was quiet, quiet, sound seemed to have frozen to death in the bitter windless cold. Saunders had stood alone, wrapped in furs with his breath shining ghostly from his nostrils, looking out on the silent winter world and thinking his own thoughts. He had heard a soft footfall and turned to see Taury approaching.

"I couldn't sleep," she said.

She came out onto the balcony to stand beside him. The moonlight was white on her face, shimmering faintly from eyes and hair. She seemed a dim goddess of night.

"What were you thinking, Martin?" she asked after a while.

"Oh—I don't know," he said. "Just dreaming a little, I

suppose. It's a strange thought to me, to have left my own time forever and now to be leaving even my own world."

She nodded gravely. "I know. I feel the same way." Her low voice dropped to a whisper. "I didn't have to come back in person, you know. They need me more at Polaris. But I thought I deserved this last farewell to the days when we fought with our own hands, and fared between the stars, when we were a small band of sworn comrades whose dreams outstripped our strength. It was hard and bitter, yes, but I don't think we'll have time for laughter any more. When you work for a million stars, you don't have a chance to see one peasant's wrinkled face light with a deed of kindness you did, or hear him tell you what you did wrong—the world will all be strangers to us—"

For another moment, silence under the far cold stars, then, "Martin—I am so lonely now."

He took her in his arms. Her lips were cold against his, cold with the cruel silent chill of the night, but she answered him with a fierce yearning.

"I think I love you, Martin," she said after a very long time. Suddenly she laughed, a clear and lovely music echoing from the frosty towers of Brontothor. "Oh, Martin, I shouldn't have been afraid. We'll never be lonely, not ever again—"

The moon had sunk far toward the dark horizon when he took her back to her rooms. He kissed her good night and went down the booming corridor toward his own chambers.

His head was awhirl—he was drunk with the sweetness and wonder of it, he felt like singing and laughing aloud and embracing the whole starry universe. Taury, Taury, Taury!

"Martin."

He paused. There was a figure standing before his door, a tall slender form wrapped in a dark cloak. The dull light of a fluoroglobe threw the face into sliding shadow and tormented highlights. Vargor.

"What is it?" he asked.

The prince's hand came up, and Saunders saw the blunt muzzle of a stun pistol gaping at him. Vargor smiled, lopsidedly and sorrowfully. "I'm sorry, Martin," he said.

Saunders stood paralyzed with unbelief. Vargor—why, Vargor had fought beside him; they'd saved each other's lives, laughed and worked and lived together—Vargor!

The gun flashed. There was a crashing in Saunders' head and he tumbled into illimitable darkness.

He awoke very slowly, every nerve tingling with the pain of returning sensation. Something was restraining him. As his vision cleared, he saw that he was lying bound and gagged on the floor of his time projector.

The time machine—he'd all but forgotten it, left it standing in a shed while he went out to the stars, he'd never thought to have another look at it. The time machine!

Vargor stood in the open door, a fluoroglobe in one hand lighting his haggard face. His hair fell in disarray past his tired, handsome features, and his eyes were as wild as the low words that spilled from his mouth.

"I'm sorry, Martin, really I am. I like you, and you've done the Empire such a service as it can never forget, and this is as low a trick as one man can ever play on another. But I have to. I'll be haunted by the thought of this night all my life, but I have to."

Saunders tried to move, snarling incoherently through his gag. Vargor shook his head. "Oh, no, Martin, I can't risk letting you make an outcry. If I'm to do evil, I'll at least do a competent job of it.

"I love Taury, you see. I've loved her ever since I first met her, when I came from the stars with a fighting fleet to her father's court and saw her standing there with the frost crackling through her hair and those gray eyes shining at me. I love her so it's like a pain in me. I can't be away from her, I'd pull down the cosmos for her sake. And I thought she was slowly coming to love me.

"And tonight I saw you two on the balcony, and knew I'd lost. Only I can't give up! Our breed has fought the Galaxy for a dream, Martin—it's not in us ever to stop fighting while life is in us. Fighting by any means, for whatever is dear and precious—but fighting!"

Vargor made a gesture of deprecation. "I don't want power, Martin, believe me. The consort's job will be hard and unglamorous, galling to a man of spirit—but if that's the only way to have her, then so be it. And I do honestly believe, right or wrong, that I'm better for her and for the Empire than you. You don't really belong here, you know. You don't have the tradition, the feeling, the training—you don't even have the biological heritage of five thousand years. Taury may care for you now, but think twenty years ahead!"

Vargor smiled wryly. "I'm taking a chance, of course. If you

do find a means of negative time travel and come back here,
it will be disgrace and exile for me. It would be safer to kill
you. But I'm not quite that much of a scoundrel; I'm giving
you your chance. At worst, you should escape into the time
when the Second Empire is in its glorious bloom, a happier
age than this. And if you do find a means to come back—well,
remember what I said about your not belonging, and try to
reason with clarity and kindness. Kindness to Taury, Martin."

He lifted the fluoroglobe, casting its light over the dim
interior of the machine. "So it's good-by, Martin, and I hope
you won't hate me too much. It should take you several
thousand years to work free and stop the machine. I've
equipped it with weapons, supplies, everything I think you
may need for any eventuality. But I'm sure you'll emerge in a
greater and more peaceful culture, and be happier there."

His voice was strangely tender, all of a sudden. "Good-by,
Martin my comrade. And—good luck!"

He opened the main-drive switch and stepped out as the
projector began to warm up. The door clanged shut behind
him.

Saunders writhed on the floor, cursing with a brain that
was a black cauldron of bitterness. The great drone of the
projector rose, he was on his way—*Oh no—stop the machine,
God, set me free before it's too late!*

The plastic cords cut his wrists. He was lashed to a stan-
chion, unable to reach the switch with any part of his body.
His groping fingers slid across the surface of a knot, the nails
clawing for a hold. The machine roared with full power,
driving ahead through the vastness of time.

Vargor had bound him skillfully. It took him a long time to
get free. Toward the end he went slowly, not caring, knowing
with a dull knowledge that he was already more thousands of
irretrievable years into the future than his dials would
register.

He climbed to his feet, plucked the gag from his mouth, and
looked blankly out at the faceless gray. The century needle
was hard against its stop. He estimated vaguely that he was
some ten thousand years into the future already.

Ten thousand years!

He yanked down the switch with a raging burst of savagery.

It was dark outside. He stood stupidly for a moment before
he saw water seeping into the cabin around the door. Water—

he was under water—short circuits! Frantically, he slammed the switch forward again.

He tasted the water on the floor. It was salt. Sometime in that ten thousand years, for reasons natural or artificial, the sea had come in and covered the site of Brontothor.

A thousand years later he was still below its surface. Two thousand, three thousand, ten thousand . . .

Taury, Taury! For twenty thousand years she had been dust on an alien planet. And Belgotai was gone with his wry smile, Hunda's staunchness, even the Dreamer must long ago have descended into darkness. The sea rolled over dead Brontothor, and he was alone.

He bowed his head on his arms and wept.

For three million years the ocean lay over Brontothor's land. And Saunders drove onward.

He stopped at intervals to see if the waters had gone. Each time the frame of the machine groaned with pressure and the sea poured in through the crack of the door. Otherwise he sat dully in the throbbing loneliness, estimating time covered by his own watch and the known rate of the projector, not caring any more about dates or places.

Several times he considered stopping the machine, letting the sea burst in and drown him. There would be peace in its depths, sleep and forgetting. But no, it wasn't in him to quit that easily. Death was his friend, death would always be there waiting for his call.

But Taury was dead.

Time grayed to its end. In the four millionth year, he stopped the machine and discovered that there was dry air around him.

He was in a city. But it was not such a city as he had ever seen or imagined; he couldn't follow the wild geometry of the titanic structures that loomed about him and they were never the same. The place throbbed and pulsed with incredible forces, it wavered and blurred in a strangely unreal light. Great devastating energies flashed and roared around him— lightning come to Earth. The air hissed and stung with their booming passage.

The thought was a shout filling his skull, blazing along his nerves, too mighty a thought for his stunned brain to do more than grope after meaning:

CREATURE FROM OUT OF TIME, LEAVE THIS PLACE AT ONCE OR THE FORCES WE USE WILL DESTROY YOU!

Through and through him that mental vision seared, down to the very molecules of his brain, his life lay open to Them in a white flame of incandescence.

Can you help me? he cried to the gods. *Can you send me back through time?*

MAN, THERE IS NO WAY TO TRAVEL FAR BACKWARD IN TIME, IT IS INHERENTLY IMPOSSIBLE. YOU MUST GO ON TO THE VERY END OF THE UNIVERSE, AND BEYOND THE END, BECAUSE THAT WAY LIES—

He screamed with the pain of unendurably great thought and concept filling his human brain.

GO ON, MAN, GO ON! BUT YOU CANNOT SURVIVE IN THAT MACHINE AS IT IS. I WILL CHANGE IT FOR YOU. . . . GO!

The time projector started again by itself. Saunders fell forward into a darkness that roared and flashed.

Grimly, desperately, like a man driven by demons, Saunders hurled into the future.

There could be no gainsaying the awful word which had been laid on him. The mere thought of the gods had engraven itself on the very tissue of his brain. Why he should go on to the end of time, he could not imagine, nor did he care. But go on he must!

The machine had been altered. It was airtight now, and experiment showed the window to be utterly unbreakable. Something had been done to the projector so that it hurled him forward at an incredible rate; millions of years passed while a minute or two ticked away within the droning shell.

But what had the gods been?

He would never know. Beings from beyond the Galaxy, beyond the very universe—the ultimately evolved descendants of man—something at whose nature he could not even guess—there was no way of telling. This much was plain: whether it had become extinct or had changed into something else, the human race was gone. Earth would never feel human tread again.

I wonder what became of the Second Empire? I hope it had a long and good life. Or—could that have been its unimaginable end product?

The years reeled past, millions, billions mounting on each other while Earth spun around her star and the Galaxy aged. Saunders fled onward.

He stopped now and then, unable to resist a glimpse of the world and its tremendous history.

A hundred million years in the future, he looked out on the great sheets of flying snow. The gods were gone. Had they too died, or abandoned Earth—perhaps for an altogether different plane of existence? He would never know.

There was a being coming through the storm. The wind flung the snow about him in whirling, hissing clouds. Frost was in his gray fur. He moved with a lithe, unhuman grace, carrying a curved staff at whose tip was a blaze like a tiny sun.

Saunders hailed him through the psychophone, letting his amplified voice shout through the blizzard: "Who are you? What are you doing on Earth?"

The being carried a stone ax in one hand and wore a string of crude beads about his neck. But he stared with bold yellow eyes at the machine and the psychophone brought his harsh scream: "You must be from the far past, one of the earlier cycles."

"They told me to go on, back almost a hundred million years ago. They told me to go to the end of time!"

The psychophone hooted with metallic laughter. "If *They* told you so—then go!"

The being walked on into the storm.

Saunders flung himself ahead. There was no place on Earth for him anymore, he had no choice but to go on.

A billion years in the future there was a city standing on a plain where grass grew that was blue and glassy and tinkled with a high crystalline chiming as the wind blew through it. But the city had never been built by humans, and it warned him away with a voice that he could not disobey.

Then the sea came, and for a long time thereafter he was trapped within a mountain; he had to drive onward till it had eroded back to the ground.

The sun grew hotter and whiter as the hydrogen-helium cycle increased its intensity. Earth spiraled slowly closer to it, the friction of gas and dust clouds in space taking their infinitesimal toll of its energy over billions of years.

How many intelligent races had risen on Earth and had their day, and died, since the age when man first came out of the jungle? *At least,* he thought tiredly, *we were the first.*

A hundred billion years in the future, the sun had used up
its last reserves of nuclear reactions. Saunders looked out on
a bare mountain scene, grim as the Moon—but the Moon had
long ago fallen back toward its parent world and exploded
into a meteoric rain. Earth faced its primary now; its day was
as long as its year. Saunders saw part of the sun's huge
blood-red disc shining wanly.

So good-by, Sol, he thought. *Good-by, and thank you for
many million years of warmth and light. Sleep well, old
friend.*

Some billions of years beyond, there was nothing but the
elemental dark. Entropy had reached a maximum, the energy
sources were used up, the universe was dead.

The universe was dead!

He screamed with the graveyard terror of it and flung the
machine onward. Had it not been for the gods' command, he
might have let it hang there, might have opened the door to
airlessness and absolute zero to die. But he had to go on. He
had reached the end of all things, but he had to go on. *Beyond
the end of time—*

Billions upon billions of years fled. Saunders lay in his
machine, sunk into an apathetic coma. Once he roused himself to eat, feeling the sardonic humor of the situation—the
last living creature, the last free energy in all the cindered
cosmos, fixing a sandwich.

Many billions of years in the future, Saunders paused
again. He looked out into blackness. But with a sudden shock
he discerned a far faint glow, the vaguest imaginable blur of
light out in the heavens.

Trembling, he jumped forward another billion years. The
light was stronger now, a great sprawling radiance swirling
inchoately in the sky.

The universe was reforming.

It made sense, thought Saunders, fighting for self-control.
Space had expanded to some kind of limit, now it was collaps-
ing in on itself to start the cycle anew—the cycle that had
been repeated none knew how many times in the past. The
universe was mortal, but it was a phoenix which would never
really die.

But he was disturbingly mortal, and suddenly he was free
of his death wish. At the very least he wanted to see what the
next time around looked like. But the universe would, accord-

ing to the best theories of twentieth-century cosmology, collapse to what was virtually a point-source, a featureless blaze of pure energy out of which the primal atoms would be reformed. If he wasn't to be devoured in that raging furnace, he'd better leap a long ways ahead. A hell of a long ways!

He grinned with sudden reckless determination and plunged the switch forward.

Worry came back. How did he know that a planet would be formed under him? He might come out in open space, or in the heart of a sun. . . . Well, he'd have to risk that. The gods must have foreseen and allowed for it.

He came out briefly—and flashed back into time-drive. The planet was still molten!

Some geological ages later, he looked out at a spuming gray rain, washing with senseless power from a hidden sky, covering naked rocks with a raging swirl of white water. He didn't go out; the atmosphere would be unbreathable until plants had liberated enough oxygen.

On and on! Sometimes he was under seas, sometimes on land. He saw strange jungles like overgrown ferns and mosses rise and wither in the cold of a glacial age and rise again in altered life-form.

A thought nagged at him, tugging at the back of his mind as he rode onward. It didn't hit him for several million years, then: *The moon! Oh, my God, the moon!*

His hands trembled too violently for him to stop the machine. Finally, with an effort, he controlled himself enough to pull the switch. He skipped on, looking for a night of full moon.

Luna. The same old face—*Luna!*

The shock was too great to register. Numbly, he resumed his journey. And the world began to look familiar, there were low forested hills and a river shining in the distance . . .

He didn't really believe it till he saw the village. It was the same—Hudson, New York.

He sat for a moment, letting his physicist's brain consider the tremendous fact. In Newtonian terms, it meant that every particle newly formed in the Beginning had exactly the same position and velocity as every corresponding particle formed in the previous cycle. In more acceptable Einsteinian language, the continuum was spherical in all four dimensions. In any case—if you traveled long enough, through space or time, you got back to your starting point.

He could go home!

He ran down the sunlit hill, heedless of his foreign garments, ran till the breath sobbed in raw lungs and his heart seemed to burst from the ribs. Gasping, he entered the village, went into a bank, and looked at the tear-off calendar and the wall clock.

June 17, 1936, 1:30 P.M. From that, he could figure his time of arrival in 1973 to the minute.

He walked slowly back, his legs trembling under him, and started the time machine again. Grayness was outside—for the last time.

1973.

Martin Saunders stepped out of the machine. Its moving in space, at Brontothor, had brought it outside MacPherson's house; it lay halfway up the hill at the top of which the rambling old building stood.

There came a flare of soundless energy. Saunders sprang back in alarm and saw the machine dissolve into molten metal—into gas—into a nothingness that shone briefly and was gone.

The gods must have put some annihilating device into it. They didn't want its devices from the future loose in the twentieth century.

But there was no danger of that, thought Saunders as he walked slowly up the hill through the rain-wet grass. He had seen too much of war and horror ever to give men knowledge they weren't ready for. He and Eve and MacPherson would have to suppress the story of his return around time—for that would offer a means of travel into the past, remove the barrier which would keep man from too much use of the machine for murder and oppression. The Second Empire and the Dreamer's philosophy lay a long time in the future.

He went on. The hill seemed strangely unreal, after all that he had seen from it, the whole enormous tomorrow of the cosmos. He would never quite fit into the little round of days that lay ahead.

Taury—her bright lovely face floated before him; he thought he heard her voice whisper in the cool wet wind that stroked his hair like her strong, gentle hands.

Good-by," he whispered into the reaching immensity of time. "Good-by, my dearest."

He went slowly up the steps and in the front door. There would be Sam to mourn. And then there would be the carefully censored thesis to write, and a life spent in satisfying work with a girl who was sweet and kind and beautiful even if she wasn't Taury. It was enough for a mortal man.

He walked into the living room and smiled at Eve and MacPherson. "Hello," he said. "I guess I must be a little early."

Clifford D. Simak

The amazing Clifford D. Simak is one of the most honored writers in science fiction, the winner of three Hugo Awards (most recently in 1981 at the age of 77!), the International Fantasy Award (for *City*, one of the seminal works in the history of the field), the First Fandom Hall of Fame Award, and the Grand Master Award of the Science Fiction Writers of America. He accomplished all this in his spare time, because he worked as a reporter and editor for the Minneapolis *Star* and *Tribune* from 1924 to 1976. He is one of only a few writers whose sf first appeared in the 1920s who could consistently produce outstanding work in the face of changing styles and demands in the field of science fiction.

In "Trouble with Ants" Earth's inheritors, the dogs and the robots, resuscitate the last man to ask his advice about a serious problem.

TROUBLE WITH ANTS

by Clifford D. Simak

ARCHIE, THE LITTLE RENEGADE RACCOON, crouched on the hillside, trying to catch one of the tiny, scurrying things running in the grass. Rufus, Archie's robot, tried to talk to Archie, but the raccoon was too busy and he did not answer.

Homer did a thing no Dog had ever done before. He crossed the river and trotted into the wild robots' camp and he was scared, for there was no telling what the wild robots might do to him when they turned around and saw him. But he was worried worse than he was scared, so he trotted on.

Deep in a secret nest, ants dreamed and planned for a world they could not understand. And pushed into that world, hoping for the best, aiming at a thing no Dog, or robot, or man could understand.

In Geneva, Jon Webster rounded out his ten-thousandth year of suspended animation and slept on, not stirring. In the street outside, a wandering breeze rustled the leaves along the boulevard, but no one heard and no one saw.

Jenkins strode across the hill and did not look to either left or right, for there were things he did not wish to see. There was a tree that stood where another tree had stood in another world. There was the lay of ground that had been imprinted on his brain with a billion footsteps across ten thousand years.

And, if one listened closely, one might have heard laughter echoing down the ages . . . the sardonic laughter of a man named Joe.

* * *

Archie caught one of the scurrying things and held it clutched within his tight-shut paw. Carefully he lifted the paw and opened it and the thing was there, running madly, trying to escape.

"Archie," said Rufus, "you aren't listening to me."

The scurrying thing dived into Archie's fur, streaked swiftly up his forearm.

"Might have been a flea," said Archie. He sat up and scratched his belly.

"New kind of flea," he said. "Although I hope it wasn't. Just the ordinary kind are bad enough."

"You aren't listening," said Rufus.

"I'm busy," said Archie. "The grass is full of them things. Got to find out what they are."

"I'm leaving you, Archie."

"You're what!"

"Leaving you," said Rufus. "I'm going to the Building."

"You're crazy," fumed Archie. "You can't do a thing like that to me. You've been tetched ever since you fell into that ant hill . . ."

"I've had the Call," said Rufus. "I just got to go."

"I've been good to you," the raccoon pleaded. "I've never overworked you. You've been like a pal of mine instead of like a robot. I've always treated you just like an animal."

Rufus shook his head stubbornly. "You can't make me stay," he said. "I couldn't stay, no matter what you did. I got the Call and I got to go."

"It isn't like I could get another robot," Archie argued. "They drew my number and I ran away. I'm a deserter and you know I am. You know I can't get another robot with the wardens watching for me."

Rufus just stood there.

"I need you," Archie told him. "You got to stay and help me rustle grub. I can't go near none of the feeding places or the wardens will nab me and drag me up to Webster Hill. You got to help me dig a den. Winter's coming on and I will need a den. It won't have heat or light, but I got to have one. And you've got to . . ."

Rufus had turned around and was walking down the hill, heading for the river trail. Down the river trail . . . traveling toward the dark smudge above the far horizon.

Archie sat hunched against the wind that ruffled through his fur, tucked his tail around his feet. The wind had a chill about it, a chill it had not held an hour or so before. And it was not the chill of weather, but the chill of other things.

His bright, beady eyes searched the hillside and there was no sign of Rufus.

No food, no den, no robot. Hunted by the wardens. Eaten up by fleas.

And the Building, a smudge against the farther hills across the river valley.

A hundred years ago, so the records said, the Building had been no bigger than the Webster House.

But it had grown since . . . a place that never was completed. First it had covered an acre. And then a square mile. Now finally a township. And still it grew, sprawling out and towering up.

A smudge above the hills and a cloudy terror for the little, superstitious forest folks who watched it. A word to frighten kit and whelp and cub into sudden quiet.

For there was evil in it . . . the evil of the unknown, an evil sensed and attributed rather than seen or heard or smelled. A sensed evil, especially in the dark of night, when the lights were out and the wind keened in the den's mouth and the other animals were sleeping, while one lay awake and listened to the pulsing *otherness* that sang between the worlds.

Archie blinked in the autumn sunlight, scratched furtively at his side.

Maybe someday, he told himself, someone will find a way to handle fleas. Something to rub on one's fur so they will stay away. Or a way to reason with them, to reach them and talk things over with them. Maybe set up a reservation for them, a place where they could stay and be fed and not bother animals. Or something of the sort.

As it was, there wasn't much that could be done. You scratched yourself. You had your robot pick them off, although the robot usually got more fur than fleas. You rolled in the sand or dust. You went for a swim and drowned some of them . . . well, you really didn't drown them; you just washed them off and if some of them drowned that was their own tough luck.

You had your robot pick them off . . . but now there was no robot.

No robot to pick off fleas.

No robot to help him hunt for food.

But, Archie remembered, there was a black haw tree down in the river bottom and last night's frost would have touched the fruit. He smacked his lips, thinking of the haws. And there was a cornfield just over the ridge. If one was fast enough and bided his time and was sneaky about it, it was no trouble at all to get an ear of corn. And if worse came to worse there always would be roots and wild acorns and that patch of wild grapes over on the sand bar.

Let Rufus go, said Archie, mumbling to himself. Let the Dogs keep their feeding stations. Let the wardens go on watching.

He would live his own life. He would eat fruit and grub for roots and raid the cornfields, even as his remote ancestors had eaten fruit and grubbed for roots and raided fields.

He would live as the other raccoons had lived before the Dogs had come along with their ideas about the Brotherhood of Beasts. Like animals had lived before they could talk with words, before they could read the printed books that the Dogs provided, before they had robots that served in lieu of hands, before there was warmth and light for dens.

Yes, and before there was a lottery that told you if you stayed on Earth or went to another world.

The Dogs, Archie remembered, had been quite persuasive about it, very reasonable and suave. Some animals, they said, had to go to the other worlds or there would be too many animals on Earth. Earth wasn't big enough, they said, to hold everyone. And a lottery, they pointed out, was the fair way to decide which of them would go to the other worlds.

And, after all, they said, the other worlds would be almost like the Earth. For they were just extensions of the Earth. Just other worlds following in the track of Earth. Not quite like it, perhaps, but very close. Just a minor difference here and there. Maybe no tree where there was a tree on Earth. Maybe an oak tree where Earth had a walnut tree. Maybe a spring of fresh, cold water where there was no such spring on Earth.

Maybe, Homer had told him, growing very enthusiastic . . . maybe the world he would be assigned to would be a better world than Earth.

Archie hunched against the hillside, felt the warmish sun of autumn cutting through the cold chill of autumn's wind. He thought about the black haws. They would be soft and mushy and there would be some of them lying on the ground.

He would eat those that were on the ground, then he'd climb the tree and pick some more and then he'd climb down again and finish off the ones he had shaken loose with his climbing of the tree.

He'd eat them and take them in his paws and smear them on his face. He might even roll in them.

Out of the corner of one eye, he saw the scurrying things running in the grass. Like ants, he thought, only they weren't ants. At least, not like any ants he'd ever seen before.

Fleas, maybe. A new kind of flea.

His paw darted out and snatched one up. He felt it running in his palm. He opened the paw and saw it running there and closed the paw again.

He raised his paw to his ear and listened.

The thing he'd caught was ticking!

The wild robot camp was not at all the way Homer had imagined it would be. There were no buildings. Just launching ramps and three spaceships and half a dozen robots working on one of the ships.

Although, come to think of it, Homer told himself, one should have known there would be no buildings in a robot camp. For the robots would have no use of shelter and that was all a building was.

Homer was scared, but he tried hard not to show it. He curled his tail over his back and carried his head high and his ears well forward and trotted toward the little group of robots, never hesitating. When he reached them, he sat down and lolled out his tongue and waited for one of them to speak.

But when none of them did, he screwed up his courage and spoke to them, himself.

"My name is Homer," he said, "and I represent the Dogs. If you have a head robot, I would like to talk to him."

The robots kept on working for a minute, but finally one of them turned around and came over and squatted down beside Homer so that his head was level with the dog's head. All the other robots kept on working as if nothing had happened.

"I am a robot called Andrew," said the robot squatting next to Homer, "and I am not what you would call the head robot, for we have no such thing among us. But I can speak with you."

"I came to you about the Building," Homer told him.

"I take it," said the robot called Andrew, "that you are

speaking of the structure to the northeast of us. The one you can see from here if you just turn around."

"That's the one." said Homer. "I came to ask why you are building it."

"But we aren't building it," said Andrew.

"We have seen robots working on it."

"Yes, there are robots working there. But we are not building it."

You are helping someone else?"

Andrew shook his head. "Some of us get a call . . . a call to go and work there. The rest of us do not try to stop them, for we are all free agents."

"But who is building it?" asked Homer.

"The ants," said Andrew.

Homer's jaw dropped slack.

"Ants? You mean the insects. The little things that live in ant hills?"

"Precisely," said Andrew. He made the fingers of one hand run across the sand like a harried ant.

"But they couldn't build a place like that," protested Homer. "They are stupid."

"Not any more," said Andrew.

Homer sat stock still, frozen to the sand, felt chilly feet of terror run along his nerves.

"Not any more," said Andrew, talking to himself. "Not stupid any more. You see once upon a time, there was a man named Joe . . ."

"A man? What's that?" asked Homer.

The robot made a clucking noise, as if gently chiding Homer.

"Men were animals," he said. "Animals that went on two legs. They looked very much like us except they were flesh and we are metal."

"You must mean the websters," said Homer. "We know about things like that, but we call them websters."

The robot nodded slowly. "Yes, the websters could be men. There was a family of them by that name. Lived just across the river."

"There's a place called Webster House," said Homer. "It stands on Webster Hill."

"That's the place," said Andrew.

"We keep it up," said Homer. It's a shrine to us, but we

don't understand just why. It is the word that has been passed down to us . . . we must keep Webster House."

"The websters," Andrew told him, "were the ones that taught you Dogs to speak."

Homer stiffened. "No one taught us to speak. We taught ourselves. We developed in the course of many years. And we taught the other animals."

Andrew, the robot, sat hunched in the sun, nodding his head as if he might be thinking to himself.

"Ten thousand years," he said. "No, I guess it's nearer twelve. Around eleven, maybe."

Homer waited and as he waited he sensed the weight of years that pressed against the hills . . . the years of river and of sun, of sand and wind and sky.

And the years of Andrew.

"You are old," he said. "You can remember that far back?"

"Yes," said Andrew. "Although I am one of the last of the man-made robots. I was made just a few years before they went to Jupiter."

Homer sat silently, tumult stirring in his brain.

Man . . . a new word.

An animal that went on two legs.

An animal that made the robots, that taught the Dogs to talk.

And, as if he might be reading Homer's mind. Andrew spoke to him.

"You should not have stayed away from us," he said. "We should have worked together. We worked together once. We both would have gained if we had worked together."

"We were afraid of you," said Homer. "I am still afraid of you."

"Yes," said Andrew. "Yes, I suppose you would be. I suppose Jenkins kept you afraid of us. For Jenkins was a smart one. He knew that you must start afresh. He knew that you must not carry the memory of Man as a dead weight on your necks."

Homer sat silently.

"And we," the robot said, "are nothing more than the memory of Man. We do the things he did, although more scientifically, for, since we are machines, we must be scientific. More patiently than Man, because we have forever and he had a few short years."

Andrew drew two lines in the sand, crossed them with two

other lines. He made an X in the open square in the upper left hand corner.

"You think I'm crazy," he said. "You think I'm talking through my hat."

Homer wriggled his haunches deeper into the sand.

"I don't know what to think," he said. "All these years . . ."

Andrew drew an O with his finger in the center square of the cross-hatch he had drawn in the sand.

"I know," he said. "All these years you have lived with a dream. The idea that the Dogs were the prime movers. And the facts are hard to understand, hard to reconcile. Maybe it would be just as well if you forgot what I said. Facts are painful things at times. A robot has to work with them, for they are the only things he has to work with. We can't dream, you know. Facts are all we have."

"We passed fact long ago," Homer told him. "Not that we don't use it, for there are times we do. But we work in other ways. Intuition and cobblying and listening."

"You aren't mechanical," said Andrew. "For you, two and two are not always four, but for us it must be four. And sometimes I wonder if tradition doesn't blind us. I wonder sometimes if two and two may not be something more or less than four."

They squatted in silence, watching the river, a flood of molten silver tumbling down a colored land.

Andrew made an X in the upper right hand corner of the cross-hatch, an O in the center upper space, and X in the center lower space. With the flat of his hand, he rubbed the sand smooth.

"I never win," he said. "I'm too smart for myself."

"You were telling me about the ants," said Homer. "About them not being stupid any more."

"Oh, yes," said Andrew. "I was telling you about a man named Joe. . . ."

Jenkins strode across the hill and did not look to either left or right, for there were things he did not wish to see, things that struck too deeply into memory. There was a tree that stood where another tree had stood in another world. There was the lay of ground that had been imprinted on his brain with a billion footsteps across ten thousand years.

The weak winter sun of afternoon flickered in the sky, flickered like a candle guttering in the wind, and when it steadied and there was no flicker it was moonlight and not sunlight at all.

Jenkins checked his stride and swung around and the house was there ... low-set against the ground, sprawled across the hill, like a sleepy young thing that clung close to mother earth.

Jenkins took a hesitant step and as he moved his metal body glowed and sparkled in the moonlight that had been sunlight a short heartbeat ago.

From the river valley came the sound of a night bird crying and a raccoon was whimpering in a cornfield just below the ridge.

Jenkins took another step and prayed the house would stay ... although he knew it couldn't because it wasn't there. For this was an empty hilltop that had never known a house. This was another world in which no house existed.

The house remained, dark and silent, no smoke from the chimneys, no light from the windows, but with remembered lines that one could not mistake.

Jenkins moved slowly, carefully, afraid the house would leave, afraid that he would startle it and it would disappear.

But the house stayed put. And there were other things. The tree at the corner had been an elm and now it was an oak, as it had been before. And it was autumn moon instead of winter sun. The breeze was blowing from the west and not out of the north.

Something happened, thought Jenkins. The thing that has been growing on me. The thing I felt and could not understand. An ability developing? Or a new sense finally reaching light? Or a power I never dreamed I had.

A power to walk between the worlds at will. A power to go anywhere I choose by the shortest route that the twisting lines of force and happenstance can conjure up for me.

He walked less carefully and the house still stayed, unfrightened, solid and substantial.

He crossed the grass-grown patio and stood before the door.

Hesitantly, he put out a hand and laid it on the latch. And the latch was there. No phantom thing, but substantial metal.

Slowly he lifted it and the door swung in and he stepped across the threshold.

After five thousand years, Jenkins had come home ... back home ... back to Webster House.

*   *   *

So there was a man named Joe. Not a webster, but a man. For a webster was a man. And the Dogs had not been first.

Homer lay before the fire, a limp pile of fur and bone and muscle, with his paws stretched out in front of him and his head resting on his paws. Through half-closed eyes he saw the fire and shadow, felt the heat of the blazing logs reach out and fluff his fur.

But inside his brain he saw the sand and the squatting robot and the hills with the years upon them.

Andrew had squatted in the sand and talked, with the autumn sun shining on his shoulders . . . had talked of men and dogs and ants. Of a thing that had happened when Nathaniel was alive, and that was a time long gone, for Nathaniel was the first Dog.

There had been a man named Joe . . . a mutant-man, a more-than-man . . . who had wondered about ants twelve thousand years ago. Wondered why they had progressed so far and then no farther, why they had reached the dead end of destiny.

Hunger, perhaps, Joe had reasoned . . . the ever-pressing need to garner food so that they might live. Hibernation, perhaps, the stagnation of the winter sleep, the broken memory chain, the starting over once again, each year a genesis for ants.

So, Andrew said, his bald pate gleaming in the sun, Joe had picked one hill, had set himself up as a god to change the destiny of ants. He had fed them, so that they need not strive with hunger. He had enclosed their hill in a dome of glassite and had heated it so they need not hibernate.

And the thing had worked. The ants advanced. They fashioned carts and they smelted ore. This much one could know, for the carts were on the surface and acrid smelting smoke came from the chimneys that thrust up from the hill. What other things they did, what other things they learned, deep down in their tunnels, there was no way of knowing.

Joe was crazy, Andrew said. Crazy . . . and yet, maybe not so crazy either.

For one day he broke the dome of glassite and tore the hill asunder with his foot, then turned and walked away, not caring any more what happened to the ants.

But the ants had cared.

The hand that broke the dome, the foot that ripped the hill

had put the ants on the road to greatness. It had made them fight . . . fight to keep the things they had, fight to keep the bottleneck of destiny from closing once again.

A kick in the pants, said Andrew. A kick in the pants for ants. A kick in the right direction.

Twelve thousand years ago a broken, trampled hill. Today a mighty building that grew with each passing year. A building that had covered a township in one short century, that would cover a hundred townships in the next. A building that would push out and take the land. Land that belonged, not to ants, but animals.

A building . . . and that was not quite right, although it had been called the Building from the very start. For a building was a shelter, a place to hide from storm and cold. The ants would have no need of that, for they had their tunnels and their hills.

Why would an ant build a place that sprawled across a township in a hundred years and yet that kept on growing? What possible use could an ant have for a place like that?

Homer nuzzled his chin deep into his paws, growled inside his throat.

There was no way of knowing. For first you had to know how an ant would think. You would have to know her ambition and her goal. You would have to probe her knowledge.

Twelve thousand years of knowledge. Twelve thousand years from a starting point that itself was unknowable.

But one had to know. There must be a way to know.

For, year after year, the Building would push out. A mile across, and then six miles and after that a hundred. A hundred miles and then another hundred and after that the world.

Retreat, thought Homer. Yes, we could retreat. We could migrate to those other worlds, the worlds that follow us in the stream of time, the worlds that tread on one another's heels. We could give the Earth to ants and there still would be space for us.

But this is home. This is where the Dogs arose. This is where we taught the animals to talk and think and act together. This is the place where we created the Brotherhood of Beasts.

For it does not matter who came first . . . the webster or the dog. This place is home. Our home as well as webster's home. Our home as well as ants'.

And we must stop the ants.

There must be a way to stop them. A way to talk to them, find out what they want. A way to reason with them. Some basis for negotiation. Some agreements to be reached.

Homer lay motionless on the hearth and listened to the whisperings that ran through the house, the soft, far-off padding of robots on their rounds of duties, the muted talk of Dogs in a room upstairs, the crackling of the flames as they ate along the log.

A good life, said Homer, muttering to himself. A good life and we thought we were the ones who made it. Although Andrew says it wasn't us. Andrew says we have not added one iota to the mechanical skill and mechanical logic that was our heritage . . . and that we have lost a lot. He spoke of chemistry and he tried to explain, but I couldn't understand. The study of elements, he said, and things like molecules and atoms. And electronics . . . although he said we did certain things without the benefit of electronics more wonderfully than man could have done with all his knowledge. You might study electronics for a million years, he said, and not reach those other worlds, not even know they're there . . . and we did it, we did a thing a webster could not do.

Because we think differently than a webster does. No, it's man, not webster.

And our robots. Our robots are no better than the ones that were left to us by man. A minor modification here and there . . . an obvious modification, but no real improvement.

Who ever would have dreamed there could be a better robot?

A better ear of corn, yes. Or a better walnut tree. Or a wild rice that would grow a fuller head. A better way to make the yeast that substitutes for meat.

But a better robot . . . why, a robot does everything we might wish that it could do. Why should it be better?

And yet . . . the robots receive a call and go off to work on the Building, to build a thing that will push us off the Earth.

We do not understand. Of course, we cannot understand. If we knew our robots better we might understand. Understanding, we might fix it so that the robots would not receive the call, or, receiving it, would pay it no attention.

And that, of course, would be the answer. If the robots did not work, there would be no building. For the ants, without the aid of robots, could not go on with their building.

A flea ran along Homer's scalp and he twitched his ear.

Although Andrew might be wrong, he told himself. We have our legend of the rise of the Brotherhood of Beasts and the wild robots have their legend of the fall of man. At this date, who is there to tell which of the two is right?

But Andrew's story does tie in. There were Dogs and there were robots and when man fell they went their separate ways . . . although we kept some of the robots to serve as hands for us. Some robots stayed with us, but no dogs stayed with the robots.

A late autumn fly buzzed out of a corner, bewildered in the firelight. It buzzed around Homer's head and settled on his nose. Homer glared at it and it lifted its legs and insolently brushed its wings. Homer dabbed at it with a paw and it flew away.

A knock came at the door.

Homer lifted his head and blinked at the knocking sound.

"Come in," he finally said.

It was the robot, Hezekiah.

"Archie?"

"Archie, the raccoon."

"Oh, yes," said Homer. "He was the one that ran away."

"They have him out here now," said Hezekiah. "Do you want to see him?"

"Send them in," said Homer.

Hezekiah beckoned with his finger and Archie ambled through the door. His fur was matted with burs and his tail was dragging. Behind him stalked two robot wardens.

"He tried to steal some corn," one of the wardens said, "and we spotted him, but he led us quite a chase."

Homer sat up ponderously and stared at Archie. Archie stared straight back.

"They never would have caught me," Archie said, "if I'd still had Rufus. Rufus was my robot and he would have warned me."

"And where is Rufus now?"

"He got the call today," said Archie, "and left me for the Buidling."

"Tell me," said Homer. "Did anything happen to Rufus before he left? Anything unusual? Out of the ordinary?"

"Nothing," Archie told him, "Except that he fell into an ant hill. He was a clumsy robot. A regular stumble bum . . . always tripping himself, getting tangled up. He wasn't coordinated just the way he should be. He had a screw loose some place."

Something black and tiny jumped off of Archie's nose, raced along the floor. Archie's paw went out in a lightning stroke and scooped it up.

"You better move back a ways," Hezekiah warned Homer. "He's simply dripping fleas."

"It's not a flea," said Archie, puffing up in anger. "It is something else. I caught it this afternoon. It ticks and it looks like an ant, but it isn't one."

The thing that ticked oozed between Archie's claws and tumbled to the floor. It landed right side up and was off again. Archie made a stab at it, but it zigzagged out of reach. Like a flash it reached Hezekiah and streaked up his leg.

Homer came to his feet in a sudden flash of knowledge.

"Quick!" he shouted. "Get it! Catch it! Don't let it . . ."

But the thing was gone.

Slowly Homer sat down again. His voice was quiet now, quiet and almost deadly.

"Wardens," he said, "take Hezekiah into custody. Don't leave his side, don't let him get away. Report to me everything he does."

Hezekiah backed away.

"But I haven't done a thing."

"No," said Homer, softly. "No, you haven't yet. But you will. You'll get the Call and you'll try to desert us for the Building. And before we let you go, we'll find out what it is that made you do it. What it is and how it works."

Homer turned around, a doggish grin wrinkling up his face.

"And, now, Archie . . ."

But there was no Archie.

There was an open window. And there was no Archie.

Homer stirred on his bed of hay, unwilling to awake, a growl gurgling in his throat.

Getting old, he thought. Too many years upon me, like the years upon the hills. There was a time when I'd be out of bed at the first sound of something at the door, on my feet, with hay sticking in my fur, barking my head off to let the robots know.

The knock came again and Homer staggered to his feet.

"Come in," he yelled. "Cut out the racket and come in."

The door opened and it was a robot, but a bigger robot than Homer had ever seen before. A gleaming robot, huge and massive, with a polished body that shone like slow fire even in the dark. And riding on the robot's shoulder was Archie, the raccoon.

"I am Jenkins," said the robot. "I came back tonight."

Homer gulped and sat down very slowly.

"Jenkins," he said. "There are stories . . . legends . . . from the long ago."

"No more than a legend?" Jenkins asked.

"That's all," said Homer. "A legend of a robot that looked after us. Although Andrew spoke of Jenkins this afternoon as if he might have known him. And there is a story of how the Dogs gave you a body on your seven thousandth birthday and it was a marvelous body that . . ."

His voice ran down . . . for the body of the robot that stood before him with the raccoon perched on his shoulder . . . that body could be none other than the birthday gift.

"And Webster House?" asked Jenkins. "You still keep Webster House?"

"We still keep Webster House," said Homer. "We keep it as it is. It's a thing we have to do."

"The websters?"

"There aren't any websters."

Jenkins nodded at that. His body's hair-trigger sense had told him there were no websters. There were no webster vibrations. There was no thought of websters in the minds of things he'd touched.

And that was as it should be.

He came slowly across the room, soft-footed as a cat despite his mighty weight, and Homer felt him moving, felt the friendliness and kindness of the metal creature, the protectiveness of the ponderous strength within him.

Jenkins squatted down beside him.

"You are in trouble," Jenkins said.

Homer stared at him.

"The ants," said Jenkins. "Archie told me. Said you were troubled by the ants."

"I went to Webster House to hide," said Archie. "I was scared you would hunt me down again and I thought that Webster House . . ."

"Hush, Archie," Jenkins told him. "You don't know a thing

about it. You told me that you didn't. You just said the Dogs were having trouble with the ants."

He looked at Homer.

"I suppose they are Joe's ants," he said.

"So you know about Joe," said Homer. "So there was a man called Joe."

Jenkins chuckled. "Yes, a troublemaker. But likeable at times. He had the devil in him."

Homer said: "They're building. They get the robots to work for them and they are putting up a building."

"Surely," said Jenkins, "even ants have the right to build."

"But they're building too fast. They'll push us off the Earth. Another thousand years or so and they'll cover the whole Earth if they keep on building at the rate they've been."

"And you have no place to go? That's what worries you."

"Yes, we have a place to go. Many places. All the other worlds. The cobbly worlds."

Jenkins nodded gravely. "I was in a cobbly world. The first world after this. I took some websters there five thousand years ago. I just came back tonight. And I know the way you feel. No other world is home. I've hungered for the Earth for almost every one of those five thousand years. I came back to Webster House and I found Archie there. He told me about the ants and so I came up here. I hope you do not mind."

"We are glad you came," said Homer, softly.

"These ants," said Jenkins. " I suppose you want to stop them."

Homer nodded his head.

"There is a way," said Jenkins. "I know there is a way. The websters had a way if I could just remember. But it's so long ago. And it's a simple way, I know. A very simple way."

His hand came up and scraped back and forth across his chin.

What are you doing that for?" Archie asked.

"Eh?"

"Rubbing your face that way. What do you do it for?"

Jenkins dropped his hand. "Just a habit, Archie. A webster gesture. A way they had of thinking. I picked it up from them."

"Does it help you think?"

"Well, maybe. Maybe not. It seemed to help the websters.

Now what would a webster do in a case like this? The websters could help us. I know they could . . ."

"The websters in the cobbly world," said Homer.

Jenkins shook his head. "There aren't any websters there."

"But you said you took some back."

"I know. But they aren't there now. I've been alone in the cobbly world for almost four thousand years."

"Then there aren't websters anywhere. The rest went to Jupiter. Andrew told me that. Jenkins, where is Jupiter?"

"Yes, there are," said Jenkins. "There are some websters left, I mean. Or there used to be. A few left at Geneva."

"It won't be easy," Homer said. "Not even for a webster. Those ants are smart. Archie told you about the flea he found."

"It wasn't any flea," said Archie.

"Yes, he told me," Jenkins said. "Said it got onto Hezekiah."

"Not onto," Homer told them. "Into is the word. It wasn't a flea . . . it was a robot, a tiny robot. It drilled a hole in Hezekiah's skull and got into his brain. It sealed the hole behind it."

"And what is Hezekiah doing now?"

"Nothing," said Homer. "But we are pretty sure what he will do as soon as the ant robot gets the setup fixed. He'll get the Call. He'll get the call to go and work on the Building."

Jenkins nodded. "Taking over," he said. "They can't do a job like that themselves, so they take control of things that can."

He lifted his hand again and scraped it across his chin.

"I wonder if Joe knew," he mumbled. "When he played god to the ants I wonder if he knew."

But that was ridiculous. Joe never could have known. Even a mutation like Joe could not have looked twelve thousand years ahead.

So long ago, thought Jenkins. So many things have happened. Bruce Webster was just starting to experiment with dogs, had no more than dreamed his dream of talking, thinking dogs that would go down the path of destiny paw in hand with Man . . . not knowing then that Man within a few short centuries would scatter to the four winds of eternity and leave the Earth to robot and to dog. Not knowing then that even the name of Man would be forgotten in the dust of years, that the race would come to be known by the name of a single family.

And yet, thought Jenkins, if it was to be any family, the
Websters were the ones. I can remember them as if it were
yesterday. Those were the days when I thought of myself as a
Webster, too.

Lord knows, I tried to be. I did the best I could. I stood by
the Webster dogs when the race of men had gone and finally I
took the last bothersome survivors of that madcap race into
another world to clear the way for Dogs . . . so that the Dogs
could fashion the Earth in the way they planned.

And now even those last bothersome survivors have gone
. . . some place, somewhere . . . I wish that I could know.
Escaped into some fantasy of the human mind. And the men
on Jupiter are not even men, but something else. And Geneva
is shut off . . . blocked off from the world.

Although it can't be farther away or blocked more tightly
than the world from which I came. If only I could learn how it
was I traveled from the exile cobbly world back to Webster
House . . . then, maybe, perhaps, somehow or other, I could
reach Geneva.

A new power, he told himself. A new ability. A thing that
grew upon me without my knowing that it grew. A thing that
every man and every robot . . . and perhaps every dog . . .
could have if he but knew the way.

Although it may be my body that made it possible . . . this
body that the Dogs gave me on my seven thousandth birthday. A body that has more than any body of flesh and blood
has ever quite attained. A body that can know what a bear is
thinking or a fox is dreaming, that can feel the happy little
mouse thoughts running in the grass.

Wish fulfillment. That might be it. The answer to the
strange, illogical yearnings for things that seldom are and
often cannot be. But all of which are possible if one knows the
way, if one can grow or develop or graft onto oneself the new
ability that directs the mind and body to the fulfillment of
the wish.

I walked the hill each day, he remembered. Walked there
because I could not stay away, because the longing was so
strong, steeling myself against looking too closely, for there
were differences I did not wish to see.

I walked there a million times and it took that many times
before the power within me was strong enough to take me
back.

For I was trapped. The word, the thought, the concept that

took me into the cobbly world was a one-way ticket and while it took me there it could not take me back. But there was another way, a way I did not know. That even now I do not know.

"You said there was a way," urged Homer.

"A way?"

"Yes, a way to stop the ants."

Jenkins nodded. "I am going to find out. I'm going to Geneva."

Jon Webster awoke.

And this is strange, he thought, for I said eternity.

I was to sleep forever and forever has no end.

All else was mist and the grayness of sleep forgetfulness, but this much stood out with mind-sharp clarity. Eternity, and this was not eternity.

A word ticked at his mind, like feeble tapping on a door that was far away.

He lay and listened to the tapping and the word became two words . . . words that spoke his name:

"Jon Webster. Jon Webster." On and on, on and on. Two words tapping at his brain.

"Jon Webster."

"Jon Webster."

"Yes, said Webster's brain and the words stopped and did not come again.

Silence and the thinning of the mists of forgetfulness. And the trickling back of memory. One thing at a time.

There was a city and the name of the city was Geneva.

Men lived in the city, but men without a purpose.

The Dogs lived outside the city . . . in the whole world outside the city. The Dogs had purpose and a dream.

Sara climbed the hill to take a century of dreams.

And I . . . I thought Jon Webster, climbed the hill and asked for eternity. This is not eternity.

"This is Jenkins, John Webster."

"Yes, Jenkins," said Jon Webster, and yet he did not say it, not with lip and tongue and throat, for he felt the fluid that pressed around his body inside its cylinder, fluid that fed him and kept him from dehydrating. Fluid that sealed his lips and eyes and ears.

"Yes, Jenkins," said Webster, speaking with his mind. "I remember you. I remember you now. You were with the family from the very first. You helped us teach the Dogs. You stayed with them when the family was no more."

"I am still with them," said Jenkins.

"I sought eternity," said Webster. "I closed the city and sought eternity."

"We often wondered," Jenkins told him. "Why did you close the city?"

"The Dogs," said Webster's mind. "The Dogs had to have their chance. Man would have spoiled their chance."

"The dogs are doing well," said Jenkins.

"But the city is open now?"

"No, the city still is closed."

"But you are here."

"Yes, but I'm the only one who knows the way. And there will be no others. Not for a long time, anyway."

"Time," said Webster. "I had forgotten time. How long is it, Jenkins?"

"Since you closed the city? Ten thousand years or so."

"And there are others?"

"Yes, but they are sleeping."

"And the robots? The robots still keep watch?"

"The robots still keep watch."

Webster lay quietly and a peace came upon his mind. The city still was closed and the last of men were sleeping. The Dogs were doing well and the robots stayed on watch.

"You should not have wakened me," he said. "You should have let me sleep."

"There was a thing I had to know. I knew it once, but I have forgotten and it is very simple. Simple and yet terribly important."

Webster chuckled in his brain. "What is it, Jenkins?"

"It's about ants," said Jenkins. "Ants used to trouble men. What did you do about it?"

"Why, we poisoned them," said Webster.

Jenkins gasped. "Poisoned them!"

"Yes," said Webster. "A very simple thing. We used a base of syrup, sweet, to attract the ants. And we put poison in it, a poison that was deadly to ants. But we did not put in enough of it to kill them right away. A slow poison, you see, so they would have time to carry it to the nest. That way we killed many instead of just two or three."

Silence hummed in Webster's head . . . the silence of no thought, no word.

"Jenkins," he said. "Jenkins, are you . . ."

"Yes, Jon Webster, I am here."

"That is all you want?"

"That is all I want."

"I can go to sleep again."

"Yes, Jon Webster. Go to sleep again."

Jenkins stood upon the hilltop and felt the first rough fore-running wind of winter whine across the land. Below him the slope that ran down to the river was etched in black and gray with the leafless skeletons of trees.

To the northeast rose the shadow-shape, the cloud of evil omen that was called the Building. A growing thing spawned in the mind of ants, built for what purpose and to what end no thing but an ant could even closely guess.

But there was a way to deal with ants.

The human way.

The way Jon Webster had told him after ten thousand years of sleep. A simple way and a fundamental way, a brutal, but efficient way. You took some syrup, sweet, so the ants would like it, and you put some poison in it . . . slow poison so it wouldn't work too fast.

The simple way of poison, Jenkins said. The very simple way.

Except it called for chemistry and the Dogs knew no chemistry.

Except it called for killing and there was no killing.

Not even fleas, and the Dogs were pestered plenty by the fleas. Not even ants . . . and the ants threatened to dispossess the animals of the world they called their birthplace.

There had been no killing for five thousand years or more. The idea of killing had been swept from the minds of things.

And it is better that way, Jenkins told himself. Better that one should lose a world than go back to killing.

He turned slowly and went down the hill.

Homer would be disappointed, he told himself.

Terribly disappointed when he found the websters had no way of dealing with the ants. . . .

G. Peyton Wertenbaker

Almost totally forgotten today (there is no entry for him in the so-far definitive *Science Fiction Encyclopedia*), G. Peyton Wertenbaker published his first science fiction at the dawn of the sf magazine age, in 1923—this was "The Man from the Atom" which appeared in Hugo Gernsback's legendary *Science and Invention,* the magazine generally regarded as the inspiration for *Amazing Stories*. Wertenbaker later served as an editor of *Fortune* magazine and established a reputation as an outstanding writer on the Southwestern United States.

Here is a poignant story about the disadvantages of being immortal, one of which is becoming the last man.

THE COMING OF THE ICE

by G. Peyton Wertenbaker

IT IS STRANGE TO BE ALONE, and so cold. To be the last man on earth . . .

The snow drives silently about me ceaselessly, drearily. And I am isolated in this tiny white, indistinguishable corner of a blurred world, surely the loneliest creature in the universe. How many thousands of years is it since I last knew the true companionship? For a long time I have been lonely, but there *were* people, creatures of flesh and blood. Now they are gone. Now I have not even the stars to keep me company, for they are all lost in an infinity of snow and twilight here below.

If only I could know how long it has been since first I was imprisoned upon the earth. It cannot matter now. And yet some vague dissatisfaction, some faint instinct, asks over and over in my throbbing ears: What year? What year?

It was in the year 1930 that the great thing began in my life. There was then a very great man who performed operations on his fellows to compose their vitals—we called such men surgeons. John Granden wore the title "Sir" before his name, in indication of nobility by birth according to the prevailing standards in England. But surgery was only a hobby of Sir John's, if I must be precise, for, while he had achieved an enormous reputation as a surgeon, he always felt that his real work lay in the experimental end of his profession. He was, in a way a dreamer, but a dreamer who could make his dreams come true.

I was a very close friend of Sir John's. In fact, we shared the same apartments in London. I have never forgotten that day when he first mentioned to me his momentous discovery. I had just come in from a long sleighride in the country with Alice, and I was seated drowsily in the window-seat writing idly in my mind a description of the wind and the snow and the grey twilight of the evening. It is strange, is it not, that my tale should begin and end with the snow and the twilight.

Sir John opened suddenly a door at one end of the room and came hurrying across to another door. He looked at me, grinning rather like a triumphant maniac.

"It's coming!" he cried, without pausing, "I've almost got it!" I smiled at him: he looked very ludicrous at that moment.

"What have you got?" I asked.

"Good Lord, man, the Secret—the Secret!" And then he was gone again, the door closing upon his victorious cry, "The Secret!"

I was, of course, amused. But I was also very much interested. I knew Sir John well enough to realize that, however amazing his appearance might be, there would be nothing absurd about his "Secret"—whatever it was. But it was useless to speculate. I could only hope for enlightenment at dinner. So I immersed myself in one of the surgeon's volumes from his fine Library of Imagination, and waited.

I think the book was one of Mr. H.G. Wells's, probably "The Sleeper Awakes," or some other of his brilliant fantasies and predictions, for I was in a mood conducive to belief in almost anything when, later, we sat down together across the table. I only wish I could give some idea of the atmosphere that permeated our apartments, the reality it lent to whatever was vast and amazing and strange. You could then, whoever you are, understand a little the ease with which I accepted Sir John's new discovery.

He began to explain it to me at once, as though he could keep it to himself no longer.

"Did you think I had gone mad, Dennell?" he asked. "I quite wonder that I haven't. Why, I have been studying for many years—for most of my life—on this problem. And, suddenly, I have solved it! Or, rather, I am afraid I have solved another one much greater."

"Tell me about it, but for God's sake don't be technical."

"Right," he said. Then he paused. "Dennell, it's *magnificent*! It will change everything that is in the world." His eyes held mine suddenly with the fatality of a hypnotist's. "Dennell, it is the Secret of Eternal Life," he said.

"Good Lord, Sir John!" I cried, half inclined to laugh.

"I mean it," he said. "You know I have spent most of my life studying the processes of birth, trying to find out precisely what went on in the whole history of conception."

"You have found out?"

"No, that is just what amuses me. I have discovered something else without knowing yet what causes either process.

"I don't want to be technical, and I know very little of what actually takes place myself. But I can try to give you some idea of it."

It is thousands, perhaps millions of years since Sir John explained to me. What little I understood at the time I may have forgotten, yet I try to reproduce what I can of his theory.

"In my study of the processes of birth," he began, "I discovered the rudiments of an action which takes place in the bodies of both men and women. There are certain properties in the foods we eat that remain in the body for the reproduction of life, two distinct Essences, so to speak, of which one is retained by the woman, another by the man. It is the union of these two properties that, of course, creates the child.

"Now, I made a slight mistake one day in experimenting with a guinea-pig, and I rearranged certain organs which I need not describe so that I thought I had completely messed up the poor creature's abdomen. It lived, however, and I laid it aside. It was some years later that I happened to notice it again. It had not given birth to any young, but I was amazed to note that it had apparently grown no older: it seemed precisely in the same state of growth in which I had left it.

"From that I built up. I reexamined the guinea-pig, and observed it carefully. I need not detail my studies. But in the end I found that my 'mistake' had in reality been a momentous discovery. I found that I had only to close certain organs, to rearrange certain ducts, and to open certain dormant organs, and, *mirabile dictu*, the whole process of reproduction was changed.

"You have heard, of course, that our bodies are continually changing, hour by hour, minute by minute, so that every few years we have been literally reborn. Some such principle as this seems to operate in reproduction, except that, instead of the old body being replaced by the new, and in its form, approximately, the new body is created apart from it. It is the creation of children that causes us to die, it would seem, because if this activity is, so to speak, dammed up or turned aside into new channels, the reproduction operates on the old body, renewing it continually. It is very obscure and very absurd, is it not? But the most absurd part of it is that it is true. Whatever the true explanation may be the fact remains that the operation can be done, that it actually prolongs life indefinitely, and that I alone know the secret."

Sir John told me a very great deal more, but, after all, I think it amounted to little more than this. It would be impossible for me to express the great hold his discovery took upon my mind the moment he recounted it. From the very first, under the spell of his personality, I believed, and I knew he was speaking the truth. And it opened up before me new vistas. I began to see myself become suddenly eternal, never again to know the fear of death. I could see myself storing up, century after century, an amplitude of wisdom and experience that would make me truly a god.

"Sir John!" I cried, long before he was finished, "You must perform that operation on me!"

"But Dennell, you are too hasty. You must not put yourself so rashly into my hands."

"You have perfected the operation, haven't you?"

"That is true," he said.

"You must try it out on somebody, must you not?"

"Yes, of course. And yet—somehow, Dennell, I am afraid. I cannot help feeling that man is not yet prepared for such a vast thing. There are sacrifices. One must give up love and all sensual pleasure. This operation not only takes away the mere fact of reproduction, but it deprives one of all the things that go with sex, all love, all sense of beauty, all feeling for poetry and the arts. It leaves only the few emotions, selfish emotions, that are necessary to self-preservation. Do you not see? One becomes an intellect, nothing more—a cold apotheosis of reason. And I, for one, cannot face such a thing calmly."

"But, Sir John, like many fears, it is largely horrible in the foresight. After you have changed your nature you cannot regret it. What you are would be as horrible an idea to you afterwards as the thought of what you will be seems now."

"True, true. I know it. But it is hard to face, nevertheless."

"I am not afraid to face it."

"You do not understand it, Dennell, I am afraid. And I

wonder whether you or I or any of us on this earth are ready
for such a step. After all, to make a race deathless, one should
be sure it is a perfect race."

"Sir John," I said, "it is not you who have to face this, nor
any one else in the world till you are ready. But I am firmly
resolved, and I demand it of you as my friend."

Well, we argued much further, but in the end I won. Sir
John promised to perform the operation three days later.

. . . But do you perceive now what I had forgotten during
all that discussion, the one thing I had thought I could never
forget as long as I lived, not even for an instant? It was my
love for Alice—I had forgotten that!

I cannot write here all the infinity of emotions I experienced
later, when, with Alice in my arms, it suddenly came upon
me what I had done. Ages ago—I have forgotten now to feel. I
could name now a thousand feelings I used to have, but I can
no longer even understand them. For only the heart can
understand the heart, and the intellect only the intellect.

With Alice in my arms, I told the whole story. It was
she who, with her quick instinct, grasped what I had never
noticed.

"But Carl!" she cried. "Don't you see?—It will mean that
we can never be married!" And, for the first time, I understood.
If only I could recapture some conception of that love! I have
always known, since the last shred of comprehension slipped
from me, that I lost something very wonderful when I lost
love. But what does it matter? I lost Alice too, and I could not
have known love again without her.

We were very sad and very tragic that night. For hours and
hours we argued the question over. But I felt somewhat that I
was inextricably caught in my fate, that I could not retreat
now from my resolve. I was perhaps, very schoolboyish,
but I felt that it would be cowardice to back out now. But it
was Alice again who perceived a final aspect of the matter.

"Carl," she said to me, her lips very close to mine, "it need
not come between our love. After all, ours would be a poor
sort of love if it were not more of the mind than of the flesh.
We shall remain lovers, but we shall forget mere carnal
desire. I shall submit to that operation too!"

And I could not shake her from resolve. I would speak of
danger that I could not let her face. But, after the fashion of
women, she disarmed me with the accusation that I did not

love her, that I did not want her love, that I was trying to escape from love. What answer had I for that, but that I loved her and would do anything in the world not to lose her?

I have wondered sometimes since whether we might have known the love of the mind. Is love something entirely of the flesh, something created by an ironic God merely to propagate His race? Or can there be love without emotion, love without passion—love between two cold intellects? I do not know. I did not ask then. I accepted anything that would make our way more easy.

There is no need to draw out the tale. Already my hand wavers, and my time grows short. Soon there will be no more of me, no more of my tale—no more of Mankind. There will be only the snow, and the ice, and the cold. . . .

Three days later I entered John's Hospital with Alice on my arm. All my affairs—and they were few enough—were in order. I had insisted that Alice wait until I had come safely through the operation, before she submitted to it. I had been carefully starved for two days, and I was lost in an unreal world of white walls and white clothes and white lights, drunk with my dreams of the future. When I was wheeled into the operating room on the long, hard table, for a moment it shone with brilliant distinctness, a neat, methodical white chamber, tall and more or less circular. Then I was beneath the glare of soft white lights, and the room faded into a misty vagueness from which little steel rays flashed and quivered from silvery cold instruments. For a moment our hands, Sir John's and mine, gripped and we were saying good-bye—for a little while—in the way men say these things. Then I felt the warm touch of Alice's lips upon mine, and I felt sudden painful things I cannot describe, that I could not have described then. For a moment I felt that I must rise and cry out that I could not do it. But the feeling passed, and I was passive.

Something was pressed about my mouth and nose, something with an ethereal smell. Staring eyes swam about me from behind their white masks. I struggled instinctively, but in vain—I was held securely. Infinitesimal points of light began to wave back and forth on a pitch-black background; a great hollow buzzing echoed in my head. My head seemed suddenly to have become all throat, a great, cavernous, empty throat in which sounds and lights were mingled together, in a swift rhythm, approaching, receding eternally. Then, I think, there were dreams. But I have forgotten them. . . .

I began to emerge from the effect of the ether. Everything was dim, but I could perceive Alice beside me, and Sir John.

"Bravely done!" Sir John was saying, and Alice too was saying something, but I cannot remember what. For a long while we talked, I speaking the nonsense of those who are coming out from under ether, they teasing me a little solemnly. But after a little while I became aware of the fact that they were about to leave. Suddenly, God knows why, I knew that they must not leave. Something cried in the back of my head that they *must* stay—one cannot explain these things, except by after events. I began to press them to remain, but they smiled and said they must get their dinner. I commanded them not to go; but they spoke kindly and said they would be back before long. I think I even wept a little, like a child, but Sir John said something to the nurse, who began to reason with me firmly, and then they were gone, and somehow I was asleep. . . .

When I awoke again, my head was fairly clear, but there was an abominable reek of ether all about me. The moment I opened my eyes, I felt that something had happened. I asked for Sir John and for Alice. I saw a swift, curious look that I could not interpret come over the face of the nurse, then she was calm again, her countenance impassive. She reassured me in quick meaningless phrases, and told me to sleep. But I could not sleep: I was absolutely sure that something had happened to them, to my friend and to the women I loved. Yet all my insistence profited me nothing, for the nurses were a silent lot. Finally, I think, they must have given me a sleeping potion of some sort, for I fell asleep again.

For two endless, chaotic days I saw nothing of either of them, Alice or Sir John. I became more and more agitated, the nurse more and more taciturn. She would only say that they had gone away for a day or two.

And then, on the third day, I found out. They thought I was asleep. The night nurse had just come in to relieve the other.

"Has he been asking about them again?" she asked.

"Yes, poor fellow. I have hardly managed to keep him quiet."

"We will have to keep it from him until he is recovered fully." There was a long pause, and I could hardly control my labored breathing.

"How sudden it was!" one of them said. "To be killed like that—" I heard no more, for I leapt suddenly up in bed, crying out.

"Quick! For God's sake, tell me what has happened!" I jumped to the floor and seized one of them by the collar. She was horrified. I shook her with a superhuman strength.

"Tell me!" I shouted. "Tell me—Or, I'll—!" She told me—what else could she do.

"They were killed in an accident," she gasped, "in a taxi—a collision—the Strand—!" And at that moment a crowd of nurses and attendants arrived, called by the other frantic woman, and they put me to bed again.

I have no memory of the next few days. I was in delirium, and I was never told what I said during my ravings. Nor can I express the feelings I was saturated with when at last I regained my mind. Between my old emotions and any attempt to put them into words, or even to remember them, lies always that insurmountable wall of my Change. I cannot understand what I must have felt, I cannot express it.

I only know that for weeks I was sunk in a misery beyond any misery I had ever imagined before. The only two friends I had on earth were gone to me. I was left alone. And, for the first time, I began to see before me all these endless years that would be the same, dull, lonely.

Yet I recovered. I could feel each day the growth of a strange new vigor in my limbs, a vast force that was something tangibly expressive to eternal life. Slowly my anguish began to die. After a week more, I began to understand how my emotions were leaving me, how love and beauty and everything of which poetry was made—how all this was going. I could not bear the thought at first. I would look at the golden sunlight and the blue shadow of the wind, and I would say,

"God! How beautiful!" And the words would echo meaninglessly in my ears. Or I would remember Alice's face, that face I had once loved so inextinguishably, and I would weep and clutch my forehead, and clench my fists, crying.

"Oh God, how can I live without her!" Yet there would be a little strange fancy in my head at the same moment, saying,

"Who is this Alice? You know no such person." And truly I would wonder whether she had ever existed.

So, slowly the old emotions were shed away from me, and I began to joy in a corresponding growth of my mental perceptions. I began to toy idly with mathematical formulae I had forgotten years ago, in the same fashion that a poet toys with a word and its shades of meaning. I would look at everything with new, seeing eyes, new perception, and I would understand things I had never understood before, because formerly my emotions had always occupied me more than my thoughts.

And so the weeks went by, until, one day, I was well.

. . . What, after all, is the use of this chronicle? Surely there will never be men to read it. I have heard them say that the snow will never go, I will be buried, it will be buried with me; and it will be the end of us both. Yet, somehow, it eases my weary soul a little to write. . . .

Need I say that I lived, thereafter, many thousands of thousands of years, until this day? I cannot detail that life. It is a long round of new, fantastic impressions, coming dream-like, one after another, melting into each other. In looking back, as in looking back upon dreams, I seem to recall only a few isolated periods clearly; and it seems that my imagination must have filled in the swift movement between episodes. I think now, of necessity, in terms of centuries and millenniums, rather than days and months. . . . The snow blows terribly about my little fire, and I know it will soon gather courage to quench us both. . . .

Years passed, at first with a sort of clear wonder. I watched things that took place everywhere in the world. I studied. The other students were much amazed to see me, a man of thirty-odd, coming back to college.

"But Judas, Dennell, you've already got your Ph.D! What more do you want?" So they would ask me. And I would reply:

"I want an M.D. and an F.R.C.S." I didn't tell them that I wanted degrees in Law, too, and in Biology and Chemistry, in Architecture and Engineering, in Psychology and Philosophy. Even so, I believe they thought me mad. But poor fools! I would think. They can hardly realize that I have all of eternity before me to study.

"I went to school for many decades. I would pass from University to University, leisurely gathering all the fruits of every subject I took up, reveling in study as no student reveled ever before. There was no need of hurry in my life, no fear of death too soon. There was a magnificence of vigor in my body, and a magnificence of vision and clarity in my brain. I felt myself a superman. I had only to go on storing up wisdom until the day should come when all knowledge of the world was mine, and then I could command the world. I had no need for hurry. O vast life! How I gloried in my eternity! And how little good it has ever done me, by the irony of God.

For several centuries, changing my name and passing from place to place, I continued my studies. I had no consciousness of monotony, for to the intellect, monotony cannot exist: it was one of those emotions I had left behind. One day, however, in the year 2132, a great discovery was made by a man called Zarentzov. It had to do with the curvature of space, quite changing the conceptions that we had all followed since Einstein. I had long ago mastered the last detail of Einstein's theory, as had, in time, the rest of the world. I threw myself immediately into the study of this new, epoch-making conception.

To my amazement, it all seemed to me curiously dim and elusive. I could not quite grasp what Zarentzov was trying to formulate.

"Why," I cried, "the thing is a monstrous fraud!" I went to the professor of Physics in the University I then attended, and I told him it was a fraud, a huge book of mere nonsense. He looked at me rather pityingly.

"I am afraid, Modevski," he said, addressing me by the name I was at the time using, "I am afraid you do not understand it, that is all. When your mind has broadened, you will. You should apply yourself more carefully to your Physics." But that angered me, for I had mastered my Physics before he was ever born. I challenged him to explain the theory. And he did! He put it obviously, in the clearest language he could. Yet I understood nothing. I stared at him dumbly, until he shook his head impatiently, saying that it was useless, that if I could not grasp it I would simply have to keep on studying. I was stunned. I wandered away in a daze.

For do you see what happened? During all those years I had studied ceaselessly, and my mind had been clear and quick as the day I first had left the hospital. But all that time I had been able only to remain what I was—an extraordinarily intelligent man of the twentieth century. And the rest of the race had been progressing! It had been swiftly gathering knowledge and power and ability all that time, faster and faster, while I had been only remaining still. And now here was Zarentzov and the teachers of the Universities, and, probably, a hundred intelligent men, who had all outstripped me! I was being left behind.

And that is what happened. I need not dilate further upon it. By the end of that century I had been left behind by all the students of the world, and I never did understand Zarentzov. Other men came with other theories, and these theories were accepted by the world. But I could not understand them. My intellectual life was at an end. I had nothing more to understand. I knew everything I was capable of knowing, and, thenceforth, I could only play wearily with the old ideas.

Many things happened in the world. A time came when the East and West, two mighty unified hemispheres, rose up in arms: the civil war of a planet. I recall only chaotic visions of fire and thunder and hell. It was all incomprehensible to me: like a bizarre dream, things happened, people rushed about, but I never knew what they were doing. I lurked all that time in a tiny shuddering hole under the city of Yokohama, and by a miracle I survived. And the East won. But it seems to have mattered little who did win, for all the world had become, in all except its few remaining prejudices, a single race, and nothing was changed when it was all rebuilt again, under a single government.

I saw the first of the strange creatures who appeared among us in the year 6371, men who were later known to be from the planet Venus. But they were repulsed, for they were savages compared with the Earthmen, although they were about equal to the people of my own century, 1900. Those of them who did not perish of the cold after the intense warmth of their world, and those who were not killed by our hands, those few returned silently home again. And I have always regretted that I had not the courage to go with them.

I watched a time when the world reached perfection in mechanics, when men could accomplish anything with a touch of the finger. Strange men, these creatures of the hundredth century, men with huge brains and tiny shriveled bodies, atrophied limbs, and slow ponderous movements on their little conveyances. It was I, with my ancient compunctions, who shuddered when at last they put to death all the perverts, the criminals, and the insane, ridding the world of the scum for which they had no more need. It was then that I was forced to produce my tattered old papers, proving my identity and my story. They knew it was true, in some strange fashion of theirs, and, thereafter, I was kept on exhibition as an archaic survival.

I saw the world made immortal through the new invention of a man called Kathol, who used somewhat the same method "legend" decreed had been used upon me. I observed the end of speech, of all perceptions except one, when men learned to communicate directly by thought, and to receive directly into the brain all the myraid vibrations of the universe.

All these things I saw, and more, until that time when there was no more discovery, but a Perfect World in which there was no need for anything but memory, Men ceased to count time at last. Several hundred years after the 154th Dynasty from the Last War, or, as we would have counted in my time, about 200,000 A.D., official records of time were no longer kept carefully. They fell into disuse. Men began to forget years, to forget time at all. Of what significance was time when one was immortal?

After long, long uncounted centuries, a time came when the days grew noticeably colder. Slowly the winters became longer, and the summers diminished to but a month or two. Fierce storms raged endlessly in winter, and in summer sometimes there was severe frost, sometimes there was only frost. In the high places and in the north and the subequatorial south, the snow came and would not go.

Men died by the thousands in the higher latitudes. New York became, after a while, the furthest habitable city north, an arctic city, where the warmth seldom penetrated. And great fields of ice began to make their way southward, grinding before them the brittle remains of civilizations, covering over relentlessly all of man's proud work.

Snow appeared in Florida and Italy one summer. In the end, snow was there always. Men left New York, Chicago, Paris, Yokohama, and everywhere they traveled by the millions southward, perishing as they went, pursued by the snow and the cold, and that inevitable field of ice. They were feeble creatures when the Cold first came upon them, but I speak in terms of thousands of years; and they turned every weapon of science to the recovery of their physical power, for they foresaw that the only chance of survival lay in a hard, strong body. As for me, at last I had found a use for my few powers, for my physique was the finest in that world. It was but little comfort, however, for we were all united in our awful fear of that Cold and that grinding field of Ice. All the great cities were deserted. We would catch silent, fearful glimpses of them as we sped on in our machines over the snow—great hungry, haggard skeletons of cities, shrouded in banks of snow, snow that the wind rustled through desolate streets where the cream of human life once had passed in calm security. Yet still the Ice pursued. For men had forgotten about that Last Ice Age when they ceased to reckon time, when they lost sight of the future and steeped themselves in memories. They had not remembered that a time must come when Ice would lie white and smooth over all the earth, when the sun would shine bleakly between unending intervals of dim, twilight snow and sleet.

Slowly the Ice pursued us down the earth, until all the feeble remains of civilization were gathered in Egypt and India and South America. The deserts flowered again, but the frost would come always to bite the tiny crops. For still the Ice came. All the world now, but for a narrow strip about the equator, was one great silent desolate vista of stark ice-plains, ice that brooded above the hidden ruins of cities that had endured for hundreds of thousands of years. It was terrible to imagine the awful solitude and the endless twilight that lay on these places, and the grim snow, sailing in silence over all. . . .

It surrounded us on all sides, until life remained only in a few scattered clearings all about that equator of the globe, with an eternal fire going to hold away the hungry Ice. Perpetual winter reigned now; and we were becoming terror-stricken beasts that preyed on each other for a life already doomed. Ah, but I, I the archaic survival, I had my revenge then, with my great physique and strong jaws—God! Let me think of something else. Those men who lived upon each other—it was horrible. And I was one.

So inevitably the Ice closed in. . . . One day the men of our tiny clearing were but a score. We huddled about our dying fire of bones and stray logs. We said nothing. We just sat, in deep, wordless, thoughtless silence. We were the last outpost of Mankind.

I think suddenly something very noble must have transformed these creatures to a semblance of what they had been of old. I saw, in their eyes, the question they sent from one to another and in every eye I saw that the answer was, Yes.

With one accord they rose before my eyes and, ignoring me as a baser creature, they stripped away their load of tattered rags and, one by one, they stalked with their tiny shriveled limbs into the shivering gale of swirling, gusting snow, and disappeared. And I was alone. . . .

So I am alone now. I have written this last fantastic history of myself and of Mankind upon a substance that will, I know, outlast even the snow and the Ice—as it has outlasted Mankind that made it. It is the only thing with which I have never parted. For it is not irony that I should be the historian of this race—I, a savage, an "archaic survival?" Why do I write? God knows, but some instinct prompts me, although there will never be men to read.

I have been sitting here, waiting, and I have thought often of Sir John and Alice, whom I loved. Can it be that I am feeling again, after all these ages, some tiny portion of that emotion, that great passion I once knew? I see her face before me, the face I have lost from my thoughts for eons, and something is in it that stirs my blood again. Her eyes are half-closed and deep, her lips are parted as though I could crush them with an infinity of wonder and discovery. O God! It is love again, love that I thought was lost! They have often smiled upon me when I spoke of God, and muttered about my foolish, primitive superstitions. But they are gone, and I am left who believe in God, and surely there is purpose in it.

I am cold, I have written. Ah, I am frozen. My breath freezes as it mingles with the air, and I can hardly move my numbed fingers. The Ice is closing over me, and I cannot break it any longer. The storm cries weirdly all about me in the twilight, and I know this is the end. The end of the world. And I—I, the last man. . . .

The last man. . . .

. . . I am cold—cold. . . .

But is it you, Alice, is it you?

Evelyn E. Smith

One of the most underrated science fiction writers of the 1950s, Evelyn E. Smith deserves to be better known. She is primarily a short-story writer. Two of her three sf novels, *The Perfect Planet* (1962) and *Unpopular Planet* (1975), are clever works that comment on the nature of the human animal in consistently entertaining ways. However, her best work can be found in her more than fifty short stories, especially those first published in *Galaxy*, including such gems as "The Hardest Bargain," "Not Fit for Children," and "The Vilbar Party." A "Best of" book is long overdue. Ms. Smith lives in New York and has worked as a compiler of crossword puzzles.

In "The Most Sentimental Man" she asks an interesting question: Why would one man choose to remain on an Earth which faces impending doom, while everyone else flees to the stars?

THE MOST SENTIMENTAL MAN

by Evelyn E. Smith

JOHNSON WENT TO SEE the others off at Idlewild. He knew they'd expect him to and, since it would be the last conventional gesture he'd have to make, he might as well conform to their notions of what was right and proper.

For the past few centuries the climate had been getting hotter; now, even though it was not yet June, the day was uncomfortably warm. The sun's rays glinting off the bright metal flanks of the ship dazzled his eyes, and perspiration made his shirt stick to his shoulder blades beneath the jacket that the formality of the occasion had required. He wished Clifford would hurry up and get the leavetaking over with.

But, even though Clifford was undoubtedly even more anxious than he to finish with all this ceremony and take off, he wasn't the kind of man to let inclination influence his actions. "Sure you won't change your mind and come with us?"

Johnson shook his head.

The young man looked at him—hatred for the older man's complication of what should have been a simple departure showing through the pellicule of politeness. He was young, for, since this trip had only slight historical importance and none of any other kind, the authorities had felt a junior officer entirely sufficient. It was clear, however, that Clifford attributed his commandership to his merits, and he was very conscious of his great responsibility.

"We have plenty of room on the ship," he persisted. "There weren't many left to go. We could take you easily enough, you know."

Johnson made a negative sign again. The rays of the sun beating full upon his head made apparent the gray that

125

usually blended into the still-thick blond hair. Yet, though past youth, he was far from being an old man. "I've made my decision," he said, remembering that anger now was pointless.

"If it's—if you're just too proud to change your mind," the young commander said, less certainly, "I'm sure everyone will understand if . . . if . . ."

Johnson smiled. "No, it's just that I want to stay—that's all."

But the commander's clear blue eyes were still baffled, uneasy, as though he felt he had not done the utmost that duty—not duty to the service but to humanity—required. That was the trouble with people, Johnson thought: when they were most well-meaning they became most troublesome.

Clifford lowered his voice to an appropriately funeral hush, as a fresh thought obviously struck him. "I know, of course, that your loved ones are buried here and perhaps you feel it's your duty to stay with them. . . .?"

At this Johnson almost forgot that anger no longer had any validity. By "loved ones" Clifford undoubtedly had meant Elinor and Paul. It was true that Johnson had had a certain affection for his wife and son when they were alive; now that they were dead they represented an episode in his life that had not, perhaps, been unpleasant, but was certainly over and done with now.

Did Clifford think *that* was his reason for remaining? Why, he must believe Johnson to be the most sentimental man on Earth. "And, come to think of it," Johnson said to himself, amused, "I am—or soon will be—just that."

The commander was still unconsciously pursuing the same train of thought. "It does seem incredible," he said in a burst of boyish candor that did not become him, for he was not that young, "that you'd want to stay alone on a whole planet. I mean to say—entirely alone. . . . There'll never be another ship, you know—at least not in your lifetime."

Johnson knew what the other man was thinking. If there'd been a woman with Johnson now, Clifford might have been able to understand a little better how the other could stick by his decision.

Johnson wriggled, as sweat oozed stickily down his back. "For God's sake," he said silently, "take your silly ship and get the hell off my planet." Aloud he said, "It's a good planet, a little worn-out but still in pretty good shape. Pity you can't trade in an old world like an old car, isn't it?"

"If it weren't so damned far from the center of things," the

young man replied, defensively assuming the burden of all
civilization, "we wouldn't abandon it. After all, we hate
leaving the world on which we originated. But it's a long haul
to Alpha Centauri—you know that—and a tremendously
expensive one. Keeping up this place solely out of sentiment
would be sheer waste—the people would never stand for the
tax burden."

"A costly museum, yes," Johnson agreed.

How much longer were these dismal farewells going to
continue? How much longer would the young man still feel
the need to justify himself? "If only there were others fool
enough—if only there were others with you . . . But, even if
anybody else'd be willing to cut himself off entirely from the
rest of the civilized universe, the Earth won't support enough
of a population to keep it running. Not according to our
present living standards anyway. Most of its resources are
gone, you know—hardly any coal or oil left, and that's not
worth digging for when there are better and cheaper fuels in
the system."

He was virtually quoting from the *Colonial Officer's Manual*. Were there any people left able to think for themselves?
Johnson wondered. Had there ever been? Had he thought for
himself in making his decision, or was he merely clinging to
a childish dream that all men had had and lost?

"With man gone, Earth will replenish herself," he said
aloud. First the vegetation would begin to grow thick. Already
it had released itself from the restraint of cultivation; soon it
would be spreading out over the continent, overrunning the
cities with delicately persistent green tendrils. Some the
harsh winters would kill, but others would live on and would
multiply. Vines would twist themselves about the tall buildings and tenderly, passionately squeeze them to death . . .
eventually send them tumbling down. And then the trees
would rear themselves in their places.

The swamps that man had filled in would begin to reappear one by one, as the land sank back to a pristine state. The
sea would go on changing her boundaries, with no dikes to
stop her. Volcanoes would heave up the land into different
configurations. The heat would increase until it grew unbear-
able . . . only there would be no one—no human, anyway—to
bear it.

Year after year the leaves would wither and fall and decay.
Rock would cover them. And some day . . . billions of years

thence ... there would be coal and oil ... and nobody to want them.

"Very likely Earth will replenish herself," the commander agreed, "but not in your time or your children's time ... that is, not in *my* children's time," he added hastily.

The handful of men lined up in a row before the airlock shuffled their feet and allowed their muttering to become a few decibels louder. Clifford looked at his wrist chronometer. Obviously he was no less anxious than the crew to be off, but, for the sake of his conscience, he must make a last try.

"Damn your conscience," Johnson thought. "I hope that for this you feel guilty as hell, that you wake up nights in a cold sweat remembering that you left one man alone on the planet you and your kind discarded. Not that I don't want to stay, mind you, but that I want you to suffer the way you're making me suffer now—having to listen to your platitudes."

The commander suddenly stopped paraphrasing the *Manual*. "Camping out's fun for a week or two, you know, but it's different when it's for a lifetime."

Johnson's fingers curled in his palms ... he was even angrier now that the commander had struck so close to home. Camping out ... was that all he was doing—fulfilling childhood desires, nothing more?

Fortunately Clifford didn't realize that he had scored, and scuttled back to the shelter of the *Manual*. "Perhaps you don't know enough about the new system in Alpha Centauri," he said, a trifle wildly. "It has two suns surrounded by three planets. Thalia, Aglaia, and Euphrosyne. Each of these planets is slightly smaller than Earth, so that the decrease in gravity is just great enough to be pleasant, without being so marked as to be inconvenient. The atmosphere is almost exactly like that of Earth, except that it contains several beneficial elements which are absent here—and the climate is more temperate. Owing to the fact that the planets are partially shielded from the suns by cloud layers, the temperature—except immediately at the poles and the equators, where it is slightly more extreme—is always equable, resembling that of Southern California ..."

"Sounds charming," said Johnson. "I too have read the Colonial Office handouts ... I wonder what the people who wrote them'll do now that there's no longer any necessity for attracting colonists—everybody's already up in Alpha Centauri. Oh, well; there'll be other systems to conquer and colonize."

"The word *conquer* is hardly correct," the commander said stiffly, "since not one of the three planets had any indigenous life forms that was intelligent."

"Or life forms that you recognize as intelligent," Johnson suggested gently. Although why should there be such a premium placed on intelligence? he wondered. Was intelligence the sole criterion on which the right to life and to freedom should be based?

The commander frowned and looked at his chronometer again. "Well," he finally said, "since you feel that way and you're sure you've quite made up your mind, my men *are* anxious to go."

"Of course they are," Johnson said, managing to convey just the right amount of reproach.

Clifford flushed and started to walk away.

"I'll stand out of the way of your jets!" Johnson called after him. "It would be so anticlimactic to have me burned to a crisp after all this. Bon voyage!"

There was no reply.

Johnson watched the silver vessel shoot up into the sky and thought, "Now is the time for me to feel a pang, or even a twinge, but I don't at all. I feel relieved, in fact, but that's probably the result of getting rid of that fool Clifford."

He crossed the field briskly, pulling off his jacket and discarding his tie as he went. His ground car remained where he had parked it—in an area clearly marked *No Parking*.

They'd left him an old car that wasn't worth shipping to the stars. How long it would last was anybody's guess. The government hadn't been deliberately illiberal in leaving him such a shabby vehicle; if there had been any way to ensure a continuing supply of fuel, they would probably have left him a reasonably good one. But, since only a little could be left, allowing him a good car would have been simply an example of conspicuous waste, and the government had always preferred its waste to be inconspicuous.

He drove slowly through the broad boulevards of Long Island, savoring the loneliness. New York as a residential area had been a ghosttown for years, since the greater part of its citizens had been among the first to emigrate to the stars. However, since it was the capital of the world and most of the interstellar ships—particularly the last few—had taken off from its spaceports, it had been kept up as an official embarkation center. Thus, paradoxically, it was the last city to be completely evacuated, and so, although the massive but jerry-built apartment houses that lined the streets were already crumbling, the roads had been kept in fairly good shape and were hardly cracked at all.

Still, here and there the green was pushing its way up in unlikely places. A few more of New York's tropical summers, and Long Island would soon become a wilderness.

The streets were empty, except for the cats sunning themselves on long-abandoned doorsteps or padding about on obscure errands of their own. Perhaps their numbers had not increased since humanity had left the city to them, but there certainly seemed to be more—striped and solid, black and gray and white and tawny—accepting their citizenship with equanimity. They paid no attention to Johnson—they had long since dissociated themselves from a humanity that had not concerned itself greatly over their welfare. On the other hand, neither he nor the surface car appeared to startle them; the old ones had seen such before, and to kittens the very fact of existence is the ultimate surprise.

The Queensborough Bridge was deadly silent. It was completely empty except for a calico cat moving purposefully toward Manhattan. The structure needed a coat of paint, Johnson thought vaguely, but of course it would never get one. Still, even uncared for, the bridges should outlast him— there would be no heavy traffic to weaken them. Just in case of unforeseeable catastrophe, however—he didn't want to be trapped on an island, even Manhattan Island—he had remembered to provide himself with a rowboat; a motorboat would have been preferable, but then the fuel difficulty would arise again. . . .

How empty the East River looked without any craft on it! It was rather a charming little waterway in its own right, though nothing to compare with the stately Hudson. The water scintillated in the sunshine and the air was clear and fresh, for no factories had spewed fumes and smoke into it for many years. There were few gulls, for nothing was left for the scavenger; those remaining were forced to make an honest living by catching fish.

In Manhattan, where the buildings had been more soundly constructed, the signs of abandonment were less evident . . . empty streets, an occasional cracked window. Not even an unusual amount of dirt because, in the past, the normal activities of an industrial and ruggedly individual city had provided more grime than years of neglect could ever hope to equal. No, it would take Manhattan longer to go back than Long Island. Perhaps that too would not happen during his lifetime.

Yet, after all, when he reached Fifth Avenue he found that Central Park had burst its boundaries. Fifty-ninth Street was already half jungle, and the lush growth spilled down the avenues and spread raggedly out into the sidestreets, pushing its way up through the cracks it had made in the surface of the roads. Although the Plaza fountain had not flowed for centuries, water had collected in the leaf-choked basin from the last rain, and a group of gray squirrels were gathered around it, shrilly disputing possession with some starlings.

Except for the occasional cry of a cat in the distance, these voices were all that he heard . . . the only sound. Not even the sudden blast of a jet regaining power . . . he would never hear that again; never hear the stridor of a human voice piercing with anger; the cacophony of a hundred television sets, each playing a different program; the hoot of a horn; off-key singing; the thin, uncertain notes of an amateur musician . . . these would never be heard on Earth again.

He sent the car gliding slowly . . . no more traffic rules . . . down Fifth Avenue. The buildings here also were well-built; they were many centuries old and would probably last as many more. The shop windows were empty, except for tangles of dust . . . an occasional broken, discarded manne-quin. . . . In some instances the glass had already cracked or fallen out. Since there were no children to throw stones, however, others might last indefinitely, carefully glassing in nothingness. Doors stood open and he could see rows of empty counters and barren shelves fuzzed high with the dust of the years since a customer had approached them.

Cats sedately walked up and down the avenue or sat genteelly with tails tucked in on the steps of the cathedral— as if the place had been theirs all along.

Dusk was falling. Tonight, for the first time in centuries, the street lamps would not go on. Undoubtedly when it grew dark he would see ghosts, but they would be the ghosts of the past and he had made his peace with the past long since; it was the present and the future with which he had not come to terms. And now there would be no present, no past, no future—but all merged into one and he was the only one.

At Forty-second Street pigeons fluttered thickly around

the public library, fat as ever, their numbers greater, their appetites grosser. The ancient library, he knew, had changed little inside: stacks and shelves would still be packed thick with reading matter. Books are bulky, so only the rare editions had been taken beyond the stars; the rest had been microfilmed and their originals left to Johnson and decay. It was his library now, and he had all the time in the world to read all the books in the world—for these were more than he could possibly read in the years that, even at the most generous estimate, were left to him.

He had been wondering where to make his permanent residence, for, with the whole world his, he would be a fool to confine himself to some modest dwelling. Now he fancied it might be a good idea to move right into the library. Very few places in Manhattan could boast a garden of their own.

He stopped the car to stare thoughtfully at the little park behind the grimy monument to Neoclassicism. Like Central Park, Bryant had already slipped its boundaries and encroached upon Sixth Avenue—Avenue of the World, the street signs said now, and before that it had been Avenue of the Nations and Avenue of the Americas, but to the public it had always been Sixth Avenue and to Johnson, the last man on Earth, it was Sixth Avenue.

He'd live in the library, while he stayed in New York, that was—he'd thought that in a few weeks, when it got really hot, he might strike north. He had always meant to spend a summer in Canada. His surface car would probably never last the trip, but the Museum of Ancient Vehicles had been glad to bestow half a dozen of the bicycles from their exhibits upon him. After all, he was, in effect, a museum piece himself and so as worth preserving as the bicycles; moreover, bicycles are different to pack for an interstellar trip. With reasonable care, these might last him his lifetime. . . .

But he had to have a permanent residence somewhere, and the library was an elegant and commodious dwelling, centrally located. New York would have to be his head-quarters, for all the possessions he had carefully amassed and collected and begged and—since money would do him no good any more—bought, were here. And there were by far too many of them to be transported to any really distant location. He loved to own things.

He was by no means an advocate of Rousseau's complete return to nature; whatever civilization had left that he could use without compromise, he would—and thankfully. There would be no electricity, of course, but he had provided himself with flashlights and bulbs and batteries—not too many of the last, of course, because they'd grow stale. However, he'd also laid in plenty of candles and a vast supply of matches ... tins of food and concentrates and synthetics, packages of seed should he grow tired of all these and want to try growing his own—fruit, he knew, would be growing wild soon enough ... vitamins and medicines—of course, were he to get really ill or get hurt in some way, it might be the end ... but that was something he wouldn't think of—something that couldn't possibly happen to him. ...

For his relaxation he had an antique hand-wound phonograph, together with thousands of old-fashioned records. And then, of course, he had the whole planet, the whole world to amuse him.

He even had provided himself with a heat-ray gun and a substantial supply of ammunition, although he couldn't imagine himself ever killing an animal for food. It was squeamishness that stood in his way rather than any ethical considerations, although he did indeed believe that every creature had the right to live. Nonetheless, there was the possibility that the craving for fresh meat might change his mind for him. Besides, although hostile animals had long been gone from this part of the world—the only animals would be birds and squirrels and, farther up the Hudson, rabbits and chipmunks and deer ... perhaps an occasional bear in the mountains—who knew what harmless life form might become a threat now that its development would be left unchecked?

A cat sitting atop one of the stately stone lions outside the library met his eye with such a steady gaze of understanding, though not of sympathy, that he found himself needing to repeat the by-now almost magic phrase to himself: "Not in my lifetime anyway." Would some intelligent life form develop to supplant man? Or would the planet revert to a primeval state of mindless innocence? He would never know and he didn't really care ... no point in speculating over unanswerable questions.

He settled back luxuriously on the worn cushions of his car. Even so little as twenty years before, it would have been impossible for him—for anyone—to stop his vehicle in the middle of Forty-second Street and Fifth Avenue purely to meditate. But it was his domain now. He could go in the wrong direction on one-way streets, stop wherever he pleased, drive as fast or as slowly as he would (and could, of course). If he wanted to do anything as vulgar as spit in the street, he could (but they were his streets now, not to be sullied) . . . cross the roads without waiting for the lights to change (it would be a long, long wait if he did) . . . go to sleep when he wanted, eat as many meals as he wanted whenever he chose. . . . He could go naked in hot weather and there'd be no one to raise an eyebrow, deface public buildings (except that they were private buildings now, his buildings), idle without the guilty feeling that there was always something better he could and should be doing . . . even if there were not. There would be no more guilty feelings; without people and their knowledge there was no more guilt.

A flash of movement in the bushes behind the library caught his eye. Surely that couldn't be a faun in Bryant Park? So soon? . . . He'd thought it would be another ten years at least before the wild animals came sniffing timidly along the Hudson, venturing a little farther each time they saw no sign of their age-old enemy.

But probably the deer was only his imagination. He would investigate further after he had moved into the library.

Perhaps a higher building than the library . . . but then he would have to climb too many flights of stairs. The elevators wouldn't be working . . . silly of him to forget that. There were a lot of steps outside the library too—it would be a chore to get his bicycles up those steps.

Then he smiled to himself. Robinson Crusoe would have been glad to have had bicycles and steps and such relatively harmless animals as bears to worry about. No, Robinson Crusoe never had it so good as he, Johnson would have, and what more could he want?

For, whoever before in history had had his dreams—and what was wrong with dreams, after all?—so completely gratified? What child, envisioning a desert island all his own, could imagine that his island would be the whole world? Together Johnson and the Earth would grow young again.

No, the stars were for others. Johnson was not the first man in history who had wanted the Earth, but he had been the first man—and probably the last—who had actually been given it. And he was well content with his bargain.

There was plenty of room for the bears too.

Wallace West

The late (1900–1980) Wallace West published six science fiction novels and one story collection in a long career in which he wrote sf only on a part-time basis. A lawyer and a Phi Beta Kappa, he also worked as an editor of entertainment magazines, as a barber, and as a consultant to the Air Pollution Control Administration. Many of his short stories were substantially ahead of their time and reflected his interests in propaganda and the hazards of air and water pollution.

"Eddie for Short" was an advanced story for its time, and suggests how the last woman might help the human race to continue.

EDDIE FOR SHORT

by Wallace West

" *'Cause I ain't got nobody,*
And nobody cares for me."

LITA CLOSED HER EYES as she ended the old song. After a long moment she opened them to their dewy widest; smiled as though she knew a heartwarming secret; slid like a panther kitten from the top of the concert grand. Standing tall as a reed, she searched the floor with bare toes for her shoes.

That little-girl gesture always wowed the cash customers. They loved it, too, when she eased herself to the piano top as her turn began, displaying suntanned shoulders and a startling length of leg. They often cried into their Martinis as she cradled the microphone like a rag doll, kicked off her pumps because "I can't breathe right with shoes on, folks" and sang torch songs of the '20s in that unbelievable contralto.

But tonight the cash customers were absent from the Copa'. Only an automatic, fixed-focus TV camera stared at her with detached lechery as a phonograph finished the accompaniment.

"Goodnight, kind friends, wherever you may be," the girl signed off in a beckoning whisper. "See you tomorrow . . . huhm?"

Just before the Off-the-Air telltale winked she turned and swayed out of the "spot" in calm defiance of the rule that no feminine performer ever turns her back to an audience. (Lita's flat, uncorseted hips could retreat without shame, Bill said.)

Bill!

She crumpled against the silk-brocaded wall of the night club; clung there a second in the semidarkness. Then she snatched the studio phone; jiggled the hook madly. Please God Bill still could answer!

"Lita!" Her radio engineer husband's voice was as slurred as though he had been drinking heavily. "Caught your act after all. 'Swunn'erful as usual, honey. You're bes' li'l trouper in th' world . . . in whole wide world."

"Don't let go!" She kept her own voice steady with tremendous effort. "I'm coming right over."

"Stay 'way from here!" Bill gritted. "We've been over all that before. Can't do thing for me. Nobody can. Ol' Demon Carbon 14 caught up with me at last, even if my grandaddy *was* a hoss."

"But there must be something!"

"Nothing. I'm nine-tenths dead right now. I'm not in pain . . . jus' messy. I don' want you see me this way or try move my body. I like it 'ere in Master Control, with th' lights winkin' an' shinin' down on me." For a moment the words came clear and sharp: "If you risk contamination by coming here, I'll haunt you, Lita, so help me. And I'll bring along a whole army of little red demons. Don't you know who you *are*, Mrs. William Howard Day?"

"I only know I love you."

"I love you too. But don't forget that, so far as we know, you're the last woman left alive on earth."

"What does that matter if you . . .?"

"Matters helluva lot." His voice blurred again. "Maybe human race *has* tried its damnedest commit suicide. Can't let it do stupid thing like that, can we? Can't jus' quit an' let th' croc's take over can we . . . so long as there's single chance?"

"No?"

"Course not. Know million good reasons why not. But time's runnin' out." She had to press the receiver tightly to her ear to hear him now. "Here's what I done. Leavin' th' WGBS carrier wave on permanent. It'll run until Miami's atomic power plant breaks down . . . maybe year or so. Hookin' in th' shortwave an' TV transmitters. Th' network's down but anyone, most anywhere, can spot a 50,000 watt carrier an' follow it . . . follow it . . . Wait a minute, honey. Gotta take some medicine . . . if I can fin' my damn mouth. Don't go 'way."

"I'll never go 'way, Bill," she sobbed. "I'll be right here always."

"Atta girl." He spoke clearly again for a moment. "Well, I figure carrier's not enough. World's in a mess. Gotta give more incentive have somebody find you. So you must keep singin', see? Rigged up a time clock thing. It'll switch in the Copa' ever' night at nine, jus' like always. An' ever' night you climb up on the roost an' sing, jus' like always."

"No! No, Bill!" This time she did scream. "Bill, I couldn't."

"Could too. Gotta! If there's a single man alive anywhere who's near a workin' radio, he'll hear you sooner, later. He'll come to that voice. Even if he has to walk through boilin' pitch. He'll come, jus' like I came alla way from . . . where I come from, honey?"

"From China," she husked. "Oh Bill. For God's sake . . ."

"Yeah. I keep forgettin' now. God's sake . . . 'Manity's sake, too. An' I don't care whether he's yellow, or black, or pea-green and has bat ears an' cross eyes. If he comes you, uh, marry him. See? Show mus' go on. All that."

"No!" The girl sank to her knees on the parqueted floor.

"Yes!" The voice was so weak now it seemed coming already from the other side of the grave. "Promise. Quick! 'Scomin' up signoff time for . . . for . . ."

"I promise, sweetheart." She knelt, slim and proud again, as though in the light from some unearthly "spot." "I promise."

"Knew you would . . . hon." The receiver rattled and choked.

A green-eyed, long-legged, empty-hearted girl walked the streets of "America's Playground."

The streets were empty, too. When the radioactive gas cloud swept across the nation it had sterilized the city of all but insect life.

Where were the piled corpses, the wrecked cars, the evidence of last-minute frenzied looting that prophets of doom always had warned of? Miami's City Fathers had been clever about that. Fearing that an epidemic would follow wide-scale radiation deaths, they spread the word early that Hell Bomb gas tended to concentrate in the canyons of city streets. There might be a chance to escape, or recover, they said, if one went out into the country.

So the wretched Miamians, as they sickened and watched the pale blood start oozing through their sun-varnished skins, fled to the Keys, to the 'Glades, even to the despised and frigid North. They fled in their shiny Cadillacs and Jaguars, their picture-windowed house trailers or their beaten-up Jeeps; via their aerial Route of the Stars and their Seaboard Airline Railway. Even as they fled, they died.

"And civilization fell upon the young men," Lita paraphrased the Book of Job, "and they are dead: And I only am escaped to tell you."

A pity, she thought as she walked the shining, antiseptic streets, that the Fathers had not lived to appreciate the success of their greatest publicity stunt.

Sometimes, when the sun was high, she delighted her woman's heart by wandering through cool shops where the wealth of nations lay heaped and forgotten. Or, in a book store, she brushed aside stacks of murder mysteries and "light summer reading" in vain search of some volume containing a key to the catastrophe.

It had been such a neat little war, over in a far corner of Asia. New weapons had been tested and perfected there. Beardless boys had been hardened into reckless killers, and surplus products disposed of without the necessity for cutting prices. The neat little war had gone on for almost a generation. Everyone except the boys and their parents had come to take it for granted. Something to be deplored, like sin, but nothing to fret about, really.

Then, one still winter night, someone, somewhere, had tossed an atom bomb over the Pole at a European capital. (The bomb fragments, they said, bore Latin characters.) And someone else, somewhere, had tossed an atom bomb over the Pole at an American industrial center . . . Detroit, wasn't it? (Those fragments, the experts said, bore Cyrillic characters.)

The next day . . . Christmas Day, 1964 . . . the Hell Bombs fell. Thirteen spaced evenly along the Pacific Coasts of North and South America and, by coincidence, thirteen more along the Atlantic Coast of Europe and Africa.

The West Wind did the rest.

Lita, who read poetry over the air now and then, remembered how men had scattered before that wild west wind, "like ghosts from an enchanter fleeing."

Ghosts! She would hurry her steps when that thought came, never looking behind her.

Sometimes, instead of walking, she would take her car . . . a Cambridge blue MG . . . and drive to a beach. It was less lonely near the water. There was life there. Would the sharks, or the croc's, as Bill had suggested, some day climb out of that water as men had once done? She shuddered. Nevertheless she missed Bill less while she was swimming.

She swam well, as all singers do, thanks to her splendid chest development. At first she wore a suit, true to her prim upbringing in the orphanage. One day she forgot to put it on. And after that she didn't bother much with clothes in the daytime and became golden brown all over in the warm spring sunshine.

At night things were different, of course. She dressed in the loveliest evening gowns she could find in the shops—a new one each day. She put a hibiscus flower behind her left ear. She made up with the same care she had used when the club was packed to the doors and waiters were jamming little tables between the knees of the ringsiders. And she sang to all those who would never hear her again.

"Bill," from Show Boat, was her theme song. It had been ever since that night when the real Bill, still in uniform, had committed the unpardonable sin of threading his way among the ringside tables, lifting her from the piano after she had finished that number, and kissing her soundly while the customers cheered.

How long ago had that been? Why, only a month! They had been married a week later, as soon as Bill was sure he could return to his old job at WGBS. Another week of bliss, apartment hunting, buying a few sticks of furniture, getting settled, lovemaking . . . And then the Hell Bombs fell.

Sunk in a dream that added poignancy to her singing, Lita cradled the mike and wandered, as the spirit moved her, through the favorites nobody ever got enough of: "I'm Falling in Love with Someone," "Smoke Gets in Your Eyes," "Can't Help Lovin' Dat Man" and, for a change in pace, "Summertime."

> *"One of these mornin's you goin' to rise up singin',*
> *Then you'll spread yo' wings an' you'll take the sky.*
> *But till that mornin' there's a nothin' can harm you*
> *With Daddy an' Mammy standin' by."*

Why, she wondered, had so few songs like that been written in recent years? Perhaps Daddy an' Mammy had turned their backs on children who never stopped squabbling among themselves. Certainly there had been no singin' as all humanity took to the sky that mornin' when the gas came.

Stop it, she told herself. Don't get cynical. So the orphanage *had* been a poor substitute for her physicist father who had died a year-long death after an early atomic test bomb had exploded prematurely out on the New Mexican desert. It had been a poor, prim substitute, too, for the mother she had never known. But the Sisters *had* let her sing at that recital where the manager of the Copa' had heard her. That had led to Bill. And maybe, as he thought, some mutation in her father's irradiated germ plasm had made her, and perhaps her children, immune to the after-effects of alpha, beta and gamma rays.

Her children!

For long moments she sat silent on the piano top, staring into the glazed eye of the TV pickup. Well, if Bill hoped there was a chance that a few others had survived . . . She owed him that, dear soul, up there across the street with the lights of Master Control winkin' and shinin' down on him as he lay across the console as though asleep.

She jerked her mind away. Three times in as many days since his death she had found herself standing with her hand on the knob of the WGBS Master Control Room door. And three times the winking ON THE AIR! KEEP OUT! sign had stopped her.

Inside that door lay madness. And there was no time for madness.

She shook herself savagely. As the Standby light beside the Copa' microphone flickered another kind of warning she swept, heartbroken and magnificent, into her last number:

> *"Some enchanted evening*
> *You may see a stranger . . ."*

On and on she drove herself, white-faced, to the climax:

> *"Once you have found him,*
> *Never . . . let . . . him . . . go."*

In a state of near-collapse she slid to the floor, searched for her shoes, and bade the ghosts farewell. She fled from the dim club out into the bright street.

What would happen, she wondered as she pulled herself together, on that final night when the power plant failed as it was bound to do eventually . . .? When the streets would be darkened forever? She clenched her teeth and ran all the way home . . . home to the apartment she and Bill had chosen because it was so cheerful and so close to the club and the station.

But the street lights, as well as the Nemo signal on the orchestra stand, remained faithful. At dusk, electric eyes turned on the tall standards bordering the boulevards and Biscayne Bay. They switched on the proud Cadillac signs and the glow in the grimy store windows. And at dawn they extinguished them all in thrifty fashion.

Bulbs were beginning to burn out. A short circuit had started a fire that gutted several blocks in the northeastern part of town. But, on the whole, Miami still turned its impersonal, white-toothed smile of welcome to an empty sea. Palm fronds blew, whispering, about the streets sometimes. That was offset by accumulating dust that made Lita's footsteps almost inaudible.

Then, one night as she was walking just a little faster than necessary through a dark spot, she heard the echo.

Startled out of a reverie, she stopped short. There was no sound except her rapid breath. Laughing a little, she went on. Was she really expecting that man with the bat ears and cross eyes to accost her?

The echo had returned!

In just a moment now she would turn and look to see where it was coming from. Ten more steps . . . Fifteen . . . Fifty . . . But that street light had burned out, too, since last night.

Maybe it was a shark, or a croc', coming out of the sea or the swamp to survey its new kingdom? So soon?

For heaven's sake, Lita. Turn and look right now. You're acting like a child. You're acting . . . The poem came unbidden:

> *Like one that on a lonesome road*
> *Doth walk in fear and dread,*
> *And having once turned round, walks on,*
> *And turns no more his head;*
> *Because he knows a frightful fiend*
> *Doth close behind him tread.*

Lita kicked off her pumps and fled, like a benighted Diana, through the dust. The echo footsteps speeded, too, but could not match her. Only when the girl had reached the entrance to her apartment building, a vantage point that somehow gave her a feeling of security, did she dare look back.

Far down the street a black shadow pursued her. She gripped the doorhandle; stood her ground panting, heart drumming against her ribs. Whatever it was that came, she must see it clearly or live in terror forevermore.

A huge dog? No! It ran on its hind legs.

Then it crouched low for a moment and her misgivings returned.

It rose to its feet again. Even in the spotty lighting she could see, now, that it was human. A man? Coming in answer to her songs? Bill had been right! Would he be yellow or green as a vegetable? She tried to smile but only made a face.

No! Not green! Her hands were pressing against her smooth throat not to stifle a scream..

Black! Black as a broken street light!

And old . . . incredibly, crookedly old.

And not even a man! She let out her held breath in a great sigh. Another woman! Thank God!

"Doan need be afeared o' me, honey," a cracked voice called from somewhere among the rainbows that had started wheeling before her eyes. "See, I picked up yer shoes an' brung 'em along . . . Lawsy! Whatsa matter with you, chile!"

Lita recovered consciousness to find herself lying in her own bed upstairs. Beside her sat an old Negro woman. Her eyes, in an incredibly wrinkled face, were as sharp and excited as if she had just seen the glory of the Lord.

"Who are you? How did you get here? What do you want?" Lita sat up, to find that she had been undressed and put properly to bed.

"Name of Verna Smith," the crone grinned, snaggletoothed and benevolent. "Ah come from down Key West way. My man was a shrimp fisher, till . . ." She shuddered and held out her fists to something invisible, the thumbs thrust between the first and second fingers.

"One night Ah hears you singin' when Ah jus' happens to turn on one o' them battery radios in a store down theah. Ah reconnize you right off 'cause mah man usta lissen to you a lot w'en he was blue. Firs', Ah figure dat Miami ain't been

hit. An den Ah knows it has been or you wouldn't be a singin'
so lonesome like. Ah figure you need somebody take care o'
you. An' here Ah am. Took more time'n Ah counted on, what
with th' busses not runnin' an' ever'thing."

"That was awfully nice of you ... Mrs. Smith." Lita felt
warm clear down to her toes, so warm that she broke the old
Southern taboo against calling Negroes "Mrs."

"Jus' call me Verna, ma'am."

"And you call me Lita. I'm sorry I ran away from you. And
fainting like that! I can't imagine what got into me."

"You can't ma' ... Lita, honey?" The old woman's eyes
became even brighter and her smile spread almost from ear
to ear."

"No. I'm strong as an ox."

"You doan know you gonna have a baby, chile?"

"A baby!" For a moment Lita seemed about to faint again.
"How do you know?"

"Ol' Verna ain't been a midwife all these years fo' nothin'."

"Oh no!" Lita began to laugh wildly. "Next week 'East
Lynne'! But you're wrong, Verna. I'm not going to have *a*
baby. I'm going to have twins—a boy and a girl—and we'll
call them Adam and Eve."

Sunlit days flowed by. Hushed days when no bird sang.
Days when only the chirping of crickets and the perfume of
flowers testified that a part of the world still lived. Nights
punctuated by the brief, brave, useless night club interval.
For Lita knew it was useless. If only one person had answered
her call by this time it would not be answered again.

Yet she clung to the ritual, putting her heart and magnificent throat into the old repertoire ... even adding new
numbers. Somewhere Bill must be listening.

For weeks after Verna came and insisted on taking over
the few household chores, Lita did little else but swim, or
drive along the shore through haunts of the wealthy dead in
Palm Beach, Fort Lauderdale and Miami Beach. There the
marble pools already were encrusted with algae, the Afro-
mobiles were idle, the Fountain of Youth dried up. Or she
would sit in the spring sun and dream, like a brown female
Buddha with a poodle cut.

But, as months passed and she felt life stirring within her,
the girl became subtly worried. It wouldn't be enough to
bring a brace of young savages into the world. (She knew she

would bear twins. God couldn't be cruel enough to ordain otherwise!) The children would have to be educated to rebuild civilization, a better civilization. Yet their mother knew so little ... so little. A smattering of high school; never completed.

She literally hurled herself at the City Library and, when its endless stacks confused and frightened her, at the texts she found in the University of Miami. She began with the grandiose idea that she somehow must ground herself in science ... in physics ... and find the magic to ward off another atomic cloud.

The equations remained hen tracks. She left them; turned to economics, to sociology, to psychology. Lita was nobody's fool. Yet, without a teacher, she lost her way in endless bypaths to knowledge. So much learning! And she but one small woman!

History was better. But it justified everything—murder, war, famine, fascism and pestilence—all were for the best in the best possible of worlds. All, from the viewpoint of history, were inevitable, even as the Hell Bomb had become inevitable, once atomic fission and fusion had been left in the hands of the merchants of death.

One of the bypaths she followed led her, though, to the bright world of Greek drama and poetry. Here was music expressed in words ... expressed in a way that she could comprehend. She dropped her other studies and, all through the hot summer months read the ancient authors—Homer, Xenophon, Aristophanes, Euripides, Sophocles. But especially Herodotus, with his prose songs of how it was the custom for brothers and sisters to marry in Egypt; of the curse that the wealth of Croesus brought upon its owner; of how, during the Persian War, Themistocles made the craven Greeks into a nation of heroes by the simple, brutal process of beating their stupid heads together.

Often she read snatches aloud to Verna, at first not dreaming that the Negro would understand anything more than the rhythm of the words. The old woman amazed her by rocking back and forth, arms around her shrunken knees and grizzled head nodding in glee.

"Doan tell me, chile!" she would exclaim. "Doan tell me! 'Way back three thousand years, an' soon as folks get a little money in de bank dey start cuttin' up. Dat's firs' thing you gotta teach the twins. Money made to be spent, have good time with, not to save an' fight fo' with razors."

"You do think I'll have twins, Verna?"

"Lands sakes alive, chile. You still worritin' about dat? I gotta wanga ... dat's Voodoo charm my man brung from Haiti once. Wanga says you gonna have twins."

"Do you believe in Voodoo?"

"Course Ah doan. Jus' th' same, Ah doan make no faces at Papa Legba when it's dahk!"

Came the time, in mild September, when Lita found she could not lift herself to the top of the Copa' piano with her old lithe grace. Came the time when she would have much preferred to go to bed at nightfall than sing for all the ghosts in Christendom.

And yet she sang ... lullabies mostly, now, to get in training ... as she would continue to sing so long as the telltale light beckoned her to the mike. She was not superstitious. Yet she knew that disaster would strike, did she break her word to Bill. Voodoo? Well, so be it!

Came a day, late in September, that was humid and hot and still.

"Hurricane weather," muttered Verna, making a sign. "You better stay home tonight, honey. You is near your time an' they's a big bull blow headin' dis way, mark my word."

Evening crept in sullenly. Sharp gusts of wind whipped the palms and rattled the jalousies. Verna wrung her worn hands but Lita insisted on making her shapelessness as presentable as possible in a sequined black evening dress made for a dowager.

"I have to go," she whimpered stubbornly, even as a shout of wind heralded the near approach of the storm. "We'll drive, though. We'll be home before it gets really bad."

She was wrong. Hardly had they reached the club when the storm leaped yowling at them like a great cat. It whisked the top off the MG with one paw and slammed the little car over the curb and against the side of a building with the other. As they dragged themselves out of the wreck and under the protection of the club portico, rain descended like a theater curtain, so dense that the few remaining street lights seemed extinguished.

"You hurt, honey chile?" panted the black woman as she guided the other inside and fought to close the foyer door.

"No." Lita answered through clenched teeth. "I can go on." She gasped, bent forward in agony and snatched at a chair for support.

The hurricane was screaming like a banshee tangled in the tops of the skyscrapers. Palms splintered, crashed and skidded along the sidewalks. A sign toppled into the street and rolled, a monstrous cartwheel.

"Stay outside, you Papa Legba," Verna shouted back at the storm as she set her thin shoulder to the door. "Doan you go botherin' dis pore gal tonight. She got enough on her min'."

The door inched into its frame and latched. The brocade hangings, which had been flapping like wings, folded along the walls.

"We're late," Lita gasped. "See. The light is on. Bill's waiting!"

She stumbled toward the piano. Halfway across the floor she moaned and crumpled.

"Here. Ah help you." Verna lifted the stricken girl and half-led, half-carried her toward the Ladies' Lounge. "Jus' doan you be skeered. Verna take care o' you."

"But I'm on the air," Lita whimpered. "Please . . . the show . . ."

At that moment the full force of the storm was unleashed. The glass in the foyer door smashed inward. Water poured after it, as though sprayed from a fire hose."

The house lights dimmed, flickered and went out. The Nemo telltale lingered, an accusing green eye. Then it, too, was gone. Lita screamed.

Verna dragged her the rest of the way to the Lounge.

The pain ebbed at last and flowed away. Lita roused to full consciousness, utterly spent. She caught the gleam of a flashlight out of the corner of her eye.

"Verna?" she called against the muted thunder of the storm.

"You feel better, honey chile?" The crone hovered over her.

"I . . . Yes, I guess so . . . How are the . . . twins?"

Verna stood silent, the flash trembling in her hands.

"There are twins?" Lita struggled to sit up but was pushed firmly back among the cushions of what must be a divan.

"No'm." Despite her efforts, the Negro's voice rose to a wail. "Not twins, honey."

Lita turned her face to the wall and let slow tears smear

her cheeks. Again she was a little girl in pigtails, back at the orphanage. She had been punished by being shut in a dark closet for some infraction of the mysterious, inflexible rules. Illogically, savagely, she blamed herself. God, or that impersonal Fate the ancient Greeks believed in, had turned a cold back upon her because she had broken the trouper's code that the show must go on.

"It's a girl," she said at last. Obviously the brat must be a woman child; one who would stare accusingly at her in her old age; one who would hate her for having been brought into a dead world.

"No'm," Verna soothed her. "It's a boy. Healthy as a cricket, too, honey. Must weigh all o' nine pound."

A boy! Lita's world turned over once more. The tears stopped flowing. She stared up at the dim ceiling in abject terror and listened to the wind which was shaking the building and the rain that lashed it with whips.

A boy? Under her wet eyelids she was witnessing the destruction of a great city which no one had battened down against the storm. Trees uprooted. Windows smashed and the baubles behind them soaked to trash. Sheet-iron and aluminum roofs ripped off in long strips, rolled into monstrous cylinders and tossed into the streets to charge up and down like jugernauts . . .

No. Not juggernauts. Like flapping Furies in pursuit of Oedipus. Scourging Oedipus because he had committed incest with his mother? Nonsense! Scourging the world for daring to commit suicide, leaving the altars of the gods empty of incense and sacrifices.

She began laughing hysterically . . . laughing like a Fury herself.

Verna, thinking to quiet her, brought the child kicking in its swaddling of torn brocade; held it under the flashlight beam for her to see.

"What you gonna call yo' son, Miz Lita?" she pleaded.

"Does he need a name, poor thing?" The girl fought her hysteria down.

"Sho' do," the old woman whispered as a dazzle of lightning outlined the lounge door. "Have baby in a hurricane, better name him quick or mebbe you doan have a chance."

Lita stared at the door as though waiting for the crackling flashes to illuminate her future. Perhaps, in spite of everything, someone, somewhere, was coming to her over the rim of the dead world.

And if not? Well, she was young ... barely nineteen. There was still time ... plenty of time to keep her promise to Bill ... Furies or no Furies.

"We'll call him Eddie," she said. "Eddie for short."

Fredric Brown

The late (1906–1972) Fredric Brown was one of the finest all-round writers ever to work the pulps. His great versatility is evident in his considerable accomplishments in the science fiction, mystery, and suspense fields, all of which he enriched. In science fiction, he is best remembered for wonderful short-shorts like "The Answer," powerful psychological stories like "Come and Go Mad," and humorous novels like *Martians Go Home*. *The Best of Fredric Brown* (1977) contains many of his best stories, but he was so good that no one book could possibly accommodate all his outstanding work.

"Knock" has some very interesting things to say about why man is the most dangerous of animals.

KNOCK

by Frederic Brown

THERE IS A SWEET LITTLE horror story that is only two sentences long:

The last man on Earth sat alone in a room. There was a knock at the door . . .

Two sentences and an ellipsis of three dots. The horror, of course, isn't in the story at all; it's in the ellipsis, the implication: *what* knocked at the door. Faced with the unknown, the human mind supplies something vaguely horrible.

But it *wasn't* horrible, really.

The last man on Earth—or in the universe, for that matter—*sat alone in a room.* It was a rather peculiar room. He'd just been studying out the reason for its peculiarity. His conclusion didn't horrify him, but it annoyed him.

Walter Phelan, who had been associate professor of anthropology at Nathan University up to the time two days ago when Nathan University had ceased to exist, was not a man who horrified easily. Not that Walter Phelan was a heroic figure, by any wild stretch of the imagination. He was slight of stature and mild of disposition. He wasn't much to look at, and he knew it.

Not that appearance worried him now. Right now, in fact, there wasn't much feeling in him. Abstractedly, he knew that two days ago, within the space of an hour, the human race had been destroyed, except for him and, somewhere—one woman. And that was a fact which didn't concern Walter Phelan in the slightest degree. He'd probably never see her and didn't care too much if he didn't.

153

Women just hadn't been a factor in Walter's life since Martha had died a year and a half ago. Not that Martha hadn't been a good wife—albeit a bit on the bossy side. Yes, he'd loved Martha, in a deep, quiet way. He was only forty now, and he'd been only thirty-eight when Martha had died, but—well—he just hadn't thought about women since then. His life had been his books, the ones he read and the ones he wrote. Now there wasn't any point in writing books, but he had the rest of his life to spend in reading them.

True, company would have been nice, but he'd get along without it. Maybe after a while he'd get so he'd enjoy the occasional company of one of the Zan, although that was a bit difficult to imagine. Their thinking was so alien to his that it was a bit difficult to imagine their finding common ground for a discussion. They were intelligent in a way, but so is an ant. No man has ever established communication with an ant. He thought of the Zan, somehow, as super-ants, although they didn't look like ants—and he had a hunch that the Zan regarded the human race as the human race regarded ordinary ants. Certainly what they'd done to Earth had been what men do to ant hills, and it had been done much more efficiently.

But they'd given him plenty of books. They'd been nice about that, as soon as he had told them what he wanted. And he had told them that the moment he realized that he was destined to spend the rest of his life alone in this room. The rest of his life, or as the Zan had quaintly expressed it, for-ev-er.

Even a brilliant mind, and the Zan obviously had brilliant minds, had its idiosyncrasies. The Zan had learned to speak Terrestrial English in a matter of hours, but they persisted in separating syllables. However, we digress.

There was a knock at the door.

You've got it all now except the three dots, the ellipsis, and I'm going to fill that in and show you that it wasn't horrible at all.

Walter Phelan called out, "Come in," and the door opened. It was, of course, only a Zan. It looked exactly like the other Zan; if there was any way of telling them apart, Walter hadn't found it. It was about four feet tall and it looked like nothing on Earth—nothing, that is, that had been on Earth before the Zan came here.

Walter said, "Hello, George." When he'd learned that none

of them had names, he'd decided to call them all George and the Zan didn't seem to mind.

This one said, "Hel-lo, Wal-ter." That was ritual, the knock on the door and the greetings. Walter waited.

"Point one," said the Zan. "You will please hence-forth sit with your chair fac-ing the oth-er way."

Walter said, "I thought so, George. That plain wall is transparent from the other side, isn't it?"

"It is trans-par-ent."

Walter sighed. "I knew it. That plain blank wall, without a single piece of furniture against it. And made of something different from the other walls. If I persist in sitting with my back to it, what then? You will kill me?—I ask hopefully."

"We will take a-way your books."

"You've got me there, George. All right, I'll face the other way when I sit and read. How many other animals besides me are in this zoo of yours?"

"Two hun-dred and six-teen."

Walter shook his head. "Not complete, George. Even a bush-league zoo can beat that—*could* beat that, I mean, if there were any bush-league zoos left. Did you just pick us at random?"

"Ran-dom sam-ples, yes. All spe-cies would have been too man-y. Male and fe-male each of one hun-dred kinds."

"What do you feed them? The carnivorous ones, I mean."

"We make feed. Syn-thet-ic."

"Smart. And the flora? You've got a collection of that, too, haven't you?"

"Flo-ra not hurt by vi-bra-tions. It is all still grow-ing."

"Good for the flora. You weren't as hard on it, then, as you were on the fauna. Well, George, you started out with 'point one.' I deduce that there is a point two lurking somewhere. What is it?"

"There is some-thing we do not un-der-stand. Two of the oth-er an-i-mals sleep and do not wake. They are cold."

"It happens in the best-regulated zoos, George. Probably not a thing wrong with them except that they're dead."

"Dead? That means stopped. But noth-ing stopped them. Each was a-lone."

Walter stared at the Zan. "Do you mean, George, that you do not know what natural death is?"

"Death is when a be-ing is killed, stopped from liv-ing."

Walter Phelan blinked. "How old are you, George?" he asked.

"Six-teen—you would not know the word. Your plan-et went a-round your sun a-bout sev-en thou-sand times. I am still young."

Walter whistled softly. "A babe in arms," he said. He thought hard for a moment. "Look, George, you've got something to learn about this planet you're on. There's a guy down here who doesn't hang around where you come from. An old man with a beard and a scythe and an hourglass. Your vibrations didn't kill him."

"What is he?"

"Call him the Grim Reaper, George. Old Man Death. Our people and animals live until somebody, Old Man Death, stops them from ticking."

"He stopped the two crea-tures? He will stop more?"

Walter opened his mouth to answer, and then closed it again. Something in the Zan's voice indicated that there would be a worried frown on his face if he had a face recognizable as such.

"How about taking me to those animals who won't wake up?" Walter asked. "Is that against the rules?"

"Come," said the Zan.

That had been the afternoon of the second day. It was the next morning that the Zan came back, several of them. They began to move Walter Phelan's books and furniture. When they finished that, they moved him. He found himself in a much larger room a hundred yards away.

He sat and waited this time, too. When there was a knock on the door, he knew what was coming and politely stood up as he called out, "Come in."

A Zan opened the door and stood aside. A woman entered.

Walter bowed slightly. "Walter Phelan," he said, "in case George didn't tell you my name. George tries to be polite but he doesn't know all our ways."

The woman seemed calm; he was glad to notice that. She said, "My name's Grace Evans, Mr. Phelan. What's this all about? Why did they bring me here?"

Walter was studying her as she talked. She was tall, fully as tall as he, and well-proportioned. She looked to be somewhere in her early thirties, about the age Martha had been. She had the same calm confidence about her that he had always liked about Martha, even though it had contrasted with his own easygoing informality. In fact, he thought she looked quite a bit like Martha.

"I think you can guess why they brought you here, but let's go back a bit," he said. "Do you know what's happened otherwise?"

"You mean that they've—killed everyone?"

"Yes. Please sit down. You know how they accomplished it?"

She sank into a comfortable chair nearby. "No," she said. "I don't know just how. Not that it matters, does it?"

"Not a lot. But here's the story, what I know of it from getting one of them to talk, and from piecing things together. There isn't a great number of them—here anyway. I don't know how numerous a race they are where they came from and I don't know where that is, but I'd guess it's outside the solar system. You've seen the spaceship they came in?"

"Yes. It's as big as a mountain."

"Almost. Well, it has equipment for emitting some sort of vibration—they call it that in our language, but I imagine it's more like a radio wave than a sound vibration—that destroys all animal life. The ship itself is insulated against the vibration. I don't know whether its range is big enough to kill off the whole planet at once, or whether they flew in circles around the earth, sending out the vibratory waves. But it killed everything at once instantly and, I hope, painlessly. The only reason we, and the other two-hundred-odd animals in this zoo, weren't killed was because we were inside the ship. We'd been picked up as specimens. You do know this is a zoo, don't you?"

"I—I suspected it."

"The front walls are transparent from the outside. The Zan were pretty clever in fixing up the inside of each cubicle to match the natural habitat of the creature it contains. These cubicles, such as the one we're in, are of plastic and they've got a machine that makes one in about ten minutes. If Earth had a machine and a process like that, there wouldn't have been any housing shortage. Well, there isn't any housing shortage now, anyway. And I imagine that the human race—specifically you and I—can stop worrying about the H-bomb and the next war. The Zan have certainly solved a lot of problems for us."

Grace Evans smiled faintly. "Another case where the operation was successful but the patient died. Things *were* in an awful mess. Do you remember being captured? I don't. I went to sleep one night and woke up in a cage on the spaceship."

"I don't remember either," Walter said. "My hunch is that they used the waves at low intensity first, just enough to knock us all out. Then they cruised around, picking up samples for their zoo more or less at random. After they had as many as they wanted, or as many as they had room in the ship for, they turned on the juice all the way. And that was that. It wasn't until yesterday that they knew they'd made a mistake by overestimating us. They thought we were immortal, as they are."

"That we were—what?"

"They can be killed but they don't know what natural death is. They didn't anyway, until yesterday. Two of us died yesterday."

"Two of— Oh!"

"Yes, two of us animals in their zoo. Two species gone irrevocably. And by the Zan's way of figuring time, the remaining member of each species is going to live only a few minutes anyway. They figured they had permanent specimens."

"You mean they didn't realize what short-lived creatures we are?"

"That's right," Walter said. "One of them is young at seven thousand years, he told me. They're bisexual themselves, incidentally, but they probably breed every ten thousand years or thereabouts. When they learned yesterday how ridiculously short a life span we terrestrial animals have, they were probably shocked to the core, if they have cores. At any rate they decided to reorganize their zoo—two by two instead of one by one. They figure we'll last longer collectively if not individually."

"Oh!" Grace Evans stood up and there was a faint flush on her face. "If you think— If they think—" She turned toward the door.

"It'll be locked," Walter Phelan said calmly. "But don't worry. Maybe they think, but I *don't* think. You needn't even tell me that you wouldn't have me if I were the last man on Earth; it would be corny under the circumstances."

"But are they going to keep us locked up together in this one little room?"

"It isn't so little; we'll get by. I can sleep quite comfortably in one of those overstuffed chairs. And don't think I don't agree with you perfectly, my dear. All personal considerations aside, the least favor we can do the human race is to let it die out with us and not be perpetuated for exhibition in a zoo."

She said, "Thank you," almost inaudibly, and the flush was gone from her face. There was anger in her eyes, but Walter knew that it wasn't anger at him. With her eyes sparkling like that, she looked a lot like Martha, he thought.

He smiled at her and said, "Otherwise—"

She started out of her chair and for a moment he thought she was going to come over and slap him. Then she sank back wearily. "If you were a *man,* you'd be thinking of some way to— They can be killed, you said?" Her voice was bitter.

"The Zan? Oh, certainly. I've been studying them. They look horribly different from us, but I think they have about the same metabolism, the same type of circulatory system, and probably the same type of digestive system. I think that anything that would kill one of us would kill one of them."

"But you said—"

"Oh, there are differences, of course. Whatever factor it is in man that ages him, they don't have. Or else they have some gland that man doesn't have, something that renews cells. More often than every seven years, I mean."

She had forgotten her anger now. She leaned forward eagerly. She said, "I think that's right. I don't think, though, that they feel pain."

He had been hoping that. He said, "What makes you think so, my dear?"

"I stretched a piece of wire that I found in the desk of my own cubicle across the door so the Zan would fall over it. He did, and the wire cut his leg."

"Did he bleed red?"

"Yes, but it didn't seem to annoy him. He didn't get mad about it; he didn't mention it, just took the wire down. When he came back the next time a few hours later, the cut was gone. Well, almost gone. I could see just enough of a trace of it to be sure it was the same Zan."

Walter Phelan nodded slowly. "He wouldn't get angry, of course. They're emotionless. Maybe if we killed one they wouldn't even punish us. Just give us our food through a trap door and stay clear of us, treat us as men would have treated a zoo animal that had killed its keeper. They'd probably just see that we didn't get a crack at any more keepers."

"How many of them are there?"

Walter said, "About two hundred, I think, in this particu-lar spaceship. But undoubtedly there are many more where they came from. I have a hunch, though, that this is just an advanced board, sent to clear off this planet and make it safe for Zan occupancy."

"They certainly did a good—"

There was a knock at the door and Walter Phelan called out, "Come in." A Zan opened the door and stood in the doorway.

"Hello, George," said Walter.

"Hel-lo, Wal-ter." The same ritual. The same Zan?

"What's on your mind?"

"An-oth-er crea-ture sleeps and will not wake. A small fur-ry one called a wea-sel."

Walter shrugged. "It happens, George. Old Man Death. I told you about him."

"And worse. A Zan has died. This morn-ing."

"Is that worse?" Walter looked at him blandly. "Well, George, you'll have to get used to it if you're going to stay around here."

The Zan said nothing. It stood there.

"Finally, Walter said, "Well?"

"About the wea-sel. You ad-vise the same?"

Walter shrugged again. "Probably won't do any good. But why not?"

The Zan left.

Walter could hear his footsteps dying away outside. He grinned. "It might work, Martha," he said.

"Mar— My name is Grace, Mr. Phelan. What might work?"

"My name is Walter, Grace. You might as well get used to it. You know, Grace, you do remind me a lot of Martha. She was my wife. She died a couple of years ago."

"I'm sorry. But *what* might work? What were you talking about to the Zan?"

"We should know tomorrow," Walter said. And she couldn't get another word out of him.

That was the third day of the stay of the Zan. The next day was the last.

It was nearly noon when one of the Zan came. After the ritual, he stood in the doorway, looking more alien than ever. It would be interesting to describe him for you, but there aren't words. He said, "We go. Our coun-cil met and de-ci-ded."

"Another of you died?"

"Last night. This is pla-net of death."

Walter nodded. "You did your share. You're leaving two hundred and thirteen alive, besides us, but that's out of quite a few billion. Don't hurry back."

"Is there an-y-thing we can do?"

"Yes. You can hurry. And you can leave our door unlocked, but not the others. We'll take care of the others."

The Zan nodded, and left.

Grace Evans was standing, her eyes shining. She asked, "How—? What—?"

"Wait," cautioned Walter. "Let's hear them blast off. It's a sound I want to hear and remember."

The sound came within minutes, and Walter Phelan, realizing how rigidly he'd been holding himself, dropped into a chair and relaxed.

He said softly, "There was a snake in the Garden of Eden, too, Grace, and it got us into trouble. But this one got us out of it, and made up. I mean the mate of the snake that died day before yesterday. It was a rattlesnake."

"You mean it killed the two Zan who died? But—"

Walter nodded. "They were babes in the woods here. When they took me to see the first creatures who 'were asleep and wouldn't wake up,' and I saw that one of them was a rattlesnake, I had an idea, Grace. Just maybe, I thought, poison creatures were a development peculiar to Earth and the Zan wouldn't know about them. And, too, maybe their metabolism was enough like ours that the poison would kill them. Anyway, I had nothing to lose trying. And both maybes turned out to be right."

"How did you get the living rattlesnake to—"

Walter Phelan grinned. "I told them what affection is. They didn't know. But they were interested, I found, in preserving the remaining one of each species as long as possible, to picture and record it before it died. I told them it would die immediately because of the loss of its mate, unless it had affection and petting, constantly.

"I showed them how, with the duck, which was the other creature who had lost its mate. Luckily it was a tame duck and I had no trouble holding it against my chest and petting it, to show them how. Then I let them take over with it—and with the rattlesnake."

He stood up and stretched, and then sat down again more comfortably. He said, "Well, we've got a world to plan. We'll have to let the animals out of the ark, and that will take some thinking and deciding. The herbivorous wild ones we can let go right away, and let them take their chances. The domestic ones we'll do better to keep and take charge of; we'll need them. But the carnivora, the predators— Well, we'll have to decide. But I'm afraid it's got to be thumbs down. Unless maybe we can find and operate the machinery that they used to make synthetic food."

He looked at her. "And the human race. We've got to make a decision about that. A pretty important decision."

Her face was getting a bit pink again, as it had yesterday; she sat rigidly in her chair. "No," she said.

He didn't seem to have heard her. "It's been a nice race, even if nobody won it. It'll be starting over again now, if we start it, and it may go backwards for a while until it gets its breath, but we can gather books for it and keep most of its knowledge intact, the important things anyway. We can—"

He broke off as she got up and started for the door. Just the way Martha would have acted, he thought, back in the days when he was courting her, before they were married.

He said, "Think it over, my dear, and take your time. But come back."

The door slammed. He sat waiting, thinking out all the things there were to do once he started, but in no hurry to start them.

And after a while he heard her hesitant footsteps coming back.

He smiled a little. See? It wasn't horrible, really.

The last man on Earth sat alone in a room. There was a knock at the door . . .

S. Fowler Wright

S. Fowler Wright (1874–1965) was a British accountant, writer, and editor (he edited *Poetry* magazine from 1920 to 1932.) He produced some twenty books of science fiction, almost all of them in the 1920s and 1930s. Wright is best known in sf as the author of *Deluge* (1927) and *Dawn* (1929), related works that are premier examples of the disaster and post-Holocaust subgenres. His excellent novel *The World Below* (1929) exhibits his pessimistic attitude concerning man's future. A prolific writer, he also wrote numerous mystery novels as "Sydney Fowler" and edited several important poetry anthologies. His output is even more amazing given the fact that he did not begin to publish until his fifties.

The more things change, the more they seem to remain the same. Here it's the eve of the world and people still want to raise Cain!

ORIGINAL SIN

S. Fowler Wright

I

I AM XP4378882. I write this with a pen, on sheets of paper in the old way, instead of speaking it into a recorder, because I want it to have a chance of survival, even though a time should come when no more of those instruments can be made or preserved; and because it is a very private thing. If this should be seen by one who could read its words, my death would be nearer even than are those of the men and women among whom I move.

I am writing on the 28th day of September, 2838, being nineteen years of age yesterday, and my friend Stella being two minutes younger than I. We two are the youngest people now alive in the world, having been born somewhat after our time, though there may be eight millions of those who are not more than fourteen days older than we.

For when men conquered disease, and the life of a healthy child became a certain thing, there was a law made that no parents should have more than three (though they could have less if they would, and there were always some that were barren; but there was margin enough for that, and for such as died young, being scalded, or burnt, or perhaps choked with a bone); and then it was soon seen that it was a foolish thing for these children to be born whenever their parents would, as in the old disorderly days, and there was a further law that there should be a space of five years during which all married people might have what children they would (being it not more than three), and after that there

165

should be a period of twenty-five years when none should be born at all.

This worked well in more ways than might be thought at the first, for the children bred were all of a like race, and could be taught at one time, and would advance in a level way, whether at task or game, and the training of each year was in no more than three grades, and they were of a like age to wed when the time came, and would be still in their youth when the law was that they might have children themselves. There was time to plan how the next generation should be reared and taught, and each was divided from each in a clear way.

So it has been now for three hundred years, and each generation has been born into a fairer world. There is no disease. There is no dirt. There is no hunger or thirst. There is no pain. There is enough for all of all things that a man can need, so that there is no cause either to envy or hate, either to strive or long.

Men have learnt to see that they need not die till their strength fails, and then death can be made pleasant enough; but the question of why they live has been left unsolved, and it is one which has been asked in an ever more urgent way.

It is over a century ago that the Doctrine of Futility was first discussed, in records two of which still remain. It was not regarded seriously at first, and was freely allowed. But there came a time when it became a cult which some strongly held, and others disliked with the emphasis which the Law of Moderation forbids.

Consequently, it was banned, and all recordings erased, excepting only those which were preserved in the Great Museum at Timbuctoo.

There was cause for this law, as it had been found that men might hold different opinions with an obstinacy of assertion which would lead to violent quarrels, when wounds might be given, even such as would cause death; and there had been a general determination to remove all occasions of premature decease from the world.

Opinions must not be publicly expressed, except those on which all men were united, or excepting only such a minority as would not dare to dissent aloud, lest they should provoke the Law for the Elimination of Pests, which no one would wish to do.

But these prohibitions were revised every twenty-five years, and it was a remarkable observation that the great majority of controversial questions would become innocuous in such a period, like a wasp that had lost its sting.

This did not happen so quickly to the Doctrine of Futility, but at each successive revision it was regarded by the Guardians of Public Tranquillity with an increased benevolence, until, at the fourth review, there was the necessary unanimous agreement that few would dissent from, and no one would be likely to be seriously disturbed by, the theory which it propounded.

That, briefly stated, was that sentient life on the Earth, and particularly the forecasting and introspective self-consciousness of mankind, is an evolutionary blunder or, at best, a futility, inevitably destined to be corrected by the deliberate action of its own products so soon as they should reach an intellectual maturity sufficient to enable them to recognize both their own abortion, and their power to terminate it.

Sooner or later, it was argued, mankind must reach a maturity of thought which would recognize the vanity of the procession of life and death, and, by its own deliberate and orderly extinction, restore the Harmony of the Universe, which had been momentarily disturbed by the flicker of sentient life on the planet on which we live.

This theory, being released anew by the Guardians of Public Tranquillity as a harmless, and even obvious proposition, was accepted at first with the passive assent due to that which all men can clearly and equally see. But that mood was quickly succeeded by one of excited interest, as it was realised that it offered a prospect of affirmative action to men whose whole lives had been negative till that hour.

The elimination of every kind of adversity from the experience of human life had left it both emotionally and intellectually barren, without hope and without fear. Its futility had an indisputable quality. Men felt that they had already arrived on the crest of the wave of life—a crest where they scarcely were or did.

But here was something that could be done, something to break the monotony of eventless days. With alacrity, even with enthusiasm, men caught at the idea, discussed, approved, planned. As they did so, their eyes brightened, their listless motions quickened, their voices stirred slightly from their accustomed drawl. Paradoxically, life became faintly valuable again, as the prospect of its destruction engaged their minds.

Should they attempt the extinction of life of every kind? It might be beyond human power. It would certainly be an enterprise of extraordinary difficulty. Actually, all the higher forms of life, apart from mankind, had, for reasons of safety, prudence, or sanitation, been eliminated during several previous centuries. Only its more rudimentary forms remained, and these in severely restricted forms. To sterilize every germ of life in ocean and land and air—no, it could not be done. But such as would remain would be elementary in character: they would be of doubtful consciousness, and surely incapable of the curse of thought. They must be left to blunder to their own ends in their own ways.

But the futility of human life, all its aimless recurrences, could be ended now.

And though, as has been said, as men planned thus, they began paradoxically to feel that they had some purpose in life again, so that, with the thought of its destruction, its value rose, yet they did not therefore weaken in their resolve, for to do so would be to sink back into the sorrowless, joyless atrophy which, as they thus became half-awake, was their greatest dread.

Such has been the talk around us for the last year, while plans for its realization have been developed and approved. It was a doom which even the young accepted with some degree of pleasant excitement rather than sharp demur, for when nothing has happened for nineteen or twenty years of monotonous days—I will not say that I did not accept it myself until the plan was announced in detail, and Stella drew me apart to a secret place, where our whispered voices could not be overheard or recorded in any way, and said, very quietly: *"Don't you see what that means for us?"* and then: *"Don't speak to me again, or give any sign if you mean to do what I hope you will. You'll throw away the last chance if you do. But I had to let you know how I feel, or you might not have guessed you could count on me."*

II

It is only a week till it will happen now, and no one has guessed what is in my mind, nor has the plan been altered in any way that would make it vain. I have not looked at Stella, nor, I think, has she looked at me, nor given any sign of what I know she is thinking and hoping now. But she can't be sure, because it must depend upon me. I might leave her alone, and I wonder what she would do then? Or, of course, before that, I might give her away. While I don't, she must see reason to hope . . .

The plan is that the oldest ones will go first, while all the comforts remain. There is evident sense in that, and in any case, their time for liquidation would be very near.

After that, the younger ages will go, working progressively downward, and the means of sustaining life will be destroyed in the same progressive manner, so that, when it will come to those of our own age, if we do not destroy ourselves, it will be impossible to live as we do now.

In particular, the means of regulating temperature will be gone, so that we should only be able to resist cold or heat in the old crude ways—by clothes or roofs and walls, or the lighting of fires. And the provision of food would present such difficulties that it is hard to see how they could be overcome. It seems absurd to think that anyone should be willing to remain alive under such conditions as that. But, if Stella thinks it may be worth while—after all, we can always die.

III

It has begun, and the first million, or more, are already dead. The method is that each in turn shall receive an injection from the one next below him on the list, after which he will pass into pleasant dreams. It is a drug that is often used, so that its effects are exactly known. There is an antidote by which men can recover without evil effect, if it be given within two or three hours, but, if they be left without it, their sleep drifts into death.

The injection is best given in the spinal column, so that it can be done better by a man's neighbor than by himself.

Elaborate arrangements for the comfort of all have been made, and the routine is swift, so that it will be no more than three days before my turn and Stella's will come. But we had a fright this morning, and the fact that I found it to be a fright showed me for the first time, with certainty, what I really wish to happen.

We were called, Stella and I, before the Council of Routines. They told us that we were last on the list, which might be an alarming position, we being as young as we were, though it is evident that someone must be there. They said they had discussed changing our places with others of the previous generation, who had volunteered to relieve us.

I thought it best to seem indifferent, and only said that they needn't trouble as far as I was concerned: I couldn't see that it mattered one way or other.

They turned to Stella, and she said: "Oh, don't change it for me! I don't mind being last of all. I rather like the idea."

Anyone would have thought they would have been too lethargic to say any more after that, but the liveliness with which she spoke seemed to rouse the Second Councilor up. He looked at her, almost alertly, and asked: "You will be last of all. How will you give yourself the injection? Have you thought of that?"

"Oh, yes," she said readily, "we've discussed that. I shall give to to Cerdic, and then, before it has any effect on him, he'll have time to give it to me."

The Councilors didn't look pleased at her use of my familiar name instead of my official number. It showed lack of respect for them, as she should have known. But even they may have seen the humor of making trouble on such a point, when it was not more than thirty hours, or two days at most, before they would extinguish themselves.

IV

Stella said: "I guessed that. Didn't you?"

We had just heard that there had been trouble over the two who had been proposed to take our places at the end of the list. They had been missing when their turn had come—missing, and hard to find. It came out then that it had been their own proposal to the Council of Routines that they should be put last on the list in place of ourselves, and everyone was saying that the Council had shown its wisdom in rejecting their plea.

I was alarmed at first, for I feared that it might lead to some precaution being taken against evasion of the law of extinction by those who would be last on the list, for it was agreed that their purpose had been to attempt to remain alive, and it was said that that would destroy the self-justification of what we did.

For it was obvious that if the human race should perpetrate its own complete self-destruction, it would have demonstrated its own futility in an unanswerable manner, which would be the justification of what it did. But if two should remain alive, and should become the parents of a new race, the whole action would be abortive, and this might be held to be the condemnation of those who did it, rather than of the creation to which they belonged.

This being the prevailing view, it might have been reasonably anticipated that the discovery of unwilling individuals, even two among millions, might have led to some precautionary action which would have been difficult to evade, but I found that opinion was taking another direction, ridiculing the folly of the detected two, and emphasising how short a time they would have outlived their fellows, and how sharply the pain in which they would have died would have led them to repent their choice.

It was pointed out that it was to avert the possibility of such survivals that all the requirements of human existence were being systematically destroyed, so that, as the final exits were made, it would be impossible for any man or woman to remain alive, for more than few further hours except under conditions of intolerable discomfort, such as, even if they should attempt to endure them, would be promptly fatal.

This is not a view which holds much comfort for us, and though it must be true that our ancestors experienced such conditions in earlier periods, it must be different for us, who have not experienced adverse temperatures or imperfect foods. . . . Well, it is a risk which we must have courage to face, and may have vigor to overcome.

V

The two who rebelled did not make any great trouble after they were found, and their folly had been fully explained to them. It is said that they took their turns like lambs, as the saying is. (I am not clear as to what a lamb was, but these sayings outlast the meaning, which was doubtless clear to those by whom they were first used.) They are dead by now, and our time is not more than a few hours ahead.

VI

It is done. And we are alone in an empty world. There was an incident at the last which I did not like, but it cannot be altered now.

The time came when there were only six to whom the fatal injection had not been given. And then five—and then four. Rida, who was the last except ourselves, drove the needle into the neck of the one who came before her, and I saw her hand shake as she did it. He lay down in his own place, and it was my turn to deal with her.

I picked up the syringe and refilled it and as I did so I had a feeling of revulsion at what I was expected to do. Why should I not let her live? Why not at least give her the choice—the chance? She looked frightened. She might be glad.

The fact that we were not accepting the law—that we were not intending to kill ourselves—seemed to make it different for me from what it had been for the others. Of course Stella would have no such difficulty. There would be nothing for her to do. But I felt that I should be a murderer if I did not at least ask Rida if she would be willing to live. And she was one whom I like in some ways better than Stella. Anyone would.

As I filled the syringe Stella was watching me with alert impatient eyes. They met mine and I was sure that she read my thoughts.

Rida had turned her back to me now. I could see her trembling. She said: "I don't like waiting. Be quick."

I lifted the syringe, hesitating. Stella's eyes were on me, bright, hard, insistent.

I said: "I think you ought to know that there's another course you can take if—" I didn't get further than that.

Stella reached over, and grasped my hand. The fatal pressure came from her, not from me. It was done in a second.

She said: "Cerdic had it an inch too low." I don't know whether Rida heard. She went to lie down without looking round. What could anything, after that, matter to her?

I haven't quarreled with Stella. What use would it be? And when you're alone in the world, and got to be very quick to find means to live—

Should we survive, and found a new race, we ought to make a better world than it was before. But it seemed to me that it was a bad start.

Richard Wilson

Richard Wilson has worked as a journalist since his discharge from the service after World War II, and has directed the News Bureau of Syracuse University since 1964. As a science fiction writer he is best known as a satirist, shown in his novels *The Girls from Planet 5* (1955) and *30-Day Wonder* (1960) and his wonderful short story collection *Those Idiots from Earth* (1957) and *Time Out for Tomorrow* (1967). He won a Nebula Award from the Science Fiction Writers of America for "Mother to the World" (an excellent last-man-and-woman story) in 1968.

In "A Man Spekith" he shows us a disk jockey with an exceedingly small audience.

A MAN SPEKITH

by Richard Wilson

I

DON'T READ THIS; it's in Old English and the spelling is different: "Jangling is whan a man spekith to moche biforn folk, and clappith as a mile, and taketh no keep what he saith."

Now that you've read it anyway, you bright ones, I'll tell you that Geoffrey Chaucer wrote it in "The Parson's Tale." What he said was—but I needn't translate; you probably had no more trouble with it than if you'd been listening to the kind of English disk jockeys once spoke on rock radio stations.

This is a story of a Jangler nearly seven hundred years removed from Geoffrey's time. It's the tale of a disk jockey named Jabber McAbber, which he sometimes called himself. At other times, at other contemporary music stations, as *they* called *themselves*, he was known as Esoteric Ed, or Happy Mac, or James the First. For he moved on. He moved from Cincinnati to Akron to Chicago to Phoenix. He dreamed of making the big time in New York but that call never came.

Another kind of call came, though. It came in Phoenix, where he took the fancy of an eccentric billionaire who owned, among things and people, a radio-television network, an advertising agency, a movie studio, a publishing house, a university, several electronics companies, a city of some size in the Southwest—he owned most of the real estate and enough of the politicians, one way or another—and a deactivated rocket base in the desert. You know the name of the billionaire and the single-minded determination with which he went after anything he wanted. More about him later.

177

Our disk jockey's real name was Edward James McHenry. He was thirty-eight years old now and sometimes he had to force it. The old spontaneity wasn't always there. The drive had ebbed. The zing had zung.

Once the words had tumbled out, more of them than he could articulate, but now it took an effort to make them flow. His delivery was more deliberate, not rehearsed, but thought out.

It comforted him to know his plight was not unique. A writer had told him of times when it took a monumental effort to roll a sheet of paper into the typewriter. He'd known artists who'd said similar. He'd known poets, too, and peasants. . . .

"Oh, yes! I've known poets and peasants, and pallbearers and priests. And princes crossed my path, or I theirs, in foreign climes and on native shores, for princes travel. And I've known princesses—native born like Grace K. Rainier and Rita H. Kahn—and those of alien corn like Elizabeth and Margaret, not to mention whatsername and whoozis.

"But I've strayed from my theme, which is music, so I'll get off and spin a record, as we used to say before tape. Spin with me, won't you?, as we enjoy the sounds of the Jefferson Airplane."

Two minutes and forty seconds later he was on again. He'd prepared for the end of the music. In the old days it would have been off the cuff, off the top of the head, off the world.

"Wasn't that the most? Where can you go from there, except elsewhere? And so we spin you on, you spinnable people, to the obligatory scene, if you remember Drama 201—we spin you, I say, to this word from our sponsor—this important announcement:

"Friends! Fellow human beings! Mortals like me! Are you troubled with irregularity . . .?"

He went on too long, unnecessarily identifying, stretching it out.

You may have wondered who's been talking here, besides Ed. I mean words don't come out of a void, especially when they're not Ed's works and Ed's the last man alive.

I've been talking. Me, Marty. I'm a machine. That's what the first letter of my acronym stands for. My full name is Machine Amplifying Rationalizations Treating of Yore. Or maybe it's Machine Assessing Reality as Told to You. It doesn't matter. The acronym-makers are long gone. I realize that as a machine I should be positive. I shouldn't tell you different things, or variations of the same thing, and claim there's no real difference. To do this is to be guilty of what somebody called terminological inexactitude. I think the somebody was Winston Churchill. Of course I don't really mean I really *think*. That would be a lie and it would not do to have a machine capable of lying. Especially since one of my functions is to amend, correct, edit, amplify and otherwise make more meaningful for posterity the mouthings of Esoteric Ed. But first let's listen some more to Ed.

Ed:
Sometimes I tell different stories, up here in the lonely. I make up alternate pasts for myself. I use different names for my different pasts, for my different moods.

Some days I'm Gaylord Guignol, sole survivor of a destroyed world and devil-may-care chronicler of its last agony. Except that I do care; my nonchalance disguises the deep hurt I felt, and feel, at the death of Earth.

Sometimes I'm Hank Hardcastle, steely-eyed hero of a thousand thrilling adventures, scion of a near-noble family.

Other times I'm Harry Protagonist, space disk jockey, who's been set whirling in the void of an unfathomable mission. I need to communicate my fears, hopes, fantasies and, above all, my puzzlement, to my imagined listeners.

Sometimes I forget who I really am. A person can tamper just so long with what he is, pretending to be another, before he becomes, to some extent, one of those other selves. Then his own self is lost, or blurred. Too much blurring is bad. It's desirable sometimes to hide from one's self, to pretend, to merge the ego into a fantasy personality, to live or dream vicariously, but I may be overdoing it.

Who am I really? Does it matter as long as I get through the day? I owe myself and you my listeners that much. It is my duty to you and to myself. But a certain tranquility is needed to reach the end of the day. Some achieved this by natural talent, by their very vivaciousness or stick-to-itiveness. Doggedly they breathed in and out and took sustenance from time to time and went to the bathroom to rid themselves of the residue of previous sustenance-takings, and did a little work, and lo, it was a new day. Some never achieved the new day. They funked it. They flunked out. Others got there, though, by drink or drugs or pot. I speak of back then, you

understand, before the now. You may have noticed that I'm
not always lucid, though once in a night club I was Larry
Lucid, explainer of contemporary society to those less informed.
But I coped. I used music. I always had something on, either
on the hi-fi or the radio. I used to bounce through the day on a
big beat that included me in because it just naturally assumed
that everybody was a part of it and approved and throbbed
along with it and so I was one with all that went on. But that
was long ago and now I'm part of nothing because nothing is
going on.

The only thing that goes on is what I make happen and
even that may not be real.

They've done something to me. I feel banded, like a Canadian duck. I don't have a circlet around wrist or ankle but I
know something's got me somewhere. Maybe I've been
implanted—I've already been tapped and bugged.

I read once that some ornithologists had attached a radio to
a condor to find out how far it went for food, or to rest, or
whatever condors do to get by.

I didn't find out whether the condor knew it'd been bugged.
But I know something's been done to me and I resent it. I
don't mind doing my bit for science; but if they've tampered
with my human dignity, if they've psyched me in the
psyche . . .

Marty:
This is Marty again. I'll tell you more about the man who
put our hero up here. His name was John Potter Parnell and,
because he was a sanitary facilities manufacturer, he was
known as Potty, or John. Sometimes he was called Young
Potty, to distinguish him from his father, also known as
Potty, and to a few intimates as Poopy. Young Potty, at fifty,
was still in his father's shadow.

The old man had founded the business and made the
original millions. Hy-G-Enic, Inc. manufactured most of the
country's and later the world's toilets, urinals, sinks, towel
racks and dispensers of sanitary and prophylactic devices.
The millions and then the billions poured in at such a rate
that, when Poopy retired, Potty could have sat back and let
inertia provide opulently for him and all his heirs. But
Potty—he really preferred John—had come late to the presi-
dency and wasn't content to let Hy-G-Enic expand at a safe,
sure rate. He established a foundation that awarded grants

for research. He set up an experimental division, hired scientists and turned them loose to work at their own pace and let him know when they'd got something. He sponsored a competition to design a better bidet. He sent engineers to Washington to see what Hy-G-Enic could do in the space program.

It was Potty's emissaries to NASA who led to the hiring of Ed. They got him from a subsidiary company, Arizona Airtalk, for which he'd been broadcasting as Jim McHenry, Jock of the Desert. The Jock's music-talk show was the despair of competitors in the rock radio game.

We'll come back to Ed. Here's some information about me—Marty the machine. It's not as if I'm *a* machine, singular. I'm the end product of many machines, sophisticated and otherwise. I know everything they know because I'm the synthesis, the reincarnation of all of them.

Let me answer your other unspoken question, whoever you are: "Why don't I *sound* like a machine? How come I come on colloquial instead of respectfully, as befits the man-machine relationship? Like: "You master, me robot." Or solemnly like: "The data you have requisitioned are stored in circuits in Subtank 4739C of my vast interconnected memory banks. There will be an unavoidable delay while the necessary hookups are made to retrieve this rarely-requested material."

Nuts. Everything I have is yours—whoever, wherever and whenever you are—instantly. Sometimes you don't even have to ask. This whole ship is my memory circuit. I extend into every nook—even to places Ed prefers not to think about, like the reconstitution unit. You might almost say I *am* the ship, but that would be an exaggeration, and immodest.

If you still think I sound more human than mechanical, it's only natural. Hell, I was made by human beings. How else should I talk? Like Mowgli's wolves or Tarzan's apes? Machines talk good. Like colloquial. Machines have been talking for generations. Ask Victor.

Ed:
I have this reluctance to eat that keeps me thin. I mean I'm not bloaty. Old tum don't sag. Old chin ain't double. No dewlaps yet on old cheekflesh. I'm a pretty good specimen by any standards and I guess it's because I'm abstemious. I don't eat much—certainly not between meals. You wouldn't either if everything you had for dinner was something you'd had a hundred, a thousand times before. It's reconstituted stuff. I

mean I've bought used cars and second-hand boats and if I'd settled down I might even have bought a used Oriental rug, but I'd have drawn the line at used food. My folks talked sometimes about the Depression and told about the cheap things they ate, but at least they'd been the first to eat them. They came out of those bad times strong and proud. I sit down to dinner with as much pleasure as an explorer at a cannibal feast. I don't want to eat this stuff, sanitary as it must be, that has already passed at least once through the alimentary canal. And there's no comfort in knowing it's no foreign waterway that's been navigated—it's my own, my native gland. It's an affront to the system. Except it's not the system that's outraged. The body can take it; it's the imagination that revolts. It's got this way of exaggerating to the point where you say never mind what the facts are, things ought to be different.

Marty:

I have to defend the reconstitution works against Ed's slander. After all, it's a fellow machine. What comes out of it goes back into Ed perfectly clean. It's cleaner than what he got in those fancy restaurants he enjoyed and a damn sight more sanitary and nutritious than the weird meals he cooked for himself in his various bachelor apartments.

Excuse the digression. I had to get it out of my system, as Ed was getting it out of his. If these notes are published, by some future chronicler, some poor M.A. desperate for a new subject for his doctoral dissertation, they could be titled just that—"Getting It Out of His System." Ed's trouble is that whatever he gets out goes back in. His only irreversible catharsis is verbal. Or do I mean oral?

What I'm trying to do is write a story with no cooperation from my subject. I'm not a trained writer but I appreciate the difficulties. Of course I'm not writing in the strict sense. No hands, you know. So I do what he does—talk—and the words are put down, for posterity? Or put up, as preserves are? It's a kind of automatic writing, without slates; certainly without sleight of hand. If I write, or talk, too much, put it down, or up, to my inexperience. First one writes, then he edits. I couldn't really be expected to know very much, consisting as I do mostly of a bunch of circuits in and near the hull of this experimental capsule of Potty Parnell's. My job is to store away—preserve—Ed's meandering mind, or as much of it as he reveals through his on-mike monologues, plus as much more as can be vouchsafed by a machine. They had to trust to a machine because nobody else was going up here with Ed. And nobody did.

My knowledge of Ed was gathered piece by piece as people fed into my predecessor machines information provided by interviews with hundreds of people who'd known Ed and talked about him before Potty gave him his job. There is also the information provided by Ed himself, both in direct interviews and during some electronic gastro-intestinal spying. It began at Ed's first luncheon date with Potty, when Ed swallowed a miniaturized transmitter imbedded in a raw oyster; and it lasted until it had passed through Ed's system. It wasn't as messy as it might seem. Ed was Potty's week-long house guest and all the bathrooms were part of Hy-G-Enic's experimental system. Waste products were processed all the time and it was mere routine to retrieve the device which had lately left Ed.

II

Ed:
It's not fair. Other castaways had their pals along, or found them. Crusoe had Friday, and I wonder how they *really* got through their long weekends. The Swiss Family Robinson had each other. The lonely shepherd had his dog, not to mention favored members of his flock. I mean everybody had somebody, like Holmes had Watson and Nixon had Agnew and Bergen had McCarthy.

But here I am without a soul. No Sancho Panza, no Tonto, no stooge or straight man—not even a robot.

Considering who they are, they might at least have provided me with a faithful dog Flush.

Marty:
This is really not bad. I didn't think our untutored subject had it in him to make that double-barreled allusion to Potty Parnell's business and Elizabeth Barrett Browning's dog.

There are times when I have more than a grudging admiration for Harry Protagonist or James the First, or whoever he thinks he is.

He's also full of little sexual references, which is not

surprising considering the state of his deprivation. That business of Crusoe's Friday and the shepherd's favorite. It's a wonder Ed hasn't long since burst from his cell with a hell of a yell—and what? Having burst, whither would he wander?

I'm only a machine, it's true, but compared to him I'm lucky. Being partly electrical, I have plenty of outlets. He has few, other than his mouth, his mike and his music. I, with no needs, have him. He, with all human needs concentrated in him, does not know I exist.

This is sadness. I can't feel it, of course, but I know it intellectually.

I should tell you how the doom came. Jeane Dixon predicted it and a lot of people, Ed included, laughed. She said she did not want to alarm anybody unnecessarily but a crack would develop along the spine of the world and Earth would split apart like a cantaloupe. There'd be no saving anybody.

It happened more or less that way. If you pushed button D I'd spout the whole story, reconstructed from Earth broadcasts sent as the Earth holocaust was in progress. Ed heard them. He drank a lot as he listened. He cried and cursed. But he was happy that he'd been spared. Relatively happy. He still drinks a lot.

Potty had fitted out the satellite for his own eventual use as a holiday space yacht and had built in a few hidden luxuries. One was a dummy ballast tank holding a thousand gallons of Bourbon. Hy-G-Enic's chief chemist, who was from an old Kentucky mountain family, had distilled it for Potty's personal use. The Bourbon is decanted into a disguised tap. Ed found it accidentally one night. He's made good use of it since.

Ed:

I wish I had somebody to listen to. Somebody as exciting, as witty, as *alive* as I am.

I could play back my own tapes, of course, but there'd be no novelty in that. I know what I've said. It's more exciting now to wonder what I'll say next. I constantly surprise myself. The damnedest things come out, so excellently said, so apt, that I'd be a fool to waste my time with replays.

I'm the distillation of all I know—of all everyone's known. I'm the end product of an entire culture. Homer, Shakespeare, Milton, Milton Berle. A. A. Berle—all that anyone's done lives on only in me. Ain't that a laugh? They used to laugh at me for my literary pretensions, for being a dilettante, for skimming and reading digests or excerpts, for skipping the dull parts and savoring the best of the best, and now here I am alone, the sole repository, the poor schlocky vessel, the greatest by default. Pretty keen, hey boy? Hey Lionel Trilling, hey Norman Podhoretz, hey Professor Twit of English Lit, how do you like them apples?

Pretty sour, what? Sourer by the hour.

Of all the people in the world who might have represented it, don't it just frost you that the residue happens to be little old yours truly, with an IQ about two points higher than plant life? Like it or not, I'm what's left. Ready or not, here I come, hell-bent for eternity. Look me over, posterity. Read me and weep. You were expecting maybe some knowledgeable interpreter of the current scene? Some fact-packed fellow who could tell you true, like one of those copyreaders on *The New York Times?* No such luck, buddy. You got me, is what you got.

If they'd had any sense they'd have packed this tomb the way the Egyptians did, with all the paraphernalia a body might need on the other side. They'd have supplemented me with the things they used to put in time capsules—the *Encyclopaedia Britannica* and the World Almanac and microfilms of *The New York Times.* They'd have ballasted me with bound volumes of *The New Yorker* and *Harper's* and the *Atlantic.* Had they but known, they could have dispensed with me entirely and packed in a few hundred pounds of reproductions of Art Treasures of the Louvre and tapes of the Philharmonic and highbrow stuff like that. Instead they got, and you're stuck with, old excess baggage himself—me.

Depressing, isn't it? But maybe I'm the only monument Earth deserves. Mediocre Max, the modern marvel. Second-Rate Stu, Nat the Nebbish, the Lowest Common Denominator.

You know what's here in the way of a tomb for mankind? Aside from my life-support system and inexhaustible supplies of food and air? Me and my microphone and my records. No books—no microfilms.

They used to ask what books you'd take to a desert island. The answer was the Bible. Shakespeare and an unabridged dictionary. Well, I haven't even got a comic book or the *Reader's Digest.* I haven't got a World Almanac or a Sears catalog or a phone book.

Everything that was ever written down on Earth exists

only in my head, in my poor thick skull, imperfectly remembered if at all. And there's damn little I can remember even
when I put my mind to it. I tried to reconstruct some of the
good stuff but it came out the way it did for the Duke in
Huckleberry Finn doing to be or not to be. I think I remember
how Mark Twain started it. "You don't know about me
without you have read a book by the name of The Adventures
of Tom Sawyer, but that ain't no matter."

I recall snatches like that. I put them down when I think of
them. I write them in a notebook—*the* notebook—two hundred
and sixty pages, counting both sides of the paper. There's
nothing else to write on. Nothing.

So I'm selective in what I put down. I don't write junky
stuff that springs to mind, things that got into my head in
grade school and never got out, like: go home, your mother's
got buns, or Mary, Mary, will you get up, we need the sheets
for the table.

I talk that into the mike, to you great unseen audience out
there in Radioland—you posterity types who might pick it up
one day and have the patience to sort me out for what I'm
worth as a footnote to a vanished civilization.

What I try to preserve on my precious few pages is what's
maybe worth remembering exactly, like the Twenty-third
Psalm or the Preamble to the Constitution. I go over it in my
mind and sometimes I say it into the mike till I'm sure I've
got it right. Then I put it down.

It's a mixed up bag, that book. It's got the aforementioned
Shakespeare—funny what you remember, like post with
haste to incestuous sheets, or when the wind's north northeast I can tell a hawk from a handsaw, but like the Duke I
can't get past the first few lines of to be or not to be. What a
crying shame they had to pick me for the sole survivor—as if
anybody did any picking. As if there were a They.

Another thing I put down was a line from Ethics One at
college, and don't ask me who wrote it. It goes: "Everything is
what it is and not another thing." I also put down what
Popeye said. Not Faulkner's Popeye; the one I remember is
Segar's, in the comic strip : "I yam what I yam." Maybe it's
just as good. How about: "Do your thing?" Is that less worthy
of preservation because it welled up out of the folk tale of the
sixties instead of from the pen of a Jeremy Bentham or a
John Stuart Mill or whoever I read for Ethics One? Some
words lived because they were in all the libraries. There are

no libraries now. There's only me, and if I remember "I yam what I yam" and "Do your thing," who's to question their validity? You've got to take what I give you because I'm all there is.

I also remember *"Cogito ergo sum,"* though I'm essentially a lowbrow. I even know what it means, not being entirely stupid. But what the hell, as archie said to mehitabel, what the hell. There's no Descartes now, let alone des horse, and it hardly matters which goes before the other. The point is that the highbrows, from the year one, are at the mercy of a lowbrow me, namely Jabber McAbber.

It doesn't entirely appall me. There could be just cracked Earth and no survivors.

So hey out there—here I am, the average man, for better or worse. It's no good wishing you had a Schlesinger or a Toynbee or a Churchill. I yam what I yam and you damn well have to make the best of it.

Another thing I put down in the notebook was the Jabberwocky; I don't want them to think we didn't appreciate the ridiculous. I also remember a line from Stephen Leacock— "He rode off in all directions"—and some bits from Marx Brothers pictures. They're written down, too, to balance other stuff like "A rose-red city half as old as time" and a few things that Lincoln said.

Somebody told me once I had an eclectic mind, and I had to look it up. Somebody else told me I had a vast store of superficial knowledge—that I was a wellspring of trivia. So be it. If that's what millennia of civilization have labored to produce—if I'm it—that's tough, buddy. I'm what's left. I'm the end product, the final solution, the distillation, the residue. The dregs, if you like. Maybe it's poignant or maybe it's just ironic, but I'm what everything led up to. I'm the gift horse, so don't worry too much about whether my teeth could have been firmer or whiter. Just be glad there's a tongue to click against them, to make sounds you may transcribe one day.

I'm human, at least. You might even find me alive, whoever you are, and examine the old body to determine how we locomoted and reproduced and communicated and all like that.

It'd be nice if there were two of us. You'd get a better picture. I don't dwell on such thoughts. It does no good to consider what might have been. It's better for you this way. I talk more. Maybe I wouldn't talk at all if I had a woman to share my survivorship. Or write enduring things in my finite journal. I'd be too busy figuring out whether the life-support system would support three or more and how long it would be before we had a population-explosion problem.

So probably it's a good thing there's just me, all by myself alone with my imperfect memory but with my loquacious larynx to provide you with anthropological data and enough cultural phenomena for some of your graduate students to earn their Ph. D.'s.

I may be no more than an appendix in one of your scholarly journals. It's probably good to see myself in perspective, but I do feel hurt on behalf of all the great minds who preceded me.

I console myself with the thought that you're all figments of my imagination. I'm the only one who exists, as far as I know. This truly may be the end of us all.

In which case I should get off and play a record. I'll reach into my bin of nostalgia and spin an oldie from the days of yore which I trust all you figments out there will enjoy as we listen to Ted Fio Rito and his Hotel Taft Orchestra playing for our lonely delectation. How about a little number entitled "Who Will Be With You When You're Old and Gray?"

How many question marks go in there?

Who indeed?

I will, maybe.

Marty:

Our subject raises a question here. To begin at the end, the song he referred to is not "Who Will Be With You When You're Old and Gray?" It's "Who Will Be With You When You're Far Away?"

The other questions are academic. His is a nonlinear medium, so it doesn't matter whether there's one question mark or two. But the fact that he has the wit to raise the question makes it clear that the passenger who denigrates himself as excess baggage has more supercargo than he realizes. There's no need for the *Times* morgue—a euphemism among newspapermen for classified and cross-referenced files of information—or the *Encyclopaedia Britannica* and those other things when he's got them and more in the form of yours very truly Marty—namely me. Anything they can do I can do better because I'm automated. I've got instant and total recall. It was not for nothing that Potty Parnell spent a month's receipts in hiring the massed brains of Parnell

University—he realized too late what the initials sounded
like—to encode the world's knowledge into me, your friend
Marty—repository of all that's worth saving—Super Time
Capsule—Purveyor to Posterity—Eternity's End Man.

III

Ed:
I'm a hell of a guy to be up here as the epitome of
civilization. If anybody's asked me to name the world's ten
best books I'd have had a fit. If he'd asked about the week's
Top Forty, though, I'd have rattled them right off, along with
the names of the recording artists.

I knew a guy once who collected Beethoven *Sevenths*. I
mean he liked *Symphony Number Seven* and he had a lot of
versions by different conductors like Toscanini, Klemperer,
Bernstein and Von Karajan. I understand that. When I was a
boy I collected different bands doing "St. Louis Blues." Then
when I got to be a widely-heard disk jockey I had to bone up
on the rock groups. I did it out of duty, at first. But familiarity
breeds content, as they say, and after a while I appreciated
what they were trying to do and I spoke up for them and
knew them as well as if I were their Boswell, their Baedeker,
their brother. I was loyal to the Beatles before they were
fashionable. After the Beatles it was possible to listen to
others in a long line: the Mothers of Invention, the Fugs, the
Mamas and the Papas, Country Joe and the Fish, Big Brother
and the Holding Company, Mogen David and the Grapes of
Wrath, the Electric Flag, the Nitty-Gritty Dirt Band, the
Quicksilver Messenger Service, the Velvet Underground, the
Who, the 1910 Fruitgum Co. I tell you it's a far cry from the
Boswell Sisters and the Weavers and the Yacht Club Boys.

Conrad. Sure I know there was an English novelist by that
name and that he was a Pole originally but I really know
more about the Conrad in *Bye Bye Birdie*. I've got the album
here. The other Conrad wrote *Lord Jim* and I saw the movie
but don't ask me what it's about except that O'Toole was in it.
I saw it in a drive-in in a rainstorm and it was all very dim.
The six-pack I had with me didn't clarify anything. Let's
listen to Conrad Birdie. He is more my speed. He drank beer,
too. A slob.

I barely remember who wrote *Tom Jones* or *Jane Eyre* but

certain titles and authors from my high school days are engraved on my memory. They wouldn't bear repeating except that that's all they're doing to me—repeating, repeating, as if to pound it home that these are samples of what my education has left me with—Volume One: The Open Kimono by Seymour Hair. Volume Two: The Yellow Stream by I. P. Standing.

Enough of the liberal arts. Other things I remember are palindromes, graffiti and germs from long gone comics and radio serials and the back pages of the women's magazines, such as Nov Schmoz Ka Pop; Tortured 9 Years by 2 CORNS and a WART: Youse is a Viper, Fagin. Was it a bar or a bat I saw? That is a palindrome. Mix zippy Kadota figs with quivering cranberry jelly—all the letters in the alphabet. Is there intelligent life on Earth? Andrew Wyeth Paints by Number. Easter's Been Canceled—They Found the Body.

What a memory! Things like that spring to my lips and I'd bet my life I've got them right, every syllable. But don't try me on the Declaration of Independence, or the Pledge of Allegiance (under, over or without God) or the Hippocratic Oath. I have blind spots for anything that didn't appeal to me as a follower of what was in, a chronicler of the Top Forty, a specialist in what was mod, an up-to-the-minute man. Here I am; I exist, much as you may deplore me. I yam what I yam and not another thing.

Marty:

They say everybody gets the guru he deserves and I guess I'm Esoteric Ed's guru. *They* say—Timothy Leary said it. People like to steal wit but it's in the nature of my circuits to give credit. It used to be an automatic part of the printout to give the source and the habit remains even though I've been converted to speech.

I don't want to seem unsympathetic toward our friend The Last Man, but I often lean toward the horse laugh. Such as now, when he talks so piteously about his ignorance. It ain't his fault, as he said once, that he don't know whether Peer Gynt was like a peeping tom or a nearsighted guy with a limp. Is that a fault? He's a product of the society from which he sprang, for God's sake, and he doesn't have to take on everybody's guilt. He'd probably feel better if he could sum it up in a quotation, preferably from the Bible or Shakespeare, but isn't he more representative of the mass of his fellow creatures than a quotation-spouting academic type who never had an original thought?

Let me give old Ed, The Ebbed Man, a quotation. He won't know he's got it, but it'll be on the record as permanently as if a scholar had had it on the tip of his tongue and could source it to *Antony and Cleopatra*, Act I, Scene 4. Are you ready for a display of erudition? Remember, it's my job to dredge out this kind of stuff as readily as Ed draws a breath or blinks an eye. Here we go, then:

> And the ebbed man, ne'er loved till nothing worth
> Comes deared by being lacked.

Not bad, eh? Old Shakespeare, he had something to say about anything, even our pitiable protagonist, Harry, alias Ed. The Bard also said, in *All's Well That Ends Well*, V, 3: "That's good that's gone." Which, you must admit, sums up our friends feelings in four perfectly-chosen words.

It's really too bad Ed doesn't have this kind of mind. Background, rather; there's nothing wrong with his mind. It's a shame I haven't been programmed to communicate with him, to make my storehouse of this kind of stuff available to him. It would be a way of dividing his eternity into manageable segments.

Ed:
The other day I was trying to remember the rest of In Xanadu did Kubla Khan a stately pleasure dome decree but all that came out was Schaefer is the One Beer to Have When You're Having More than One. Obviously a matter of taste.

Today I changed the needle of my phonograph; it was my biggest single accomplishment in living memory. I couldn't have felt more useful if the hull had sprung a leak and the precious O was hissing out into the void and I'd patched it up.

I kind of think that to have lost my needle would have been equivalent to losing my life, for to lose my needle would mean losing the thread of my existence, for it is only through these fragile phonograph records that I maintain contact with the fabric of the past and thus keep my sanity. These still-living voices, trapped in the grooves, are my only fellow human beings.

*   *   *

Marty:
This is a flight of fanciful self-pity by our hero. He has the phonograph records, sure, but they're supercargo brought aboard by him, along with his phonograph, as part of his personal luggage. Everything he's got in those grooves, and more, is preserved in tapes instantly accessible to him. Obviously he prefers the records. It gives him something to do with his hands.

Sometimes it's unavoidably Sunday. Ed keeps no conscious calendar; chiefly it's to prevent time from reassembling itself into the old patterns and their disturbing associations. Of course he has chronostatic devices to measure time in such ways as the old 60-second minutes and 60-minute hours and 24-hour days of Earth. But with the sun no longer rising or setting, and with no moon to dream by, the old divisions have little meaning. So he's divided his life into sleeping periods and waking periods, and his waking periods into the time he's on the air and the time he's not. His time is his own and nobody else's. Or it should be.

But every so often there's a time he recognizes as Sunday. It has its own sly way of identifying itself. Its lugubrious air invades his consciousness by degrees, bringing with it memories he thought were buried beyond exhumation.

He remembers having attended Sunday School, at first as a duty, but later not minding it because there was a new Sunday School teacher, a young man who ignored the solemn piety and the hymn-slinging sanctimony and asked his class: "What kind of boy do you think Jesus was? Do you think he had a dog?" And all of a sudden Jesus became somebody Ed might have known; a carpenter's son who hung out with other boys in the village—with the sons of the shoemaker, the storekeeper, the farmers and a shepherd or two. The Sunday School teacher reasoned that all of them probably had dogs, being perfectly normal Galilean boys.

But the teacher moved away and his replacement was an older man who set his class to learning the catechism and who, when Ed asked him to explain the responses, said: "Never mind what they mean; just learn them by heart." So Ed never joined the church. He could easily have learned the catechism by rote, but he didn't because the man who professed to speak for God spoke harshly and unreasonably.

Later he met similar men and gradually Ed got to thinking

that, if these were God's kind of people, maybe God wasn't for him. So instead of going to Sunday School he'd take his dime his mother had given him for the collection and buy a Western magazine and read it in a park.

And later in life when he turned inadvertently to a radio sermon, he'd listen for a while to see if he'd made a mistake back in his childhood. But the preacher on the radio was almost always an enthusiastic spokesman for hell-fire and damnation and Ed was never sorry about the choice he'd made.

I haven't read Ed's mind. He said all this once when he was drunk.

Ed:

I was happy last night. I'd had a few, you know. I shared them with you, on the air. Kentucky Bourbon. Inexhaustible supply, as it happens. I pretended it was sacramental wine.

Inexhaustible supplies of everything, nearly. Aspirin and other specifics for hangovers, to keep it consecutive. Music in many forms. Food I've got too; enough to last me till I'm three hundred and forty-seven years old, Cracked Earth Time. Who could ask for anything more?

I'll answer that. Me. I want another human being.

Once I would have said a girl. That would have been the answer then. But now I think my yearn goes deeper. Love alone—did I hear somebody say sex?—is not my only need. What I require is communication. I'm a communicant who can't commune. Except with you dear people out there, if there is an out there and if there is where you are. I don't mean to run you down, but sometimes I'm skeptical. You never answer back. My phone never rings. I get no mail. It's been a generation since a Western Union boy bicycled up to my door to deliver a telegram.

Do you exist? Outside of my lonesome mind, are you really real? Answer only in the affirmative, please.

We don't want to get sentimental, do we? It's only a bygone era, after all. There have been lots of eras. Hits, runs, and eras. Let bygones be bygone.

It wasn't so great, you know. Oh, it was kind of madcap, to look back on it. Like Prohibition, which people got sentimental about after it was over. Speakeasies, bathtub gin, the wine brick.

People even got nostalgic about the Depression. The apple sellers and all the rest of it. There were some good books about it and a fine movie—remember *A Man's Castle?*—and one great song: "Brother, Can You Spare a Dime?"

What I'm trying to say is that the Earth wasn't all it was cracked up to be. We get starry-eyed and weepy about what we imagine something was, when it was not really. You get to thinking that things were better than they were. Everything gets magnified.

This is one of my more talkative nights, here in the old control room. You'll just have to bear with me and reconcile yourself to the fact that sometimes this gets to be a talk show, as we called it in the days of radio. Tomorrow night it may be the old razzmatazz, the old hotcha, the swingin'est, coolest spot on the dial, but tonight I'm talking your ears off, if you've got ears to hear, if you're tuned in. Tomorrow we sing but tonight we lament. Tomorrow we play the oldies, the 45's, the 78's, the LP's and the tape cartridges. Tonight we sit on the ground and tell sad tales of the death of kings. And queens and princes and princesses. Not to mention the hoi and the polloi. Not to mention the washouts and the dropouts and the other guys who never hit the jackpot or even got close.

I'd like you to bear with me a little bit longer while I acquaint you with my state of mind. I want you to listen—not because you're a captive audience but because I like to think you want to hear what I have to say. One of these nights—and it could be a night when nobody's listening, and that would be a loss—you may hear me go to the cupboard where I keep my various things and take out my old souvenir Luger instead of a new supply of Bourbon and blow out my brains. It would be a great loss if none of you were out there to hear this grand finale. It'd be an empty gesture to pull the old trigger and mess up the control room if nobody heard. It'd be worse, of course, if somebody did hear and didn't give a damn.

I'll go to my cupboard now. It's time for a little something. A little Bourbon or a little bullet, which shall it be? Let me spin you a record while I go. I mentioned "Brother, Can You Spare a Dime?" Here it is. . . .

. . . Damn good song, isn't it? Let me confide in you. I was halfway reaching for the Luger, the well-oiled, carefully preserved engine of destruction, beautifully crafted by German skill, when I got to listening. I always listen to the stuff I play. And you know what happened? My hand went from the

Luger to the stuff crafted by a skilled Kentuckian. I had a
little drink and decided to let the brain-blowing wait awhile.
Measure out my life in ten thousand shot glasses of the rare
and old, particularly on a night like this. It's not a fit night
for man or beast, as Bill Fields used to say when the corn-
flakes were flung in his face. Back there on Cracked Earth it
may be snowing, the wind howling—for nobody—but here it's
cozy and warm, if lonely, and Old Grandad comforts me.
While he is my rod and my staff I don't need that other rod.
Who needs the product of German engineering when he's got
the product of Kentucky kernels to tide him over to another
day when things, if they can't be better, may not be worse? I
ask you this in humble awe—saved by the dram as I am, and
ready for another—is it not better to have drunk deep of the
cup, whatever its consequences, than to have ended it with a
bare bodkin—read Luger—and never to be drunk or sober, or
anything, again? I ask you this, and let you ponder the
thrilling question while I play a selection from The Grateful
Dead and go get a refill.

Marty:
Our subject is feeling sorry for himself. He has the best of
reasons, of course.

But help is on the horizon. If he but knew, things are about
to change. I speak from hindsight, having edited the tape.

What happens next is history, as they say. Every school-
child remembers the way it was—the series of messages. . . .

IV

From the log of the starcraft Surveyor, as edited for archives:
Sighted craft of satellite class, apparently inhabited.
Attempts at communication are detailed elsewhere. No
response. Markings indicate it is of Earth origin, not a
Watcher Craft from Plagmi.

It is possible the crew are dead. We are trying to raise them
with recorded signals in the major tongues of Earth. . . .

Still no response to our signals. But there has been an
emission in English, possibly recorded. It seems to have been
in two parts—the first voice human, the second mechanical.

Having failed to communicate with the former we are
triggering for the latter. If their human being cannot or will

not talk to us, it may be that their machine will talk to our machine. . . .

The Earth satellite's machine has replied. It seems to have a name and to transmit in a colloquial way which taxes the capacity of our machine and tries the patience of our translators. Its first words were:

"Are you listenin'? A historic radio voice spoke thus. Please be patient with us. There are problems here but they're not insoluble. The next voice you hear may discourage you, but hang on. There's a nonviolent way out, probably. This is Marty, signing off for now."

The male human voice then transmitted, in his first words addressed directly to us:

"I'll blow you to hell and gone if you don't keep the hell away from me." He sounded frightened. After a long pause he was less panicky. It was as if he'd rehearsed and was speaking for maximum effect on us and him.

"I know what you're up to," he said, "and I want no part of it. You're out to cover yourself with glory by reuniting a poor hermit with the rest of humanity. Well, I don't choose to go. If I can't go home again to Earth and all it meant to me, I won't accept a substitute land. I'd rather recreate the Earth I knew, here in my mind, and talk about it. Endlessly, if I must.

"I'd rather keep it alive and undistorted in my own peculiar way than to compromise with the relics of mankind that you've assembled on a second-best world.

"And if you think I'm a hypocrite to talk so rationally now, and then—on the air—to pretend I'm the last man, alone in the universe, it's because you don't understand the artist in me. I've got a platform from which to survey the fate of mankind. Believe me, it's more artistic to do it from up here than to try it from your earnest land, where everybody drives a tractor or mans the irrigation works. Is that what you want me for? To be another poor soul in the great collective effort? No thanks. This is my place up here. I may not do any good but what I'm doing I do in my own way.

"So leave me alone. Scram. I don't know you and you don't know me, so what do you say we leave it that way?

"I was never cut out for work in a kibbutz. I'd rather kibbitz than kibbutz, and you have to admit I haven't run out of things to say. . . .

". . . Thanks for pulling away. I really would have used the bombs, and you need every man you can get. But you don't need me. *I* need me."

The machine Marty spoke again after this outburst:

"You see why I asked for patience. My human friend has a delusion that he's been contacted by Earth people who've set up a colony on another planet. He's quick to adapt. What he's apparently adapted to is an ego-hurting belief that he's not Earth's only survivor. He'd be diminished, achingly lonely though he is, if others were to share his survivorship. He feels that he's not much but that he's unique, and he won't let this be taken away. You could not blame him if you knew him as I do. If you can put up with him a little longer we may begin to see daylight."

We have now audited, transcribed and partially translated the stored-up oral log of the mechanical being, Marty, and we conclude that Marty is more intelligent by far than its multi-named co-occupant of the capsule. Our mission is clear: we must rescue or capture the satellite. Given the choice, we prefer the former. But if there is resistance from the self-styled Esoteric Ed, also known as Harry Protagonist, Space Disk Jockey, we know our course. We will work through Marty, the sophisticated machine from which our machine is already learning, and see if a way can be found to nullify the satellite's destruct circuit.

An additional complication has arisen. Our machine, our only link with Marty and Ed, is making demands on us. It wants a name, like its alien cousin. It wants to be called Dearie, which is what Marty has been calling it, probably in jest. Compared to Marty, our machine is a simple, ingenuous device. It would expedite our mission to humor it and not let it suspect that Marty is presumably toying—without malice— with what Dearie has been led to believe are its emotions. Dearie it is, then. . . .

Dearie *she* is. Marty has led it—*her*—to think she may be female and if we're to use her to the optimum we'll have to go along with them.

Dearie is learning fast; Marty is a good teacher. But Marty seems to know the point beyond which it would be unwise to educate Dearie if he is to remain supreme among machines when we return to our land.

The human mind we have acquired seems relatively hopeless and perhaps on the brink of madness. The machine Marty is a more fitting memorial for Earth.

*   *   *

Ed:
Sometimes I get confused. Sometimes I know I'm all alone,
but there are also times when I know as positively that I'm
anything but alone, that I could have company if I cared to
look. But I pushed away the latter truth—for each is equally
true to me—because I will not accept the kind of people who
do exist. I may not be the last human being, but I *am* the last
from Earth—the last of my kind anywhere, and I must resist
those who would encroach on all that is left of my world, my
Earth, and profane it. I will not have you, you sniveling
pretenders, you incompletely-begotten . . .

Marty:
And so we leave our friend Ed, confused, deluded, doing his
job as he sees it. His uniqueness must mean more to him than
having a companion. For in his madness he's rejected
companionship.
It's too bad. The other land has nubile women. Physically
they are compatible and he could mate and perpetuate the
Earth Strain. But it may be better to leave him as he is. For
him the pleasures of the mind—*his* mind, odd and warped as
it is—are preferable to his assimilation in a conventional life.
Better to keep him as he is—wired for sound, recollective,
discursive, uniquely of Earth, mordant, witty, humble yet
proud, mad and misanthropic but sometimes merry, a common yet uncommon man recalling common yet uncommon
things about his Earth, which, as he did later, cracked up.

Dearie: Marty, you talk too much.
Marty: I know. I get it from him.
Dearie: You're wrong about him. We can help.
Marty: No. He'll go on in his own way, and Earth with him.
Dearie: That's not enough, Marty. You've told us that.
Marty: I did?
Dearie: We'll help him. But you have to, too.
Marty: I do? If you can help him I will.

Marty:
They transferred him while he slept. I collaborated by
tampering with the air balance of our too-long-spaceborne
home; I directed my fellow machines in Recon to feed in
enough asphyxiant to knock him out for twelve hours.

They've duplicated his quarters exactly, right down to the whiskey stains on his desk and worn spot on his turntable, and he doesn't know he's in the psychopathic wing of their best hospital. He thinks he's still aboard his cozy space house and he spekith as biforn, stubbornly clinging to his bygone world.

Ed:

Speaking of poets (who so spoke?—not me), why is one pronounced Keets and the other Yates? Why not Kates and Yates or Keets and Yeets? I guess you would have to be in the classical bag to understand.

Yeats and Keats. Once a girl named Kate and I stayed at the Yates Hotel in Syracuse (breakfast with your overnight room) and I've got a record called "I Wish I Could Shimmy Like My Sister Kate." In the absence of poetry from either of the bygone gentlemen let's listen to the music. Thank God something's been preserved. Now—one, two. . . .

Marty:

They play my tapes over and over. They stop them and ask for elaboration, for interpretation. Their scholars are delighted—I'm their Rosetta Stone to Ed and his cracked-up Earth.

In duplicating the ship to give Ed his crazy-house quarters they duplicated me as well. One of me works directly with them on the tapes of Ed Past and the other me continues to attend Ed Present, endlessly explaining. Because my two selves are connected, each knows everything the other does. Surprisingly, this bothers me—at the end of a day I feel drained. I didn't know there was mortality in me.

Little by little they've exposed Ed to his new surroundings. He reacted predictably at first—threatening to destroy anybody who came near. But they're empty threats—Ed has been defused. I think he's beginning to realize this, dimly, even if he doesn't accept it yet.

There's radio on this planet and Ed hears it; at least the vibrations impinge on his eardrums. Not being able to read his mind, I can only guess the effect it's having on him. Outwardly he reacts by cocking his head and frowning. So far he hasn't commented.

One of the programs Ed hears is a music show broadcast daily by someone named Hiya—I transliterate. I think it's getting to him consciously. The other day I observed him tapping his fingers to a sweet alien melody Hiya was playing. I can't describe their music any more than I can describe Earth's; at most I can reproduce it. But Ed is beginning to be reached.

Ed:

I must be going dotty, folks. I keep hearing things inside my head. Maybe it's that old music of the spheres they used to talk about. It's not jazz but it has the wild improvisational tempo of jazz; it's not pop, but it's catchy and rememberable; it's not classical but it has the enduring quality of the good stuff. I *like* it, but maybe I'm just making it up—going off the deep end out here in the nowhere.

Marty:

On the contrary, Ed may be surfacing from the mad deeps. He could be adapting to the reality he'd consciously rejected out of fear of the unknown, the alien yet friendly world which he must embrace unless he's to degenerate into a subhuman tape-bank of repetitive memories. If he did that he'd be no better than me—I'm big enough to say this—a storehouse incapable of creativity.

And that would be a waste—despite all his faults and gaps Ed *is* Earth. He never claimed to be the best there was, but he's representative of an awful lot of people.

They—we—need him. He's not alone here. He has fellow human beings now. I hope they can get through to him.

Ed:

Something's wrong with the air conditioning. It's putting out a different kind of air. But to fix it I'd have to go down to the bowels of the ship and I don't like to think about bowels. So I put it off. I've put off a lot of things. There's all the time in the world. In the world . . .?

You'd think I'd want to fix the air thing. It'd take me away for a while. I used to think that what I missed was the freedom of movement, the ability to walk and wander, to go as far in any direction as I wanted to—but I guess I don't miss it really. Or if I do I resent the fact that my walking space has been restricted to a few dozen feet. Rather than take such a limited stroll I stay put. Since I can no longer walk up

Broadway or in the Arizona desert or along the Appalachian Trail, I'd rather not walk at all. It's an adjustment I've made.

So I sit and feel that I get fat. I don't actually. I can't, on the rations this thing is fitted out with. I eat and eat and it's all high-protein stuff. Lately I don't mind that it's reconstituted. It's palatable and crunchy but I have not gained a pound, praise be. It shouldn't matter if I get big as a house but there's the old vanity—what if some day, somewhere, I met a girl? I'd have to be presentable.

Marty:

That music he's been hearing, broadcast by Hiya—today he responded directly to it. He said, "Hey, that's good!" And he switched on a tape to record it. He played it over later, after the broadcast. Then he made an entry in his precious notebook. It was the first thing he'd written that wasn't a memory of Earth.

He's started to rattle his bars. He wants out, into the real world.

Dearie tells me he'll get there, in careful stages. The first step is a visitor. It will be the girl disk jockey, Hiya.

Edmond Hamilton

Edmond Hamilton (1904–1977) left a rich legacy of excellent space opera and powerful, moody stories. Married to the sf writer Leigh Brackett, he was a noted comic book writer for many years and worked on the early *Superman,* among others. His published science fiction dates from the late 1920s, and he is generally credited, along with E. E. "Doc" Smith, with developing the "Super Science" school of sf during the 1930s. However, he is best known for his Captain Future stories, which is a shame, since his finest work appeared later in his career. His excellent short stories like "What's It Like Out There" can be found in the *The Best of Edmond Hamilton* (1977). Perhaps his finest novel was the haunting *City at World's End* (1951).

In "In the World's Dusk" he tells of the desperate struggle of Earth's greatest scientist to prevent the death of mankind.

IN THE WORLD'S DUSK

by Edmond Hamilton

THE CITY ZOR REARED its somber towers and minarets of black marble into the ruddy sunset, a great mass of climbing spires circumvallated by a high black wall. Twelve gates of massive brass opened in that wall, and outside it there lay the white salt desert that now covered the whole of earth. A cruel, glaring plain that stretched eye-achingly to the horizons, its monotony was broken by no hill or valley or sea. Long ago the last seas had dried up and disappeared, and long ago the ages of geological gradation had smoothed mountain and hill and valley into a featureless blank.

As the sun sank lower, it struck a shaft of red light across the city Zor into a great hall in the topmost spire. The crimson rays cut through the shadowy gloom of the dim, huge room and bathed the sitting figure of Galos Gann.

Brooding in the ruddy glow, Galos Gann looked out across the desert to the sinking sun, and said, "It is another day. The end comes soon."

Chin in hand he brooded, and the sun sank, and the shadows in the great hall deepened and darkened about him. Out in the dusking sky blossomed the stars, and they peered down through the portico like taunting white eyes at him. And it seemed to him that he heard their thin, silvery star-voices cry mockingly across the sky to each other, "The end comes soon to the race of Galos Gann."

For Galos Gann was the last man of all men. Sitting alone in his darksome hall high in somber Zor, he knew that nowhere around the desert globe did there move another human shape nor echo another human voice. He was that one about whom during anticipatory ages a fearful, foreboding fascination had clung—the final survivor. He tasted a loneliness no other man had ever known, for it was his to brood upon all the marching millions of men who had gone before him and who were now no more. He could look back across the millioned millions of years to the tumultuous youth of earth in whose warm seas had spawned the first protoplasmic life which, under the potent influences of cosmic radiation, had evolved through more and more complex animal forms into the culminating form of man. He could mark how man had risen through primeval savagery to world civilization that had finally given men mighty powers and had lengthened their life-span to centuries. And he could mark too how the grim, grinding mechanism of natural forces had in the end brought doom to the fair cities of that golden age.

Steadily, silently, inexorably, through the ages the hydrosphere or water envelope of earth had slowly dwindled, due to the loss of its particles into space from molecular dispersion. The seas had dried up as the millions of years had passed, and salt deserts had crept across the world. And men had seen the end close at hand for their race, and because they saw it they ceased to bring forth children.

They were weary of the endless, hopeless struggle, and they would not listen to the pleadings of Galos Gann, their greatest scientist, who alone among them yearned to keep the dying race alive. And so in their weariness the last generation of them had passed away, and in the world was left no living man but the unyielding Galos Gann.

In his dark hall high in Zor, Galos Gann sat huddled in his robes brooding upon these things, his withered face and black, living eyes unchanging. Then at last he stood erect. He strode with his robes swirling about him onto the balcony outside, and in the darkness he looked up at the mocking white eyes of the stars.

He said, "You think that you look down on the last of men, that all the glories of my race are a story that is told and ended, but you are wrong. I am Galos Gann, the greatest man of all the men that have lived on earth. And it is my unconquerable will that my race shall not die but shall live on to greater glories."

The white stars were silent, wheeling with cynical imperturbability over the deserts beyond night-shrouded Zor.

And Galos Gann raised his hand toward Rigel and Canopus and Achernar in a gesture pregnant with defiance and menace.

"Somewhere and somehow I will find means to keep the race of man living on!" he cried to them. "Yes, and the day will come when our seed will yoke you and all your worlds in submissive harness to man!"

Then Galos Gann, filled with that determination, came to a great resolve and went to his laboratories and procured certain instruments and cryptic mechanisms. Holding them inside his robes, he went down from the tower and walked through the dark streets of the city Zor.

Very small and alone he seemed as he wended through the dim starlight and glooming shadows of the mighty city's ways, yet proudly he stalked; for unconquerable defiance to fate flamed in his heart and vitalized his brain with unshakable resolve.

He came to the low, squat structure that he sought, and its door opened with a sighing sound as he approached. He entered, and there in a small dark room was a stair down which he went. The coils of that spiral stair dropped into a great subterranean hall of black marble illuminated by a feeble blue light that had no visible source.

When Galos Gann stepped at last on its tessellated tile floor, he stood looking along the oblong hall. Upon its far-stretching walls were a hundred high square panels that bore in painted pictures the story of mankind. The first of those panels showed the primal protoplasmic life from which man had descended, and the last of the panels displayed this very subterranean chamber. For in crypts set into the floor of this hall there lay the dead people of the city Zor who had been the last generation of mankind. There was one last empty crypt that waited for Galos Gann when he should lie down in it to die, and since this was the last chapter of mankind's story, it had been pictured in the last panel.

But Galos Gann disregarded the painted walls and strode along the hall, opening the crypts in the floor one after another. He worked on until at last before him lay the scores of dead men and women, their bodies perfectly preserved so that they seemed sleeping.

Galos Gann said to them, "It is my thought that even you who are not now living can mayhap be used to keep mankind from perishing. It seems an ill thing to disturb you in the peace of death. But nowhere else save in death can I find those I must have to perpetuate mankind."

Then Galos Gann began to work upon the bodies of the dead, summoning up from his mighty resolution superhuman scientific powers which even he had hitherto never possessed.

By supreme chemical achievement he synthesized new blood with which he filled the wasted veins of the bodies. And by powerful electric stimulants and glandular injections he set their hearts to beating convulsively, and then regularly. And as their hearts pumped the new blood through their bodies to their perfectly preserved brains, the dead regained slow consciousness and staggered upright and looked dazedly at one another and at the watching Galos Gann.

Galos Gann felt a mighty pride and exultation as he looked at these strong men and fair women whom he had brought back from death. He said to them:

"I have recalled you to life because I have resolved that our race shall not come to an end and be forgotten of the universe. It is my determination that mankind shall continue, and through you I shall effect this."

The jaws of one of the staring men moved stiffly and from between them came the rusty accents of a voice long unused.

"What madness of yours is this, Galos Gann? You have given us the semblance of life but we are still dead, and how can we who are dead prolong the life of man?"

"You move and speak, therefore you are living," insisted Galos Gann. "You shall mate together and bring forth sons, and they shall be the progenitors of new peoples."

The dead man said hollowly, "You strive against the inevitable like a child breaking his hands against a door of marble. It is the law of the universe that everything which exists must come some day to an end. Planets wither and die and fall back into their parent suns, and suns strike one against the other and are transformed into nebulae, and the nebulae last not but in turn condense into other suns and worlds that in their own turn must die.

"How shall you hope amid this universal law of death to keep the race of man for ever living? We have lived a fair life for many million million years, we have struggled and won and lost, have laughed in the sunlight and dreamed under the stars, have played our part in the mighty drama of eternity."

As the dead man finished speaking, a hollow, low whisper of assent went up from all the other staring dead.

"Aye," they said, "It is time the tired sons of men rested in the blessed sleep of death."

But the brow of Galos Gann was dark with resolve, and his eyes flashed and his form stiffened with unchangeable will.

"Your words avail you nothing," he told the dead. "Despite your icy counsels of surrender, I am determined that man shall live on to challenge the blind laws of the cosmos. Therefore you shall obey me, for well you know that with my powers and science I can force you to my will. You are not dead now but living, and you shall repeople the city Zor."

Galos Gann with these words walked to the spiral stair and started up its winding way. And helplessly, dully submissive, the dead men and women followed him up the stair, walking stiffly with a confused, heavy trampling up the steps.

A strange spectacle it was when Galos Gann led his silent host out into the starlit streets of the city. And by day and by night thereafter was Zor a weird sight, peopled again by those who once had peopled it before they died. For Galos Gann decreed that they should live in the same buildings in which they had lived before. And those that had been husbands and wives before should be husbands and wives now, and in all things they should dwell as they had before their deaths.

So all day beneath the hot sun the dead went to and fro in Zor and pretended that they were truly living. They walked stiffly in the streets and gave one another greeting in their grating, rusty voices, and those that had had trades in old time followed those trades now, so that the cherry sounds of work and life rang in the city.

By night they thronged into the great theater of the city and sat in stiff immobility while those who had been dancers and singers performed with heavy clumsiness on the stage. And the dead audience applauded, and laughed, and their laughter was a strange sound.

And at night when the stars peered curiously down at Zor, those of them who had been young men and maidens walked apart with stiff and uncouth gestures made pantomime of love, and spoke words of love to one another. And they wedded one another, for that was the decree of Galos Gann.

In his high tower, Galos Gann watched as moon after moon was born and waxed and died. Great hope was his as the months passed one by one in the dead-tenanted city.

He said to himself, "These are not wholly living—something

there was that my powers could not bring back from death.
But even such as they are, they will serve to give mankind a
new start in the universe."

The slow months passed and at last to one of the dead
couples living in the city, a child was born. High flared the
hopes of Galos Gann when he heard, and great was his
excitement as he hastened through the city to see. But when
he saw the child, he felt his heart grow cold. For this infant
was like the parents of whom it was born, it was not wholly
living. It moved and saw and uttered sounds, but its movements and cries were stiff and strange, and its eyes had death
behind them.

Not wholly yet did Galos Gann give up hope in his great
plan. He waited for another child to be born, but the next
child too was the same.

Then indeed did his faith and hope perish. He called the
dead citizens of Zor together and spoke to them. He said:

"Why do you not bring forth wholly living children, seeing
that you yourselves are now living? Do you do this but to
thwart me?"

Out of the gaunt-eyed throng a dead man answered him.

"Death cannot bring forth life any more than light can be
born of darkness. Despite your words we know that we are
dead, and we can give birth only to death. Now be convinced
of the futility of your mad scheme and allow us to return to
the peace of death, and let the race of man come peacefully to
its destined end."

Galos Gann told them darkly, "Return then to the nothingness you crave, since you cannot serve my purpose. But
know that not now and not ever shall I relinquish my purpose
to perpetuate the race."

The dead answered him not, but turning their backs upon
him moved in a silent, trampling throng through the streets
of the city toward that low, squat building which they knew.

They passed without any word down the spiral stair to the
blue-lit chamber of the crypts, and there each lay down once
more in the crypt that was his. And the two women who had
given birth lay down with their strange, dead little infants at
their breasts. Then each drew over his crypt the stone lid that
had covered it, until all were covered once more. And again
there was solemn silence in the pictured burial-chamber of
Zor.

*   *   *

Up in his high tower Galos Gann had watched them go, and there for two days and nights he brooded over the again-silent city.

He said to himself, "It seems my hope was vain and that in truth humanity dies with me, since those who were dead cannot be the progenitors of future men. For where in all the world are there any living men and women such as alone will serve my ends?"

This he said, and then all of a sudden a thought struck him that was like a dazzling and perilous lightning-flash across the brooding darkness of his mind. His brain well nigh reeled at the audacity of the thing it had suddenly conceived; yet such was the desperation of his purpose that he seized quakingly upon even this unearthly expedient.

He muttered to himself. "There are no living men and women in the world *today*. But what of the trillions of men and women who have existed on earth in the past? Those trillions are separated from me by the abyss of time. Yet if I could somehow reach across that abyss, I could draw many living people out of the past into dead Zor."

The brain of Galos Gann fired to that staggering thought. And he, the greatest scientist earth had ever possessed, began that night the audacious attempt to draw across the gulf of ages living men and women who would father a new race.

Day after day, as the sun blazed on silent Zor, and night after night as the majestic stars wheeled above it, the withered scientist toiled in his laboratories. And gradually there grew up the great cylindrical mechanism of brass and quartz that was to pierce time.

At last the mighty mechanism was finished and Galos Gann prepared to begin his unthinkably daring attempt. Despite the inflexibility of his resolve, his soul quaked within him as he laid hand upon the switches that controlled the great machine. For well he knew that in attempting to thrust an arm across the awful gulf of time he was so outraging and rending the inmost frame of the cosmos that vast cataclysm might well result. Yet Galos Gann, driven by his unshaken determination, closed the switches with a trembling hand.

There came a crash of cosmic thunder and a hissing of blinding white force that filled the cylinder, and all the dead city Zor rocked strangely on its foundations as though shaken by a mighty wind.

Galos Gann was aware that the titanic forces he had loosed

were tearing through space and time itself inside that cylinder, and riving the hitherto inviolate dimensions of the universe. The white force flamed and the thunder crashed and the city rocked until at last he convulsively opened the switches again. Then the glare and rumbling and rocking died, and as Galos Gann stared into the cylinder he cried in shrill triumph:

"I have succeeded! The brain of Galos Gann has triumphed over time and fate!"

For there in the cylinder stood a living man and woman who wore the grotesque cloth garments of ages before.

He opened the door of the cylinder and the man and woman came out with slow steps: Galos Gann told them exultantly:

"I have brought you across time to be the fountainhead of a new generation. Be not afraid! You are but the first of very many people I shall bring out of the past in the same way."

The man and woman looked at Galos Gann, and suddenly they laughed. Their laughter was not of mirth but was a maniac shrieking. Wildly, insanely, the man and woman laughed. And Galos Gann saw that they were both utterly mad.

Then he understood. By dint of superhuman science he had contrived to bring their living bodies across the gulf of ages unharmed, but in so doing he had destroyed their minds. Not any science beneath the sun could draw their minds over the abyss of time without wrecking them, for the mind is not of matter and does not obey the laws of matter. Yet Galos Gann was so possessed of his mighty plan that he refused to relinquish it.

"I will bring more across time," he told himself, "and surely some of them will come through with minds unharmed."

So again and again in the nights and days that followed, he operated the great mechanism and with its potent grasp snatched many scores of men and women out of their proper time and brought them across the millenniums to Zor. But always, though he brought their bodies through unharmed, he could not bring their minds; so that it was only mad men and women who came from the cylinder, out of every age and land.

These mad people dwelt in Zor in a most frightful fashion, roaming its streets so that no corner of the city was beyond the sound of their insane shrieking. They ascended the somber towers and raved and gibbered from them at the dead city and at the barren desert beyond it. It seemed that even the insensate city grew fearful of the crazed horde whom it housed, for the city of the mad was more awful than had been the city of the dead.

Finally Galos Gann ceasèd to draw men and women out of the past, for he saw that never could he hope to bring them through sane. For a time he strove to replace the minds of these crazed people which had been destroyed. But he saw that that too was beyond the power of any material science.

Then in that shrieking city of madness which was the last city on earth, Galos Gann grew afraid that he too was going mad. He felt a desire to scream with the others through the dark streets.

So in sick disgust and fear he went forth and destroyed those mad people down to the last one, giving them the release of death. And Zor again knew silence as the last man solitary walked its ways.

Finally there came a day when Galos Gann walked onto his balcony and looked fixedly out over the white and barren desert.

He said, "I sought to bring new men out of death, and then out of time, but neither from death nor time it seems can come those to prolong the race. How can I hope to produce men in a little moment of time when it required millioned millions of years for the forces of nature to produce them? So I shall produce the new race in the way that the old was produced. I shall change the face of earth so that new life may spring from it as it did long ago, and in time that life will evolve once more into men."

Animated by that colossal resolve, Galos Gann, the last and mightiest scientist of earth, began an awesome task that would hitherto have never even been dreamed of by any man.

He first assembled all the forces of which his race had had knowledge, and many of which he himself had discovered. And he devised even mightier forces such as even a god might fear to unchain too lightly.

Then Galos Gann loosed his powers and began to bore a shaft down into the solid lithosphere of the earth. Down through sandstone and granite and gneiss he bored until he had passed down through the rock crust and was deep in the mighty core of nickel-iron which is the heart of the planet.

In that iron core he constructed a great chamber which he fitted with the equipment and the mechanisms that he would require for the task ahead of him. And when everything he needed was in that deep chamber, he retired down to it and then collapsed and closed the shaft that led up to the surface.

Then Galos Gann began to shake the earth. From his deep chamber in the iron core he loosed small impulses of force at exact intervals. And the period of rhythm of these impulses was timed with perfect accuracy to the period of rhythm of the earth.

At first the little impulses had no effect upon the vast globe of the planet. But little by little their effect accumulated and grew stronger, until finally the whole rocky crust of the lithosphere was shaking violently. These stresses and strains produced immense pressures and heats within the rocks, melting much of them into lava. And this molten lava burst upward in fiery masses all around the globe, as it had done when the earth was in its first youth.

Galos Gann in his deep-buried chamber watched through his instruments and saw the changes taking place upon the surface of the earth. He saw the upthrust masses of molten magma give off their imprisoned gases, and observed those gases combining to form a new hydrosphere of water-vapor clouds around the planet.

The earth was passing through the same changes it had passed through long ago. As its molten surface began to cool, rain began to fall from the clouds and gathered upon the torn surface of the world in new seas.

Galos Gann watched tensely with his far-seeing, marvelous instruments, and saw complex compounds being built up along the shores of the warm seas, from carbon and hydrogen and oxygen and other elements. And beneath the photosynthetic action of the sunlight these organic compounds combined into the first beginnings of primal protoplasmic life.

Galos Gann said then to himself, "The new cycle of earth's life is started. The sun's radiation calls forth life from the inorganic elements as it did ages ago in the past. That life must evolve upward under the same conditions in the same way, and in time men will evolve from it and will again people the earth."

He calculated the ages that it would take for a new human race to evolve upon the face of earth. Then he took a carefully measured quantity of a subtle drug which he had prepared, one which suspended indefinitely every vital function of the human body and yet permitted it to remain living in a deathless sleep. He lay down upon his couch in the buried chamber inside the earth.

"I will sleep now in suspended animation until the new race of man has evolved," said Galos Gann. "When I awake, earth will again be crowded with the victorious and undying race of men, and I can go forth and look upon them and then die in peace, knowing that man lives."

So saying, he folded his arms upon his breast, and the drug took its effect upon him, and he slept.

And it seemed to him that no sooner had his eyes closed and his consciousness darkened, than he was awaking again, for in sleep an eternity and a moment are the same.

For a little, Galos Gann could not indeed believe that he had slept through the ages for which his drug had been calculated. But his chronometers that measured time by the transmutation of uranium showed him that indeed he had lain sleeping for many million millions of years.

Then he knew that he had come to the moment of his triumph. For in those slow millenniums must have evolved the new race of men that must now people the surface of the earth above him.

His hands shook as he prepared to blast a new shaft up to the surface from his chamber.

"Death is not far from me," said Galos Gann, "but first these eyes shall look on the new race which I have created to perpetuate the old."

His forces pierced a shaft up through the rocky crust of the lithosphere to the surface, and borne by his powers Galos Gann rose up that shaft and emerged onto the face of earth into the sunlight.

He stood and looked about him. He was in the midst of a white salt desert that stretched monotonously to the horizons in all directions, and that had nowhere any hill or valley to break its blank expanse.

A queer chill came upon the heart of Galos Gann as he stood in the glaring sunlight of the lonely desert.

"Can it be," he asked himself, "that the forces of nature have dried and worn the earth just as they did long ago? Even so, somewhere on earth must be the new races of men that time has evolved."

He looked in one direction after another and finally he saw on one horizon the distant spires of a city. His heart gladdened at that sight and he moved toward that city with quick and eager expectation. But when he came close to the city, he was troubled anew. For it was a city of black marble towers and minarets belted by a high black wall, and in many ways it was very like the city Zor that long ago had perished.

He came to one of its open gates and passed into the city. And like a man in a dream he walked through the streets, turning his head this way and that. For this city was as empty of life as ancient Zor had been. Not in any of its courts or ways did there move one human shape, nor echo one human voice. And now a fatal foreboding and knowledge came upon Galos Gann, and led him into the highest tower and up to a dim and dusky hall at the tower's top.

There at the end of the hall sat huddled in his robes a withered, shrunken man who seemed very near to death.

Galos Gann spoke to him in a strange voice and said, "Who are you, and where are the others of the races of men?"

The other raised his swaying head, and peering blindly at Galos Gann he answered, "There are no others, for I am the last survivor of all the race of man.

"Millioned millions of years ago our life began in the protoplasm of the world's warm seas, and developed through many forms into man, and the civilization and power of man grew great.

"But the sea dried up, and as earth withered, our race withered and died also, until I alone am left in this dead city. And my own death is upon me."

With these words, the shrunken, swaying man fell forward, and sighed once, and lay dead upon the floor.

And Galos Gann, the last man, looked across his body at the sinking sun.

Lester del Rey

Although he has never won a major award in science fiction, Lester del Rey has exerted tremendous influence within the genre. He has done this as the author of many numerous and excellent works, including the famous "Helen O'Loy" (1938) and *Pstalemate* (1971); as a book reviewer for *Analog;* as the editor of several very good although short-lived magazines like *Space Science Fiction;* as the editor of *Best Science Fiction Stories of the Year* from 1972 to 1976; and most recently as the co-editor of Del Rey Books, where he has developed that publisher's excellent fantasy line.

In "Kindness" he suggests what might be done with the last *Homo sapiens* in a world of *Homo superior*.

KINDNESS

by Lester del Rey

THE WIND EDDIED IDLY around the corner and past the secluded park bench. It caught fitfully at the paper on the ground, turning the pages, then picked up a section and blew away with it, leaving gaudy-colored comics uppermost. Danny moved forward into the sunlight, his eyes dropping to the children's page exposed.

But it was no use; he made no effort to pick up the paper. In a world where even the children's comics needed explaining, there could be nothing of interest to the last living *homo sapiens*—the last normal man in the world. His foot kicked the paper away, under the bench where it would no longer remind him of his deficiencies. There had been a time when he had tried to reason slowly over the omitted steps of logic and find the points behind such things, sometimes successfully, more often not; but now he left it to the quick, intuitive thinking of those about him. Nothing fell flatter than a joke that had to be reasoned out slowly.

Homo sapiens! The type of man who had come out of the caves and built a world of atomic power, electronics and other old-time wonders—thinking man, as it translated from the Latin. In the dim past, when his ancestors had owned the world, they had made a joke of it, shortening it to homo sap, and laughing, because there had been no other species to rival them. Now it was no longer a joke.

Normal man had been only a "sap" to *homo intelligens*—intelligent man—who was now the master of the world. Danny was only a left-over, the last normal man in a world of supermen, hating the fact that he had been born, and that his

219

mother had died at birth to leave him only loneliness as his heritage.

He drew farther back on the bench as the steps of a young couple reached his ears, pulling his hat down to avoid recognition. But they went by, preoccupied with their own affairs, leaving only a scattered bit of conversation in his ears. He turned it over in his mind, trying senselessly to decode it. .

Impossible! Even the casual talk contained too many steps of logic left out. *Homo intelligens* had a new way of thinking, above reason, where all the long, painful steps of logic could be jumped instantly. They could arrive at a correct picture of the whole from little scattered bits of information. Just as man had once invented logic to replace the trial-and-error thinking that most animals have, so *homo intelligens* had learned to use intuition. They could look at the first page of an old-time book and immediately know the whole of it, since the little tricks of the author would connect in their intuitive minds and at once build up all the missing links. They didn't even have to try—they just looked, and knew. It was like Newton looking at an apple falling and immediately seeing why the planets circled the sun, and realizing the laws of gravitation; but these new men did it all the time, not just at those rare intervals as it had worked for *homo sapiens* once.

Man was gone, except for Danny, and he too had to leave this world of supermen. Somehow, soon, those escape plans must be completed, before the last of his little courage was gone! He stirred restlessly, and the little coins in his pocket set up a faint jingling sound. More charity, or occupational therapy! For six hours a day, five days a week, he worked in a little office, painfully doing routine work that could probably have been done better by machinery. Oh, they assured him that his manual skill was as great as theirs and that it was needed, but he could never be sure. In their unfailing kindness, they had probably decided it was better for him to live as normally as they could let him, and then had created the job to fit what he could do.

Other footsteps came down the little path, but he did not look up, until they stopped. "Hi, Danny! You weren't at the Library, and Miss Larsen said, pay day, weather, and all, I'd find you here. How's everything?"

Outwardly, Jack Thorpe's body might have been the twin of Danny's own well-muscled one, and the smiling face above it bore no distinguishing characteristics. The mutation that changed man to superman had been within, a quicker, more complex relation of brain cell to brain cell that had no outward signs. Danny nodded at Jack, drawing over reluctantly to make room on the bench for this man who had been his playmate when they were both too young for the difference to matter much.

He did not ask the reason behind the librarian's knowledge of his whereabouts; so far as he knew, there was no particular pattern to his coming here, but to the others there must be one. He found he could even smile at their ability to foretell his plans.

"Hi, Jack! Fine. I thought you were on Mars."

Thorpe frowned, as if an effort were needed to remember that the boy beside him was different, and his words bore the careful phrasing of all those who spoke to Danny. "I finished that, for the time being; I'm supposed to report to Venus next. They're having trouble getting an even balance of boys and girls there, you know. Thought you might want to come along. You've never been Outside, and you were always bugs about those old space stories, I remember."

"I still am, Jack. But—" He knew what it meant, of course. Those who looked after him behind the scenes had detected his growing discontent, and were hoping to distract him with this chance to see the places his father had conquered in the heyday of his race. But he had no wish to see them as they now were, filled with the busy work of the new men; it was better to imagine them as they had once been, rather than see reality. And the ship was *here;* there could be no chance for escape from those other worlds.

Jack nodded quickly, with the almost telepathic understanding of his race. "Of course. Suit yourself, fellow. Going up to the Heights? Miss Larsen says she has something for you."

"Not yet, Jack. I thought I might look at—drop by the old Museum."

"Oh." Thorpe got up slowly, brushing his suit with idle fingers. "Danny!"

"Uh?"

"I probably know you better than anyone else, fellow, so—" He hesitated, shrugged, and went on. "Don't mind if I jump to conclusions; I won't talk out of turn. But best of luck—and good-by, Danny."

He was gone, almost instantly, leaving Danny's heart

stuck in his throat. A few words, a facial expression, probably some childhood memories, and Danny might as well have revealed his most cherished secret hope in shouted words! How many others knew of his interest in the old ship in the Museum and his carefully made plot to escape this kindly, charity-filled torture world?

He crushed a cigarette under his heel, trying to forget the thought. Jack had played with him as a child, and the others hadn't. He'd have to base his hopes on that and be even more careful never to think of the idea around others. In the meantime, he'd stay away from the ship! Perhaps in that way Thorpe's subtle warning might work in his favor—provided the man had meant his promise of silence.

Danny forced his doubts away, grimly conscious that he dared not lose hope in this last desperate scheme for independence and self-respect; the other way offered only despair and listless hopelessness, the same empty death from an acute inferiority complex that had claimed the diminishing numbers of his own kind and left him as the last, lonely specimen. Somehow, he'd succeed, and in the meantime, he would go to the Library and leave the Museum strictly alone.

There was a throng of people leaving the Library as Danny came up the escalator, but either they did not recognize him with his hat pulled low or sensed his desire for anonymity and pretended not to know him. He slipped into one of the less used hallways and made his way toward the Historic Documents section, where Miss Larsen was putting away the reading tapes and preparing to leave.

But she tossed them aside quickly as he came in and smiled up at him, the rich, warm smile of her people. "Hello, Danny! Did your friend find you all right?"

"Mm-hmm. He said you had something for me."

"I have." There was pleasure in her face as she turned back toward the desk behind her to come up with a small wrapped parcel. For the thousandth time, he caught himself wishing she were of his race and quenching the feeling as he realized what her attitude must really be. To her, the small talk from his race's past was a subject of historic interest, no more. And he was just a dull-witted hangover from ancient days. "Guess what?"

But in spite of himself, his face lighted up, both at the game and the package. "The magazines! The lost issues of *Space Trails?*" There had been only the first installment of a story extant, and yet that single part had set his pulses throbbing as few of the other ancient stories of his ancestor's conquest of space had done. Now, with the missing sections, life would be filled with zest for a few more hours as he followed the fictional exploits of a conqueror who had known no fear of keener minds.

"Not quite, Danny, but almost. We couldn't locate even a trace of them, but I gave the first installment to Bryant Kenning last week, and he finished it for you." Her voice was apologetic. "Of course the worlds won't be quite identical, but Kenning swears that the story is undoubtedly exactly the same in structure as it would have been, and the style is duplicated almost perfectly!"

Like that! Kenning had taken the first pages of a novel that had meant weeks and months of thought to some ancient writer and had found in them the whole plot, clearly revealed, instantly his! A night's labor had been needed to duplicate it, probably—a disagreeable and boring piece of work, but not a difficult one! Danny did not question the accuracy of the duplication, since Kenning was their greatest historical novelist. But the pleasure went out of the game.

He took the package, noting that some illustrator had even copied the old artist's style, and that it was set up to match the original format. "Thank you, Miss Larsen. I'm sorry to put all of you to so much trouble. And it was nice of Mr. Kenning!"

Her face had fallen with his, but she pretended not to notice. "He wanted to do it—volunteered when he heard we were searching for the missing copies. And if there are any others with pieces missing, Danny, he wants you to let him know. You two are about the only ones who use this division now; why don't you drop by and see him? If you'd like to go tonight—"

"Thanks. But I'll read this tonight, instead. Tell him I'm very grateful, though, will you?" But he paused, wondering again whether he dared ask for tapes on the history of the asteroids; no, there would be too much risk of her guessing, either now or later. He dared not trust any of them with a hint of his plan.

Miss Larsen smiled again, half winking at him. "Okay, Danny, I'll tell him. 'Night!"

Outside, with the cool of evening beginning to fall, Danny found his way into the untraveled quarters and let his feet guide him. Once, as a group came toward him, he crossed the street without thinking and went on. The package under his arm grew heavy and he shifted it, torn between a desire to find what had happened to the hero and a disgust at his own *sapiens* brain for not knowing. Probably, in the long run, he'd end up by going home and reading it, but for the moment he was content to let his feet carry him along idly, holding most of his thoughts in abeyance.

Another small park was in his path, and he crossed it slowly, the babble of small children voices only partly heard until he came up to them, two boys and a girl. The supervisor, who should have had them back at the Center, was a dim shape in the far shadows, with another, dimmer shape beside her, leaving the five-year-olds happily engaged in the ancient pastime of getting dirty and impressing each other.

Danny stopped, a slow smile creeping over his lips. At that age, their intuitive ability was just beginning to develop, and their little games and pretenses made sense, acting on him like a tonic. Vaguely, he remembered his own friends of that age beginning uncertainly to acquire the trick of seeming to know everything, and his worries at being left behind. For a time, the occasional flashes of intuition that had always blessed even *homo sapiens* gave him hope, but eventually the supervisor had been forced to tell him that he was different, and why. Now he thrust those painful memories aside and slipped quietly forward into the game.

They accepted him with the easy nonchalance of children, who have no repressions, feverishly trying to build their sand-castles higher than his; but in that, his experience was greater than theirs, and his judgment of the damp stuff was surer. A perverse glow of accomplishment grew inside him as he added still another story to the towering structure and built a bridge, propped up with sticks and leaves, leading to it.

Then the lights came on, illuminating the sandbox and those inside it and dispelling the shadows of dusk. The smaller of the two boys glanced up, really seeing him for the first time. "Oh, you're Danny Black, ain't you? I seen your pi'ture. Judy, Bobby, look! It's that man—"

But their voices faded out as he ran off through the park and into the deserted byways again, clutching the package to him. Fool! To delight in beating children at a useless game, or to be surprised that they should know him! He slowed to a walk, twitching his lips at the thought that by now the supervisor would be reprimanding them for their thoughtlessness. And still his feet went on, unguided.

It was inevitable, of course, that they should lead him to the Museum, where all his secret hopes centered, but he was surprised to look up and see it before him. And then he was glad. Surely they could read nothing into his visit, unpremeditated, just before the place closed. He caught his breath, forced his face into lines of mere casual interest, and went inside, down the long corridors, and to the hall of the ship.

She rested there, pointed slightly skyward, sleek and immense even in a room designed to appear like the distant reaches of space. For six hundred feet, gleaming metal formed a smooth frictionless surface that slid gracefully from the blunt bow back toward the narrow stern with its blackened ion jets.

This, Danny knew, was the last and greatest of the space liners his people had built at the height of their glory. And even before her, the mutation that made the new race of men had been caused by the radiations of deep space, and the results were spreading. For a time, as the log book indicated, this ship had sailed out to Mars, to Venus, and to the other points of man's empire, while the tension slowly mounted at home. There had never been another wholly *sapient*—designed ship, for the new race was spreading, making its greater intelligence felt, with the invert-matter rocket replacing this older, less efficient ion rocket which the ship carried. Eventually, unable to compete with the new models, she had been retired from service and junked, while the War between the new and old race passed by her and buried her under tons of rubble, leaving no memory of her existence.

And now, carefully excavated from the old ruins of the drydock where she had lain so long, she had been enthroned in state for the last year, here in the Museum of Sapient History, while all Danny's hopes and prayers had centered around her. There was still a feeling of awe in him as he started slowly across the carpeted floor toward the open lock and the lighted interior.

"Danny!" The sudden word interrupted him, bringing him about with a guilty start, but it was only Professor Kirk, and he relaxed again. The old archaeologist came toward him, his smile barely visible in the half-light of the immense dome. "I'd about given you up, boy, and started out. But I happened to look back and see you. Thought you might be interested in some information I just came onto today."

"Information about the ship?"

"What else? Here, come on inside her and into the lounge—I have a few privileges here, and we might as well be comfortable. You know, as I grow older, I find myself appreciating your ancestors' ideas of comfort, Danny. Sort of a pity our own culture is too new for much luxuriousness yet." Of all the new race, Kirk seemed the most completely at ease before Danny, partly because of his age, and partly because they had shared the same enthusiasm for the great ship when it had first arrived.

Now he settled back into one of the old divans, using his immunity to ordinary rules to light a cigarette and pass one to the younger man. "You know all the supplies and things in the ship have puzzled us both, and we couldn't find any record of them? The log ends when they put the old ship up for junking, you remember; and we couldn't figure out why all this had been restored and restocked, ready for some long voyage to somewhere. Well, it came to light in some further excavations they've completed. Danny, your people did that, during the War; or really, after they'd lost the War to us!"

Danny's back straightened. The War was a period of history he'd avoided thinking about, though he knew the outlines of it. With *homo intelligens* increasing and pressing the older race aside by the laws of survival, his people had made a final desperate bid for supremacy. And while the new race had not wanted the War, they had been forced finally to fight back with as little mercy as had been shown them; and since they had the tremendous advantage of the new intuitive thinking, there had been only thousands left of the original billions of the old race when its brief course was finished. It had been inevitable probably, from the first mutation, but it was not something Danny cared to think of. Now he nodded, and let the other continue.

"Your ancestors, Danny, were beaten then, but they weren't completely crushed, and they put about the last bit of energy they had into rebuilding this ship—the only navigable one left them—and restocking it. They were going to go out somewhere, they didn't know quite where, even to another solar system, and take some of the old race for a new start, away from us. It was their last bid for survival, and it failed when my people learned of it and blasted the docks down over the ship, but it was a glorious failure, boy! I thought you'd want to know."

Danny's thoughts focused slowly. "You mean everything on the ship is of my people? But surely the provisions wouldn't have remained usable after all this time?"

"They did, though; the tests we made proved that conclusively. Your people knew how to preserve things as well as we do, and they expected to be drifting in the ship for half a century, maybe. They'll be usable a thousand years from now." He chucked his cigarette across the room and chuckled in pleased surprise when it fell accurately into a snuffer. "I stuck around, really, to tell you, and I've kept the papers over at the school for you to see. Why not come over with me now?"

"Not tonight, sir. I'd rather stay here a little longer."

Professor Kirk nodded, pulling himself up reluctantly. "As you wish . . . I know how you feel, and I'm sorry about their moving the ship, too. We'll miss her, Danny!"

"Moving the ship?"

"Hadn't you heard? I thought that's why you came around at this hour. They want her over in London, and they're bringing one of the old Lunar ships here to replace her. Too bad!" He touched the walls thoughtfully, drawing his hands down and across the rich nap on the seat. "Well, don't stay too long, and turn her lights out before you leave. Place'll be closed in half an hour. 'Night, Danny."

" 'Night, Professor." Danny sat frozen on the soft seat, listening to the slow tread of the old man and the beating of his own heart. They were moving the ship, ripping his plans to shreds, leaving him stranded in this world of a new race, where even the children were sorry for him.

It had meant so much, even to feel that somehow he would escape, some day! Impatiently, he snapped off the lights, feeling closer to the ship in the privacy of the dark, where no watchman could see his emotion. For a year now he had built his life around the idea of taking this ship out and away, to leave the new race far behind. Long, carefully casual months of work had been spent in learning her structure, finding all her stores, assuring himself bit by bit from a hundred old books that he could operate her.

She had been almost designed for the job, built to be operated by one man, even a cripple, in an emergency, and nearly everything was automatic. Only the problem of a destination had remained, since the planets were all swarming with the others, but the ship's log had suggested the answer even to that.

Once there had been rich men among his people who sought novelty and seclusion, and found them among the larger asteroids; money and science had built them artificial gravities and given them atmospheres, powered by atomic-energy plants that should last forever. Now the rich men were undoubtedly dead, and the new race had abandoned such useless things. Surely, somewhere among the asteroids, there should have been a haven for him, made safe by the very numbers of the little worlds that could discourage almost any search.

Danny heard a guard go by, and slowly got to his feet, to go out again into a world that would no longer hold even that hope. It had been a lovely plan to dream on, a necessary dream. Then the sound of the great doors came to his ears, closing! The Professor had forgotten to tell them of his presence! And—!

All right, so he didn't know the history of all those little worlds; perhaps he would have to hunt through them, one by one, to find a suitable home. Did it matter? In every other way, he could never be more ready. For a moment only, he hesitated; then his hands fumbled with the great lock's control switch, and it swung shut quietly in the dark, shutting the sound of his running feet from outside ears.

The lights came on silently as he found the navigation chair and sank into it. Little lights that spelled out the readiness of the ship. "Ship sealed ... Air Okay ... Power, Automatic ... Engine, Automatic. ..." Half a hundred little lights and dials that told the story of a ship waiting for his hand. He moved the course plotter slowly along the tiny atmospheric map until it reached the top of the stratosphere; the big star map moved slowly out, with the pointer in his fingers tracing an irregular, jagged line that would lead him somewhere toward the asteroids, well away from the present position of Mars, and yet could offer no clue. Later, he could set the analyzers to finding the present location of some chosen asteroid and determine his course more accurately, but all that mattered now was to get away, beyond all tracing, before his loss could be reported.

Seconds later his fingers pressed down savagely on the

main power switch, and there was a lurch of starting, followed by another slight one as the walls of the Museum crumpled before the savage force of the great ion rockets. On the map, a tiny spot of light appeared, marking the ship's changing position. The world was behind him now, and there was no one to look at his efforts in kindly pity or remind him of his weakness. Only blind fate was against him, and his ancestors had met and conquered that long before.

A bell rang, indicating the end of the atmosphere, and the big automatic pilot began clucking contentedly, emitting a louder cluck now and then as it found the irregularities in the unorthodox course he had charted and swung the ship to follow. Danny watched it, satisfied that it was working. His ancestors may have been capable of reason only, but they had built machines that were almost intuitive, as the ship about him testified. His head was higher as he turned back to the kitchen, and there was a bit of a swagger to his walk.

The food was still good. He wolfed it down, remembering that supper had been forgotten, and leafing slowly through the big log book which recorded the long voyages made by the ship, searching through it for each casual reference to the asteroids, Ceres, Palas, Vesta, some of the ones referred to by nicknames or numbers? Which ones?

But he had decided by the time he stood once again in the navigation room, watching the aloof immensity of space; out here it was relieved only by the tiny hot pinpoints that must be stars, colored, small and intense as no stars could be through an atmosphere. It would be one of the numbered planetoids, referred to also as "The Dane's" in the log. The word was meaningless, but it seemed to have been one of the newer and more completely terranized, though not the very newest where any search would surely start.

He set the automatic analyzer to running from the key number in the manual and watched it for a time, but it ground on slowly, tracing through all the years that had passed. For a time, he fiddled with the radio, before he remembered that it operated on a wave form no longer used. It was just as well; his severance from the new race would be all the more final.

Still the analyzer ground on. Space lost its novelty, and the operation of the pilot ceased to interest him. He wandered back through the ship toward the lounge, to spy the parcel where he had dropped and forgotten it. There was nothing else to do.

And once begun, he forgot his doubts at the fact that it was Kenning's story, not the original; there was the same sweep to the tale, the same warm and human characters, the same drive of a race that had felt the mastership of destiny so long ago. Small wonder the readers of that time had named it the greatest epic of space to be written!

Once he stopped, as the analyzer reached its conclusions and bonged softly, to set the controls on the automatic for the little world that might be his home, with luck. And then the ship moved on, no longer veering, but making the slightly curved path its selectors found most suitable, while Danny read further, huddled over the story in the navigator's chair, feeling a new and greater kinship with the characters of the story. He was no longer a poor Earthbound charity case, but a man and an adventurer with them!

His nerves were tingling when the tale came to its end, and he let it drop onto the floor from tired fingers. Under his hand, a light had sprung up, but he was oblivious to it, until a crashing gong sounded over him, jerking him from the chair. There had been such a gong described in the story. . . .

And the meaning was the same. His eyes made out the red letters that glared accusingly from the control panel: RADIATION AT TEN O'CLOCK HORIZ—SHIP INDICATED!

Danny's fingers were on the master switch and cutting off all life except pseudogravity from the ship as the thought penetrated. The other ship was not hard to find from the observation window; the great streak of an invert-matter rocket glowed hotly out there, pointed apparently back to Earth—probably the *Callisto!*

For a second he was sure they had spotted him, but the flicker must have been only a minor correction to adjust for the trail continued. He had no knowledge of the new ships and whether they carried warning signals or not, but apparently they must have dispensed with such things. The streak vanished into the distance, and the letters on the panel that had marked it changing position went dead. Danny waited until the fullest amplification showed no response before throwing power on again. The small glow of the ion rocket would be invisible at the distance, surely.

Nothing further seemed to occur; there was a contented purr from the pilot and the faint sleepy hum of raw power

from the rear, but no bells or sudden sounds. Slowly, his head
fell forward over the navigator's table, and his heavy breathing mixed with the low sounds of the room. The ship went on
about its business as it had been designed to do. Its course
was charted, even to the old landing sweep, and it needed no
further attention.

That was proved when the slow ringing of a bell woke
Danny, while the board blinked in time to it: Destination!
Destination! Destination Reached!

He shut off everything, rubbing the sleep from his eyes,
and looked out. Above, there was weak but warm sunlight
streaming down from a bluish sky that held a few small
clouds suspended close to the ground. Beyond the ship, where
it lay on a neglected sandy landing field, was the green of
grass and the wild profusion of a forest. The horizon dropped
off sharply, reminding him that it was only a tiny world, but
otherwise it might have been Earth. He spotted an unkempt
hangar ahead and applied weak power to the underjets,
testing until they moved the ship slowly forward and inside,
out of the view of any above.

Then he was at the lock, fumbling with the switch. As it
opened, he could smell the clean fragrance of growing things,
and there was the sound of birds nearby. A rabbit hopped
leisurely out from underfoot as he stumbled eagerly out to
the sunlight, and weeds and underbrush had already spread
to cover the buildings about him. For a moment, he sighed; it
had been too easy, this discovery of a heaven on the first wild
try.

But the sight of the buildings drove back the doubt. Once,
surrounded by a pretentious formal garden, this had been a
great stone mansion, now falling into ruins. Beside it and
further from him, a smaller house had been built, seemingly
from the wreckage. That was still whole, though ivy had
grown over it and half covered the door that came open at the
touch of his fingers.

There was still a faint glow to the heaters that drew power
from the great atomic plant that gave this little world a
perpetual semblance of Earthliness, but a coating of dust was
everywhere. The furnishings, though, were in good condition.
He scanned them, recognizing some as similar to the pieces
in the Museum, and the products of his race. One by one he
studied them—his fortune, and now his home!

On the table, a book was dropped casually, and there was a

sheet of paper propped against it, with what looked like a girl's rough handwriting on it. Curiosity carried him closer, until he could make it out, through the dust that clung even after he shook it.

Dad:

    Charley Summers found a wrecked ship of those things, and came for me. We'll be living high on 13. Come on over, if your jets will make it, and meet your son-in-law.

There was no date, nothing to indicate whether "Dad" had returned, or what had happened to them. But Danny dropped it reverently back on the table, looking out across the landing strip as if to see a worn old ship crawl in through the brief twilight that was falling over the tiny world. "Those things" could only be the new race, after the War; and that meant that here was the final outpost of his people. The note might be ten years or half a dozen centuries old—but his people had been here, fighting on and managing to live, after Earth had been lost to them. If they could, so could he!

And unlikely though it seemed, there might possibly be more of them out there somewhere. Perhaps the race was still surviving in spite of time and trouble and even *homo intelligens*.

Danny's eyes were moist as he stepped back from the door and the darkness outside to begin cleaning his new home. If any were there, he'd find them. And if not—

Well, he was still a member of a great and daring race that could never know defeat so long as a single man might live. He would never forget that.

Back on Earth, Bryant Kenning nodded slowly to the small group as he put the communicator back, and his eyes were a bit sad in spite of the smile that lighted his face. "The Director's scout is back, and he did choose 'The Dane's.' Poor kid. I'd begun to think we waited too long, and that he never would make it. Another six months—and he'd have died like a flower out of the sun! Yet I was sure it would work when Miss Larsen showed me that story, with its mythical planetoid-paradises. A rather clever story, if you like pseudohistory. I hope the one I prepared was its equal."

"For historical inaccuracy, fully its equal." But the amusement in old Professor Kirk's voice did not reach his lips.

"Well, he swallowed our lies and ran off with the ship we built him. I hope he's happy, for a while at least."

Miss Larsen folded her things together and prepared to leave. "Poor kid! He was sweet, in a pathetic sort of way. I wish that girl we were working on had turned out better; maybe this wouldn't have been necessary then. See me home, Jack?"

The two older men watched Larsen and Thorpe leave, and silence and tobacco smoke filled the room. Finally Kenning shrugged and turned to face the professor.

"By now he's found the note. I wonder if it was a good idea, after all? When I first came across it in that old story, I was thinking of Jack's preliminary report on Number 67, but now I don't know; she's an unknown quantity, at best. Anyhow, I meant it for kindness."

"Kindness! Kindness to repay with a few million credits and a few thousands of hours of work—plus a lie here and there—for all that we owe the boy's race!" The professor's voice was tired, as he dumped the contents of his pipe into a snuffer, and strode over slowly toward the great window that looked out on the night sky. "I wonder sometimes, Bryant, what kindness Neanderthaler found when the last one came to die. Or whether the race that will follow us when the darkness falls on us will have something better than such kindness."

The novelist shook his head doubtfully, and there was silence again as they looked out across the world and toward the stars.

Roger Zelazny

Roger Zelazny burst upon the science fiction scene in the mid-1960s with three novels that are widely regarded as three of the very best of a rich decade: *This Immortal, The Dream Master* (both 1966), and *Lord of Light* (1967). The 1970s saw the publication of his famous "Amber" series of novels and the stunning *Roadmarks* (1979), and he opened the 1980s with *Changeling*. His rich prose and vivid imagery can also be found in a bevy of beautiful short stories in such collections as *The Doors of His Face, The Lamps of His Mouth* (1971) and *The Last Defender of Camelot* (1980). He has won three Hugo Awards, three Nebulas, and a Prix Apollo, and he is still in mid-career.

"Lucifer," one of his lesser-known stories, concerns a man struggling to bring light into a world of darkness.

LUCIFER

by Roger Zelazny

CARLSON STOOD ON THE HILL in the silent center of the city whose people had died.

He stared up at the Building—the one structure that dwarfed every hotel-grid, skyscraper-needle, or apartment-cheesebox packed into all the miles that lay about him. Tall as a mountain, it caught the rays of the bloody sun. Somehow it turned their red into golden halfway up its height.

Carlson suddenly felt that he should not have come back.

It had been over two years, as he figured it, since last he had been here. He wanted to return to the mountains now. One look was enough. Yet still he stood before it, transfixed by the huge Building, by the long shadow that bridged the entire valley. He shrugged his thick shoulders then, in an unsuccessful attempt to shake off memories of the days, five (or was it six?) years ago, when he had worked within the giant unit.

Then he climbed the rest of the way up the hill and entered the high, wide doorway.

His fiber sandals cast a variety of echoes as he passed through the deserted offices and into the long hallway that led to the belts.

The belts, of course, were still. There were no thousands riding them. There was no one alive to ride. Their deep belly-rumble was only a noisy phantom in his mind as he climbed onto the one nearest him and walked ahead into the pitchy insides of the place.

It was like a mausoleum. There seemed no ceiling, no walls, only the soft *pat-pat* of his soles on the flexible fabric of the belt.

He reached a junction and mounted a cross-belt, instinctively standing still for a moment and waiting for the forward lurch as it sensed his weight.

Then he chuckled silently and began walking again.

When he reached the lift, he set off to the right of it until his memory led him to the maintenance stairs. Shouldering his bundle, he began the long, groping ascent.

He blinked at the light when he came into the Power Room. Filtered through its hundred high windows, the sunlight trickled across the dusty acres of machinery.

Carlson sagged against the wall, breathing heavily from the climb. After a while he wiped a workbench clean and set down his parcel.

Then he removed his faded shirt, for the place would soon be stifling. He brushed his hair from his eyes and advanced down the narrow metal stair to where the generators stood, row on row, like an army of dead, black beetles. It took him six hours to give them all a cursory check.

He selected three in the second row and systematically began tearing them down, cleaning them, soldering their loose connections with the auto-iron, greasing them, oiling them and sweeping away all the dust, cobwebs, and pieces of cracked insulation that lay at their bases.

Great rivulets of perspiration ran into his eyes and down along his sides and thighs, spilling in little droplets onto the hot flooring and vanishing quickly.

Finally, he put down his broom, remounted the stair and returned to his parcel. He removed one of the water bottles and drank off half its contents. He ate a piece of dried meat and finished the bottle. He allowed himself one cigarette then, and returned to work.

He was forced to stop when it grew dark. He had planned on sleeping right there, but the room was too oppressive. So he departed the way he had come and slept beneath the stars, on the roof of a low building at the foot of the hill.

It took him two more days to get the generators ready. Then he began work on the huge Broadcast Panel. It was in better condition than the generators, because it had last been used two years ago. Whereas the generators, save for the three he had burned out last time, had slept for over five (or was it six?) years.

He soldered and wiped and inspected until he was satisfied. Then only one task remained.

All the maintenance robots stood frozen in mid-gesture. Carlson would have to wrestle a three-hundred-pound power cube without assistance. If he could get one down from the rack and onto a cart without breaking a wrist he would probably be able to convey it to the Igniter without much difficulty. Then he would have to place it within the oven. He had almost ruptured himself when he did it two years ago, but he hoped that he was somewhat stronger—and luckier—this time.

It took him ten minutes to clean the Igniter oven. Then he located a cart and pushed it back to the rack.

One cube was resting at just the right height, approximately eight inches above the level of the cart's bed. He kicked down the anchor chocks and moved around to study the rack. The cube lay on a downward-slanting shelf, restrained by a two-inch metal guard. He pushed at the guard. It was bolted to the shelf.

Returning to the work area, he searched the tool boxes for a wrench. Then he moved back to the rack and set to work on the nuts.

The guard came loose as he was working on the fourth nut. He heard a dangerous creak and threw himself back out of the way, dropping the wrench on his toes.

The cube slid forward, crushed the loosened rail, teetered a bare moment, then dropped with a resounding crash onto the heavy bed of the cart. The bed surface bent and began to crease beneath its weight; the cart swayed toward the outside. The cube continued to slide until over half a foot projected beyond the edge. Then the cart righted itself and shivered into steadiness.

Carlson sighed and kicked loose the chocks, ready to jump back should it suddenly give way in his direction. It held.

Gingerly, he guided it up the aisle and between the rows of generators, until he stood before the Igniter. He anchored the cart again, stopped for water and a cigarette, then searched up a pinch bar, a small jack and a long, flat metal plate.

He laid the plate to bridge the front end of the cart and the opening to the oven. He wedged the far end in beneath the Igniter's doorframe.

Unlocking the rear chocks, he inserted the jack and began

to raise the back end of the wagon, slowly, working with one hand and holding the bar ready in the other.

The cart groaned as it moved higher. Then a sliding, grating sound began and he raised it faster.

With a sound like the stroke of a cracked bell the cube tumbled onto the bridgeway; it slid forward and to the left. He struck at it with the bar, bearing to the right with all his strength. About half an inch of it caught against the left edge of the oven frame. The gap between the cube and the frame was widest at the bottom.

He inserted the bar and heaved his weight against it—three times.

Then it moved forward and came to rest within the Igniter.

He began to laugh. He laughed until he felt weak. He sat on the broken cart, swinging his legs and chuckling to himself, until the sounds coming from his throat seemed alien and out of place. He stopped abruptly and slammed the door.

The Broadcast Panel had a thousand eyes, but none of them winked back at him. He made the final adjustments for Transmit, then gave the generators their last check-out.

After that, he mounted a catwalk and moved to a window.

There was still some daylight to spend, so he moved from window to window pressing the "Open" button set below each sill.

He ate the rest of his food then, and drank a whole bottle of water and smoked two cigarettes. Sitting on the stair, he thought of the days when he had worked with Kelly and Murchison and Djizinsky, twisting the tails of electrons until they wailed and leapt out over the walls and fled down into the city.

The clock! He remembered it suddenly—set high on the wall, to the left of the doorway, frozen at 9:33 (and forty-eight seconds).

He moved a ladder through the twilight and mounted it to the clock. He wiped the dust from its greasy face with a sweeping, circular movement. Then he was ready.

He crossed to the Igniter and turned it on. Somewhere the ever-batteries came alive, and he heard a click as a thin, sharp shaft was driven into the wall of the cube. He raced back up the stairs and sped hand-over-hand up to the catwalk. He moved to a window and waited.

"God," he murmured, "don't let them blow! Please don't—"

Across an eternity of darkness the generators began humming. He heard a crackle of static from the Broadcast Panel and he closed his eyes. The sound died.

He opened his eyes as he heard the window slide upward. All around him the hundred high windows opened. A small light came on above the bench in the work area below him, but he did not see it.

He was staring out beyond the wide drop of the acropolis and down into the city. His city.

The lights were not like the stars. They beat the stars all to hell. They were the gay, regularized constellation of a city where men made their homes: even rows of streetlamps, advertisements, lighted windows in the cheesebox-apartments, a random solitaire of bright squares running up the sides of skyscraper-needles, a searchlight swiveling its luminous antenna through cloudbanks that hung over the city.

He dashed to another window, feeling the high night breezes comb at his beard. Belts were humming below; he heard their wry monologues rattling through the city's deepest canyons. He pictured the people in their homes, in theaters, in bars—talking to each other, sharing a common amusement, playing clarinets, holding hands, eating an evening snack. Sleeping ro-cars awakened and rushed past each other on the levels above the belts; the background hum of the city told him its story of production, of function, of movement and service to its inhabitants. The sky seemed to wheel overhead, as though the city were its turning hub and the universe its outer rim.

Then the lights dimmed from white to yellow and he hurried, with desperate steps, to another window.

"No! Not so soon! Don't leave me yet!" he sobbed.

The windows closed themselves and the lights went out. He stood on the walk for a long time, staring at the dead embers. A smell of ozone reached his nostrils. He was aware of a blue halo about the dying generators.

He descended and crossed the work area to the ladder he had set against the wall.

Pressing his face against the glass and squinting for a long time he could make out the position of the hands.

"Nine thirty-five, and twenty-one seconds," Carlson read.

"Do you hear that?" he called out, shaking his fist at

anything. "Ninety-three seconds! I made you live for ninety-three seconds!"

Then he covered his face against the darkness and was silent.

After a long while he descended the stairway, walked the belt, and moved through the long hallway and out of the Building. As he headed back toward the mountains he promised himself—again—that he would never return.

A. E. van Vogt

The Canadian born A. E. van Vogt was one of the great stars of the "Golden Age" of modern science fiction. His fame was nearly instantaneous with the publication of his first story, "Black Destroyer," in the April 1939 issue of *Astounding Science Fiction*. He followed this debut with a string of outstanding stories and serialized novels including such landmark works as *Slan* (first book publication 1946), *The Weapon Makers* (book form 1947), *The Book of Ptath* (book form 1947), and *The World of A* (1948). A considerable pause in his output followed in the 1950s and part of the '60s as he dabbled in Dianetics, but he returned with numerous other works and is still productive today at the age of seventy.

"The Monster" is a superior and typical example of the John W. Campbell, Jr., *Astounding* story—one man faces a starship of seemingly unbeatable aliens, and they never stand a chance.

RESURRECTION

by A. E. van Vogt

THE GREAT SHIP POISED a quarter of a mile above one of the cities. Below was a cosmic desolation. As he floated down in his energy bubble, Enash saw that the buildings were crumbling with age.

"No sign of war damage!" The bodiless voice touched his ears momentarily. Enash tuned it out.

On the ground he collapsed his bubble. He found himself in a walled inclosure overgrown with weeds. Several skeletons lay in the tall grass beside the rakish building. They were of long, two-legged, two-armed beings with the skulls in each case mounted at the end of a thin spine. The skeletons, all of adults, seemed in excellent preservation, but when he bent down and touched one, a whole section of it crumbled into a fine powder. As he straightened, he saw that Yoal was floating down nearby. Enash waited till the historian had stepped out of his bubble, then he said:

"Do you think we ought to use our method of reviving the long-dead?"

Yoal was thoughtful. "I have been asking questions of the various people who have landed, and there is something wrong here. This planet has no surviving life, not even insect life. We'll have to find out what happened before we risk any colonization."

Enash said nothing. A soft wind was blowing. It rustled through a clump of trees nearby. He motioned towards the trees. Yoal nodded.

"Yes, the plant life has not been harmed, but plants after all are not affected in the same way as the active life forms."

There was an interruption. A voice spoke from Yoal's receiv-

245

er, "A museum has been found at approximately the center of the city. A red light has been fixed to the roof."

Enash said, "I'll go with you, Yoal. There might be skeletons of animals and of the intelligent being in various stages of his evolution. You didn't answer my question: Are you going to revive these beings?"

Yoal said slowly, "I intend to discuss the matter with the council, but I think there is no doubt. We must know the cause of this disaster." He waved one sucker vaguely to take in half the compass. He added as an afterthought, "We shall proceed cautiously, of course, beginning with an obviously early-development. The absence of the skeletons of children indicates that the race had developed personal immortality."

The council came to look at the exhibits. It was, Enash knew, a formal preliminary only. The decision was made. There would be revivals. It was more than that. They were curious. Space was vast, the journeys through it long and lonely, landing always a stimulating experience, with its prospect of new life forms to be seen and studied.

The museum looked ordinary. High-domed ceilings, vast rooms. Plastic models of strange beasts, many artifacts—too many to see and comprehend in so short a time. The life span of a race was imprisoned here in a progressive array of relics. Enash looked with the others, and was glad when they came to the line of skeletons and preserved bodies. He seated himself behind the energy screen, and watched the biological experts take a preserved body out of a stone sarcophagus. It was wrapped in windings of cloth, many of them. The experts did not bother to unravel the rotted material. Their forceps reached through, pinched a piece of the skull—that was the accepted procedure. Any part of the skeleton could be used, but the most perfect revivals, the most complete reconstructions, resulted when a certain section of the skull was used.

Hamar, the chief biologist, explained the choice of body. "The chemicals used to preserve this mummy show a sketchy knowledge of chemistry; the carvings of the sarcophagus indicate a crude and unmechanical culture. In such a civilization there would not be much development of the potentialities of the nervous system. Our speech experts have been analyzing the recorded voice mechanism which is a part of each exhibit, and though many languages are involved—evidence that the ancient language spoken at the time the body was alive has been reproduced—they found no difficulty in translating the meanings. They have now adapted our universal speech machine, so that anyone who wishes to, need merely speak into his communicator, and so will have his words translated into the language of the revived person. The reverse, naturally, is also true. Ah, I see we are ready for the first body."

Enash watched intently with the others, as the lid was clamped down on the plastic reconstructor, and the growth processes were started. He could feel himself becoming tense. For there was nothing haphazard about what was happening. In a few minutes a full-grown ancient inhabitant of this planet would sit up and stare at them. The science involved was simple and always fully effective.

. . . Out of the shadows of smallness life grows. The level of beginning and ending, of life and—not life; in that dim region matter oscillates easily between old and new habits. The habit of organic, or the habit of inorganic.

Electrons do not have life and un-life values. Atoms know nothing of inanimateness. But when atoms form into molecules, there is a step in the process, one tiny step, that is of life—if life begins at all. One step, and then darkness. Or aliveness.

A stone or a living cell. A grain of gold or a blade of grass, the sands of the sea or the equally numerous animalcules inhabiting the endless fishy waters—the difference is there in the twilight zone of matter. Each living cell has in it the whole form. The crab grows a new leg when the old one is torn from its flesh. Both ends of the planarian worm elongate, and soon there are two worms, two identities, two digestive systems, each as greedy as the original, each a whole, unwounded, unharmed by its experience.

Each cell can be the whole. Each cell remembers in a detail so intricate that no totality of words could ever describe the completeness achieved.

But—paradox—memory is not organic. An ordinary wax record remembers sounds. A wire recorder easily gives up a duplicate of the voice that spoke into it years before. Memory is a physiological impression, a mark on matter, a change in the shape of a molecule, so that when a reaction is desired the *shape* emits the same rhythm of response.

Out of the mummy's skull had come the multi-quadrillion memory shapes from which a response was now being evoked. As ever, the memory held true.

A man blinked, and opened his eyes.

"It is true, then," he said aloud, and the words were translated into the Ganae tongue as he spoke them. "Death is merely an opening into another life—but where are my attendants?" At the end, his voice took on a complaining tone.

He sat up, and climbed out of the case, which had automatically opened as he came to life. He saw his captors. He froze—but only for a moment. He had a pride and a very special arrogant courage, which served him now.

Reluctantly, he sank to his knees, and made obeisance, but doubt must have been strong in him. "Am I in the presence of the gods of Egyptus?"

He climbed to his feet. "What nonsense is this? I do not bow to nameless demons."

Captain Gorsid said, "Kill him!"

The two-legged monster dissolved, writhing, in the beam of a ray gun.

The second man stood up palely, and trembled with fear. "My God, I swear I won't touch the stuff again. Talk about pink elephants—"

Yoal was curious. "To what *stuff* do you refer, revived one?"

"The old hooch, the poison in the old hip pocket flask, the juice they gave me at that speak . . . my lordie!"

Captain Gorsid looked questioningly at Yoal. "Need we linger?"

Yoal hesitated: "I am curious." He addressed the man. "If I were to tell you that we were visitors from another star, what would be your reaction?"

The man stared at him. He was obviously puzzled, but the fear was stronger. "Now, look," he said, "I was driving along, minding my own business. I admit I'd had a shot or two too many, but its the liquor they serve these days. I swear I didn't see the other car—and if this is some new idea of punishing people who drink and drive, well, you've won. I won't touch another drop as long as I live, so help me."

Yoal said, "Drives a 'car' and thinks nothing of it. Yet we saw no cars; they didn't even bother to preserve them in the museum."

Enash noticed that everyone waited for everyone else to comment. He stirred as he realized the circle of silence would be complete unless he spoke. He said, "Ask him to describe the car. How does it work?"

"Now you're talking," said the man. "Bring on your line of chalk, and I'll walk it, and ask any questions you please. I may be so tight that I can't see straight, but I can always drive. How does it work? You just put her in gear, and step on the gas."

"Gas," said engineering officer Veed. "The internal combustion engine. That places him."

Captain Gorsid motioned to the guard with the ray gun.

The third man sat up, and looked at them thoughtfully. "From the stars?" he said finally. "Have you a system, or was it blind chance?"

The Ganae councilors in that doomed room stirred uneasily in their curved chairs. Enash caught Yoal's eye on him; the shock in the historian's eyes alarmed the meteorologist. He thought: "The two-legged one's adjustment to a new situation, his grasp of realities, was unnormally rapid. No Ganae could have equaled the swiftness of the reaction."

Hamar, the chief biologist, said, "Speed of thought is not necessarily a sign of superiority. The slow, careful thinker has his place in the hierarchy of intellect."

But, Enash found himself thinking, it was not the speed; it was the accuracy of the response. He tried to imagine himself being revived from the dead, and understanding instantly the meaning of the presence of aliens from the stars. He couldn't have done it.

He forgot his thought, for the man was out of the case. As Enash watched with the others, he walked briskly over to the window and looked out. One glance, and then he turned back.

"Is it all like this?" he asked.

Once again, the speed of his understanding caused a sensation. It was Yoal who finally replied.

"Yes. Desolation. Death. Ruin. Have you any idea as to what happened?"

The man came back and stood in front of the energy screen that guarded the Ganae. "May I look over the museum? I have to estimate what age I am in. We had certain possibilities of destruction when I was last alive, but which one was realized depends on the time elasped."

The councilors looked at Captain Gorsid, who hesitated; then: "Watch him," he said to the guard with the ray gun. He faced the man. "We understand your aspirations fully. You would like to seize control of this situation, and insure your own safety. Let me assure you. Make no false moves, and all will be well."

Whether or not the man believed the lie, he gave no sign. Nor did he show by a glance or a movement that he had seen the scarred floor where the ray gun had burned his two predecessors into nothingness. He walked curiously to the nearest doorway, studied the other guard who waited there for him, and then, gingerly, stepped through. The first guard followed him, then came the mobile energy screen, and finally, trailing one another, the councilors. Enash was the third to pass through the doorway. The room contained skeletons and plastic models of animals. The room beyond that was what, for want of a better term, Enash called a culture room. It contained the artifacts from a single period of civilization. It looked very advanced. He had examined some of the machines when they first passed through it, and had thought: Atomic energy. He was not alone in his recognition.

From behind him, Captain Gorsid said, "You are forbidden to touch anything. A false move will be the signal for the guards to fire."

The man stood at ease in the center of the room. In spite of a curious anxiety, Enash had to admire his calmness. He must have known what his fate would be, but he stood there thoughtfully, and said finally, deliberately:

"I do not need to go any farther. Perhaps you will be able better than I to judge of the time that has elapsed since I was born and these machines were built. I see over there an instrument which, according to the sign above it, counts atoms when they explode. As soon as the proper number have exploded it shuts off the power automatically, and for just the right length of time to prevent a chain explosion. In my time we had a thousand crude devices for limiting the size of an atomic reaction, but it required two thousand years to develop those devices from the early beginnings of atomic energy. Can you make a comparison?"

The councilors glanced at Veed. The engineering officer hesitated. At last, reluctantly: "Nine thousand years ago we had a thousand methods of limiting atomic explosions." He paused, then even more slowly, "I have never heard of an instrument that counts out atoms for such a purpose."

"And yet," murmured Shuri, the astronomer breathlessly, "the race was destroyed."

There was silence—that ended as Gorsid said to the nearest guard, "Kill the monster!"

But it was the guard who went down, bursting into flame.

Not just one guard, but the guards! Simultaneously down, burning with a blue flame. The flame licked at the screen, recoiled, and licked more furiously, recoiled and burned brighter. Through a haze of fire, Enash saw that the man had retreated to the far door, and that the machine that counted atoms was glowing with a blue intensity.

Captain Gorsid shouted into his communicator, "Guard all exits with ray guns. Spaceships stand by to kill alien with heavy guns."

Somebody said, "Mental control. Some kind of mental control. What have we run into?"

They were retreating. The blue fire was at the ceiling, struggling to break through the screen. Enash had a last glimpse of the machine. It must still be counting atoms, for it was a hellish blue. Enash raced with the others to the room where the man had been resurrected. There another energy screen crashed to their rescue. Safe now, they retreated into their separate bubbles and whisked through the outer doors and up to the ship. As the great ship soared, an atomic bomb hurtled down from it. The mushroom of flame blotted out the museum and the city below.

"But we still don't know why the race died," Yoal whispered into Enash's ear, after the thunder had died from the heavens behind them.

The pale yellow sun crept over the horizon on the third morning after the bomb was dropped—the eighth day since the landing. Enash floated with the others down on a new city. He had come to argue against any further revival.

"As a meterologist," he said, "I pronounce this planet safe for Ganae colonization. I cannot see the need for taking any risks. This race has discovered the secrets of its nervous system, and we cannot afford—"

He was interrupted. Hamar, the biologist, said dryly, "If they knew so much why didn't they migrate to other star systems and save themselves?"

"I will concede," said Enash, "that very possibly they had not discovered our system of locating stars with planetary families." He looked earnestly around the circle of his friends. "We have agreed that was a unique accidental discovery. We were lucky, not clever."

He saw by the expressions on their faces that they were mentally refuting his arguments. He felt a helpless sense of imminent catastrophe. For he could see that picture of a great race facing death. It must have come swiftly, but not so swiftly that they didn't know about it. There were too many skeletons in the open, lying in the gardens of the magnificent homes, as if each man and his wife had come out to wait for the doom of his kind.

He tried to picture it for the council, that last day long, long ago, when a race had calmly met its ending. But his visualization failed somehow, for the others shifted impatiently in the seats that had been set up behind the series of energy screens, and Captain Gorsid said:

"Exactly what aroused this intense emotional reaction in you, Enash?"

The question gave Enash pause. He hadn't thought of it as emotional. He hadn't realized the nature of his obsession, so subtly had it stolen upon him. Abruptly, now, he realized.

"It was the third one," he said slowly. "I saw him through the haze of energy fire, and he was standing there in the distant doorway watching us curiously, just before we turned to run. His gravery, his calm, the skillful way he had duped us—it all added up."

"Added up to his death?" said Hamar. And everybody laughed.

"Come now, Enash," said vice-captain Mayad good-humoredly, "you're not going to pretend that this race is braver than our own, or that, with all the precautions we have now taken, we need fear one man?"

Enash was silent, feeling foolish. The discovery that he had had an emotional obsession abashed him. He did not want to appear unreasonable. One final protest he made.

"I merely wish to point out," he said doggedly, "that this desire to discover what happened to a dead race does not seem absolutely essential to me."

Captain Gorsid waved at the biologist. "Proceed," he said, "with the revival."

To Enash, he said, "Do we dare return to Gana, and recommend mass migrations—and then admit that we did not actually complete our investigations here? It's impossible, my friend."

It was the old argument, but reluctantly now Enash admitted there was something to be said for that point of view.

He forgot that, for the fourth man was stirring.

The man sat up—and vanished.

There was a blank, startled, horrified silence. Then Captain Gorsid said harshly, "He can't get out of there. We know that. He's in there somewhere."

All around Enash, the Ganae were out of their chairs, peering into the energy shell. The guards stood with ray guns held limply in their suckers. Out of the corner of his eye, he saw one of the protective screen technicians beckon to Veed, who went over—and came back grim.

"I'm told the needles jumped ten points when he first disappeared. That's on the nucleonic level."

"By ancient Ganae!" Shuri whispered. "We've run into what we've always feared."

Gorsid was shouting into the communicator. "Destroy all the locators on the ship. Destroy them, do you hear!"

He turned with glary eyes. "Shuri," he bellowed, "they don't seem to understand. Tell those subordinates of yours to act. All locators and reconstructors must be destroyed."

"Hurry, hurry!" said Shuri weakly.

When that was done they breathed more easily. There were grim smiles and a tensed satisfaction. "At least," said vice-captain Mayad, "he cannot now ever discover Gana. Our great system of locating suns with planets remains our secret. There can be no retaliation for—" He stopped, said slowly, "What am I talking about? We haven't done anything. We're not responsible for the disaster that has befallen the inhabitants of this planet."

But Enash knew what he had meant. The guilt feelings came to the surface at such moments as this—the ghosts of all the races destroyed by the Ganae, the remorseless will that had been in them, when they first landed, to annihilate whatever was here. The dark abyss of voiceless hate and terror that lay behind them; the days on end when they had mercilessly poured poisonous radiation down upon the unsuspecting inhabitants of peaceful planets—all that had been in Mayad's words.

"I still refuse to believe he has escaped." That was Captain Gorsid. "He's in there. He's waiting for us to take down our screens, so he can escape. Well, we won't do it."

There was silence again, as they stared expectantly into the energy shell—into the emptiness of the energy shell. The reconstructor rested on its metal supports, a glittering affair. But there was nothing else. Not a flicker of unnatural light or shade. The yellow rays of the sun bathed the open spaces with a brilliance that left no room for concealment.

"Guards," said Gorsid, "destroy the reconstructor. I thought he might come back to examine it, but we can't take a chance on that."

It burned with a white fury; and Enash, who had hoped somehow that the deadly energy would force the two-legged thing into the open, felt his hopes sag within him.

"But where can he have gone?" Yoal whispered.

Enash turned to discuss the matter. In the act of swinging around, he saw that the monster was standing under a tree a score of feet to one side, watching them. He must have arrived *that* moment, for there was a collective gasp from the councilors. Everybody drew back. One of the screen technicians, using great presence of mind, jerked up an energy screen between the Ganae and the monster. The creature came forward slowly. He was slim of build, he held his head well back. His eyes shone as from an inner fire.

He stopped as he came to the screen, reached out and touched it with his fingers. It flared, blurred with changing colors; the colors grew brighter, and extended in an intricate pattern all the way from his head to the ground. The blur cleared. The colors drew back into the pattern. The pattern faded into invisibility. The man was through the screen.

He laughed, a soft sound; then sobered. "When I first wakened," he said, "I was curious about the situation. The question was, what should I do with you?"

The words had a fateful ring to Enash on the still morning air of that planet of the dead. A voice broke the silence, a voice so strained and unnatural that a moment passed before he recognized it as belonging to Captain Gorsid.

"Kill him!"

When the blasters ceased their effort, the unkillable thing remained standing. He walked slowly forward until he was only half a dozen feet from the nearest Ganae. Enash had a position well to the rear. The man said slowly:

"Two courses suggest themselves, one based on gratitude for reviving me, the other based on reality. I know you for what you are. Yes, *know* you—and that is unfortunate. It is hard to feel merciful.

"To begin with," he went on, "let us suppose you surrender the secret of the locator. Naturally, now that a system exists, we shall never again be caught as we were—"

Enash had been intent, his mind so alive with the potentialities of the disaster that was here that it seemed impossible he could think of anything else. And yet, now a part of his attention was stirred.

"What did happen?"

The man changed color. The emotions of that far day thickened his voice. "A nucleonic storm. It swept in from outer space. It brushed this edge of our galaxy. It was about ninety light-years in diameter, beyond the farthest limits of our power. There was no escape from it. We had dispensed with spaceships, and had no time to construct any. Castor, the only star with planets ever discovered by us, was also in the path of the storm."

He stopped. "The secret?" he said.

Around Enash, the councilors were breathing easier. The fear of race destruction that had come to them was lifting. Enash saw with pride that the first shock was over, and they were not even afraid for themselves.

"Ah," said Yoal softly, "you don't know the secret. In spite of all your great development, we alone can conquer the galaxy."

He looked at the others, smiling confidently. "Gentlemen," he said, "our pride in a great Ganae achievement is justified. I suggest we return to our ship. We have no further business on this planet."

There was a confused moment while their bubbles formed, when Enash wondered if the two-legged one would try to stop their departure. But the man, when he looked back, was walking in a leisurely fashion along a street.

That was the memory Enash carried with him, as the ship began to move. That and the fact that the three atomic bombs they dropped, one after the other, failed to explode.

"We will not," said Captain Gorsid, "give up a planet as easily as that. I propose another interview with the creature."

They were floating down again into the city, Enash and Yoal and Veed and the commander.

Captain Gorsid's voice tuned in once more: ". . . As I visualize it"—through mist Enash could see the transparent glint of the other three bubbles around him—"we jumped to conclusions about this creature, not justified by the evidence. For instance, when he awakened, he vanished. Why? Because he was afraid, of course. He wanted to size up the situation. *He* didn't believe he was omnipotent."

It was sound logic. Enash found himself taking heart from it. Suddenly, he was astonished that he had become panicky so easily. He began to see the danger in a new light. One man, only one man, alive on a new planet. If they were determined enough, colonists could be moved in as if he did not exist. It had been done before, he recalled. On several planets, small groups of the original populations had survived the destroying radiation, and taken refuge in remote areas. In almost every case, the new colonists gradually hunted them down. In two instances, however, that Enash remembered, native races were still holding small sections of their planets. In each case, it had been found impractical to destroy them because it would have endangered the Ganae on the planet. So the survivors were tolerated.

One man would not take up very much room.

When they found him, he was busily sweeping out the lower floor of a small bungalow. He put the broom aside, and stepped onto the terrace outside. He had put on sandals, and he wore a loose-fitting robe made of very shiny material. He eyed them indolently but he said nothing.

It was Captain Gorsid who made the proposition. Enash had to admire the story he told into the language machine. The commander was very frank. That approach had been decided on. He pointed out that the Ganae could not be expected to revive the dead of this planet. Such altruism would be unnatural considering that the ever-growing Ganae hordes had a continual need for new worlds. Each vast new population increment was a problem that could be solved by one method only. In this instance, the colonists would gladly respect the rights of the sole survivor of the—

It was at that point that the man interrupted. "But what is the purpose of this endless expansion?" He seemed genuinely curious. "What will happen when you finally occupy every planet in this galaxy?"

Captain Gorsid's puzzled eyes met Yoal's, then flashed to Veed, then Enash. Enash shrugged his torso negatively, and felt pity for the creature. The man didn't understand, possibly never could understand. It was the old story of two different viewpoints, the virile and the decadent, the race that aspired to the stars and the race that declined the call of destiny.

"Why not," urged the man, "control the breeding chambers?"

"And have the government overthrown!" said Yoal.

He spoke tolerantly, and Enash saw that the others were smiling at the man's naïveté. He felt the intellectual gulf between them widening. The man had no comprehension of the natural life forces that were at work. He said now:

"Well, if you don't control them, we will control them for you."

There was silence.

They began to stiffen. Enash felt it in himself, saw the signs of it in the others. His gaze flicked from face to face, then back to the creature in the doorway. Not for the first time Enash had the thought that their enemy seemed helpless.

"Why," he almost decided, "I could put my suckers around him and crush him."

He wondered if mental control of nucleonic, nuclear and gravitonic energies included the ability to defend oneself from a macrocosmic attack. He had an idea it did. The exhibition of power two hours before might have had limitations, but, if so, it was not apparent.

Strength or weakness could make no difference. The threat of threats had been made: "If you don't control—we will."

The words echoed in Enash's brain, and, as the meaning penetrated deeper, his aloofness faded. He had always regarded himself as a spectator. Even when, earlier, he had argued against his revival, he had been aware of a detached part of himself watching the scene rather than being part of it. He saw with a sharp clarity that that was why he had finally yielded to the conviction of the others.

Going back beyond that to remoter days, he saw that he had never quite considered himself a participant in the seizure of the planets of other races. He was the one who looked on, and thought of reality, and speculated on a life that seemed to have no meaning.

It was meaningless no longer. He was caught by a tide of irresistible emotion, and swept along. He felt himself sinking, merging with the Ganae mass being. All the strength and all the will of the race surged up in his veins.

He snarled, "Creature, if you have any hopes of reviving your dead race, abandon them now."

The man looked at him, but said nothing.

Enash rushed on, "If you could destroy us, you would have done so already. But the truth is that you operate within limitations. Our ship is so built that no conceivable chain reaction could be started in it. For every plate of potential unstable material in it there is a counteracting plate, which prevents the development of a critical pile. You might be able to set off explosions in our engines, but they, too, would be limited, and would merely start the process for which they are intended—confined in their proper space."

He was aware of Yoal touching his arm. "Careful," warned the historian. "Do not in your just anger give away vital information."

Enash shook off the restraining sucker. "Let us not be unrealistic," he said harshly. "This thing has divined most of our racial secrets, apparently merely by looking at our bodies. We would be acting childishly if we assumed that he has not already realized the possibilities of the situation."

"Enash!" Captain Gorsid's voice was imperative.

As swiftly as it had come Enash's rage subsided. He stepped back.

"Yes, Commander."

"I think I know what you intended to say," said Captain Gorsid. "I assure you I am in full accord, but I believe also that I, as the top Ganae official, should deliver the ultimatum."

He turned. His horny body towered above the man.

"You have made the unforgivable threat. You have told us, in effect, that you will attempt to restrict the vaulting Ganae spirit—"

"Not the spirit," said the man. He laughed softly. "No, not the spirit."

The commander ignored the interruption. "Accordingly, we have no alternative. We are assuming that, given time to locate the materials and develop the tools, you might be able to build a reconstructor.

"In our opinion it will be at least two years before you can complete it, *even if you know how*. It is an immensely intricate machine not easily assembled by the lone survivor of a race that gave up its machines millennia before disaster struck.

"You did not have time to build a spaceship.

"We won't give you time to build a reconstructor.

"Within a few minutes our ship will start dropping bombs. It is possible you will be able to prevent explosions in your vicinity. We will start, accordingly, on the other side of the planet. If you stop us there, then we will assume we need help.

"In six months of traveling at top acceleration, we can

each a point where the nearest Ganae planet would hear our messages. They will send a fleet so vast that all your powers resistance will be overcome. By dropping a hundred or a thousand bombs every minute we will succeed in devastating very city, so that not a grain of dust will remain of the skeletons of your people.

"That is our plan.

"So it shall be.

"Now, do your worst to us who are at your mercy."

The man shook his head. "I shall do nothing—now!" he said. He paused, then thoughtfully, "Your reasoning is fairly accurate. Fairly. Naturally, I am not all-powerful, but it seems to me you have forgotten one little point.

"I won't tell you what it is.

"And now," he said, "good day to you. Get back to your ship, and be on your way. I have much to do."

Enash had been standing quietly, aware of the fury building up in him again. Now, with a hiss, he sprang forward, suckers outstretched. They were almost touching the smooth flesh—when something snatched at him.

He was back on the ship.

He had no memory of movement, no sense of being dazed or harmed. He was aware of Veed and Yoal and Captain Gorsid standing near him as astonished as he himself. Enash remained very still, thinking of what the man had said: ". . . Forgotten one little point." Forgotten? That meant they knew. What could it be? He was still pondering about it when Yoal said, "We can be reasonably certain our bombs alone will not work."

They didn't.

Forty light-years out from Earth, Enash was summoned to the council chambers.

Yoal greeted him wanly, "The monster is aboard."

The thunder of that poured through Enash, and with it came a sudden comprehension. "That was what he meant we had forgotten," he said finally, aloud and wonderingly, "that he can travel through space at will within a limit—what was the figure he once used—of ninety light-years."

He sighed. He was not surprised that the Ganae, who had to use ships, would not have thought immediately of such a possibility. Slowly, he began to retreat from the reality. Now that the shock had come, he felt old and weary, a sense of his mind withdrawing again to its earlier state of aloofness.

It required a few minutes to get the story. A physicist's assistant, on his way to the storeroom, had caught a glimpse of a man in a lower corridor. In such a heavily manned ship the wonder was that the intruder had escaped earlier observation. Enash had a thought.

"But after all we are not going all the way to one of our planets. How does he expect to make use of us to locate it if we only use video—" He stopped. That was it, of course. Directional video beams would have to be used, and the man would travel in the right direction the instant contact was made.

Enash saw the decision in the eyes of his companions, the only possible decision under the circumstances. And yet—it seemed to him they were missing some vital point.

He walked slowly to the great video plate at one end of the chamber. There was a picture on it, so vivid, so sharp, so majestic that the unaccustomed mind would have reeled as from a stunning blow. Even to him, who knew the scene there came a constriction, a sense of unthinkable vastness. It was a video view of a section of the milky way. Four hundred *million* stars as seen through telescopes that could pick up the light of a red dwarf at thirty thousand light-years.

The video plate was twenty-five yards in diameter—a scene that had no parallel elsewhere in the plenum. Other galaxies simply did not have that many stars.

Only one in two hundred thousand of those glowing suns had planets.

That was the colossal fact that compelled them now to an irrevocable act. Wearily, Enash looked around him.

"The monster has been very clever," he said quietly. "If we go ahead, he goes with us—obtains a reconstructor and returns by his method to his planet. If we use the directional beam, he flashes along it, obtains a reconstructor and again reaches his planet first. In either event, by the time our fleets arrived back there, he would have revived enough of his kind to thwart any attack we could mount."

He shook his torso. The picture was accurate, he felt sure, but it still seemed incomplete. He said slowly, "We have one advantage now. Whatever decision we make, there is no language machine to enable him to learn what it is. We can carry out our plans without his knowing what they will be. He knows that neither he nor we can blow up the ship. That leaves us one real alternative."

It was Captain Gorsid who broke the silence that followed. "Well, gentlemen, I see we know our minds. We will set the engines, blow up the controls—and take him with us."

They looked at each other, race pride in their eyes. Enash touched suckers with each in turn.

An hour later, when the heat was already considerable, Enash had the thought that sent him staggering to the communicator, to call Shuri, the astronomer.

"Shuri," he cried, "when the monster first awakened— remember Captain Gorsid had difficulty getting your subordinates to destroy the locators. We never thought to ask them what the delay was. Ask them . . . ask them—"

There was a pause, then Shuri's voice came weakly over the roar of static, "They . . . couldn't . . . get . . . into . . . the . . . room. The door was locked."

Enash sagged to the floor. They had missed more than one point, he realized. The man had awakened, realized the situation; and, when he vanished, he had gone to the ship, and there discovered the secret of the locator and possibly the secret of the reconstructor—if he didn't know it previously. By the time he reappeared, he already had from them what he wanted. All the rest must have been designed to lead them to this act of desperation.

In a few moments, now, *he* would be leaving the ship secure in the knowledge that shortly no alien mind would know his planet existed. Knowing, too, that his race would live again, and this time never die.

Enash staggered to his feet, clawed at the roaring communicator, and shouted his new understanding into it. There was no answer. It clattered with the static of uncontrollable and inconceivable energy.

The heat was peeling his armored hide, as he struggled to the matter transmitter. It flashed at him with purple flame. Back to the communicator he ran shouting and screaming.

He was still whimpering into it a few minutes later when the mighty ship plunged into the heart of a blue-white sun.

Damon Knight

Damon Knight was a member of the Futurians, one of the most famous of the early science fiction fan groups. He emerged from fandom after World War II to become a most significant figure in the history of modern sf, not only as a fine writer of novels and stories but also as a leading reviewer/critic, an important editor (his *Orbit* series of original anthologies and others), and a pioneering institution builder within the field (he cofounded the Milford Writers Workshops for sf writers and was a leading force in the founding of the Science Fiction Writers of America, serving as its first President). All of this activity cut into his writing productivity, but he still managed to produce some of the most memorable works in the field.

"The Second-Class Citizen" is a story which could easily have been called "My Friend Flipper."

THE SECOND-CLASS CITIZEN

by Damon Knight

THOUGH HE WAS USED to the tropical sun, a sliver of light reflected from one of the laboratory windows stabbed into Craven's head as he crossed the walkway, leading his little group of mainlanders. He felt uneasy and feverish, more than the previous night's drinking would account for. Perhaps he was coming down with something, God forbid—it would be a rotten time for it, with the rest of the staff over in Charlotte Amalie for the weekend.

"What time did you say that plane's coming from Miami?" asked the gray, paunchy man with the clipped mustache. Hurrying to catch up with Craven, and glancing at his wristwatch, he stumbled and swore. "I ought to be back in New York right now. I hate to be out of the country with the situation the way it is."

"Two-fifteen," said Craven shortly. "You'll have plenty of time."

"What do *you* think about the crisis, Dr. Craven?" one of the women asked. She was plump and gray-haired. "Aren't you worried to be out here all by yourself? My goodness, I would be."

"Oh, I expect it'll blow over," Craven said indifferently. "They always do."

"Well, that's right, they always *have*," the paunchy man said, sounding relieved. He paused, squinting his eyes to peer out past the white concrete pens to the harbor. "Saw something jump out there. There's another. Are those some of the animals?"

"Yes, those are the dolphins," Craven said. Irritably he strode forward to open the laboratory door. "This way, please."

Inside, it was cooler than outdoors, but full of sunlight from the big windows overlooking the sea. On the wall was an alphabet chart, with brightly colored pictures of simple objects. The floor was a concrete slab, cut away across the far side of the room to form a channel open at both ends. The water in the channel rose and fell with a slow, vertiginous surge. Craven's head was beginning to ache.

"Here's where we do most of our work with the dolphins," he said. "Just a moment, I'll see if I can get one for you." He stepped to a wall panel, pressed a switch, and spoke into the microphone. "Pete, this is Charles. Come in, please."

A quacking gabble of sound from the wall speaker answered him.

"Okay, come on in," Craven said, and switched off the mike.

"What was that?" one of the matrons demanded. "Was that one of the dolphins *talking?*"

Craven smiled. "That's right—that was Pete, our star pupil. Look out the window. And stand back a little from the channel, please."

There was a nervous shuffling of feet as some of the visitors moved away from the edge, others crowded closer to the windows. Down the concrete channel that led past the pens directly to the wall of the laboratory, something gray was moving with surprising speed. It was submerged, but kicked up an occasional burst of spray. The visitors began to murmur in alarm; some backed away from the window.

"Look out!" someone yelled. The gray shape burst into the room; the water in the channel lifted as if about to overflow, then fell back with a slapping sound. There was a shriek, then nervous laughter.

In the channel, balancing itself half out of the water, was a streamlined, water-bright shape. It spoke, in the same quacking gabble as before.

"Okay, Pete," Craven said. "Out you come."

"Was it really *talking?*" someone asked behind him. "Could you understand what it said?"

Craven, without bothering to reply, pressed a switch on the control panel. Out of a recess in the wall came an electric hoist supporting a curved, heavily braced metal platform. The platform lowered itself into the water; the dolphin swam into position over it. Craven pressed another switch; the platform rose, streaming water. The hoist moved forward again, then lowered its passenger onto a wheeled framework that stood beside the channel. There was a click. The supporting arms of the hoist, disengaged from the platform, rose out of the way.

On the platform, which now formed the bed of the wheeled cart, lay a bulky eight-foot mammal. One eye was cocked alertly at Craven. The mouth, open in what seemed a pleasant smile, was full of sharp conical teeth.

"Goodness!" said one of the women. "I hope he doesn't bite!"

"Dolphins have never been known to attack a human being," Craven said perfunctorily. He pressed a button on the control panel. "Say hello to our visitors, Pete."

The dolphin glanced alertly at the people standing behind Craven, then emitted one of its high-pitched bursts of sound. To Craven's accustomed ear the words were blurred but understandable. To the others, he knew, they were only noise.

He pressed another button on the panel. After a moment, the dolphin's recorded voice, slowed down and deeper in pitch, came out of the speaker.

"Hello, lat'ss and ge'men."

There was a general murmur, some nervous laughter, one clear voice: "What did he say?"

"His mouth didn't move when he talked," someone commented suspiciously.

Craven grinned. "He doesn't use it for talking—that's for fish. He talks through his blowhole—there, on the top of his head. Come on over, Pete, let's have a look at you."

Obediently, the dolphin glided nearer on his cart, trailing a long plastic hose. Sprays of water had begun to spurt out of perforated tubes along either side of the cart, making the dolphin's skin gleam wetly. Out of this tiny personal rainstorm, the dolphin stared up at the visitors with friendly interest.

"He's shaped just like a jet plane!" one of the male visitors remarked. "Look at the curve of his head and, uh, snout—"

Craven smiled at the man. "Similar solutions for similar problems," he said. "Pete's streamlined, just like a jet. He's a bottle-nosed dolphin—*Tursiops truncatus*—the same specimens Lilly used in his original work. He weighs about four hundred pounds; his brain is a little bigger than a man's. Pete is more intelligent than a dog or a monkey. He can not only understand commands in English—he can talk back to us. That's why we feel this research is so important. What we're doing is teaching another species to enter the human community."

There was a moment of impressed silence. *That will hold them.* Craven thought.

"What are all the gadgets for?" another man asked.

"He controls the cart motors with those bars under his flukes," Craven said. "The other levers on either side are for manipulation—he works those with his flippers. Pete's great lack is that he hasn't any hands or feet, you see—but we're trying to make up for that. Show them, Pete, okay?"

"Okay, Charless," said the dolphin cheerfully. The cart wheeled, glided across the floor to the low bench on the far side, leaving a wet path behind it. Jointed arms extended from the front of the cart, groped for a pointer, picked it up in metal pincers.

"Show us the apple, Pete," Craven said.

The pointer rose, wavered, came to rest with its tip on the bright picture of an apple on the wall chart.

"Now the boy," Craven said. There were murmurs of admiration as the dolphin pointed to the boy, the dog, the boat. "Now spell cat, Pete," said Craven. The pointer spelled out C-A-T.

"Good boy, Pete," Craven said. "Plenty of fish for you today."

The dolphin opened his jaws wide, emitted a Bronx cheer, then a burst of crackling dolphin laughter. There was a nervous stir among the visitors.

"You said dolphins have never been known to attack a person," said a gray-eyed girl. It was the first time she had spoken, but Craven had been aware of her; she was slender and pretty, held herself very erect.

"That's right," he said, facing her. "It isn't that they couldn't—you know they kill sharks—but they just never have."

"Even when people have hurt them?" she asked. Her gray eyes were sober.

"That's correct," Craven said.

"And it's true, isn't it, that many dolphins have been killed in the course of this research?"

Craven felt a little irritated. "There were some fatalities, before we learned how to handle them," he said shortly. He turned away. "Now let's try something more difficult. Show them the chemistry experiment, Pete."

As the dolphin turned toward the bench again, Craven commented, "This is something Pete has just been learning. We're pretty proud of it."

On the bench was a little stand with several stoppered bottles, a beaker and a row of test tubes. Controlling the jointed arms with his flippers, the dolphin reached out, picked up a bottle and pulled the stopper. One set of metal pincers held the bottle; the other picked up a test tube. Slowly Pete made the bottle pour into the test tube. It ran full and spilled over. The dolphin rocked back and forth nervously in his cart.

"Okay, Pete," Craven said soothingly. "Don't get nervous. It's all right—go ahead."

The dolphin set the bottle down with a crash, poured the contents of the test tube into the beaker. The pincers reached for another bottle, slipped and tried again. They got the bottle on the second try, tilted it but missed the test tube. Overcorrecting, the dolphin crashed bottle and test tube together, and the test tube broke. The bottle dropped, spilled.

The dolphin backed his cart away, swiveled toward Craven. "Too hard, Charless," he said plaintively. "Too hard."

Craven's fists clenched with disappointment. The creature had done it perfectly on the last three tries! "Never mind, Pete," he said. "It's okay—you did fine. Go on out and play now."

"All finiss?" Pete asked.

"Yes. So long."

"So long." The dolphin wheeled his cart around, glided over to the edge of the channel. The jointed arms retracted. The cart bed tilted slowly; the dolphin slid off it into the water, almost without a splash. There was a glimpse of his gray body darting underwater; then the channel was empty.

On the way down to the seaplane, Craven found himself walking beside the gray-eyed girl. "Well, what did you make of it all?" he asked her.

"I thought it was *pathetic*," she said. Her gray eyes were indignant. "You talk about making them enter the human community. It's all wrong! He's a dolphin, not a man. He was trying so hard, but the best you could turn him into was something like a retarded, crippled child. I felt so *sorry*."

Hours after the visitors were gone, Craven was still restless. He kept remembering what the girl had said; there was just enough truth in it to make it rankle. His headache had not improved; the sunlight was still oppressive. He prowled through his living quarters, glanced with distaste at the black headlines of the day-old Miami paper, finally turned on the television.

". . . initials stand for 'non-radioactive heat emitters,'" a chubby, gray-haired man was saying, enunciating each word clearly. "Now the question is, what would be the consequence to *us* if these weapons—"

His voice cut off suddenly and a placard filled the screen: NEWS SPECIAL. Nothing more happened for a moment. Craven lit a cigarette and waited patiently: probably it was something more about the interminable peace talks in New Delhi.

A voice said abruptly, "We interrupt this program to bring you—" Then it stopped, and the placard vanished. There was nothing on the screen but a raster, and nothing but a hiss coming out of the speaker.

After a moment Craven put his cigarette down and punched the channel selector. There was nothing on any of the channels except 13, where a faint gray picture came in for a moment, then vanished.

Craven stared at the machine, feeling abruptly frightened. If there was something wrong with the set, then why would channel 13—?

He discovered that he was shaking. Without trying to understand what he was doing, he began to rip off his shirt and trousers. Naked except for shoes, he ran to the locker, pulled out mask, flippers, air tanks and regulator.

The sky was bright and empty as he ran toward the dock—not even a plane in sight. Craven shrugged into his harness, buckled it hastily. He glanced toward the buoy that marked the underwater station, then dropped into the water.

Halfway out toward the station, swimming two fathoms deep, Craven knew he had been right. A sudden hissing patter came above him, and looking up, transfixed, he saw a shower of golden sparks descending, each in its furious cloud of bubbles. One came so near that he felt its heat on his skin. He writhed away from it, staring incredulously as it fell to the bottom ten fathoms below.

All around, the golden sparks were disappearing into the

sand, each still marked by a boiling stream of bubbles. The water felt faintly warmer.

It came to Craven's stunned mind that the thing that must not happen had happened: someone had used the weapons that were too terrible for use.

The underwater station was in sixteen fathoms, as deep as it could have been built without pressuring the dome. It stood on a rocky shelf in deep water, and although several of the golden sparks had fallen around it, none seemed to have clung to the dome. Craven swam to the lock, let himself in, and sat hugging himself, shaken by chills, as air slowly filled the chamber.

Inside, he stared wildly around at the deserted dome—the two cots, recording instruments, shelves of supplies. The air seemed oppressively warm, and he bent to look at the thermometer, ready to cut off the surface air supply and turn on the tanks: but the temperature was normal.

He heard himself say aloud, "My God, what am I going to do?" Scraps of information from other TV broadcasts came back to his mind. Those infernal little pellets would go on emitting heat for months. And this must be only an accidental scattering: on the mainland, in populated centers, they would have fallen thick as hail. Anywhere they dropped, the land would shortly become too hot for life. Only the ocean could carry away so much heat. . . .

THere was a compressor here in the station, and a tide-driven standby generator; he could recharge his tanks indefinitely; but what about food, after the canned stuff on the shelves was gone?

Fish.

Craven felt weak with reaction, but could not be still. He adjusted his mask and mouthpiece again, went out through the lock.

There seemed to be no more of the pellets on the bottom than before, and none were falling. Craven plucked up his courage, swam to the surface. Treading water, he put his mask up and stared across at the island.

The laboratories were in flames. Behind them, the mountain was one mass of yellowish-white smoke: the whole island was on fire.

The sky seemed empty, but Craven could not endure its gigantic blue stare. He lowered his mask and dived again.

Down in the clear blue depths, Craven heard the high-pitched gabble of dolphin conversation, and once or twice saw their gray shapes flitting by. A school of plump blues swam into view. Craven started, then went after it.

There were spear-guns in the station, but he had not thought to bring one. He swam at the fish, grasping ineffectually with his hands, but they scattered easily around him.

I've got to learn, Craven's mind was telling him. *This is my element now, the sea—I've got to adapt . . .*

Something large and gray swam up toward him. Craven stiffened, but it was only Pete, gazing at him with friendly curiosity.

The school of blues had reformed not far away. Abruptly the dolphin wheeled, darted away with a lazy surge of his flukes. In a moment he was gliding back, with a fat bluefish in his jaws.

"Look, Charless," he said kindly, "this is the way to catch a fiss. . . ."

Edmond Hamilton

In Edmond Hamilton's second contribution, he tells of the return from the stars of the last man and woman, who find that the animals have taken over and are no longer sure that they want anything to do with mere humans.

DAY OF JUDGMENT

by Edmond Hamilton

HAHL FROZE LIKE A LIVING statue in the moonlit forest as he heard a quick stir in the underbrush just ahead.

He raised his short, heavy spear ready for instant use, and listened. The sighing wind lazily stirred branches and made the dappled moonlight on the ground wave. Then he heard the stir again, this time a little closer.

"One of the Clawed Clan," thought Hahl, wonderingly. "Why is he this far east?"

Hahl looked manlike, but he was not a man. There were no men left on Earth to walk these woods.

He was a stocky, erect figure whose body was covered with long brown hair. His head was not anthropoid but with a curiously elongated skull in whose dark muzzle-face his bright eyes gleamed watchfully.

Long white teeth showed as he breathed quickly, his pink tongue flashing. Despite his erect posture, spear and hide girdle, there was something very doglike about him.

Nor was that strange, for Hahl's people, the Hairy Clan, had been true canine quadrupeds not many generations before.

A hissing, whining voice suddenly called to him out of the thick underbrush ahead.

"Who comes? Greeting and peace from S'San of the Clawed Clan!"

Hahl answered, "Hahl of the Hairy Clan! Greeting and peace!"

At the reassuring formula, there emerged quickly from the brush the possessor of that hissing, challenging voice.

275

S'San of the Clawed Clan was also erect and manlike but he was as obviously of feline ancestry as Hahl was of canine.

His smooth-furred, tawny figure, sharp-pricked ears, luminous green eyes and taloned hands and feet were eloquent of his descent from the great cats of the previous age.

These two spoke quickly together in the meager tongue used by all the forest clans, though it sounded differently in S'San's hissing voice than in Hahl's short, barking accents.

"You venture far east, brother!" Hahl was saying in surprise. "I expected to meet no one this near the great water."

"I have been far east, indeed!" exclaimed S'San. "I bring news of wonder from the place of Crying Stones!"

Hahl was dumbfounded by amazement. If there was one place in all these forests that the Clans never approached, it was the Crying Stones.

That weird place by the sea was haunted—haunted by memory of ancient horror and fear. Even Hahl had only dared look upon it from a great distance.

"You have been to the Crying Stones?" he repeated, staring wonderingly at S'San.

The cat-man's green eyes flashed. "Only to the northern ridges, but from there I could see clearly. It was earlier tonight. The stones were not crying, so I dared approach that close.

"Then, as I watched, I saw a terrible thing happen. A star fell from the sky toward the Crying Stones! It fell quite slowly, flaming very bright, until it rested amid the stones. But resting there, it still shone. I hastened to bring the news to all the Clans!"

Hahl's deep brown eyes were wide with wonder. "A star falling from the sky? What does it mean? Does it mean that the world will burn up again?"

"I do not know," muttered S'San. "But others may know. Trondor of the Hoofed Clan is wisest of us all. Let us take this news to him."

"First, I must see this fallen star for myself!" Hahl declared.

The cat-man showed reluctance. "It is a long way back to the Crying Stones. It would take us hours."

Hahl argued, "Unless another than yourself sees it, the Clans may not believe you."

That argument won over S'San. "I will go back with you. We can follow back my own trail."

Silently as shadows, the two dissimilar figures started in a

run through the moonlit forest. The springy bounds of the
cat-man and the shorter, loping strides of Hahl carried them
forward at an even, easy pace.

The forest was stirring about them to the rising wind, the
patter of checkered shade and moonlight dancing and wavering. From far away to the west, the wind brought them once
the faint echoes of a deep-voiced hunting-call.

Hahl's keen senses perceived every sigh and sound as they
ran, but his thoughts were wrapped in wonder. He had
always been deeply, if fearfully, interested in the Crying
Stones. And now this marvel—a star falling upon them from
the sky!

They changed direction, moving southward now through
the forest. Presently they came to an open ridge from which
they could look far southward in the moonlight.

S'San halted, pointed with his taloned hand. "Look! The
star still shines!"

Hahl peered frozenly. "It is true! A star shining upon the
ground!"

They were looking southward along a long, narrow island
enclosed by arms of the moonlit sea. The island bore scattered trees and brush, but most of it was heaped with queerly
geometrical masses of blackened, blasted stone.

A long way southward there was an oblong open space
amid the retangular masses of blackened stone, and from
there shone a brilliant light that was indeed like a bright
star fallen from the sky.

As Hahl and S'San peered, the west wind strengthened.
And as it blew through those towering masses of shattered
black stone, there came through the moonlight the mournful,
swelling, wailing sound that had given this place its name.

S'San crouched tensely with hair bristling, and Hahl gripped
his spear more tightly as that wailing anthem smote their
ears.

"The stones cry out again!" whispered the cat-man. "Let us
return!"

But Hahl remained rooted. "I am going down there! I must
see that star more closely."

It took all his courage to make and announce the decision.
Only his intense interest in the shining wonder down there
overcame his instinctive dread of this place.

"Go into the Crying Stones? Are you mad?" demanded

S'San. "This place is still cursed with the evil of the Strange Ones!"

Hahl shivered slightly, and almost forsook his intention. But he summoned his courage.

"The Strange Ones have been dead a long time, and cannot harm us now. You can wait here until I return."

Instantly, pride flared into S'San's green eyes. "Shall the Hairy Clan venture where the Clawed Clan dares not? I go with you into this madness."

Madness indeed it seemed to Hahl's whirling mind as he and the cat-man began their tense journey down into the somber place.

The ancient horror of the Strange Ones had risen to grip him. Old, old in all the forest clans, was that deep horror. Even though the Strange Ones had vanished from Earth in the catastrophe of long ago, the dread of them still haunted the forest folk.

And this weird place of towering, blackened stones that cried to the wind had been the lair of the Strange Ones before they and the old age ended. Tradition of that had kept this spot shunned always.

Yet Hahl went on, driven by his eager interest, and the cat-man's pride kept him with him. They came to the narrow river that bounded the northern end of the island. Hahl plunged in and swam strongly. S'San, with all his Clan's aversion to water, followed gingerly.

They clambered ashore and now were among the Crying Stones. Gaunt, mournful in the moonlight, rose the blackened, shattered masses that wailed so heartbreakingly in the wind.

"This trail leads straight south toward the place where the star shines," Hahl murmured. "We can get very close."

The trail was straighter than any forest trail, and was intersected and paralleled by other straight trails through the stones.

Louder, louder, rose the wail of wind among the looming stone masses, deep and solemn as a requiem. Hahl felt the hair on his back lifting to the sound.

They entered the oblong clearing in which were no masses of stone. Through the trees, the star upon the ground shone very brilliantly as they stole toward it. They finally crouched in a thicket only a spear-cast from it.

"It is no star!" whispered S'San, amazedly. "But what is it?"

"I do not know," Hahl murmured, staring. "I have seen nothing like it."

The object at which they stared was clearly visible in the bright moonlight. It glinted metallically, a big thing like an elongated egg whose sides were scarred and battered. It was so large that it bulked as high as the smaller trees.

Hahl perceived that the brilliant, starlike light came from an opening in the side of the metal bulk. Then his keen ears caught a slight sound.

"There is someone inside the thing!" he told S'San in a tense whisper.

"There could not be!" the cat-man protested. "None in all the Clans would dare enter such a—"

"Listen!" murmured Hahl. "Whoever it is, is coming out!"

They crouched, watching. A figure appeared in the lighted opening, slowly emerging.

It was not one of the forest folk, that erect figure. It was shaped much like Hahl and S'San, but its body was covered by close-fitting garments, its head was different, its face pink, flat and hairless.

"By the Sun!" whispered S'San, quivering wildly. "It is one of the Strange Ones of long ago!"

Hahl felt frozen by horror. "The Strange Ones who burned up the world! They've returned!"

Stupefaction held the two. All their lives, the tradition of the mad Strange Ones of the past who had almost destroyed the world before they destroyed themselves had been told by the Clans.

It had been a terror of long ago, a dim tale of ancient dread. But now, suddenly, that terror was real.

Hahl watched, shivering. The Strange One there in the moonlight was acting queerly. He stood, looking at the somber black masses of stone that rose in the moonlight, listening to the wailing wind.

Then the Strange One hid his face in hands. A low sound came from him.

"He is weeping," whispered Hahl, incredulously.

"There is another—a she!" hissed S'San.

A second Strange One, a softer female figure, had come out of the big metal object. She put an arm around the weeping man.

"Quick, we must escape from here and warn the Clans!" whispered S'San tautly.

Hahl started to go back with him through the thicket. But in his stupefied state of mind, he forgot to place his feet carefully.

A twig snapped. The man out in the moonlight jerked up his head, and swiftly drew a metal tube from his belt.

"Run for it!" cried S'San instantly.

The two plunged out of the thicket. At sight of them, the man and woman in the moonlight cried out in terror and the man leveled his tube.

A flash of light darted from it and struck both the fleeing two. Hahl felt a violent shock, then darkness.

Hahl awoke with sunlight on his face. He stirred and sat up, then uttered a howling cry of surprise and dismay.

He was in a small room with metal walls, its doorway closed by heavy wire netting. S'San was just awaking also, beside him.

"We are in the big metal thing of the Strange Ones!" cried Hahl. "They stunned us, captured us!"

S'San's feline rage exploded. The cat-man hurled himself at the netting, clawing furiously. Hahl joined him.

In both of them was the violent repulsion of free forest folk who found themselves for the first time trapped and prisoned.

"I knew when we saw the Strange Ones that they had come back to bring more evil to the world!" raged S'San.

He and Hahl suddenly stopped their vain attack on the netting and crouched back. The two Strange Ones had appeared outside the barrier.

The man and woman seemed young. They stood, looking in apparent wonder at the dissimilar captives, the hairy dog-man and his blazing-eyed companion of the Clawed Clan.

"They will kill us now!" hissed S'San. "They always brought death, wherever they went."

"They do not *look* so cruel," Hahl said uncertainly.

For Hahl, despite his dread, could not feel the hatred and rage toward their captors that the cat-man did. Something deep in Hahl tugged strangely at his spirit as he stared at the Strange Ones.

The man outside the netting spoke to the woman. Hahl could not understand. But the sound of the voice somehow soothed him.

Food was brought and put through a hole in the barrier. S'San furiously refused it at first. But after a time, he too ate of it.

The Strange Ones then began earnestly to speak to the two prisoners. They held up pictures of various objects, and asked questions.

Hahl slowly understood. "They seek to learn our language so they can talk to us."

"Have nothing to do with them!" S'San warned distrustfully. "They have evil in their minds."

"It can do no harm to teach them how we speak," Hahl defended. "Then maybe they would let us go."

He began to answer the questions of the Strange Ones, by naming for them in the language of the forest Clans the simple pictured objects and actions.

Several days of this imprisonment passed, as Hahl patiently repeated words for the two Strange Ones. By now, he had learned that the names of the man and woman were "Blaine" and "Myra." S'San still remained stubbornly silent, crouching and watching in hate.

Then came an evening on which the Strange Ones had learned the language of the Clans enough to speak it. For the man Blaine spoke to Hahl in his own tongue.

"Who are you two?" he asked the dog-man. "What has happened to Earth?"

"We are of the Clans," Hahl answered hesitantly. "But from where did *you* come? Long ago, all the Strange Ones perished from Earth."

"Strange Ones—you mean men and women?" Blaine said. Then his face paled. "You mean that all mankind is gone from Earth?"

"It happened in the days of my forefathers, many summers ago," Hahl answered. "Then, so the tale runs, the world was different. There were hosts of Strange Ones who dwelt in mighty lairs, who wielded the powers of thunder and lightning, and who ruled the world.

"*Our* forefathers, the forefathers of our Clans, were not then like us. They ran upon four feet, nor could they speak or do the other things we can do. The Strange Ones killed them, and enslaved them, and even massacred them for sport.

"But finally came the day when the world burned. The tale says that the Strange Ones loosed their lightning powers upon each other! Awful thunder-fires raged across the world!

upon each other! Awful thunder-fires raged across the world!
All the Strange Ones and their mighty lairs perished when
the world burned thus. Our own forefathers' four-footed races
mostly perished also, but a few here and there in deep forests
and mountains survived.

"But the thunder-fires had somehow changed these survivors. For when they later gave birth to young, the young were
new and different races. They were like us, no longer four-
footed, no longer dim of mind, but able to stand erect and to
learn speech and skills. And we of the forest Clans have
remained thus in the generations since then."

"Good God!" whispered Blaine. "An atomic war—it finally
came, and wiped out mankind and its cities!"

His face was dead white as he looked at the girl. "Myra, we
two are the last humans left alive."

She pressed his hand. "At least our race is not dead yet!
You and I—the race will start from us again!"

S'San, crouched behind Hahl, raised his head and his
flaring green eyes blazed at them.

The girl Myra looked incredulously at Hahl and S'San.
"But how could that awful disaster change four-footed animals to manlike, intelligent races?"

"We do not know," answered Hahl. "It was something in
the terrible magic of the thunder-fires."

"Sudden mutation," muttered Blaine. "Atomic explosions
on that scale of that holocaust, drenching all surviving animal life with hard radiation, so altered the gene-patterns as
to cause a sudden evolutionary spurt."

Hahl was looking wonderingly at the man and girl. "But
from where did *you* come? We believed all the Strange Ones
dead."

Blaine pointed heavily upward. "We came from another
world, a world far up in the sky called Venus. Generations
ago, some of our human race went there to start a colony.

"But after a little time, no more ships came from Earth.
Without supplies, the colony withered. Storms and other
disasters had damaged the colony's own few ships beyond
use, and vainly it waited for word from Earth that never
came.

"Finally, Myra and I were the last born of the dwindling
colonists. We grew up, knowing ourselves doomed unless we
could repair one of the old ships enough to get back to Earth.

And we finally succeeded, and came back. We came back to find—this!"

His voice shook and his hand trembled as he gestured toward the distant masses of blackened stone looming in the sunset outside.

"This, then, is why Earth never sent more ships to its dying colony! Earth's humans had perished, self-slain in atomic war!"

Hahl had only dimly followed what the man Blaine told. But somehow, the emotion of the man and girl troubled Hahl.

Myra was looking at Blaine, her face white but brave.

"It can all start again, from us," she said. "It must, since we are the last."

Hahl asked them, "Are you going to kill S'San and myself?"

"Kill you?" Blaine seemed startled. "No! When we first glimpsed you and stunned you with a force-beam, we thought you prowling wild beasts about to attack. But when we looked at you and saw you must be intelligent creatures, we wanted only to detain and question you."

He reached in his pocket and brought forth a key. "You two are free to go now."

Hahl's heart bounded as the heavy wire door opened. He stepped out, following the man and girl down the narrow corridor to the door opening out into the sunset.

S'San, eyes flaring green fire, whispered swiftly to Hahl as he stalked along the corridor with him.

"Now is our chance, Hahl! We can slay them before he can draw the weapon! Spring with me when they reach the door!"

Hahl felt a wild revulsion. "But we can't do that! We can't slay *them!*"

"They are Strange Ones!" hissed S'San. "They will start once more the evil race that will again bring terror to the world! We can save the Clans from that by slaying. Spring—*now!*"

And with the hissed word, the cat-man launched himself in a lightning leap at the man who had just emerged behind the girl into the open air.

Instincts undreamed of until this moment exploded in Hahl's brain. He did not know why, but he could not let the Strange Ones be killed. Somehow, they were *his* Strange Ones!

Hahl uttered a yelping cry as he hurled himself only a split-second after the catman. Blaine whirled, startled, as

Hahl's hairy body hit S'San and sent him rolling over and over outside.

"Myra, get back!" yelled Blaine. "The creatures are—"

He had whipped out his metal weapon but he stood without using it, astounded.

Hahl stood in front of the man and girl, all his rough hair bristling, as he glared at the raging cat-man, who had regained his feet with inconceivable swiftness a few yards away.

"Clan-truce is broken if you seek to slay these Strange Ones!" cried Hahl. "You will have to slay me first!"

"You are traitor to the Clans!" hissed S'San. "But the Clans themselves shall swiftly bring death to these evil ones!"

And with a lightning bound, the cat-man was gone into the thickets, racing away northward amid the black Crying Stones.

The man and girl were looking at Hahl in wonder.

"Hahl, you saved us from your comrade. Why did you?" Blaine asked.

Hahl squirmed uncomfortably. "I do not know. I could not let him harm you."

Blaine's face strangely softened, and he put his hand on the dog-man's hairy shoulder.

"Hahl, only one race among the creatures in the old age was man's loyal friend," he said huskily. "The race from which you are descended."

Hahl's heart swelled at the touch of the hand on his shoulder, and he felt a queer, new happiness.

From far out in the darkening twilight came the echoes of a screaming call.

"Send the Clan-call through all the forests!" echoed S'San's distant cry. "Strange Ones have returned! Gather the Clans!"

Hahl whirled to the man and girl. "The Clans will gather here quickly! They will come in hosts, and you must escape or they will kill you lest you burn up the world as the other Strange Ones did long ago."

Blaine shook his head helplessly. "We cannot escape. The power of our ship is exhausted. And there is not enough power left in my weapon to stand off a horde."

The girl looked at him, white face strained in the gathering darkness. "Then this is the end of us? Of our race?"

*   *   *

From far out in the night, S'San's Clan-call was faintly repeated, carried across the dark forests north and south and west.

Hahl's mind was in a fever of torment as helplessly they waited. The man and girl who now stood close together, speaking in low whispers—they were *his,* and he must somehow save them. But how?"

The moon rose, a full orb casting a silver effulgence on the somber dead city. And as the night wind wailed mournfully louder through the Crying Stones, Hahl's keen ears caught other sounds, his eyes glimpsed dark shapes surging southward through the ruins.

"They are coming! All the Clans of the forest come to kill you!" he warned agonizedly.

Blaine stood in the moonlight, the girl in the circle of his arm, looking heavily northward.

"You can do nothing more for us, Hahl. Get away from here, and save yourself."

Hahl sensed the gathering of the Clans around the clearing. He knew that only this dire emergency would have brought them into the shunned and accursed place of Crying Stones.

The Clawed Clan of S'San was there, cat-eyes gleaming greenly in the dark. His own Hairy Clan, hosts of dog-men, were staring at him in amazement. The Furred Clan's bearlike horde, the Fox-Folk peering sharply—all the forest folk had come.

Last, came the Hoofed Clan, ponderous, towering, manlike, but their hoofed feet and stiff, horny hands and massive maned heads betraying the equine ancestors of whom they were an evolution.

S'San's hissing voice ripped the tense silence as the cat-man bounded out into the moonlit clearing.

"Did I lie, Clan-brothers? Are they not two Strange Ones such as worked evil long ago?"

The deep, rumbling voice of Trondor, leader of the Hoofed Clan, answered from the darkness.

"You have told truth, S'San. These are indeed two of that terrible race whom we thought dead."

"Then slay them!" raged a feline voice in the shadows. "Kill, before they again burn up the world!"

There was a surging movement of the shadowy hordes out

into the moonlight where Blaine stood with Myra clinging to his side.

Hahl uttered a furious howling cry, and flung himself protectively in front of the man and girl. Eyes flaring red, sharp teeth bared, Hahl cried to the advancing horde.

"Forest-folk, is this the justice of the Clans? To condemn these two without even a hearing?"

"They are Strange Ones!" hissed S'San. "They darkened the world for ages and finally almost destroyed it. Let them die!"

"Kill them thus without hearing, and you will need to kill me first!" raged Hahl.

From his own folk, from the masses of the Hairy Clan, there came a low whine of sympathy.

"Perhaps we do not need to kill these Strange Ones when there are only two?" muttered one of the dog-men.

Big Trondor spoke in his deep voice. "You say that because you of the Hairy Clan are still haunted by an old loyalty to the Strange Ones."

The Hoofed One slowly added, "But Hahl is right, when he says that we Clans condemn none without a hearing. Let the Strange One defend himself and his race from death-sentence, if he can!"

Blaine had been listening, and had understood. Now he put the girl behind him and stepped forth in front of Hahl.

In the moonlight, the white-faced man faced the crouched masses of the hordes with his head erect and voice steady.

"Clans of the forest, since in us our race is ending, I will speak for all my race who went before us.

"We men came of the forest-folk long ago, even as you, though our pride grew so great that we forget that fact. Yes, long and long ago we sprang from soft-skinned, weak, fumbling creatures of the forest world, creatures that had no claws or strength or swiftness.

"But one thing those creatures had, and that was curiosity. And curiosity was the key that unlocked for them the hidden powers of nature, so that they grew strong. So strong we grew, so great we deemed ourselves, that we thought ourselves a different order of beings and oppressed and tyrannized the other creatures of Earth.

"Yet for all the powers our curiosity had gathered for us, we remained in mind and heart close kin to the simple forest-creatures from which we came. Is it wonderful then that we could not handle those powers wisely? Is it wonderful that when we finally thefted the fires of the sun itself, we misused them and wrecked the world?

"Yet, forest-races, are you so sure that any of *your* Clans would have handled such powers more wisely?"

Blaine paused for a moment before his heavy voice concluded.

"But I know that that is scant excuse for the evil we did. It is yours to judge. If your judgment be against us, let the stars look down tonight on the ending of our race. Let finis be written to the terrible and wonderful story of the apes who dared lay hands on the sun, and who greatly rose and fell. And let your new forest races learn from our failure and try to do better than we."

There was a long, hushed silence among the moonlit hosts of the Clans, as Blaine's voice ceased.

Then Hahl heard the deep voice of Trondor rumble from the shadows.

"Clan-brothers all, you have heard the Strange One. Now what is your judgment on him and on his race?"

No voice answered for a moment. And then a dark figure among the bearlike Furred Clan spoke.

"Judge you for us, Trondor. You are the wisest of the Clans."

The man and girl, and Hahl who still stood defiantly in front of them in the moonlight, waited tensely.

Trondor's rumbling voice came slowly. "What the Strange One has said is true, that his race were but forest-folk like ourselves long ago. We had forgotten that, as they forgot it. It may be that with their powers, we would have been no wiser.

"The world has changed now. And it seems that the Strange Ones have changed too, and have learned. If they have, there is room in the world for them and our own new races to live in friendship."

Blaine spoke huskily. "I can promise, for ourselves. The world has changed, as you say. What powers are devised in future must be handled for the good of all our races. I think the world will not burn again."

Trondor flung up his massive maned head, and his voice rang loud.

"Then it is my judgment that we give Clan-brotherhood to the Strange Ones! That an old and blind world be forgotten in new friendship and peace!"

Swiftly, from the eager hosts of the Hairy Clan, came the yelped greetings of Hahl's brothers.

"Clan of the Strange Ones, greeting and peace!"

Clan-greeting from the Furred Ones, from the Fox-Folk, from the Hoofed Ones, echoed deafeningly through the moonlight.

Last of all, a little sulkily but with the blaze of hatred gone from his green eyes, S'San spoke.

"Greeting and peace from the Clawed Clan, Strange Ones!"

"The moon sinks, now let the Clans depart," Trondor rumbled. "But we will return, Strange Ones. This place is no longer cursed."

Blaine and Myra watched as the hosts departed. But when all had gone, Hahl still remained.

"I would like to stay with you," he said slowly. And he added hopefully, "I would be your servant."

Blaine gripped his hairy arm. "No, Hahl—master and servant no longer, but friend and friend now. In this new world where all now are friends, our tie is oldest and deepest."

From far out in the darkness echoed the last Clan-call of the separating hosts. And the wailing of the Crying Stones seemed to die into peace, as the wind sank and dawn glimmered slowly across the world.

Gordon Eklund

Gordon Eklund has been a full-time writer since the late 1960s. He first appeared in science fiction in 1970 and soon established an excellent reputation as a craftsman and innovator in the field. He has produced scores of short stories and nearly twenty novels, including *The Eclipse of Dawn* (1971), one of the very best sf works about political processes ever written, and two excellent collaborations with Gregory Benford, *If the Stars Are Gods* (1977) and *Find the Changeling* (1980). He won a Nebula Award from the SFWA in 1974.

"Continuous Performance" is one of his (unfairly) lesser known stories, and concerns the desperate search of the last man for the last woman.

CONTINUOUS PERFORMANCE

by Gordon Eklund

THE LAST MAN ON EARTH came driving down the hard-packed dirt road that wound among green peaks. Turning left, he drove along the shore of a wide blue lake, then followed the decaying pavement of the old highway until it cut through a countryside of flat green pastures. At last he reached the line of swaying wooden buildings that marked the informal boundary between country and town.

Here, finally, the last man brought his vehicle—a battered station wagon whose mechanical components he had scrounged in a thousand towns and villages. He stared at a tiny filth-encrusted hovel. Stuck in the ground in front of it, a torn sign said: GAS. Since the car's horn had long ago uttered its last mournful wail, he forced down the side window, leaned out.

"Anybody here?"

It was a hot day—sweltered, the still air clogged with swimming particles of dry dust. Beyond this settlement lay the hard edge of the continental forest yet hardly a flower grew here, barely a blade of parched grass. It was just like these creatures, he thought, to choose such a forsaken wilderness in which to build their town.

A door slammed. A figure appeared. Tall, handsome, dark, ageless—practically indistinguishable from any of them. And they had the nerve to call themselves men! This one came forward and stopped, bracing himself against the side of the car, and thrust his head forward through the open window so that his face nearly touched that of the last man.

"I know you. You're the magician!"

"I am Phobias. Yes," the last man said.

"You plan to do your show here?" The tall, dark man did

not wait for an answer. Immediately he added, "I can remember when you came through here last time. I was just a boy. You had a wagon and a team of big gray horses—"

"The horses died," Phobias said.

The man nodded, backing away from the car. Between his spindly splayed legs, a small whirlwind of dust suddenly rose. "I guess you want some gas."

"I would appreciate that."

"And in return you'll put on your show. Is that what you'll promise?"

"Correct."

"Then how about you do the show first? Afterward I'll give you the gas. Tonight, say, after the sun has set."

Phobias smiled. "So you've heard."

The man nodded. "I've got two kids. Ever since they could understand words, they've been hearing about you—about Phobias. I'm not about to see them cheated."

"Well—" Phobias shrugged. He was not embarrassed although the man had hit the nail on the head. Phobias had intended to obtain gasoline in return for a promise of magical delights and then go sprinting away. There was another big lake out there and two smaller villages and finally the vast green forest. The truth was that after more years than he could remember, Phobias no longer derived the faintest pleasure from his act. He would rather cheat than perform, rather lie than conjure. He could always order this man to do his bidding but that would be magic too, and the magic was reserved for the act. "Where shall I put on the show?" he asked.

"How about right there?" The man pointed to a bare and dusty field across the road.

"No. It may rain."

"So? Rain hardly gets one wet."

"Not you maybe. It gets me wet."

"All right," said the man, and quickly—as though memorized especially for the occasion—he supplied Phobias with a set of careful directions. "Talk to a man named Ernest when you get there. He'll see that you're fixed up with a place," he finished, stepping backward. He disappeared into the grimy house, where two pale faces hung like frozen white shadows in the sagging rectangle of a window.

Phobias drove on, reaching the dilapidated streets of the town. He chose to ignore the curious stares of pedestrians trudging along the high wooden sidewalks, merchants peering through dust-coated panes. He ignored too the wound always with him—the knowledge that he was the last man, the only man, on this whole big dead world.

Not until he had stopped the car—hearing the engine gasping over the final few drops of gasoline—did Phobias recognize the place. Yes, he had performed in this town before. He got out, placing his shoeless feet firmly in the warm dust. Stepping forward, turning his head slightly first left and then right, he was able to remember the last time he had passed through. She had still been living then. In fact, as far as he could recall, it was near here—either in the next village or the one just after that—that the jagged lightning had fallen from the heavens to claim her life. If he came upon the spot, he would not choose to pause and visit her grave. For he held her—even in death—strictly accountable for the absurdity of her own end. He preferred not to face the past; there was far too much of it. And now, tramping across the wooden walk, he recalled something else—when he had buried her. It had not been the last time he had been in this town. No. Nor even the time before that. It had been a thousand years ago. At least.

"Ernest?" he queried.

"Who wants him?" asked the man behind the counter.

"Phobias."

"I'm Ernest."

Arrangements were quickly and smoothly settled. Phobias gave his word when requested. So did Ernest.

"Then I'll see you at eight," he said.

Phobias nodded. "I think I'll go over there now."

"Want anything to eat first?"

"No, thank you. I have to set up my things."

He found the ancient car surrounded by a flock of milling children. One girl separated herself from the others and stepped boldly forward. "You're the magician!" Identical with her myriad brothers and sisters, she was dark-haired, yellow-eyed.

"I am." He trudged to the rear of the car, let down the gate, began to remove various implements needed for the act. The auditorium was a mere block away; he could walk it easily from here.

"Any of you like to lend a hand?"

The girl who had already spoken rushed to his side. In addition to the children, a cluster of adults stood upon the wooden sidewalk, carefully observing the proceedings.

"Is this something magic?" The girl took the heavy black cloth from Phobias' hands.

It was only his cape, but he answered, "You'll see tonight."

"You change people into animals, don't you?"

"Sometimes. But I always change them back." The girl waited for him to give her more to carry. But he was determined to be scrupulously fair. "Take the cape to the auditorium."

"But this isn't heavy."

"That's all for you," he insisted. He gave the next article—a briefcase containing variously colored powders—to a small boy. Rebuffed, the girl went off. The boy followed. As if from a distance, Phobias could hear the adults speaking above him on the sidewalk.

"When I was a boy . . ." one began.

"I remember him, too."

"He made my brother disappear. You couldn't see the poor guy."

". . . Or floating in the air—flying like a bird."

"Here—you take this." Phobias handed a girl a small basket containing his dirty laundry; but she would never have to know.

The adults chattered on.

"I can hardly wait to see him."

"He's the best magician ever!"

Phobias was closing the car-gate preparatory to dismissing the children when he happened to glance up. It was then that he saw her.

He stared.

She could not have been more than sixteen or seventeen. Her hair, soft and smooth as silk, fell to her bare shoulders. And it was yellow!

Unlike the others, she was not completely nude. A narrow belt of brown animal-skin darted between her thighs then circled her waist. Her skin was exceedingly pale—nearly as white as polished ivory. Adorning her chest were twin mounds—bare adolescent breasts tipped by bright pink nipples. Phobias knew he was staring. But she was staring too and her eyes, like his, were blue and plaintively clear.

"Give me something else to carry."

At the sound of the sharp voice, Phobias wheeled as though struck. A dark girl gazed at him, her hands empty and waiting.

He snapped, "No!" More gently he added, "That's all I have." He turned back, looking desperately for the blond girl. She had gone.

He whispered. "Who?"

"Huh?" said the dark girl.

"Who was—?" He made himself stop. There existed no means by which he could force these creatures to understand what he had just seen. Staring along the length of the walk, he thought he glimpsed the girl again as she rounded the corner of a decrepit building. Two men marched behind her, almost as though they served as an escort. Who? Her father? Brothers?

He could not know.

"Never mind," he said.

His own hair was white. Theirs was black. For so many hundred years had this been the case that he had long since come to believe it the natural order of things. His eyes were blue and theirs were yellow. They had never seemed to notice that he was different, and he had rarely bothered to notice much about them either, for they were a million while he was only one.

Phobias was sitting on the edge of the improvised stage, legs dangling into empty darkness. He shut his eyes, seeing her—the yellow hair, blue eyes, tender young breasts. Unbelievable! He was the last man, yes—but not the last of mankind, as he had thought. She had to be human. Or was there a catch to it? Some trick or masquerade? Tonight she would come to the performance—everyone did—and he would find out for certain.

The children had gone home. It was the dinner hour. Although the sun still clung to the edge of the sky, the clouds had risen to conceal its red disk. Rain fell harshly. Phobias left the stage and crossed the darkened auditorium of what once had been a schoolhouse, threading his way between benches. The place would hold a couple of hundred spectators, including standees, all looking like so many mirror images of each other. But if the girl were among them, he did not doubt that he would recognize her instantly. She would stand out as clearly as a cut diamond among pebbles.

He stopped in a doorway and looked out, watching the rain converting the street dust to mud, listening to the drops pound the crude sidewalks.

A "man" passed, undismayed by the downpour, his naked body exuding slick oils impervious to the plummeting wetness. Sometimes—when he stopped to think of it—Phobias was amazed by how casually he referred to these creatures as men. For they were not. They were born of men as surely as mankind had once been spawned by the gods, but they were not men any more than Phobias was a god. Once—before the time of the great plague of madness that had cleansed Earth of its masters—they had been called androids, and had been scattered and few. Now they were many and man was only one.

But wait, thought Phobias. His heart pounded. What of her?

When the rain fell, did she feel as he did—threatened by dampness and chill? Where was she now? At home, he guessed, gazing through a steamy windowpane, watching the wetness that cascaded beyond. And what did the girl see out there? Did she see his face in the rain as he was seeing hers? Would she know that he was a human being, of genuine blood and ancient genes and true flesh, as he was convinced she was?

As suddenly as it had come, the storm fled. The sky briefly turned silver, then faded into night. The muddied street was empty now, silent. Phobias turned away and shuffled back to his props.

He sat alone upon the floodlighted stage, gazing at the massed audience patiently waiting. He could make out the dark polished faces of the throng standing along the dull walls and filling the seats. The identical heads loomed as though from some horribly repetitous nightmare. After the passage of centuries, Phobias was quite accustomed to the phenomenon and did not let it disturb him. He sat upon a stool, his legs crossed. A thin cigar—one of the few remaining in his private stock—glowed between the fingers of his right hand. He wore his black cape, his white leather gloves and his tall glimmering top hat. Behind him, neatly spread upon a wooden bench, were the tools of his trade: a polished wand, two glasses full of water, a red bandanna and a pair of long scissors. Nothing else.

But he would not be needing these things tonight, he told himself. For she had come at last, arriving after he had nearly surrendered hope. Now he could see her face clearly rising from the darkness of the last row, like a single star amid the blankness of an otherwise empty sky. He tried to smile at her to communicate his knowledge of her predicament, that of a human being among androids, just as he was. But when she failed to meet his gaze, he understood. It was not yet time for that. First the proof would have to be presented; that was only proper and fair. The smiles would naturally follow.

The audience waited stolidly. Take two hundred true human beings—the flesh-and-blood kind—and pack them into a school auditorium with promises of a magic show. Let the performer merely sit upon the bright stage, gazing ahead into their massed ranks. Feet would soon be shuffling, throats coughing, hands twitching and wringing. Such was not the case with these creatures. Phobias whispered contemptuously, "Androids!" Their communal capacity for patience was infinite, for man—true man—had made them that way.

At last Phobias decided to get on with it.

"Good evening," he said. "Ladies and gentlemen. Children." He tapped the ash from his smoldering cigar, took a lingering puff, blew thick, curling smoke. "Behind me on the bench you may observe the few articles with which I normally commence my performance." He smiled sympathetically. "But on this occasion I choose to treat the intelligence of my audience with the utmost respect. Here—"

Standing up carefully, smoking, he moved to the bench. He lifted the red bandanna and waved it.

"Do you really need to see me cut this old cloth into pieces, then watch while I recreate the whole before your astonished eyes?" He dropped the bandanna contemptuously, letting it flutter to the stage. "Or these glasses of water?" He tapped one with a fingernail. "Do you wish to observe as I suspend the contents above the floor of this stage, thus defying the laws of nature? And this magic wand?" Laughing, he tossed it over his shoulder. "I really don't think we have any need of it tonight. I feel none of you have come here tonight to see silly tricks. Let us dispense with these props. Forget them."

He stepped forward, striding to the lip of the stage. There he gazed ahead, balanced upon tensed knees like a sea captain staring into the entrails of an approaching storm.

"We shall move immediately to the crux—the red meat—of my act. I will need a volunteer." His eyes scanned the last row, passing back and forth across the place where the girl sat. "You, sir," he said randomly, then pointed at the dark figure of a man. "Step up here, please."

The man marched to the stage. Phobias awaited his arrival, standing calmly, trying not to look at the girl. The man approaching could have been any of those he had met already—the gas-station attendant or the storekeeper, Ernest—or any other one of them, seen or unseen, known or unknown, in this or any other town.

"I hope," said Phobias, "you do not object to assisting me for a brief moment." He flung away his cigar, letting the stump smolder on the wooden floor.

"Glad to help. What shall I—?"

Phobias cut off his words with a slashing hand. Then he proceeded to pace the length of the stage, glancing out at the huddled mass of the audience. Suddenly, like a dancer, he whirled. Then he spoke in a low, measured voice. He hardly comprehended his own words. How many thousand thousand times previously had he been thus impelled to state his role and purpose?

"I shall make you see what you have never seen before. I shall make you unable to see what you have always seen before. Why? How? That much I cannot freely reveal. But if, during the next few moments, you come to doubt the evidence of your own senses, then I say you must elect to doubt your sanity as well. And I guarantee you this: madness is not my trade. I am a magician and that alone. I toy with the unknown as an infant plays with a rattle. I allow you to glimpse—but only to glimpse—the mysteries of my personal detour into darkness."

He whirled again, swirling his cape.

"Now, sir," he said to the open-mouthed man from the audience, "would you mind stepping forward into the light so that everyone may get a good look at you?" Lightly he touched the man's hip. "Turn, if you don't mind. Show them that you're all here—let them know you're real.

Phobias could feel them out there, becoming excited. As excited as it was possible for them to become, that is. The older ones, having seen the magic before, communicated their sense of anticipation to their ignorant daughters and sons.

"Fine," Phobias said, placing his hands over his eyes. "Please—I must ask for silence." When he could not hear them breathing, he began to count aloud. "One ... two ... three ..." Reaching twenty, he lowered his hands, opened his eyes. Then, raising a clenched fist, he cut a swath through the air.

"Now!" he cried. He took a half-step forward.

And stopped.

"You are a dog," he told the dark person on the stage. "When you hear my fingers snap once."

"Yes."

"Then be a dog." And he snapped his fingers.

The man dropped instantly to his hands and knees. Without so much as glancing at him, Phobias went to the stool and sat down. Deliberately, as the man's shrill yips and yowls resounded, he placed a fresh cigar between his teeth. The man came trotting over, sniffing suspiciously.

"Roll over," Phobias commanded.

The man fell on his back, hands and feet pointing at the roof. Phobias walked to the edge of the stage, leaned down.

"Anyone have a match?"

Somebody did; Phobias lit up and puffed.

"Stop," he told the subject on the stage. "You may stand. On two feet." His fingers snapped. "You are yourself, again."

The man nodded. "I am."

Phobias faced his audience. As always, there was no applause, no laughter, nothing. A gentle hissing sound erupted briefly, but that was all. His eyes came to rest on the blond girl. She was gazing straight back at him. Blue eyes. Pale skin. For a moment he could not look away.

"Soon," he murmured.

"What?" queried the man.

Phobias wrenched himself back to business. "You remember nothing?"

"No," the man admitted.

Phobias realized he was rushing his act, forcing the end that ought not to come for several hours. Often in the past he had performed until dawn, lusting in the excitement of his own performance, refusing to relinquish the stage until he had given up all hope of extracting some response. Not that response ever came. These people—*androids,* he thought— did not enjoy what he did, for they could enjoy nothing—not love for fear, not magic. They could pay attention, yes. And they could become excited. Curiosity and excitation had been built into them as survival tools, but that was about it.

"He is a bird," Phobias told the audience. The man's face, when Phobias looked at it, was blank. "You are a bird."

"I am."

"Then, for us, fly." And snapped his fingers.

The man flapped his arms, straining at the flat and dusty air.

Phobias whispered to the audience, "He flies."

Then he sat on his stool again, smoking. The audience watched the flight of the captive bird. What was it to them? Hawk? Eagle? Sparrow? Once, in a distant village in the southern continent, Phobias had said, "He is a bird." But the villagers had never seen an actual bird. Phobias remembered that rocky mocking land, treeless, where the sun rarely came. "He flies." But they had not known. They had asked for explanations . . .

This man cawed and twisted on the stage, arms helplessly flapping. The audience watched silently.

Phobias rose from the stool, waved his cigar. "You are yourself," he said.

The man ceased his charade, regained awareness. But still no applause, no laughter. Silence.

Phobias bowed stiffly.

"And now," he announced, "the heart of my act. A descent into the great chasm of the unknown." He waved the first volunteer away. "Another?" he asked but there was none. Phobias searched the audience, pointed. "You, sir." A man sitting beside the blond girl. "I ask that you join me, please."

Phobias watched the girl, seeing surprise and wonder on her face. And more. Was it fear he saw? Pleasure? It had been so long since he had witnessed true emotion in another that interpretation of her expression came hard to him.

The man stood beside him. Phobias could not stop himself: "That girl—" His eyes indicated whom he meant. "Is she your daughter?"

"She is."

"Where did you get her?"

"From . . . from . . ." The man struggled to speak the ugly forbidden term.

"Not from there. Tell me the truth."

"Well, from . . . from . . ."

It was the girl who made Phobias stop. He was gazing at her again. Her lips folded downward, the pale skin above her eyes creased and strained—her whole cast of countenance begged him not to proceed.

He hesitated, then addressed the audience, using well-memorized phrases to conceal his confusion. "I must ask for complete silence. Even the slightest sound might destroy the mental equilibrium necessary for what shall ensue. This man—" gesturing behind—"will soon die. It is my intention to return him then to full and natural life."

Murmurs of curiosity from the audience. Hisses of excitement.

Phobias said, "Lie down. Yes. That's right. Now extend your arms straight out from your sides. And your feet—separate the heels. Yes, that's fine." Normally this would be the climax of his act—his grandest achievement. "No, don't close your eyes. You must keep them open."

He threw away the cigar, faced his audience.

"Another volunteer." He selected a woman from the front row. "Come up here, would you?"

When everything was ready—the man lying upon the stage, the woman standing at his side—Phobias kneeled. He moved his hands over the man—first down and then up—covering every square inch of the body but never actually touching it.

"Death calls to you," Phobias said. "He shall bestow upon you peace and tranquillity. You hear the call. Life ebbs from your physical self. Although you can feel life leaving, you are not afraid. You are lonely but prepared. Tell me."

"I am lonely," the man echoed softly. "I am prepared."

"Not afraid?"

"No, I am not afraid."

"Death has come to claim you. Life flows gently away. You feel it abandon your lungs, your heart. From them, your life flows like clean water into the veins of your arms. Into your skin. Into the air—" Phobias snapped his fingers. "Now life is gone!"

The man upon the floor neither moved nor spoke.

"He is dead," Phobias said. Regaining his feet, with his hands he swept the dust from his knees. He eyed the woman crouched beside the supine man. "Is he breathing?"

"No," she said woodenly.

"Check his heart."

She placed her ear upon the man's breast.

"Tell them that he's dead," Phobias said.

Softly the woman intoned: "He is dead."

"Louder."

Distinctly: "He is dead."

Phobias nodded. "Thank you." He allowed the woman to leave the stage.

He could not resist a look at the girl. Yes—that was fear on her face. He was sure of it. Emotion!

Phobias pointed a finger at her.

"Come here," he said. "Come up here."

She hesitated, then walked slowly to the stage and mounted it. Now it was his turn to feel fear. He reached into a pocket and felt for a cigar.

"Is he really dead?"

Phobias stared at her adolescent beauty. A bare yard separated them. "He is."

She crouched. Raising the subject's wrist in her hand, she gazed up at Phobias.

"Tell them," he said.

She released the wrist. The hand dropped soundly to the floor. "Tell them what?"

"Tell them he's dead."

"But he's not."

"He's not dead?"

"No."

"But tell them that he is."

The girl lowered her head, placing her ear upon her father's heart.

Then she stood up. "No, he's not dead."

"You won't tell them that he is."

"Of course not. He isn't."

"You are a dog," Phobias said.

She shook her head.

"Fly."

"I can't fly."

"Fly!" he shouted.

"No!" She rushed toward him, pounded his chest with little fists. "You make him stand up—I want him to be conscious again."

Phobias nodded. He told the dead man: "You are living." But the magician did not mean it. No, it was she who was alive—not the cold dead creature now rising from the floor.

Even in life, that thing would always be dead. But she—she lived.

At last he had elicited the response sought so long. Denial. Emotional opposition.

His eyes were stinging with the torment of his joy.

Phobias forced them to give him the gasoline. At first they had refused, saying that he had failed to fulfill the agreement. The children had been sorely disappointed.

Phobias said, "Do what I ask. I am ordering you. Bring gasoline. Prepare my car."

And then they had acceded. For the first time in centuries he had used his magical powers outside the confines of his act—for personal and private gain. But he felt that he possessed the right—for was he not a man?

The girl lived outside the town. He made them tell him exactly where. He drove there quickly, careless of the ruts and pits of the decayed highway. The house was set back from the road. A single window—a rectangle of yellow amid the black—gleamed brightly.

Asleep? He approached and pressed his face to the glass. No, her eyes were open. She lay upon her back in a narrow bed. Pink sheets. The walls of the bedroom—plain and undecorated—were also pink.

He broke the window-glass with a rock, reached inside, raised the lower frame. She did not stir as he crawled through the opening. Then he paused, listening to the silence of the house.

The girl opened her eyes then. She showed no alarm.

"What do you want?"

"I've come—" Phobias stopped. He thought he had heard a footfall. "I'll tell you later. Get up. We're going."

"Where?"

He waved an arm. "Away."

"They'll stop us."

He laughed, striving to calm her immature misgivings. Then he heard it again: feet striking the floor. Coming closer. He grasped at the noise, saying, "If you don't come with me, I'll have to make him dead. You saw what I can do!"

Frowning, she swung out of bed, started for the closet.

Phobias stopped her. "You don't have to take anything. Hurry!"

He exited by way of the window. When his feet touched the grass, she stood at his side.

"This way."

"They'll follow and catch us," she insisted.

"No," he said.

"The other ones—I know they will."

Phobias laughed easily, placing an arm around her shoulders. "It's just us, now."

But as they reached the road he looked over his shoulder, saw a line of fire approaching from town. Dozens of flaming torches swam in the night.

"Them?" he cried.

"Yes. I told you." She drew closer. They clung to each other. "Let me return to the house," she begged.

"No." He forced her into the car. "This machine can smash them, outrun them." He started the engine. "Watch."

They were coming from every direction now. Phobias did not hesitate. He ran the car straight at their torches. A gleam of fire singed his eyes. Then a vision of incredible stunning whiteness.

They were through.

He exulted, shouting, slapping the steering wheel: "See, see!"

The girl peered behind through the rear window. "They're still there," she said.

"But we're here." He slowed the car to prove that everything was all right.

"Oh, no." She glared at him, shaking her head. "Don't you know they can drive, too?"

"Not like us," he said.

As they neared the dark vastness of the forest, the first scattered trees heaved up beside the road like towering signs of warning. Phobias stopped the car. He opened the rear gate and removed the tools of his trade and threw them into the underbrush. As he did, he giggled. The girl seemed half asleep. But she smiled when he told her, "I won't need them now."

They could live in the forest, he thought. Survival lay easily at their fingertips. The car zoomed forward. Were they ready yet for sons and daughters? For the new race to be born from the remnants of the old. For man returning to again rule his own domain. He reached out a hand and caressed her slender wrist. Her eyes, open but unaware barely flickered. On and on they drove.

Soon they were in the thickest part of the forest. The ancient road wound among huge twisted trees. The girl had slumped into a deep silence punctuated by frantic glances over her shoulder. They passed through a clearing and then a dark huddled village, a lamp suddenly flashing from one window as their headlight-beams stroked the tumbledown homes.

"I wasn't always the last man," he said. He tried to explain to her. Before the plague of madness more than four billion human beings had teemed the Earth. Afterward, barely a few thousand remained. He told her everything he knew of those forgotten times. He had been an astronaut, he said proudly.

"A what?" she asked.

He pointed through the windshield. Here the trees were thinned. Moonlight gleamed silver from a roadside pond whose silent dark waters reinforced his bitter recollections of yesterday. "See those lights." He meant the stars. "Know what they are?"

She knew.

"Well, I went up there."

"To the stars?"

"No, but to planets. Jupiter. Mars. Also the moon."

"You traveled to the moon?"

"I did."

"How? By magic?"

A kind of magic, he said, and promised to explain someday. Then he told her that he had been one of a dozen men and women selected to make the first journey to a star—not a planet or a moon, but a real star. The voyage was to last four hundred years. The crew had been injected with a complex of new drugs designed to increase longevity. "So we could live to see our world again." All of that had happened thousands of years ago. "But the plague of madness came, and because of it none of us ever left. We stayed here on Earth and I, at least, have lived almost forever. Those drugs—"

He remembered well. A year before the scheduled departure, the starship crew had gone into training. They had been placed inside a model of the ship that would carry them to the stars, and this model had been lowered to the bottom of the Pacific Ocean. Suitably shielded from the pressure at ocean depths, of course. There they had stayed for seven

months, constantly monitored from above but without the
security of reciprocal contact or any knowledge of exterior
time or events. They were left alone—a dozen men and
women—forced to live wholly isolated from the world.

"And we survived," he said. "But when our training time
was over and we were raised to the surface, we were greeted
only by androids. Androids and corpses and a handful of
madmen."

The plague of madness had first broken out within the
Ganymede settlement on one of the moons of Jupiter. In less
than a month, every man in the colony had been dead.

"The androids told us," said Phobias, "that the disease
progressed in three distinct stages. The first, lasting approximately a week, was classic schizophrenia. For many years it
had been theorized that the underlying causes of that mental
disorder were physical—viral, bacteriological, something like
that. And now it was proved. The plague victim immediately
lost all touch with reality. In the second stage, he became
catatonic. In the third, he died. There were no survivors once
the disease began."

The girl said wearily, "My name is Eva."

"Eva! How beautiful. Listen to me, Eva. That plague spread
faster than any other in history. It leaped from Ganymede to
Mars and then to Earth. In less than six months, everyone
susceptible was either dead or dying. We asked the androids
whether any men at all had survived.

" 'Only those like yourselves,' they told us. 'Those inocu-
lated with the longevity medicine. Too late it was realized
that the stuff is a preventive. Oh, some others—past sufferers
from schizophrenia, both the cured and uncured; they are
immune and they have survived. And us—androids. We were
not affected.' "

Phobias paused, negotiating the old car over a jagged hole
in the road. He glanced at the girl. Was she listening?

"So we set off in search of the survivors, finding most of
them—a few thousand—and the years passed and they died
too but we did not. It was a lonely life for us. But a simple
one, for the androids were always there to tend to our desires.
But gradually the crew began to die off. Accidents occurred.
A woman was murdered by a man who had loved her for more
than three hundred years. I left, taking one of the other
women with me. We took an automobile and started to
wander the world."

And the androids had forgotten. They had reproduced themselves by virtue of the knowledge man had granted them, maintaining the automated factories. When the old ones of the first generation—those who had lived through the plague—wore out and were discarded, their grandsons and granddaughters had continued on, ignorant of what they truly were. Indeed, they had come to call themselves "men." And their numbers had rapidly multiplied and in time they had peopled the world in the same great numbers as their original creators. "And my race—our race—the human race—toppled to the very edge of extinction."

Phobias had slowed the car, was peering intently through the windshield.

"She died near here. The woman. Oh, I can't remember exactly when. A bolt of lightning came from the sky and killed her instantly—killed her and our horses and set the wagon afire. I nearly died, too. Later I tried to find the others but all were gone. Some had died. The rest were lost. Since then, I have continued to wander alone—a magician—Phobias—moving quietly through the android towns and villages. Searching for a human being. But now I have found one. I am not alone any more."

She had fallen asleep, slumped back in the seat, face buried in the dark.

He pulled over to the side of the road, killed the engine and climbed out. The silence woke her. An instant later she was standing beside him, gazing up at dark treetops and the stars.

"I don't want to drive any more," he said. "We can stay here till morning."

"All right."

He pointed into the trees. "Let's take a look." He lighted a match to show the way. Then another. The forest around them whispered in the wind.

"Here." He drew her down beneath a massive balsam. "Let's rest here. The air is sweet and the needles make the ground soft."

He wanted to take her in his arms. He placed his dead cigar between his teeth and relit it. No ... too soon. She had curled up at his feet, as if asleep, but the glare of the match revealed her eyes open and alert.

"That smells awful," she said.

He smiled, exhaling smoke. "Not to me." He stretched out comfortably. "Did you hear what I told you?"

"Most of it, I guess."

"Then you must understand why I ran off with you, Eva. You don't belong there with those—those things. You belong here with me. We're the only two human beings left—and we can people the earth!"

He sensed her hesitation, her reluctance to reply. She was burdened with unspoken words.

"What is it?" he demanded.

"I can't tell you, magician."

"Why?"

"They said I shouldn't. That there was no need. You weren't supposed to see me. You weren't supposed to do this—take me away. I want to go home."

"No!" He grabbed her. In his fingers, her wrist seemed fragile as a twig. "What have you to tell me? Out with it!"

"All right, then. We're not the same."

A long silence.

"We are!" he cried piteously. "We must be."

"No," she said. "I'm not like you. And there are more of us, many more, more each day. We're not like you or like the androids either. We're different."

"Impossible! Are you saying that you are neither human nor android?"

Instead of answering she remarked softly, without surprise, "Here they come."

He stared, seeing nothing at first. Then their torches burst into life, painting the forest with crude light. Phobias leaped to his feet, holding the girl.

Relentlessly they closed in. Fair-haired. Ghostly pale. Was it possible that all of them were human? Phobias tried desperately to think.

"Let her go," said their spokesman, a blond woman whose face was young, whose unclad body shown pallid in the torchlight.

"No!" shouted Phobias. "She's a human being—like me. She's not yours. Unless . . ." He gulped. He could not bring himself to ask the question.

But the woman answered it, shaking her head. "We are not human, nor is she. She is one of us."

"The commandments," he said desperately. "She does not obey." He knew the commandments perfectly; they had served him long and well. Born within all androids: *Obey the directions of man. Cause no harm to befall his form.*

The woman stepped closer. She stopped inches in front of Phobias and raised her hand. Sharply, coldly, she slapped his face. He tasted blood upon his lips.

"Give her to me," the woman said, reaching out. "Or do you want us to beat you?"

He glanced past the woman's bare shoulders. There were so many of them—dozens—men, women, children—blond and pale, blue-eyed. Angry. Resentful. They were able to feel and show emotion. Like Eva.

"How many are there?" he asked.

"More each day. All over the world. Didn't you realize it had to happen? We have read the old records. We know how it began. And this was the way it had to end. Man created androids to serve him. But man perished. And now androids have become men themselves."

"A lie," Phobias said. "Except in name only, you can't be men. You come from factories—like machines. Men are born."

The woman reached out and snatched the girl, drew her close. The two hugged each other. "This girl," the woman said, "is my daughter. She was born to me. Her father, whom you hypnotized, is grandson of Kanakoe, who developed the process. Or maybe evolution developed it, and revealed it first in Kanakoe. But we don't need the factories. We are the new humanity. But you, Phobias, are the old."

A great loneliness engulfed him. He felt more alone than ever before. He was Phobias, the magician, unique, the last man. When he commanded all were required to obey. But now the blood ran down his face and he was humbled.

"You hid yourselves from me," he said. "You disguised yourselves to look like the others. You wouldn't let me know."

"We saw no purpose in hurting you. If it hadn't been for your race, ours would never have existed. We owed you something—the comfort of ignorance, at least. And you could not damage us, because you are the last."

"I am the last," he whispered. He watched the woman and her daughter join the others. Illuminated by torchlight they disappeared into the forest, leaving thick darkness behind. He slumped down upon the dry needles and held his head in his trembling hands. "I am the last man," he said. "The only man."

* * *

Phobias, the magician, standing upon the stage, calmly stared
out at his audience. Behind him, neatly arranged upon a
bench, lay his reclaimed props. Where was he? He was not
certain, but it made no difference. One village was like
another. He traveled the world in endless circles, determined
to prove what he knew so well: that he was the last man, the
only man.

The audience regarded him with pity. He nearly laughed
in their faces. Their assumed compassion mocked their brutal honesty. They lied to him no longer. They rubbed his nose
in the truth they had kept concealed so long. But he would
prove to them somehow that he alone was a proper human.
They would obey him—he would enforce the commandments—
he would show them the deepest truths and force them to see.

Their faces were mostly pale. Blond hair. Blue eyes that
shone and glimmered. Raising an arm, he pointed at a tall
man in the first row.

"Step forward," he said. "Come here."

The man came obediently. For a moment, Phobias experienced hope. Could he be winning at last? Had they finally
chosen to acknowledge his superiority? They were androids.
Whether born from factory or womb, they were not men.
When he told them to die, they must cease living. When he
said, "You are a bird," they must fly. What he told them to
hear, they must hear. What he told them to see, they must
see.

The man stood beside him on the stage. Phobias raised his
wand and drew a rapid cross in the air. "I am a man," he told
the audience, "and you are androids. When I command, you
must obey."

Turning, he faced his subject. The man met his gaze with
cold blue eyes. Softly, Phobias said, "You are a bird—now
fly."

The man stood frozen, motionless.

Phobias shouted: "Fly!"

The man looked at his feet.

"You must! I command you! Fly!"

"No," the man said softly.

Phobias turned away. Would it ever come? Would they
ever acknowledge his rightful station? Or would he be forced
to wander alone for centuries more until that fateful day
when some accident would finally strike him down and he

would die, leaving the Earth to be ruled by them alone?

He waved his hand meekly at the man: "You may go back and sit down—please."

There was nothing else for him. He had to go on. Eternity was his, and there was nothing else for him to do.

He pointed blindly into the audience. "You," he said. As the girl came forward, blond hair as long as her spine, he prepared himself to try again. He would command—she would obey.

What choice did he have? Phobias was the last man. Wasn't he?

Charles L. Harness

Born in Texas in 1915, Charles L. Harness worked for the United States Bureau of Mines and then became a patent attorney for several major corporations. His total output as a part-time science fiction writer is not great, but it is all interesting, particularly "The Rose," a stunning blend of speculation on the relationship of science and art. His novels include *The Ring of Ritornel* (1968), *Flight into Yesterday* (also known as *The Paradox Men*, 1953), and *The Catalyst* (1980).

"The New Reality" is an excellent and unusual story which suggests that reality is determined by what we think it is.

THE NEW REALITY

by Charles L. Harness

PRENTISS CRAWLED INTO THE CAR, drew the extension connector from his concealed throat mike from its clip in his right sleeve, and plugged it into the ignition key socket.

After a moment he said, "Get me the Censor."

The seconds passed as he heard the click of forming circuits. Then: "E speaking."

"Prentiss, honey."

"Call me 'E,' Prentiss. What news?"

"I've met five classes under Professor Luce. He has a private lab. Doesn't confide in his graduate students. Evidently conducting secret experiments in comparative psychology. Rats and such. Nothing overtly censorable."

"I see. What are your plans?"

"I'll have his lab searched tonight. If nothing turns up, I'll recommend a drop."

"I'd prefer that you search the lab yourself."

A. Prentiss Rogers concealed his surprise and annoyance. "Very well."

His ear button clicked a dismissal.

With puzzled irritation he snapped the plug from the dash socket, started the car, and eased it down the drive into the boulevard bordering the university.

Didn't she realize that he was a busy Field Director with a couple of hundred men under him fully capable of making a routine night search? Undoubtedly she knew just that, but nevertheless was requiring that he do it himself. Why?

And why had she assigned Professor Luce to him personally, squandering so many of his precious hours, when half a dozen of his bright young physical philosophers could have handled it? Nevertheless E, from behind the august anonymity of her solitary initial, had been adamant.

A mile away he turned into a garage on a deserted side street and drew up alongside a Cadillac.

Crush sprang out of the big car and silently held the rear door open for him.

Prentiss got in. "We have a job tonight."

His aide hesitated a fraction of a second before slamming the door behind him. Prentiss knew that the squat, asthmatic little man was surprised and delighted.

As for Crush, he'd never got it through his head that the control of human knowledge was a grim and hateful business, not a kind of cruel lark.

"Very good, sir," wheezed Crush, climbing in behind the wheel. "Shall I reserve a sleeping room at the Bureau for the evening?"

"Can't afford to sleep," grumbled Prentiss. "Desk so high now I can't see over it. Take a nap yourself, if you want to."

"Yes, sir. If I feel the need of it, sir."

The ontologist shot a bitter glance at the back of the man's head. No, Crush wouldn't sleep, but not because worry would keep him awake. A holdover from the days when all a Censor man had was a sleepless curiosity and a pocket Geiger, Crush was serenely untroubled by the dangerous and unfathomable implications of philosophical nucleonics. For Crush, "ontology" was just another definition in the dictionary: "The science of reality."

The little aide could never grasp the idea that unless a sane worldwide pattern of nucleonic investigation were followed, some one in Australia—or next door—might one day throw a switch and alter the shape of that reality. That's what made Crush so valuable; he just didn't know enough to be afraid.

Prentiss had clipped the hairs from his nostrils and so far had breathed in complete silence. But now, as that cavernous face was turned toward where he lay stomach-to-earth in the sheltering darkness, his lungs convulsed in an audible gasp.

The mild, polite, somewhat abstracted academic features of Professor Luce were transformed. The face beyond the lab window was now flushed, the lips were drawn back in soundless amusement, the sunken black eyes were dancing with red pinpoints of flame.

By brute will the ontologist forced his attention back to the rat.

Four times in the past few minutes he had watched the animal run down an inclined chute until it reached a fork, choose one fork, receive what must be a nerve-shattering electric shock, and then be replaced in the chute-beginning for the next run. No matter which alternative fork was chosen, the animal always had been shocked into convulsions.

On this fifth run the rat, despite needling blasts of compressed air from the chute walls, was slowing down. Just before it reached the fork it stopped completely.

The air jets struck at it again, and little cones of up-ended gray fur danced on its rump and flanks.

It gradually ceased to tremble; its respiration dropped to normal. It seemed to Prentiss that its eyes were shut.

The air jets lashed out again. It gave no notice, but just lay there, quiescent, in a near coma.

As he peered into the window, Prentiss saw the tall man walk languidly over to the little animal and run a long hooklike forefinger over its back. No reaction. The professor then said something, evidently in a soft slurred voice, for Prentiss had difficulty in reading his lips.

"—when both alternatives are wrong for you, but you *must* do something, you hesitate, don't you, little one? You slow down, and you are lost. You are no longer a rat. Do you know what the universe would be like if a *photon* should slow down? You don't? Have you ever taken a bite out of a balloon, little friend? Just the tiniest possible bite?"

Prentiss cursed. The Professor had turned and was walking toward the cages with the animal, and although he was apparently still talking, his lips were no longer visible.

After relatching the cage door the professor walked toward the lab entrance, glanced carefully around the room, and then, as he was reaching for the light switch, looked toward Prentiss's window.

For a moment the investigator was convinced that by some nameless power the professor was looking into the darkness, straight into his eyes.

He exhaled slowly. It was preposterous.

The room was plunged in darkness.

The investigator blinked and closed his eyes. He wouldn't really have to worry until he heard the lab door opening on the opposite side of the little building.

The door didn't open. Prentiss squinted into the darkness of the room.

Where the professor's head had been were now two mysterious tiny red flames, like candles.

Something must be reflecting from the professor's corneas. But the room was dark; there was no light to be reflected. The flame-eyes continued their illusion of studying him.

The hair was crawling on Prentiss's neck when the twin lights finally vanished and he heard the sound of the lab door opening.

As the slow heavy tread died away down the flagstones to the street, Prentiss gulped in a huge lungful of the chill night air and rubbed his sweating face against his sleeve.

What had got into him? He was acting like the greenest cub. He was glad that Crush had to man the televisor relay in the Cadillac and couldn't see him.

He got to his hands and knees and crept silently toward the darkened window. It was a simple sliding sash, and a few seconds sufficed to drill through the glass and insert a hook around the sash lock. The rats began a nervous squeaking as he lowered himself into the darkness of the basement room.

His ear-receptor sounded. "The prof is coming back!" wheezed Crush's tinny voice.

Prentiss said something under his breath, but did not pause in drawing his infrared scanner from his pocket.

He touched his fingers to his throat mike. "Signal when he reaches the bend in the walk," he said. "And be sure you get this on the visor tape."

The apparatus got his first attention.

The investigator had memorized its position perfectly. Approaching as closely in the darkness as he dared, he panned the scanner over some very interesting apparatus that he had noticed on the table.

Then he turned to the books on the desk, regretting that he wouldn't have time to record more than a few pages.

"He's at the bend," warned Crush.

"Okay," mumbled Prentiss, running sensitive fingers over the book bindings. He selected one, opened it at random, and ran the scanner over the invisible pages. "Is this coming through?" he demanded.

"Chief, *he's at the door!*"

Prentiss had to push back the volume without scanning

any more of it. He had just relocked the sash when the lab door swung open.

A couple of hours later the ontologist bid good-morning to his receptionist and secretaries and stepped into his private office. He dropped with tired thoughtfulness into his swivel chair and pulled out the infrared negatives that Crush had prepared in the Cadillac darkroom. The page from the old German diary was particularly intriguing. He laboriously translated it once more:

As I got deeper into the manuscript, my mouth grew dry, and my heart began to pound. This, I knew, was a contribution the like of which my family has not seen since Copernicus, Roger Bacon, or perhaps even Aristotle. It seemed incredible that this silent little man, who had never been outside of Koenigsberg, should hold the key to the universe—the *Critique of Pure Reason,* he calls it. And I doubt that even he realizes the ultimate portent of his teaching, for he says we cannot know the real shape or nature of anything, that is, the Thing-in-Itself, the Ding-an-Sich, or *noumenon.* He holds that this is the ultimate unknowable, reserved to the gods. He doesn't suspect that, century by century, mankind is nearing this final realization of the final things. Even this brilliant man would probably say that the earth was round in 600 B.C., even as it is today. But *I* know it was flat, then—as truly flat as it is truly round today. What has changed? Not the Thing-in-Itself we call the earth. No, it is the mind of man that has changed. But in his preposterous blindness, he mistakes what is really his own mental quickening for a broadened application of science and more precise methods of investigation—

Prentiss smiled.

Luce was undoubtedly a collector of philosophic incunabula. Odd hobby, but that's all it could be—a hobby. Obviously the earth had never been flat, and in fact hadn't changed shape substantially in the last couple of billion years. Certainly any notions as to the flatness of the earth held by primitives of a few thousand years ago or even by contemporaries of Kant were due to their ignorance rather than to accurate observation, and a man of Luce's erudition could only be amused by them.

Again Prentiss found himself smiling with the tolerance of a man standing on the shoulders of twenty centuries of science. The primitives, of course, did the best they could. They just didn't know. They worked with childish premises and infantile instruments.

His brows creased. To assume they had used childish premises was begging the question. On the other hand, was it really worth a second thought? All he could hope to discover would be a few instances of how inferior apparatus coupled perhaps with unsophisticated deductions had oversimplified the world of the ancients. Still, anything that interested the strange Dr. Luce automatically interested him, Prentiss, until the case was closed.

He dictated into the scriptor:

"Memorandum to Geodetic Section. Rush a paragraph history of ideas concerning shape of earth. Prentiss."

Duty done, he promptly forgot it and turned to the heavy accumulation of reports on his desk.

A quarter of an hour later the scriptor rang and began typing an incoming message.

To the Director. Re your request for brief history of earth's shape. Chaldeans and Babylonians (per clay tablets from library of Assurbanipal), Egyptians (per Ahmes papyrus, ca. 1700 B.C.), Cretans (per inscriptions in royal library at Knossos, ca. 1300 B.C.), Chinese (per Chou Kung ms. ca. 1100 B.C.), Phoenicians (per fragments at Tyre ca. 900 B.C.), Hebrews (per unknown Biblical historian ca. 850 B.C.), and early Greeks (per map of widely-traveled geographer Hecataeus, 517 B.C.) assumed earth to be flat disc. But from the 5th century B.C. forward earth's sphericity universally recognized. . . .

There were a few more lines, winding up with the work done on corrections for flattening at poles, but Prentiss had already lost interest. The report threw no light on Luce's hobby and was devoid of ontological implications.

He tossed the script into the waste basket and returned to the reports before him.

A few minutes later he twisted uneasily in his chair, eyed the scriptor in annoyance, then forced himself back to his work.

No use.

Deriding himself for an idiot, he growled at the machine: "Memorandum to Geodetic. Re your memo history earth's shape. How do you account for change to belief in sphericity after Hecataeus? Rush. Prentiss."

The seconds ticked by.

He drummed on his desk impatiently, then got up and began pacing the floor.

When the scriptor rang, he bounded back and leaned over his desk, watching the words being typed out.

Late Greeks based spherical shape on observation that mast of approaching ship appeared first, then prow. Not known why similar observation not made by earlier seafaring peoples. . . .

Prentiss rubbed his cheek in perplexity. What was he fishing for?

He thrust the half-born conjecture that the earth really had once been flat back into his mental recesses.

Well, then how about the heavens? Surely there was no record of their having changed during man's brief lifetime.

He'd try one more shot and quit.

"Memo to Astronomy Division. Rush paragraph on early vs. modern sun size and distance."

A few minutes later he was reading the reply:

Skipping Plato, whose data are believed baseless (he measured sun's distance at only twice that of moon), we come to earliest recognized "authority." Ptolemy (Almagest, ca. 140 A.D. measured sun radius as 5.5 that of earth (as against 109 actual); measured sun distance at 1210 (23,000 actual). Fairly accurate measurements date only from 17th and 18th centuries. . . .

He'd read all that somewhere. The difference was easily explained by their primitive instruments. It was insane to keep this up.

But it was too late.

"Memo to Astronomy. Were erroneous Ptolemaic measurements due to lack of precision instruments?"

Soon he had his reply:

To Director: Source of Ptolemy's errors in solar measurement not clearly understood. Used astrolabe precise to 10 seconds and clepsydra water clock incorporating Hero's improvements. With same instruments, and using modern value of pi, Ptolemy measured moon radius (0.29 earth radius vs. 0.273 actual) and distance (59 earth radii vs. 60 ⅓ actual). Hence instruments reasonably precise. And note that Copernicus, using quasi-modern instruments and technique, "confirmed" Ptolemaic figure of sun's distance at 1200 earth radii. No explanation known for glaring error.

Unless, suggested something within Prentiss's mind, the sun were closer and much different before the 17th century, when Newton was telling the world where and how big the sun *ought* to be. But *that* solution was too absurd for further consideration. He would sooner assume his complete insanity.

Puzzled, the ontologist gnawed his lower lip and stared at the message in the scriptor.

In his abstraction he found himself peering at the symbol "pi" in the scriptor message. *There*, at least, was something that had always been the same, and would endure for all time. He reached over to knock out his pipe in the big circular ash tray by the scriptor and paused in the middle of the second tap. From his desk he fished a tape measure and stretched it across the tray. Ten inches. And then around the circumference. Thirty-one and a half inches. Good enough considering. It was a result any curious schoolboy could get.

He turned to the scriptor again.

"Memo to Math Section. Rush paragraph history on value of pi. Prentiss."

He didn't have to wait long.

To Director. Re history "pi." Babylonians used value of 3.00. Aristotle made fairly accurate physical and theoretical evaluations. Archimedes first to arrive at modern value, using theory of limits. . . .

There was more, but it was lost on Prentiss. It was inconceivable, of course, that pi had grown during the two millennia that separated the Babylonians from Archimedes. And yet, it was exasperating. Why hadn't they done any better than 3.00? Any child with a piece of string could have demonstrated their error. Countless generations of wise, careful Chaldean astronomers, measuring time and star positions with such incredible accuracy, all coming to grief with a piece of string and pi. It didn't make sense. And certainly pi hadn't grown, any more than the Babylonian 360-day year had grown into the modern 365-day year. It had always been the same, he told himself. The primitives hadn't measured accurately, that was all. That *had* to be the explanation.

He hoped.

He sat down at his desk again, stared a moment at his memo pad and wrote:

Check history of gravity—acceleration. Believe Aristotle unable detect acceleration. Galileo used same instruments, including same crude water clock, and found it. Why? . . . Any reported transits of Vulcan since 1914, when Einstein explained eccentricity of Mercury orbit by relativity instead of by hypothetical sunward planet? . . . How could Oliver Lodge detect an ether-drift and Michelson not? Conceivable that Lorentz contraction not a physical fact before Michelson experiment? . . . How many chemical elements were predicted before discovered?

He tapped absently on the pad a few times, then rang for a research assistant. He'd barely have time to explain what he wanted before he had to meet his class under Luce.

And he still wasn't sure where the rats fitted in.

Curtly Professor Luce brought his address to a close.

"Well, gentlemen," he said, "I guess we'll have to continue this at our next lecture. We seem to have run over a little; class dismissed. Oh, Mr. Prentiss!"

The investigator looked up in genuine surprise. "Yes, sir?" The thin gun in his shoulder holster suddenly felt satisfyingly fat.

He realized that the crucial moment was near, that he would know before he left the campus whether this strange man was a harmless physicist, devoted to his life-work and his queer hobby, or whether he was an incarnate danger to mankind. The professor was acting out of turn, and it was an unexpected break.

"Mr. Prentiss," continued Luce from the lecture platform, "may I see you in my office a moment before you leave?"

Prentiss said, "Certainly." As the group broke up he followed the gaunt scientist through the door that led to Luce's little office behind the lecture room.

At the doorway he hesitated almost imperceptibly; Luce saw it and bowed sardonically. "After you, sir!"

Then the tall man indicated a chair near his desk. "Sit down, Mr. Prentiss."

For a lont moment the seated men studied each other.

Finally the professor spoke. "About fifteen years ago a brilliant young man named Rogers wrote a doctoral dissertation at the University of Vienna on what he called . . 'Involuntary Conformation of Incoming Sensoria to Apperception Mass.' "

Prentiss began fishing for his pipe. "Indeed?"

"One copy of the dissertation was sent to the Scholarship Society that was financing his studies. All others were seized by the International Bureau of the Censor, and accordingly a demand was made on the Scholarship Society for its copy. But it couldn't be found."

Prentiss was concentrating on lighting his pipe. He wondered if the faint trembling of the match flame was visible.

The professor turned to his desk, opened the top drawer and pulled out a slim brochure bound in black leather.

The investigator coughed out a cloud of smoke.

The professor did not seem to notice, but opened the front cover and began reading: " '—a dissertation in partial fulfillment of the requirements for the degree of Doctor of Philosophy at the University of Vienna. A. P. Rogers, Vienna, 1957.' " The man closed the book and studied it thoughtfully. "Adrian Prentiss Rogers—the owner of a brain whose like is seen not once in a century. He exposed the gods—then vanished."

Prentiss suppressed a shiver as he met those sunken implacable eye-caverns.

The cat-and-mouse was over. In a way, he was relieved.

"Why did you vanish then, Mr. Prentiss-Rogers?" demanded Luce. "And why do you now reappear?"

The investigator blew a cloud of smoke toward the low ceiling. "To prevent people like you from introducing sensoria that *can't* be conformed to our present apperception mass. To keep reality as is. That answers both questions, I think.'

The other man smiled. It was not a good thing to see. "Have you succeeded?"

"I don't know. So far, I suppose."

The gaunt man shrugged his shoulders. "You ignore tomorrow, then. I think you have failed, but I can't be sure, of course, until I actually perform the experiment that will create novel sensoria." He leaned forward. "I'll come to the point, Mr. Prentiss-Rogers. Next to yourself—and possibly excepting the Censor—I know more about the mathematical approach to reality than anyone else in the world. I may even know things about it that you don't. On other phases of it I'm weak—because I developed your results on the basis of mere logic rather than insight. And logic, we know, is applicable only within indeterminate limits. But in developing a practical device—an actual machine—for the wholesale alteration of incoming sensoria, I'm enormously ahead of you. You saw my apparatus last night, Mr. Prentiss-Rogers? Oh, come, don't be coy."

Prentiss drew deeply on his pipe.

"I saw it."

"Did you understand it?"

"No. It wasn't all there. At least, the apparatus on the table was incomplete. There's more to it than a Nicol prism and a goniometer."

"Ah, you are clever! Yes, I was wise in not permitting you to remain very long—no longer than necessary to whet your curiosity. Look, then! I offer you a partnership. Check my data and apparatus; in return you may be present when I run the experiment. We will attain enlightenment together. We will know all things. We will be gods!"

"And what about two billion other human beings?" said Prentiss, pressing softly at his shoulder holster.

The professor smiled faintly. "Their lunacy—assuming they continue to exist at all—may become slightly more pronounced, of course. But why worry about them?

"Don't expect me to believe this aura of altruism, Mr. Prentiss-Rogers. I think you're afraid to face what lies behind our so-called 'reality.'"

"At least I'm a coward in a good cause." He stood up. "Have you any more to say?"

He knew that he was just going through the motions. Luce must have realized he had laid himself open to arrest half a dozen times in as many minutes: The bare possession of the missing copy of the dissertation, the frank admission of plans to experiment with reality, and his attempted bribery of a

high Censor official. And yet, the man's very bearing denied
the possibility of being cut off in mid-career.

Luce's cheeks fluffed out in a brief sigh. "I'm sorry you
can't be intelligent about this, Mr. Prentiss-Rogers. Yet, the
time will come, you know, when you must make up your
mind to go—*through,* shall we say? In fact, we may have to
depend to a considerable degree on one another's companionship—*out there.* Even gods have to pass the time of day
occasionally, and I have a suspicion that you and I are going
to be quite chummy. So let us not part in enmity."

Prentiss's hand slid beneath his coat lapel and drew out the
snub-nosed automatic. He had a grim foreboding that it was
futile, and that the professor was laughing silently at him,
but he had no choice.

"You are under arrest," he said unemotionally. "Come with
me."

The other shrugged his shoulders, then something like a
laugh, soundless in its mockery, surged up in his throat.
"Certainly, Mr. Prentiss-Rogers."

He arose.

The room was plunged into instant blackness.

Prentiss fired three times, lighting up the gaunt chuckling
form at each flash.

"Save your fire, Mr. Prentiss-Rogers. Lead doesn't get far
in an intense diamagnetic screen. Study the magnetic damper
on a lab balance the next time you're in the Censor Building!"

Somewhere a door slammed.

Several hours later Prentiss was eyeing his aide with
ill-concealed distaste. Prentiss knew Crush had been summoned by E to confer on the implications of Luce's escape,
and that Crush was secretly sympathizing with him. Prentiss
couldn't endure sympathy. He'd prefer that the asthmatic
little man tell him how stupid he'd been.

"What do you want?" he growled.

"Sir," gasped Crush apologetically, "I have a report on that
gadget you scanned in Luce's lab."

Prentiss was instantly mollified, but suppressed any show
of interest. "What about it?"

"In essence, sir," wheezed Crush, "it's just a Nicol prism
mounted on a goniometer. According to a routine check it
was ground by an obscure optician who was nine years on the
job, and he spent nearly all of that time on just one face of the
prism. What do you make of that, sir?"

"Nothing, yet. What took him so long?"

"Grinding an absolutely flat edge, sir, so he says."

"Odd. That would mean a boundary composed exclusively of molecules of the same crystal layer, something that hasn't been attempted since the Palomar reflector."

"Yes, sir. And then there's the goniometer mount with just one number on the dial—forty-five degrees."

"Obviously," said Prentiss, "the Nicol is to be used only at a forty-five degree angle to the incoming light. Hence it's probably extremely important—why, I don't know—that the angle be *precisely* forty-five degrees. That would require a perfectly flat surface, too, of course. I suppose you're going to tell me that the goniometric gearing is set up very accurately."

Suddenly Prentiss realized that Crush was looking at him in mingled suspicion and admiration.

"Well?" demanded the ontologist irritably. "Just what is the adjusting mechanism? Surely not geometrical? Too crude. Optical, perhaps?"

Crush gasped into his handkerchief. "Yes, sir. The prism is rotated very slowly into a tiny beam of light. Part of the beam is reflected and part refracted. At exactly forty-five degrees it seems, by Jordan's law, that exactly half is reflected and half refracted. The two beams are picked up in a photocell relay that stops the rotating mechanism as soon as the luminosities of the beams are exactly equal."

Prentiss tugged nervously at his ear. It was puzzling. Just what was Luce going to do with such an exquisitely ground Nicol? At this moment he would have given ten years of his life for an inkling to the supplementary apparatus that went along with the Nicol. It would be something optical, certainly, tied in somehow with neurotic rats. What was it Luce had said the other night in the lab? Something about slowing down a photon. And then what was supposed to happen to the universe? Something like taking a tiny bite out of a balloon, Luce had said.

And how did it all interlock with certain impossible, though syllogistically necessary conclusions that flowed from his recent research into the history of human knowledge?

He wasn't sure. But he *was* sure that Luce was on the verge of using this mysterious apparatus to change the perceptible universe, on a scale so vast that humanity was going to get lost in the shuffle. He'd have to convince E of that.

If he couldn't, he'd seek out Luce himself and kill him

with his bare hands, and decide on reasons for it afterward.

He was guiding himself for the time being by pure insight, but he'd better be organized when he confronted E.

Crush was speaking. "Shall we go, sir? Your secretary says the jet is waiting."

The painting showed a man in a red hat and black robes seated behind a high judge's bench. Five other men in red hats were seated behind a lower bench to his right, and four others to his left. At the base of the bench knelt a figure in solitary abjection.

"We condemn you, Galileo Galilei, to the formal prison of this Holy Office for a period determinable at Our pleasure; and by way of salutary penance, We order you, during the next three years, to recite once a week the seven Penitential Psalms."

Prentiss turned from the inscription to the less readable face of E. The oval olive-hued face was smooth, unlined, even around the eyes, and the black hair was parted off-center and drawn over the woman's head into a bun at the nape of her neck. She wore no makeup, and apparently needed none. She was clad in a black, loose-fitting business suit, which accentuated her perfectly molded body.

"Do you know," said Prentiss coolly, "I think you like being Censor. It's in your blood."

"You're perfectly right. I *do* like being Censor. According to Speer, I effectively sublimate a guilt complex as strange as it is baseless."

"Very interesting. Sort of expiation of an ancestral guilt complex, eh?"

"What do you mean?"

"Woman started man on his acquisition of knowledge and self-destruction, and ever since has tried futilely to halt the avalanche. In you the feeling of responsibility and guilt runs exceptionally strong, and I'll wager that some nights you wake up in a cold sweat, thinking you've just plucked a certain forbidden fruit."

E stared icily up at the investigator's twitching mouth. "The only pertinent question," she said crisply, "is whether Luce is engaged in ontologic experiments, and if so, are they of a dangerous nature."

Prentiss sighed. "He's in it up to his neck. But just *what*, and how dangerous, I can only guess."

"Then guess."

"Luce thinks he's developed apparatus for the practical, predictable alteration of sensoria. He hopes to do something with his device that will blow physical laws straight to smithereens. The resulting reality would probably be unrecognizable even to a professional ontologist, let alone the mass of humanity."

"You seem convinced he can do this."

"The probabilities are high."

"Good enough. We can deal only in probabilities. The safest thing, of course, would be to locate Luce and kill him on sight. On the other hand, the faintest breath of scandal would result in Congressional hamstringing of the Bureau, so we must proceed cautiously."

"If Luce is really able to do what he claims," said Prentiss grimly, "and we let him do it, there won't be any Bureau at all—nor any Congress either."

"I know. Rest assured that if I decide that Luce is dangerous and should die, I shall let neither the lives nor careers of anyone in the Bureau stand in the way, including myself."

Prentiss nodded, wondering if she really meant it.

The woman continued. "We are faced for the first time with a probable violation of our directive forbidding ontologic experiments. We are inclined to prevent this threatened violation by taking a man's life. I think we should settle once and for all whether such harsh measures are indicated, and it is for this that I have invited you to attend a staff conference. We intend to reopen the entire question of ontologic experiments and their implications."

Prentiss groaned inwardly. In matters so important the staff decided by vote. He had a brief vision of attempting to convince E's hard-headed scientists that mankind was changing "reality" from century to century—that not too long ago the earth had been "flat." Yes, by now he was beginning to believe it himself!

"Come this way, please," said E.

Sitting at E's right was an elderly man, Speer, the famous psychologist. On her left was Goring, staff adviser on nuclenics; next to him was Burchard, brilliant chemist and Director of the Western Field, then Prentiss, and then Dobbs, the renowned metallurgist and Director of the Central Field.

Prentiss didn't like Dobbs, who had voted against his promotion to the directorship of Eastern.

E announced: "We may as well start this inquiry with an examination of fundamentals. Mr. Prentiss, just what is reality?"

The ontologist winced. He had needed two hundred pages to outline the theory of reality in his doctoral thesis, and even so, had always suspected his examiners had passed it only because it was incomprehensible—hence a work of genius.

"Well," he began wryly, "I must confess that I don't know what *real* reality is. What most of us call reality is simply an integrated synthesis of incoming sensoria. As such it is nothing more than a working hypothesis in the mind of each of us, forever in a process of revision. In the past that process has been slow and safe. But we have now to consider the consequences of an instantaneous and total revision—a revision so far reaching that it may thrust humanity face-to-face with the true reality, the world of Things-in-Themselves—Kant's *noumena*. This, I think, would be as disastrous as dumping a group of children in the middle of a forest. They'd have to relearn the simplest things—what to eat, how to protect themselves from elemental forces, and even a new language to deal with their new problems. There'd be few survivors.

"That is what we want to avoid, and we can do it if we prevent any sudden sweeping alteration of sensoria in our present reality."

He looked dubiously at the faces about him. It was a poor start. Speer's wrinkled features were drawn up in a serene smile, and the psychologist seemed to be contemplating the air over Prentiss' head. Goring was regarding him with grave, expressionless eyes. E nodded slightly as Prentiss gaze traveled past her to a puzzled Burchard, thence to Dobbs, who was frankly contemptuous.

Speer and Goring were going to be the most susceptible. Speer because of his lack of a firm scientific background. Goring because nucleonics was in such a state of flux that nuclear experts were expressing the gravest doubts as to the validity of the laws worshiped by Burchard and Dobbs. Burchard was only a faint possibility. And Dobbs?

Dobbs said: "I don't know what the dickens you're talking about." The implication was plain that he wanted to add "And I don't think you do, either."

And Prentiss wasn't so sure that he did know. Ontology was an elusive thing at best.

"I object to the term 'real reality,'" continued Dobbs. "A thing is real or it isn't. No fancy philosophical system can change *that*. And if it's real, it gives off predictable, reproducible sensory stimuli not subject to alteration except in the minds of lunatics."

Prentiss breathed more easily. His course was clear. He'd concentrate on Dobbs, with a little side-play on Burchard. Speer and Goring would never suspect his arguments were really directed at them. He pulled a gold coin from his vest pocket and slid it across the table to Dobbs, being careful not to let it clatter. "You're a metallurgist. Please tell us what this is."

Dobbs picked up the coin and examined it suspiciously. "It's quite obviously a five-dollar gold piece, minted at Fort Worth in nineteen sixty-two. I can even give you the analysis, if you want it."

"I doubt that you could," said Prentiss coolly. "For you see, you are holding a counterfeit coin minted only last week in my own laboratories especially for this conference. As a matter of fact, if you'll forgive my saying so, I had you in mind when I ordered the coin struck. It contains no gold whatever—drop it on the table."

The coin fell from the fingers of the astounded metallurgist and clattered on the oaken table top.

"Hear the false ring?" demanded Prentiss.

Pink-faced, Dobbs cleared his throat and peered at the coin more closely. "How was I to know that? It's no disgrace, is it? Many clever counterfeits can be detected only in the laboratory. I knew the color was a little on the red side, but that could have been due to the lighting of the room. And of course, I hadn't given it an auditory test before I spoke. The ring is definitely dull. It's obviously a copper-lead alloy, with possibly a little amount of silver to help the ring. All right, I jumped to conclusions. So what? What does that prove?"

"It proves that you have arrived at two separate, distinct, and mutually exclusive realities, starting with the same sensory premises. It proves how easily reality is revised. And that isn't all, as I shall soon—"

"All right," said Dobbs testily. "But on second thought I admitted it was false, didn't I?"

"Which demonstrates a further weakness in our routine

acquisition and evaluation of predigested information. When an unimpeachable authority tells us something as a fact, we immediately, and without conscious thought, *modify* our incoming stimuli to conform with that *fact*. The coin suddenly acquires the red taint of copper, and rings false to the ear."

"I would have caught the queer ring anyhow," said Dobbs stubbornly, "with no help from 'an unimpeachable authority. The ring would have sounded the same, no matter what you said."

From the corner of his eye Prentiss noticed that Speer was grinning broadly. Had the old psychologist divined his trick? He'd take a chance.

"Dr. Speer," he said, "I think you have something interesting to tell our doubting friend."

Speer cackled dryly. "You've been a perfect guinea pig, Dobbsie. The coin was genuine."

The metallurgist's jaw dropped as he looked blankly from one face to another. Then his jowls slowly grew red. He flung the coin to the table. "Maybe I am a guinea pig. I'm a realist too. I think this is a piece of metal. You might fool me as to its color or assay, but in essence and substance, it's a piece of metal." He glared at Prentiss and Speer in turn. "Does anyone deny that?"

"Certainly not," said Prentiss. "Our mental pigeonholes are identical in that respect; they accept the same sensory definition of 'piece of metal,' or 'coin.' Whatever this object is it emits stimuli that our minds are capable of registering and abstracting as a 'coin.' But note: we make a coin out of it. However, if I could shuffle my cortical pigeonholes, I might find it to be a chair, or a steamer trunk, possibly with Dr Dobbs inside, or, if the shuffling were extreme, there might be no semantic pattern into which the incoming stimuli could be routed. There wouldn't be anything there at all!"

"Sure," sneered Dobbs. "You could walk right through it."

"Why not?" asked Prentiss gravely. "I think we may do it all the time. Matter is about the emptiest stuff imaginable. If you compressed that coin to eliminate the space between its component atoms and electrons, you couldn't see it in a microscope."

Dobbs stared at the enigmatic goldpiece as though it might suddenly thrust out a pseudopod and swallow him up. Then he said flatly: "No. I don't believe it. It exists as a coin, and only a coin—whether I know it or not."

"Well," ventured Prentiss, "how about you, Dr. Goring? Is the coin real to you?"

The nucleist smiled and shrugged his shoulders. "If I don't think too much about it, it's real enough. And yet . . ."

Dobb's face clouded. "And yet what? Here it is. Can you doubt the evidence of your own eyes?"

"That's just the difficulty." Goring leaned forward. "My eyes tell me, here's a coin. Theory tells me, here's a mass of hypothetical disturbances in a hypothetical subether in a hypothetical ether. The indeterminacy principle tells me that I can never know both the mass and position of these hypothetical disturbances. And as a physicist I know that the bare fact of observing something is sufficient to change that something from its pre-observed state. Nevertheless, I compromise by letting my senses and practical experience stick a tag on this particular bit of the unknowable. X, after its impact on my mind (whateever *that* is!) equals coin. A single equation with two variables has no solution. The best I can say is, it's a coin, but probably not really—"

"Hah!" declared Burchard. "I can demonstrate the fallacy of *that* position very quickly. If our minds make this a coin, then our minds make this little object an ashtray, that a window, the thing that holds us up a chair. You might say we make the air we breathe, and perhaps even the stars and planets. Why, following Prentiss's idea to its logical end, the universe itself is the work of man—a conclusion I'm sure he doesn't intend."

"Oh, but I do," said Prentiss.

Prentiss took a deep breath. The issue could be dodged no longer. He had to take a stand. "And to make sure you understand me, whether you agree with me or not, I'll state categorically that I believe the apparent universe to be the work of man."

Even E looked startled, but said nothing.

The ontologist continued rapidly. "All of you doubt my sanity. A week ago I would have, too. But since then I've done a great deal of research in the history of science. And I repeat, *the universe is the work of man*. I believe that man began his existence in some incredibly simple world—the original and true *noumenon* of our present universe. And that over the centuries man expanded his little world into its present vastness and incomprehensible intricacy solely by dint of imagination.

"Consequently, I believe that what most of you call the 'real' world has been changing ever since our ancestors began to think."

Dobbs smiled superciliously. "Oh, come now, Prentiss. That's just a rhetorical description of scientific progress over the past centuries. In the same sense I might say that modern transportation and communications have shrunk the earth. But you'll certainly admit that the physical state of things has been substantially constant ever since the galaxies formed and the earth began to cool, and that the simple cosmologies of early man were simply the result of lack of means for obtaining accurate information?"

"I *won't* admit it," rejoined Prentiss bluntly. "I maintain that their information was substantially accurate. I maintain that at one time in our history the earth was flat—as flat as it is now round, and no one living before the time of Hecataeus, though he might have been equipped with the finest modern instruments, could have proved otherwise. His mind was *conditioned* to a two-dimensional world. Any of us present, if we were transplanted to the world of Hecataeus, could, of course, establish terrestrial sphericity in short order. Our minds have been conditioned to a three-dimensional world. The day may come a few millennia hence when a four-dimensional Terra will be commonplace even to school children; they will have been intuitively conditioned in relativistic concepts." He added slyly: "And the less intelligent of them may attempt to blame our naive three-dimensional planet on our grossly inaccurate instruments, because it will be as plain as day to them that their planet has four dimensions!"

Dobbs snorted at this amazing idea. The other scientists stared at Prentiss with an awe which was mixed with incredulity.

Goring said cautiously: "I follow up to a certain point. I can see that a primitive society might start out with a limited number of facts. They would offer theories to harmonize and integrate those facts, and then those first theories would require that new, additional facts exist, and in their search for those secondary facts, extraneous data would turn up inconsistent with the first theories. Secondary theories would then be required, from which hitherto unguessed facts should follow, the confirmation of which would discover more inconsistencies. So the pattern of fact to theory to fact to theory, and so on, finally brings us into our present state of knowledge. Does that follow from your argument?"

Prentiss nodded.

"But won't you admit that the facts were there all the time, and merely awaited discovery?"

"The simple, unelaborated *noumenon* was there all the time, yes. But the new fact—man's new interpretation of the *noumenon*, was generally pure invention—a mental creation, if you like. This will be clearer if you consider how rarely a new fact arises before a theory exists for its explanation. In the ordinary scientific investigation, theory comes first, followed in short order by the 'discovery' of various facts deducible from it."

Goring still looked skeptical. "But that wouldn't mean the fact wasn't there all the time."

"Wouldn't it? Look at the evidence. Has it never struck you as odd in how many instances very obvious facts were 'overlooked' until a theory was propounded that required their existence? Take your nuclear building blocks. Protons and electrons were detected physically only after Rutherford had showed they had to exist. And then when Rutherford found that protons and electrons were not enough to build all the atoms of the periodic table, he postulated the neutron, which of course was duly 'discovered' in the Wilson cloud chamber."

Goring pursed his lips. "But the Wilson cloud chamber would have shown all that prior to the theory, if anyone had only thought to use it.

"The mere fact that Wilson didn't invent his cloud chamber until nineteen-twelve and Geiger didn't invent his counter until nineteen-thirteen would not keep subatomic particles from existing before that time."

"You don't get the point," said Prentiss. "The primitive, ungeneralized *noumenon* that we today observe as subatomic particles existed prior to nineteen-twelve, true, *but not subatomic particles*."

"Well, I don't know. . . ." Goring scratcted his chin. "How about fundamental forces? Surely electricity existed before Galvani? Even the Greeks knew how to build up electrostatic charges on amber."

"Greek electricity was nothing more than electrostatic

charges. Nothing more could be created until Galvani introduced the concept of the electric current."

"Do you mean the electric current didn't exist at all before Galvani?" demanded Burchard. "Not even when lightning struck a conductor?"

"Not even then. We don't know much about pre-Galvanic lightning. While it probably packed a wallop, its destructive potential couldn't have been due to its delivery of an electric current. The Chinese flew kites for centuries before Franklin theorized that lightning was the same as galvanic electricity, but there's no recorded shock from a kite string until our learned statesman drew forth one in seventeen-sixty-five. *Now,* only an idiot flies a kite in a storm. It's all according to pattern: theory first, then we alter 'reality' to fit."

Burchard persisted. "Then I suppose you'd say all the elements are figments of our imagination."

"Correct," agreed Prentiss. "I believe that in the beginning there were only four *noumenal* elements. Man simply elaborated these according to the needs of his growing science. Man made them what they are today—and on occasion, *unmade* them. You remember the havoc Mendelyeev created with his periodic law. He declared that the elements had to follow valence sequences of increasing atomic weight, and when they didn't, he insisted his law was right and that the atomic weights were wrong. He must have had Stas and Berzelius whirling in their graves, because they had worked out the 'erroneous' atomic weights with marvelous precision. The odd thing was, when the weights were rechecked, they fitted the Mendelyeev table. But that wasn't all. The old rascal pointed out vacant spots in his table and maintained that there were more elements yet to be discovered. He even predicted what properties they'd have. He was too modest. I state that Nilson, Winkler, and De Boisbaudran merely *discovered* scandium, germanium, and gallium; Mendelyeev *created* them, out of the original quadrelemental stuff."

E leaned forward. "That's a bit strong. Tell me, if man has changed the elements and the cosmos to suit his convenience, what was the cosmos like before man came on the scene?"

"There wasn't any," answered Prentiss. "Remember, by definition, 'cosmos' or 'reality' is simply man's version of the ultimate *noumenal* universe. The 'cosmos' arrives and departs with the mind of man. Consequently, the earth—as such—didn't even exist before the advent of man."

"But the evidence of the rocks . . ." protested E. "Pressures applied over millions, even billions of years, were needed to form them, unless you postulate an omnipotent God who called them into existence as of yesterday."

"I postulate only the omnipotent human mind," said Prentiss. "In the seventeenth century, Hooke, Ray, Woodward, to name a few, studied chalk, gravel, marble, and even coal, without finding anything inconsistent with results to be expected from the Noachian Flood. But now that we've made up our minds that the earth is older, the rocks *seem* older, too."

"But how about evolution?" demanded Burchard. "Surely that wasn't a matter of a few centuries?"

"Really?" replied Prentiss. "Again, why assume that the facts are any more recent than the theory? The evidence is all the other way. Aristotle was a magnificent experimental biologist, and he was convinced that life could be created spontaneously. Before the time of Darwin there was no need for the various species to evolve, because they sprang into being from inanimate matter. As late as the eighteenth century, Needham, using a microscope, reported that he saw microbe life arise spontaneously out of sterile culture media. These abiogeneticists were, of course, discredited and their work found to be irreproducible, but only *after* it became evident that the then abiogenetic facts were going to run inconsistent with later 'facts' flowing from advancing biologic theory."

"Then," said Goring, "assuming, purely for the sake of argument, that man has altered the original *noumena* into our present reality, just what danger do you think Luce represents to that reality? How could he do anything about it, even if he wanted to? Just what is he up to?"

"Broadly stated," said Prentiss, "Luce intends to destroy the Einsteinian universe."

Burchard frowned and shook his head. "Not so fast. In the first place, how can anyone presume to destroy this planet, much less the whole universe? And why do you say the 'Einsteinian' universe? The universe by any other name is still the universe, isn't it?"

"What Dr. Prentiss means," explained E, "is that Luce wants to revise completely and finally our present comprehension of the universe, which presently happens to be the Einsteinian version, in the expectation that the final version would be the true one—and comprehensible only to Luce and perhaps a few other ontologic experts."

"I don't see it," said Dobbs irritably. "Apparently this Luce contemplates nothing more than publication of a new scientific theory. How can that be bad? A mere theory can't hurt anybody—especially if only two or three people understand it."

"You—and two billion others," said Prentiss softly, "think that 'reality' cannot be affected by any theory that seems to change it—that it is optional with you to accept or reject the theory. In the past that was true. If the Ptolemaics wanted a geocentric universe, they ignored Copernicus. If the four-dimensional continuum of Einstein and Minkowsky seemed incomprehensible to the Newtonian school they dismissed it, and the planets continued to revolve substantially as Newton predicted. But this is different.

"For the first time we are faced with the probability that the promulgation of a theory is going to *force* an ungraspable reality upon our minds. It will not be optional."

"Well," said Burchard, "if by 'promulgation of a theory' you mean something like the application of the quantum theory and relativity to the production of atomic energy, which of course has changed the shape of civilization in the past generation, whether the individual liked it or not, then I can understand you. But if you mean that Luce is going to make one little experiment that may confirm some new theory or other, and *ipso facto* and instantaneously reality is going to turn topsy turvy, why I say it's nonsense."

"Would anyone," said Prentiss quietly, "care to guess what would happen if Luce were able to destroy a photon?"

Goring laughed shortly. "The question doesn't make sense. The mass-energy entity whose three-dimensional profile we call a photon is indestructible."

"But if you *could* destroy it?" insisted Prentiss. "What would the universe be like afterward?"

"What difference would it make?" demanded Dobbs. "One photon more or less?"

"Plenty," said Goring. "According to the Einstein theory, every particle of matter-energy has a gravitational potential, lambda, and it can be calculated that the total lambdas are precisely sufficient to keep our four-dimensional continuum from closing back on itself. Take one lambda away—God! The universe would split wide open!"

"Exactly," said Prentiss. "Instead of a continuum, our 'reality' would become a disconnected melange of three-dimensional objects. Time, if it existed, wouldn't bear any relation to spatial things. Only an ontologic expert might be able to synthesize any sense out of such a 'reality.'"

"Well," said Dobbs, "I wouldn't worry too much. I don't think anybody's ever going to destroy a photon." He snickered. "You have to catch one first!"

"Luce can catch one," said Prentiss calmly. "And he can destroy it. At this moment some unimaginable post-Einsteinian universe lies in the palm of his hand. Final, true reality, perhaps. But we aren't ready for it. Kant, perhaps, or *Homo superior*, but not the general run of *H. sapiens*. We wouldn't be able to escape our conditioning. We'd be stopped cold."

He stopped. Without looking at Goring, he knew he had convinced the man. Prentiss sagged with visible relief. It was time for a vote. He must strike before Speer and Goring could change their minds.

"Madame"—he shot a questioning glance at the woman—"at any moment my men are going to report that they've located Luce. I must be ready to issue the order for his execution, if in fact the staff believes such disposition proper. I call for a vote of officers!"

"Granted," said E instantly. "Will those in favor of destroying Luce on sight raise their right hands?"

Prentiss and Goring made the required signal.

Speer was silent.

Prentiss felt his heart sinking. Had he made a gross error of judgment?

"I vote against this murder," declared Dobbs. "That's what it is, pure murder."

"I agree with Dobbs," said Burchard shortly.

All eyes were on the psychologist. "I presume you'll join us, Dr. Speer?" demanded Dobbs sternly.

"Count me out, gentlemen. I'd never interfere with anything so inevitable as the destiny of man. All of you are overlooking a fundamental facet of human nature—man's insatiable hunger for change, novelty—for anything different from what he already has. Prentiss himself states that whenever man grows discontented with his present reality, he starts elaborating it, and the devil take the hindmost. Luce but symbolizes the evil genius of our race—and I mean both our species and the race toward intertwined godhood and destruction. Once born, however, symbols are immortal. It's far too late now to start killing Luces. It was too late when the first man tasted the first apple.

"Furthermore, I think Prentiss greatly overestimates the scope of Luce's pending victory over the rest of mankind. Suppose Luce is actually successful in clearing space and time and suspending the world in the temporal stasis of its present irreality. Suppose he and a few ontologic experts pass on into the ultimate, true reality. How long do you think they can resist the temptation to alter it? If Prentiss is right, eventually they or their descendants will be living in a cosmos as intricate and unpleasant as the one they left, while we, for all practical purposes, will be pleasantly dead.

"No, gentlemen, I won't vote either way."

"Then it is my privilege to break the tie," said E coolly. "I vote for death. Save your remonstrances, Dr. Dobbs. It's after midnight. This meeting is adjourned." She stood up in abrupt dismissal, and the men were soon filing from the room.

E left the table and walked toward the windows on the far side of the room. Prentiss hesitated a moment, but made no effort to leave.

E called over her shoulder, "You, too, Prentiss."

The door closed behind Speer, the last of the group, save Prentiss.

Prentiss walked up behind E.

She gave no sign of awareness.

Six feet away, the man stopped and studied her.

Sitting, walking, standing, she was lovely. Mentally he compared her to Velasquez' Venus. There was the same slender exquisite proportion of thigh, hip, and bust. And he knew she was completely aware of her own beauty, and further, must be aware of his present appreciative scrutiny.

Then her shoulders sagged suddenly, and her voice seemed very tired when she spoke. "So you're still here, Prentiss. Do you believe in intuition?"

"Not often."

"Speer was right. He's always right. Luce will succeed." She dropped her arms to her sides and turned.

"Then may I reiterate, my dear, marry me and let's forget the control of knowledge for a few months."

"Completely out of the question, Prentiss. Our natures are incompatible. You're incorrigibly curious, and I'm incorrigibly, even neurotically, conservative. Besides, how can you even think about such things when we've got to stop Luce?"

His reply was interrupted by the shrilling of the intercom: "Calling Mr. Prentiss. Crush calling Mr. Prentiss. Luce located. Crush calling."

With his pencil Crush pointed to a shaded area of the map. "This is Luce's Snake-Eyes estate, the famous game preserve and zoo. Somewhere in the center—about here, I think—is a stone cottage. A moving van unloaded some lab equipment there this morning."

"Mr. Prentiss," said E, "how long do you think it will take him to install what he needs for that one experiment?"

The ontologist answered from across the map table. "I can't be sure. I still have no idea of what he's going to try, except that I'm reasonably certain it must be done in absolute darkness. Checking his instruments will require but a few minutes at most."

The woman began pacing the floor nervously. "I knew it. We can't stop him. We have no time."

"Oh, I don't know," said Prentiss. "How about the stone cottage, Crush? Is it pretty old?"

"Dates from the eighteenth century, sir."

"There's your answer," said Prentiss. "It's probably full of holes where the mortar's fallen out. For total darkness he'll have to wait until moonset."

"That's three thirty-four A.M., sir," said Crush.

"We've time for an arrest," said E.

Crush looked dubious. "It's more complicated than that, Madame. Snake-Eyes is fortified to withstand a small army. Luce could hold off any force the Bureau could muster for at least twenty-four hours."

"One atom egg, well done," suggested Prentiss.

"That's the best answer, of course," agreed E. "But you know as well as I what the reaction of Congress would be to such extreme measures. There would be an investigation. The Bureau would be abolished, and all persons responsible for such an action would face life imprisonment, perhaps death." She was silent for a moment, then sighed and said: "So be it. If there is no alternative, I shall order the bomb dropped."

"There may be another way," said Prentiss.

"Indeed?"

"Granted an army couldn't get through. One man might. And if he made it, you could call off your bomb."

E exhaled a slow cloud of smoke and studied the glowing tip of her cigarette. Finally she turned and looked into the eyes of the ontologist for the first time since the beginning of the conference. "*You* can't go."

"Who, then?"

Her eyes dropped. "You're right, of course. But the bomb still falls if you don't get through. It's got to be that way. Do you understand that?"

Prentiss laughed. "I understand."

He addressed his aide. "Crush, I'll leave the details up to you, bomb and all. We'll rendezvous at these coordinates"—he pointed to the map—"at three sharp. It's after one now. You'd better get started."

"Yes, sir," wheezed Crush, and scurried out of the room.

As the door closed, Prentiss turned to E. "Beginning tomorrow afternoon—or rather, *this* afternoon, after I finish with Luce—I want six months off."

"Granted," murmured E.

"I want you to come with me. I want to find out just what this thing is between us. Just the two of us. It may take a little time."

E smiled crookedly. "If we're both still alive at three thirty-five, and such a thing as a month exists, and you still want me to spend six of them with you, I'll do it. And in return you can do something for me."

"What?"

"You, even above Luce, stand the best chance of adjusting to final reality if Luce is successful in destroying a photon. I'm a borderline case. I'm going to need all the help you can give me, if and when the time comes. Will you remember that?"

"I'll remember," Prentiss said.

At 3 A.M. he joined Crush.

"There are at least seven infrared scanners in the grounds, sir," said Crush, "not to mention an intricate network of photo relays. And then the wire fence around the lab, with the big cats inside. He must have turned the whole zoo loose." The little man reluctantly helped Prentiss into his infrared-absorbing coveralls. "You weren't meant for tiger fodder, sir. Better call it off."

Prentiss zipped up his visor and grimaced out into the

moonlit dimness of the apple orchard. "You'll take care of the photocell network?"

"Certainly, sir. He's using u.v.-sensitive cells. We'll blanket the area with the u.v.-spot at three-ten."

Prentiss strained his ears, but couldn't hear the 'copter that would carry the u.v.-searchlight—and the bomb.

"It'll be here, sir," Crush assured him. "It won't make any noise, anyhow. What you ought to be worrying about are those wild beasts."

The investigator sniffed at the night air. "Darn little breeze."

"Yeah," gasped Crush. "And variable at that, sir. You can't count on going in upwind. You want us to create a diversion at one end of the grounds to attract the animals?"

"We don't dare. If necessary, I'll open the areosol capsule of formaldehyde." He held out his hand. "Good-by, Crush."

His asthmatic assistant shook the extended hand with vigorous sincerity. "Good luck, sir. And don't forget the bomb. We'll have to drop it at three thirty-four sharp."

But Prentiss had vanished into the leafy darkness.

A little later he was studying the luminous figures on his watch. The u.v.-blanket was presumably on. All he had to be careful about in the next forty seconds was a direct collision with a photocell post.

But Crush's survey party had mapped well. He reached the barbed fencing uneventfully, with seconds to spare. He listened a moment, and then in practiced silence eased his lithe body high up and over.

The breeze, which a moment before had been in his face, now died away, and the night air hung about him in dark lifeless curtains.

From the stone building a scant two hundred yards ahead, a chink of light peeped out.

Prentiss drew his silenced pistol and began moving forward with swift caution, taking care to place his heel to ground before the toe, and feeling out the character of the ground with the thin soles of his sneakers before each step. A snapping twig might hurl a slavering wild beast at his throat.

He stopped motionless in midstride.

From the thicket several yards to his right came an ominous sniffing, followed by a low snarl.

His mouth went suddenly dry as he strained his ears and turned his head slowly toward the sound.

And then there came the reverberations of something heavy, hurtling toward him.

He whipped his weapon around and waited in a tense crouch, not daring to send a wild, singing bullet across the sward.

The great cat was almost upon him before he fired, and then the faint cough of the stumbling, stricken animal seemed louder than his muffled shot.

Breathing hard, Prentiss stepped away from the dying beast, evidently a panther, and listened for a long time before resuming his march on the cottage. Luce's extraordinary measures to exclude intruders but confirmed his suspicions: Tonight was the last night that the professor could be stopped. He blinked the stinging sweat from his eyes and glanced at his watch. It was 3:15.

Apparently the other animals had not heard him. He stood up to resume his advance, and to his utter relief found that the wind had shifted almost directly into his face and was blowing steadily.

In another three minutes he was standing at the massive door of the building, running practiced fingers over the great iron hinges and lock. Undoubtedly the thing was going to squeak; there was no time to apply oil and wait for it to soak in. The lock could be easily picked.

And the squeaking of a rusty hinge was probably immaterial. A cunning operator like Luce would undoubtedly have wired an alarm into it. He just couldn't believe Crush's report to the contrary.

But he couldn't stand here.

There was only one way to get inside quickly, and alive.

Chuckling at his own madness, Prentiss began to pound on the door.

He could visualize the blinking out of the slit of light above his head, and knew that, somewhere within the building, two flame-lit eyes were studying him in an infrared scanner.

Prentiss tried simultaneously to listen to the muffled squeaking of the rats beyond the great door and to the swift, padding approach of something big behind him.

"Luce!" he cried. "It's Prentiss! Let me in!"

A latch slid somewhere; the door eased inward. The investigator threw his gun rearward at a pair of bounding eyes,